GET THE FIRST BOOK IN THIS SERIES FOR FREE.

Sign up for the no-spam newsletter and get *BREACH*.

Details can be found at the end of *DOGS OF DOOM*.

Copyright © 2017 Bronwyn Leroux

All the characters in this book are fictitious, and any resemblance to actual persons living or dead is purely coincidental.

All rights reserved. No part of this publication may be reproduced, stored in a retrieval system, distributed, or transmitted in any form or by any means, including photocopying, recording, or other electronic or mechanical methods, without the prior written permission of the author, except in the case of brief quotations embodied in critical reviews and certain other noncommercial uses permitted by copyright law. For permission requests, contact the author at info@bronwynleroux.com
https://bronwynleroux.com/

Cover design by Lena Yang Designs

ISBN-13: 978-1-953107-03-9

DOGS OF DOOM

BRONWYN LEROUX

CHAPTER ONE

Jaden couldn't bear it. His mother's words echoed in his head. She had told him outright not to come for them if her vision proved true. To save the world instead of them. Would Jaden really have to make such a dreadful choice?

Oblivious to his surroundings, Jaden hunched on Han's broad back as they flew south, his thoughts careening into one another, his mind reeling from his mother's revelations. He couldn't accept there were no alternatives. Wouldn't accept it. There must be another way. He would find it. And soon, because time was against him—against them.

Still unclear about precisely what it was they were supposed to do, Jaden couldn't hazard a guess on how long it might take. Meaning he should use this time to concoct a few creative solutions before things flew out of control. But the more Jaden concentrated on the problem, the more impossible it seemed. Annoyed by his lack of progress, Jaden abandoned the process, leaving his subconsciousness to work.

His gaze inevitably went to Kayla, astride Taz on his right, her long, blonde hair flowing around her stunning face as they surged toward their destination. Her presence made this ordeal infinitely more bearable. After his mother's bombshell revelation, Kayla had caught his hand as they climbed the stairs to the roof for their departure, whispering they would find a way.

It was the first time she'd initiated contact since pulling away from him that night at his Gran's. That simple touch, her belief in him, and her resolute support had made him want to pull her into his arms. At that moment, she couldn't possibly know how much he'd loved her.

Jaden's brain stuttered on the thought. *Loved her? Well, there are all kinds of love, aren't there? Friends love each other, don't they?* Jaden snarled, a low guttural sound at the base of his throat. *Now is neither the time nor place for such thoughts.* But the distress Kayla had tried so hard to hide when he'd unwittingly let go of her hand earlier that same day flashed to the forefront of his mind.

There was no mistaking her hurt. And didn't that tell him she more than liked him, if just not enough to admit it yet—even to herself? *No, I can't think like that. We have a mission to complete, and I won't complicate matters by pursuing more than friendship with Kayla before we finish this.*

Han glanced at him over his shoulder, and Jaden grimaced. He wasn't sure how the bat sensed his inner turmoil. Rubbing Han's neck, Jaden wordlessly conveyed his glider need not worry. Han accepted this because he flew on without further inquisition.

Jaden's mind returned to their departure a few hours earlier. Just as he and Kayla had hoped, their bats appeared at the exact moment they stepped out onto the Jameson's rooftop landing site with his mother. Their typically serene faces wore concern until they established the teens weren't in any immediate danger. Then they were all business, ready to rush on with the next stage of their journey.

Jaden's mother, hoping for a glimpse of the magnificent creatures after her own mother's endless gushing, was disappointed when the gliders remained invisible to her. Too addled, Jaden hadn't thought to offer his mother the relic stone. Instead, he and Kayla mumbled commiserations and indulged in fierce farewell hugs.

When Han and Taz circled lower for their pickup, Jaden warned his mother that he and Kayla would probably become as invisible as their gliders once they reunited. Despite this, his mother's shock was evident when they vanished. Jaden's last impression as they whirled away was his mother's utterly distraught face. It seared its way into his mind and distressed him even more. If only his mother had seen the gliders. Then she might be more confident in their success following her mind-blowing confession.

As Han angled them away from his mother, he discerned Jaden's anguish. After several unsuccessful attempts at cheering Jaden up, Han gave up. Now their group flew in silence, headed for the destination the book had revealed. *Soquazba*. Incredibly, the bats were familiar with the ancient name, so Jaden let them lead. He hadn't thought to question their steeds as he and Kayla bowed under the burden Clara Jameson had laid on them.

With a sigh, Jaden roused himself from his fugue. His legs were stiff, his shoulders tense. They must've been flying for longer than he'd thought. Relieved when the bats hadn't insisted on practicing their aerial skills, as was their wont, Jaden now considered whether they were just as anxious as their voyagers about completing this mission and getting on with their lives. Jaden shattered the silence accompanying them for too long. "Are we nearly there?"

"No, young one. We have some distance to go. Would you care to discuss what's troubling you?" Han's tone indicated he found Jaden's brooding disconcerting.

Jaden deliberated. *Honestly, I don't want to think about what my mom said, let alone talk about it.* Because saying the words out loud would be akin to confessing their truth, admitting defeat. However, a nagging certainty in the back of his mind said this was exactly what he should do. Growling, Jaden hailed Taz, and once the girls joined them, Jaden related his mother's dream.

Their bats listened without comment, finally understanding why their voyagers were so withdrawn.

"Thank you for sharing that, Jaden," Han murmured. "We will join with you in considering ways we might rescue your parents, without allowing you to become a captive yourself."

"Thanks, Han. I appreciate that." Jaden sighed, relieved the burden was no longer solely his to bear. Han shifted under him, surprised by his use of the bat's new abbreviated name for the first time.

The bat ruminated. "Han . . . I like it. Do you have a shorter name for Tazanna too?"

"I think Taz will do." Jaden glanced her way to witness her reaction, delighted when Han's body quaked under him with repressed mirth.

Taz graced Jaden with a bored glare. "If you must."

Did the absence of her usually scathing reproach reflect Taz's reluctance to destroy the fragile tendril of normalcy he was displaying? From the way Kayla leaned over and caressed the side of her glider's neck, Jaden suspected it was.

"Speaking of weaknesses, should we share some of the Gaptor's flaws?" Taz asked.

I'm so right about Taz's motivations, Jaden thought. She was trying to distract him by offering information. *How very sneaky.*

Kayla's broad smile confirmed her agreement with the sentiment. "That would be useful."

"Obviously, we're a lot more graceful than that floating monstrosity—" Taz began.

Jaden grinned, recognizing Taz's usual superior tone.

Kayla giggled. "Of course you are!"

Taz grinned, showing her tiny, sharp teeth, and warmed to her subject. "We're nimbler because we're smaller, permitting quicker adjustments that allow us to outmaneuver him. And we're faster across shorter distances."

Over Taz's head, Kayla grinned at Jaden, and they shared silent laughter. "Is there any area where you don't surpass the Gaptor?"

Taz measured the question, before sniffing. "I suppose I have to concede he can fly further than we can in one stretch. But his power wanes when he does. So it can be both an advantage and a disadvantage, depending on the situation."

"His power?" Kayla questioned. "You mean that EMP thing?"

"Yes. He can't sustain the blast for as long or send it out with as much power when he's tired. But it's still a potent weapon and one we should avoid."

Han cleared his throat. "Don't forget about our arcachoa."

Taz glared like he'd betrayed some secret. "Yes, then there's that. We have one, but he doesn't."

Her reluctance to divulge even that scrap of information was evident. Jaden couldn't let it slide. "Your arca—what?"

"Arcachoa," Han repeated. "It's the name for the space on our bodies made especially for your medallions."

Taz's glower was noteworthy, meaning there was definitely more to this. Jaden pressed in. "Tell us about this arcachoa."

Han's powerful shoulders rolled under Jaden when his bat shrugged at Taz with apology. Jaden smirked. Apparently, even in the gliders' world, males had to be mindful of the unpredictable female psyche.

Taz harrumphed. "If you must know, it's just below the ridge on our neck."

"Oh, like a holding space," Kayla said, exploring the fur in the region Taz had mentioned. "But why would you want to keep that a secret?"

Kayla had picked up on that too. Jaden waited for Taz's response.

"It's not exactly a holding space," Han explained when Taz didn't answer. "It serves a unique purpose."

"What?" Jaden prodded, sensing they had reached the crux of the matter.

Taz growled, and Kayla's probing fingers immediately ceased their exploration. Frowning at Han, Taz said, "This was not something I planned on sharing with you. But since the proverbial cat's out of the bag, I suppose you should know what it does, should the need ever arise for you to use it."

Jaden squirmed on Han's back. "Spit it out already."

Taz sighed. "It's difficult to explain, but essentially, when you place your medallion in the space, it allows both the glider and voyager to travel through time."

CHAPTER TWO

Jaden sputtered, sure Taz was joking. "Seriously?"

"Yes, seriously. But like the adverb you so aptly used, we should only use it in the most extreme circumstances and, even then, only when exercising every precaution."

"Like a time machine effect of sorts?" Jaden guessed this would be their only opportunity to gather information on the peculiar medallion space if Taz had any say in the matter. The moment he heard he could travel through time, an idea had formed in his mind. He needed to establish whether his plan was viable.

"I suppose so," Han said. "You move through time but don't change locations. I guess if there was such a thing as a time machine, that's how it would work."

"But unlike your mythical time machine, our time travel has two important limitations: it only functions when you're in an area containing an artifact—" Taz began.

Jaden interrupted. "An artifact? What's that?"

"An item that's present in both your world and ours."

Jaden blew out a sigh. *This is exasperating! First, Taz withholds mention of the medallion space. Then, when Han's revelation forces her to discuss it, she agrees unwillingly. And now, she's intentionally concealing something else. If she wants us to know how the medallion space functions, why isn't she telling us everything? Isn't more knowledge better than less?*

"Could you give an example?" Jaden asked in a measured tone.

Taz glanced at him, as if wondering whether he was being obnoxious. "They're difficult to define, but an example that comes to mind is your medallion."

Jaden scowled. "That's not helpful."

Han, sensing the rising tension between the two, cut in. "Start by thinking of what you might find in both our world and yours."

But it only stoked Jaden's temper. "Easy for you to say when you know what's in your world. We don't have that insight, so how do we work out whether it's something we might find in both worlds?"

"There aren't that many," Han admitted, "but an artifact would typically be something ancient and unusual in this world." He must've sensed Jaden was puzzling over something specific, because he asked, "What are you concerned about?"

Jaden snuck a calming breath. If he wanted information, he couldn't lose his temper. "Taz was clear about this only working when there's an artifact in the area. Therefore, it follows we should know exactly what an artifact is, in case we ever need to use this time jump effect. Hence the question: How do we identify an artifact?"

Taz nodded. "You're right."

Jaden blinked, sure he hadn't heard correctly. *Since when does Taz admit someone else is right?*

Taz continued. "If ever there's a pressing need to use our arcachoa, it will already be too late then to explain. Think of an artifact as something you would need or find on this quest you're on. My guess is the relic stone your grandmother gave you is also an artifact. It serves a purpose in this world but comes from ours."

Kayla's face brightened. "And the key Jaden's Gran gave him would be one too?"

"Most likely," Han answered. "But we're guessing what an artifact is as much as you are. The definition is vague. We're not deliberately trying to be obtuse. We just don't have the information."

Jaden calmed. Han's response persuaded him they were on the

same side. "Thanks, Han. I suppose we'll figure it out together if the need arises."

Han purred, and Jaden felt his pleasure. They flew for a few minutes before Jaden thought of something else. "Taz, I'm sorry. I interrupted you earlier. You said there were two limitations to the time travel. The first was that it would only happen when there was an artifact in the area. What was the second?"

"Oh yes, I'm glad you reminded me. Should you ever use our arcachoa, it will only take you to the exact time period when the artifact was in that area, not just any random time period."

"So we can't set a date to 'jump' to, like they do in the movies?" Kayla asked.

"No. The time we 'jump' to, as you so appropriately worded it, is the exact point needed to locate the artifact at that precise spot in that particular time period," Taz said.

"Then it's like the 'jump' is preset to transfer you back to the last time there was an artifact at that location?" Jaden asked.

Han smiled. "You understand."

But Taz, studying Jaden, must've perceived the hidden agenda behind his question. "Jaden, what exactly are you thinking of doing?"

"Nothing right now—only an idea I'm noodling."

Taz pursed her lips. "It's imperative you inform us before using our arcachoa. Using its effects puts both glider and voyager on an extremely hazardous path." Unsure whether she was getting through to him, she tried again. "Jaden, do you understand you shouldn't activate the arcachoa shouldn't except in the most exceptional situations, when there is absolutely no other option?"

Han nodded. "She's right. Using the arcachoa affects us both. Please don't be cavalier in thinking you can use it at any time."

Kayla's eyes sparked. "What's so dangerous?"

Taz's glare was stern. "I don't know all the adverse consequences, except that there are plenty. One of the most devastating is that you can get lost in the time period you travel to if you aren't careful. Imagine not only leaving your friends and family forever but also landing in a culture that's foreign to your own, possibly even with a language you don't understand."

"What do you mean 'lost?'" Kayla pressed.

Taz was quick to elaborate this time. "When you travel to what we could term the 'parallel past world,' you can only exist there for a limited time. If you exceed that time, you're stuck there forever, with no way of returning."

"How much time?" Jaden asked, causing the gliders to glance nervously at one another.

"It varies, and we don't really know what determines the variation," Taz confessed. "That's what makes using the arcachoa so perilous. It's impossible to know how long is too long."

"I see," Jaden muttered. A quick peek at Kayla showed even she was getting suspicious. Her next statement confirmed it.

"Jaden, please, tell us what's going on in that head of yours."

Jaden exhaled. He had accumulated enough information to conclude what he was considering was impossible. "Really, it's nothing. I thought the time travel might be useful for, uh, finding something, but now that I understand how it works, it's not an option."

"Jaden Jameson, you're still hiding something. You would never give up so quickly. Tell us what you were thinking, or so help me. I'll take your medallion away from you right now!"

Startled by her anger, Jaden tried pacifying her. "No need to get upset. I was just thinking it might be a way to help my parents."

Sympathy softened Kayla's response. "You thought you might somehow go back in time and rescue them?"

"Yes, that was my initial idea. But now that I understand how the time effect works, I know I can't get back to them, primarily because they aren't artifacts."

Jaden wanted to squirm as Kayla studied him for signs of deceit. Convinced he truly had no intention of taking whatever scheme he might have had in mind any further, she said, "Okay, but do nothing crazy before speaking to all of us first."

"Yes, ma'am," Jaden teased, touched she cared. If he wasn't such a wimp, he would tell her how much that meant to him. But he kept his mouth shut. Until she could recognize her own feelings for him, he wouldn't force her hand.

Kayla smiled, but Jaden saw her fatigue, as though all the emotions of the day had finally come crashing down and were crushing her.

Kayla moaned. "How much farther?"

"Actually, we're nearly there," Han replied. "Jaden, bring out that map of yours. It's time to set more precise bearings."

Jaden removed the wooden disc from his pocket and manipulated its various parts until the map splashed up into the surrounding air. The bats whistled appreciatively, getting their first glimpse of the spectacular map. Without the walls of Jaden's room to restrain it, it was even more impressive, floating all around them on a far larger scale. That wasn't the only difference.

Jaden and Kayla both saw it simultaneously. A prominent X had appeared. *How is that possible? Are we imagining it?* But one look at Kayla and Jaden knew they were both questioning the same variance.

Then Jaden noticed something else. As they flew, the X changed its position relative to their movement. It was guiding them, like a compass, toward their intended destination. Jaden gawked in stunned amazement.

"How on earth did they have technology like this even a hundred years ago, let alone more?" Jaden breathed.

"I don't know," Kayla whispered, awed. "Something else to add to the growing list of things we should ask Zareh the next time we see him."

Their gliders flew on, guided by the shifting X. They were no longer required to identify landmarks but surveyed their surroundings nonetheless. The terracotta-hued terrain passing beneath them had a stark beauty all of its own. Scrubby, whitewashed bushes pimpled the flat reddish base, scattered with rocky mesas and buttes of varying sizes emerging from earthy mounds of eroded soil. Larger plateaus made sporadic appearances, granting the landscape a semblance of balance.

Twenty minutes passed before Jaden noticed the bats getting antsy. "What's wrong?"

"It's almost twilight," Taz replied, her voice betraying her stress.

"And that's supposed to mean something?"

"It's prime time for Gaptor attacks," Han explained.

"Oh, something we definitely want to avoid!" Jaden responded. "Let's land and rest. My legs are aching."

"Mine too," Kayla confessed. "A break will be nice, and there's no point risking an attack when we're all tired. Besides, it'll be nice not to see that beast's ugly mug for another day if we can help it."

Taz gave a toothy smile, leading them toward a rocky outcropping rising from the barren land.

It was tough to tell in the growing darkness, but Jaden thought the outcropping would make an excellent resting place and provide shelter should the Gaptor make an appearance. He revised his thinking when he noticed the way Taz drooled at the trees skirting the eastern edge. "Those trees looking tasty?" Jaden teased.

Taz's nose twitched. "Yes, the leaves smell delectable."

Jaden chuckled. "I'm not the only one who thinks about food."

"The difference is that I don't think about it all the time," Taz retorted.

Jaden laughed. He passed his hand over the disc as they descended, and the map disappeared. The sudden absence of the soft light from the lines made it feel darker. Could it be indicative of their situation? The unexpected, pessimistic inkling made Jaden realize how exhausted he was.

Jaden amended his earlier suggestion. "On second thought, why don't we settle here for the night instead and pick it up again tomorrow? Keen as I am to get answers, I'm sacked."

Delighted agreement from the others confirmed he had made the right call. Considering their level of fatigue, the tempting prospect of relaxation was tough to resist. The day's events had taken their toll, physically, mentally, and emotionally, and the group was quiet as they dropped the last few feet.

Jaden longed to be on the ground already. He desperately needed the respite a decent night's sleep would provide—and it was the only way he'd have a hope of functioning coherently tomorrow. Who knew what they would be called to do? Shaky with fatigue by the time they touched down, Jaden slipped to the ground, too drained to eat and definitely too tired to care about the others. Dragging his sleeping shell from his backpack, Jaden tossed it onto the dusty desert floor. Wordlessly, he crawled inside, closed his eyes, and shut out all thoughts except sleep.

CHAPTER THREE

Jaden opened his eyes the next morning to find the sky sprinkled with a billion stars. He watched them wink out when bathed by the faint radiance of early dawn. Sitting up, he rubbed sleep from his eyes, noticing the gliders' absence. Probably out foraging. The thought of food made his stomach growl. He'd missed dinner last night and was ravenous.

Glancing over to where Kayla still slept, submerged in her shell, he quietly rummaged in his backpack for food. The two power bars weren't his first choice, but they would have to do. Despite chewing each mouthful a hundred times, he was still hungry. He knew he should wait for the food to make its way through his digestive system before eating more, so he tried drowning his hunger pangs with water.

Eager to do something other than think about his empty stomach, Jaden stood and stretched, observing for the first time in the half-light that their little camp was near the edge of a precipice. Wandering to the rim, he studied his surroundings.

The plateau overlooked a deep, shadowed, rocky valley. On the far side, another sheer cliff climbed to the sky. Dark holes of varying sizes, presumably caves, pockmarked the walls of the opposing cliff. *Are the cliffs concealed beneath me similarly covered?*

Strolling along the edge, Jaden absorbed the stark beauty of the empty terrain, gradually revealed in vivid purples, delicate pinks, chocolate browns, and olive greens as the sun edged above the horizon. It was stunning for a landscape devoid of conventionally appealing elements.

Hearing something, he turned and saw Kayla ambling over. Just the sight of her made his day. He grinned. Her hair, still slightly mussed from sleep, curled in waves around her gorgeous face. Her dreamy eyes and languid movements told him she wasn't quite awake yet. "Morning."

Kayla grinned. "Morning. Sleep well?" Her eyes teased his lack of etiquette at going to sleep without so much as a word to any of them.

"Yeah. I was totally wasted. Sorry if I left you hanging with the bats —no pun intended."

Kayla laughed. "No worries. Actually, we just followed suit and crashed too. Where do you think they are?"

"Out finding food. Have you eaten?"

"No, I like to wake up before I eat, but I suppose the same isn't true for you?"

"Missing a meal is never good for me. I've eaten the power bars we rationed for breakfast, but I'm still hungry."

"You could always eat what we planned for last night's dinner," Kayla proposed, giggling as Jaden pulled a face.

"It's one thing to eat tuna for dinner when you can sleep off the smell but quite another to have it for breakfast and reek of it all day."

Kayla smirked. "That depends on how hungry you are."

"You have a point." Jaden smiled. "But you'd better not complain about it later today."

Kayla drew a hand across her lips as though sealing them. Jaden chuckled, and they sauntered back to their transitory camp.

"So, what do you think that was last night?" Kayla asked while they scratched in their bags for food. Jaden raised his eyebrows, and she elaborated. "The moving 'x?'"

"Not sure. With this quest, my wild imagination has me thinking the weirder the explanation, the more likely it is that it's the right one."

"So what's your wild theory?"

"I'd guess the name in the book, Soquazba, only gave us a general idea of the area we should head toward. If we'd 'turned on' the map earlier, we might've seen when the 'x' appeared. But lacking that information, I'd go out on a limb and speculate the 'x' only materialized when we were within range of our endpoint. And to make it interesting, let's say it also only popped up because we're the 'right' people looking for it."

Kayla laughed. "Okay, remind me to not ask you difficult questions in the morning if I don't want wacky answers."

They settled on their sleeping shells with their food. It didn't take long to demolish the meager portions. Afterward, they lounged on their shells, waiting for their bats to return. Thirty minutes later, they were still waiting.

"Those bats sure are taking their sweet time," Kayla grumbled. "Let's take another look at the map. Maybe we can make sense of that 'x' and figure out how far we still have to travel."

Jaden plucked the disc from the inside pocket of his windbreaker. Two seconds later, the map floated around them. Again, the change was impossible to miss.

Gone was their two-dimensional map with its guiding "X." Instead, a three-dimensional landscape glowed in front of them, yesterday's lines shifting vertically to varying heights so they now depicted more readily recognizable features. Most notable, though, was the appearance of a dot, blinking slowly, on the highest part of the map. It reminded Jaden of a cursor on an antiquated computer monitor, waiting for a command.

Agitated by the radical change, Jaden paced. "First an 'x' and now a dot! What's next? A lightning bolt on the exact spot?"

Cradling the map in the palm of his hand, Jaden waited for the landscape to move around him as it had with the "X." The image didn't budge. *But is the dot flashing a little faster?* Convinced it was his imagination, Jaden stopped pacing and glared at the offending speck. Its tempo remained constant. Whirling, he stalked back toward their camp, monitoring the dot. And this time, when the blinking slowed unmistakably, he knew he hadn't imagined it.

He glanced at Kayla, wanting confirmation she had noticed it too, but she was staring off into the distance, searching for the bats. "Hey," Jaden called, "check this out. Follow me and watch the dot. Tell me if you think it blinks faster."

Kayla rolled her eyes. She evidently wasn't in the mood for games.

Jaden ignored her reaction. He swiveled and strode away, grinning when he heard her blow out a long sigh before stomping after him. She drew level, looking annoyed. But the annoyance faded when, almost imperceptibly, the dot blinked a little faster. Jaden's smile widened as she craned her neck to get closer, eyeing the dot like a bird watching a live snake.

The dot didn't disappoint. The further they moved from the camp, the more rapidly it flashed.

Kayla noticed Jaden's grin. Her brow furrowed. "Try going back the other way," she ordered.

Jaden complied, and the closer they got to their camp, the slower the dot pulsed.

"Hmm, I have an idea," Kayla said.

"What?"

"Did you ever play that game as a kid where you hid something from someone and then let them find it by telling them they were getting hotter or colder according to their distance from the item?"

"Who didn't?" he answered. "You think this might work the same way? That it blinks faster when we get closer and vice versa?"

"I do. Let's follow it and see where it leads."

Studying the dot, they left the camp, adjusting their course several times when it became obvious they weren't traveling in a straight line. But it wasn't long before they established their destination.

"That hill over there—you think that's where the dot is leading us?" Jaden asked.

"Yup. It's the highest point in this area, which coincides with the map."

Sure enough, the dot blinked frantically when they reached the sharp rise in elevation that marked the outer edge of the mini-butte.

"How's your climbing?" Jaden asked, indicating the squat rocky face that rose steeply, but for only a short distance.

"Guess we'll find out," Kayla muttered. She reached out and gripped a rocky bulge. "Onward and upward!"

Jaden took a moment to watch as she labored up the rock face. Climbing wasn't her forte. But she hadn't complained or backed down. He grinned. She wouldn't let him get to the top and find answers without her. He waited a little longer before scrambling up after her, making sure he stayed behind her in case she needed help. Cresting the summit, he found Kayla eyeing him deprecatingly.

"You didn't mention you were a mountain goat."

"You have little choice when you live near mountains and have friends like Markov and Stovan."

She nodded understanding and flopped onto her back to catch her breath.

Jaden moved to sit next to her. When her labored breathing eased, Jaden retrieved the disc from his zippered jacket pocket and extracted the map. As anticipated, the dot was almost a permanent mark, the period between blinks virtually invisible.

Since the only way to move was forward, they rose and advanced. The apex of the hill wasn't as flat as it had appeared from the base. The ground underfoot was uneven, strewn with rocks near the edge, giving way to lumpy mounds of earth closer to the center. Creeping forward so they didn't accidentally roll an ankle, the pair couldn't avoid noticing when the dot stopped blinking and exuded a soft, steady glow instead.

"I think we're there," Jaden murmured.

"Fat lot of use that does us; there's nothing here! What are we supposed to do now?"

Jaden examined the area. She was right. They stood on the only flat, bare piece of earth amidst the hillocky earth surrounding it. No rocks, no trees, no blaring neon sign declaring they had reached their destination. "Hmm, not sure. Any ideas?"

"Maybe it's buried?"

"Like treasure?"

Kayla rolled her eyes for the second time that day. "Have any better suggestions?"

"No, but since the area we're standing on seems to be soil, not rock, your theory has credibility."

"Wow, thanks," Kayla acknowledged, not bothering to hide her sarcasm.

Jaden grinned. She was adorable when irritated. She reminded him of an angry pixie. What would she do if he told her that? The thought made him grin all the more because she would most likely clock him.

"What are you smiling at?"

"Nothing," Jaden hummed, bending over and scratching at the soil so she wouldn't see the laughter he was struggling to suppress.

Out of the corner of his eye, he caught Kayla studying him as though she knew he wasn't telling her something. Then she sighed. Bending, she scratched alongside Jaden. Hardened by decades of weathering, the packed earth was unyielding.

"If we must dig, we'll need tools," Kayla grunted a minute later.

Agreeing it would be too much effort to go down to their camp and then realizing they had nothing helpful there anyway, they scoured the immediate area for makeshift implements. Some loose, flat rocks scattered closer to the edge appeared suitable, so they picked out a few and returned to the site, setting their chosen rocks on the ground. It was a pitiful assembly, but preferable to using their bare hands. Selecting a thin piece, narrow on one end and wide at the other, Jaden dug.

Kayla copied him, and it wasn't long before fine dust coated them. It was grueling work. The soil was baked solid, and the stones were difficult to work with. Their rough exteriors and unwieldy shapes weren't conducive to the task. But they pressed on, determined to find whatever the dot had led them to.

An hour later, Jaden noticed he wasn't the only one sweating profusely. Neither was he the only one with hands raw from the fine particles coating the stones scraping against his skin with every downward shove. They were parched and worn out. Kayla caught him staring and gave a half-shrug. In unison, they flopped onto their backs, panting.

"Maybe there's nothing here," Jaden said, uncharacteristically ready to pursue another course of action, or at the very least, entertain other ideas.

"There must be something. What other reason could there be for the dot to stop flashing and start glowing? Can you see anything else out there hinting at a different scenario?" she asked, gesturing meaningfully toward the empty area around them.

Jaden scowled, disgruntled by the prospect of more digging. "Is it possible that whatever was here isn't anymore?"

"If that were true, the soil wouldn't be concrete."

They were silent for a few moments, Jaden sensing Kayla's determination to dig more and Kayla apparently sensing his reluctance.

Jaden gave in. "Look, could we maybe agree to dig for another thirty minutes and then call it quits?"

She considered his suggestion. "Desperate as I am to find something, I'm also tired. And hungry. And thirsty. In thirty minutes, the hole will probably be deep enough to convince me nothing's buried here."

"You agree? Thirty minutes more, and then we stop?"

"Yes, another thirty minutes only. But no slacking! I didn't turn my nails into jagged stumps for nothing."

"Deal." Jaden beamed. Her request was reasonable, and with an end in sight, he felt invigorated.

Twenty-three minutes later, they hit a rock. A large one, stretching almost all the way across the opening they had made. They stopped digging, eyeing one another.

"What now?" Jaden asked.

"We still have seven minutes. Let's try pry it out. Whatever we're looking for might be under the rock."

"Not what I wanted to hear, but yeah, I agree. All we've hit so far is sand. This rock is definitely out of place."

With hopes of imminent victory, they doubled their efforts. Burrowing around the rock took an exhausting fifteen minutes. They were so focused on the task, neither noticed how large the rock was until they sat back and viewed it.

Jaden scratched his head. "We're not getting that out of there without some leverage."

"There were some trees on the eastern edge of the rocks by our camp. Maybe we could break a branch off?"

"If we could break the branch off, I doubt it would support the weight of the stone."

"Ugh!" Kayla groaned, throwing the rock she had been digging with onto one of the small mounds of earth a short distance away. "Why can't we catch a break?"

As she said this, the rock landed and made a soft, clinking sound.

Jaden's head jerked up. "Did you hear that?"

Kayla sprang to her feet and darted toward the heap, Jaden right behind.

Finding her discarded rock, Kayla snatched it and pawed at the sand underneath. A tiny, rusted bit of metal poked through. Hurriedly scrubbing away the dirt around the exposed portion, Kayla revealed part of a metal bar. Without speaking, they attacked the soil with their rocks, exposing what lay there: an antiquated, round-nosed metal shovel.

CHAPTER FOUR

Jaden groaned. "Now we find a shovel!"

Kayla grinned. "No, we found a lever."

Her face was so full of pride it was impossible not to laugh. "We did! Let's hope it's not too rusted to be of use."

Lifting the ancient tool, Jaden carried it back to the hole. With the nose of the shovel wedged under the widest part of the rock, he directed Kayla to the other side of the handle. They each applied one hand to the open end of the handle and the other hand to the metal bar leading down to the nose.

Kayla's face flushed with excitement. The dirt smearing her cheeks did nothing to diminish her appeal. Jaden felt a curious ache in his chest as he thought of the dangers they would have to face. He only hoped they would both get out of this in one piece. "Ready?"

Kayla nodded, and they pushed down. Nothing happened. Like the rock had grown roots, it clung obstinately to the earth below. Jaden was about to tell Kayla they should give the handle another jolt when, with a soft whoosh, the rock gave way, lifting a little.

Working their way around the hole, they released the rock sufficiently so they could remove it. Except Jaden didn't know how they'd manage. The rock was incredibly heavy. He discussed options with

Kayla, and in minutes, they hatched a plan. Using some smaller stones they had collected earlier, they lifted and shimmed repeatedly in a circular manner until the rock was high enough for them to coax it from the hole using the shovel. It groaned out, flipped over, and came to a stop with its dirty underside facing away from them.

Diving into the hollow, Jaden and Kayla scooped out the stones they'd used as shims . . . and found nothing. Just more sand. Which, ironically, resembled beach sand, loose and fine, nothing like the hard soil they had had to dig through to this point. Jaden snatched up the shovel and attacked the soft earth, tossing large loads over his shoulder in an almost maniacal frenzy.

When his pace slowed, Kayla took over, digging just as feverishly. Ten minutes later, Jaden took over again. But after only a few loads, he threw the shovel to the ground and stalked off. Kayla trailed him, her disappointment as keen as his own. They dropped to the ground, away from the offending hole, miserable. It was time to face the painful truth: there was nothing in the hole.

Jaden slumped onto his back, permitting his aching muscles some relief. "I don't understand. Why would the map lead us here if there was nothing to find?"

Kayla collapsed next to him. Turning his head, Jaden observed as she scratched peevishly at her birthmark. He would have to ask her about that sometime.

Sighing, Kayla said, "Maybe you were right. Whatever was there could've already been found or moved. Alternatively, it's been here for so long that it's completely disintegrated. If it was organic, it could've decomposed by now, right?"

Jaden nodded a mute agreement. While he understood her groping for a logical answer to his question, his fury rose by the minute. *Why does the map show this precise spot if there's nothing here?* They had to be missing something.

Jaden rolled his shoulders, then rotated his neck, trying to stretch the stiff muscles as he lay on the hard ground. Something flashed from the rock they'd removed, lying just behind his upturned head. Rolling onto his stomach, he squinted to get a better view. There, embedded in the rock's underside, was a second relic stone.

"Would you look at that!" he exclaimed, leaping to his feet.

Kayla twisted her head backward, lacking the energy to spring up as Jaden had. Then her eyes widened.

"Ziggety! There's another one!" Kayla shouted, bounding up to land next to Jaden in one fluid movement. Inspecting it, she asked, "How do we get it out of there?"

Winking, Jaden withdrew his Swiss army knife from the pocket in his pants. He examined the rock until he found what he was looking for. With extreme care, he inserted the tip of the blade into the tiny crack in the boulder on one side of the relic stone.

Gently, he tried prying the precious object from its prison. It didn't give. Exasperated, he removed the tip and tried again, altering the angle. But the minute space hindered maneuverability, rendering his tactic ineffective. The relic stone remained lodged. Drawing back, Jaden frowned. His blade hadn't even scratched the surface of the surrounding rock.

"How do you think they embedded the ring in the rock?" Kayla wondered aloud.

"Maybe they didn't. It's possible they buried it underneath the rock, but with time, and the rock's weight, the two melded together."

"That's plausible. Then again, whoever placed it there might have wrapped the rock around it to prevent it from being removed."

Jaden stared at her. *Is she insane?*

"What?" Kayla retorted. "Weren't you the one who told me this morning that the more improbable the explanation, the more likely it was correct?"

"You have a point—again. It just sounded so ridiculous when you said it."

Kayla laughed. "Didn't it? But I made that point for a reason. If we figure out how the ring got in there, we might find the way to get it out. The knife is useless; it didn't even mark the rock. Maybe a diamond-tipped drill bit would be the answer, but considering we don't have one of those handy, what are the alternatives?"

Jaden considered. "Going with your theory and expanding it, let's say someone from Zareh's world secured the relic stone here. If that's the case, then perhaps only someone—or something—from that world can remove it. Do you think the gliders could extract it with their talons?"

For the second time in as many minutes, Kayla laughed. "I'd like to see you asking Taz. I can already hear her complaining you're ruining her manicure."

The picture had Jaden laughing too. "Okay, so maybe not. Han would be the better option. Or we could ask him to carry the rock into the air and then drop it. He's insanely strong, so the weight wouldn't be a problem."

"Hmm, no, not such a great idea either. If we can break the rock by dropping it, the relic stone might shatter too."

Bamboozled, the teens studied the rock from various angles, as though this would impart inspiration. And oddly, it did. Jaden snapped his fingers and marched off to their pile of discarded digging stones. Searching until he found one with a relatively sharp point, he crossed back to the boulder and scraped the stone across the impervious surface.

The stone lasted all of ten seconds before it cracked and fragmented under the pressure. Jaden repeated the process with another stone, this one differing in color and texture, hoping this specimen was made of stronger stuff. But it crumbled in an even shorter time. In quick succession, he experimented with several others, all with the same unsatisfactory result.

Jaden sighed. "Well, whatever the boulder's made of, it's stronger than any of the other rocks up here." His stomach grumbled. "Let's grab lunch. I'm famished."

Kayla agreed, and they clambered down the butte and trudged back to their camp. Discouraged, they mechanically removed the sandwiches they had brought with them and began chewing.

"The bats are taking forever to come back. Where do you think they are? Surely they can't still be out foraging?" Kayla said.

"Who knows?" Jaden answered, his mind still puzzling over how they would remove the relic stone. "Maybe they figured they got us here, so there's nothing more for them to do."

"Jaden!" Kayla admonished. "They don't think like that. We're their responsibility, and I'm sure that wherever they are, they didn't just dump us here!"

Jaden rolled his eyes. "I don't really think that. I'm just being peevish. Forgive me?"

"Yes, but muzzle your mouth. If our gliders heard you, it would offend them."

Jaden nodded. For the third time that day, she made a valid point. Her astute mind continually amazed him. *No, that's not true. It's not only her mind. It's everything about her. I've never met anyone like her before.*

"What are you thinking?"

Kayla's unexpected question flustered him. She *would* catch him thinking about her. But he wasn't about to admit it. Not all of it anyway. "I was thinking about your brilliant brain. Why don't you set it to work calculating how we can remove the relic stone from that rock?"

She eyed him curiously before answering. "That's what I was doing. I was guessing the bats might have suggestions on what we could try, which made me wonder where they were. But since they aren't back, I suppose we must figure it out for ourselves."

"Bummer," Jaden grumbled. But he was relieved she hadn't asked why he'd been momentarily speechless. A random thought struck him. "Hey, where do you reckon the first relic stone came from? I mean, before it was in human hands? Was it also encased by rock?"

Without waiting for her reply, Jaden delved in his backpack for the relic stone. He had not thought to remove it when they took to the skies the previous day with their gliders. Then again, his mother's disclosures and her distraught face when they left had traumatized him.

Pushing the depressing memories aside, Jaden scrutinized every square inch of the ring for signs of forcible removal from tough sheathing. He found none. Sighing, he stowed the ring in his zippered shirt pocket in case they wanted to look at it again when they were back on the butte.

"Nothing there?" Kayla guessed, noting his downcast face.

"Nope. What have you been up to?" he asked, aware she hadn't been close.

"While you were studying your relic stone, I was collecting a few things that might help remove the other one." She gestured toward a pile of pointy instruments: a bottle opener with a fortuitous corkscrew attachment on the opposite end; a small screwdriver; a pair of tweezers; a thick metal wire from the frame of her backpack; a star-shaped earring; and a small glass bottle. Eyeing the bottle, Jaden gestured toward it inquiringly.

Kayla grinned. "Who knows? It might just release the relic stone."

Jaden had to smile. "Yeah, you never know. Should we take a cotton ball too?"

Kayla smacked him on the shoulder, but she laughed too. "Have anything you want to add before we climb that wretched hill again?"

Jaden poked around in his backpack, coming up with a pair of nail clippers, a magnet, and a paper clip. "More of the innocuous," he said when Kayla raised her eyebrows.

Refreshed by the food and their break, they made short work of the trip back to the butte. Jaden couldn't say it surprised him that the climb to the top seemed easier the second time around for Kayla. After heaving themselves onto the flat top, they retraced their path back to the overturned boulder.

Tipping their excavating tools out of the small bag they had brought them in, they unsuccessfully tried one after the other. Eventually, only the bottle remained.

"Should we smash it so we have a sharp edge to use?" Kayla asked.

"No, let's take a break and think."

They sprawled out on the ground. Jaden unzipped his pocket and retrieved the relic stone his grandmother had given him. *How had this one come to exist?* He studied it, but there were still no clues. Annoyed, he shoved the ring onto his index finger.

Boom!

Jaden flipped his hands towards his ears, but the ring distracted him midway—it was burning his finger! He altered the course his arm was taking, intent on ripping the ring off, but before he had a chance, there was a blinding flash of light, and an unseen force smashed his hand into his face.

Shell-shocked, Jaden lay there, waiting for something else to happen. But the noise had vanished. The light dimmed back to pure, desert sunshine. The air stilled. Sanity returned. A trickle of blood ran down his cheek where the ring had ripped the flesh.

Turning his head slowly toward his hand, the relic stone's altered shape astounded him. He blinked, trying to make sense of what he was seeing. Staring at the ring, his eyes regained focus. The ring hadn't changed shape. The second relic stone now supplemented it, inverting itself on the first, the two discs cemented together.

Jaden sat up gingerly. "What happened?"

"Why don't you tell me?" Kayla snapped, rubbing her elbow where it had cracked against a rock, then gesturing toward the relic stones on his finger.

"I don't know," Jaden muttered, still confused.

"Well, maybe all the light and noise had something to do with it?"

"You think?"

They began laughing. It was a mixture of relief, joy, and fatigue all rolled into one sweet, liberating sound.

Kayla finally sputtered, "Why are we laughing?"

"No idea." Jaden chortled, before another fit of laughter seized him.

When their laughter died down, Kayla said, "It seems we only needed the relic stone your grandmother gave you to get the other one out of the rock. How does that work?"

Jaden sighed, gesturing toward his medallion and the attached relic stones and then imitating something flying. "How does any of this work?"

"Right. Well, what now?"

"Get the rings apart? I don't think they're meant to remain attached."

"Really, we're flogging that horse again? I say we leave it where it is, get off this hill, and go get some dinner."

"I like where you're going with that thought—" Jaden began.

But he didn't get any further. A piercing whistle interrupted him. Two enormous shadows rushed over them, momentarily blocking the sun's heat and chilling him. Peering up, Jaden saw their gliders swooping past.

"Jump!" Han yelled, urgency imprinted along every line of his tense body. "You're in danger."

Danger? Here? Kayla's face was as blank as his own. Then, looking around, Jaden spotted it. The impossibly black shape of the Gaptor, heading straight for them. Without hesitation, he and Kayla turned and sprinted to the edge of the small hill. They leaped with abandon. Their gliders caught them in midair before speeding off in a mad dash, intent on escape.

CHAPTER FIVE

"Spittlebugs, how'd he find us?" Kayla cursed.

"Our question too!" Taz shot back. "What were you doing? Shooting flares to mark your location? He appeared from nowhere, streaking toward your exact position like a cockroach to a festering cesspool."

Kayla exchanged glances with Jaden. The only explanation was the explosive way the second relic stone removed itself from bondage. But she couldn't talk. Their gliders were moving faster than in any of their practice sessions, and Kayla had to garner every ounce of concentration just to regulate her breathing.

"Well?" Taz demanded. "What were you two up to?"

"We found another relic stone," Kayla gasped.

Taz wobbled under her in surprise. "You did? Where?"

"On that butte you rescued us from," Kayla managed, squeezing each word out with extreme effort.

"Details later. Our focus must be on eluding that beast. Can we fly faster?"

"A little, but I'm almost at my limit."

"It's impossible to avoid him at this rate. We must make for the cliffs and try outmaneuvering him there."

Taz swerved violently to the right. With her attention honed on not passing out, Kayla pitched face-first off of Taz's back. Momentarily disoriented by the fall, it took a moment before she remembered to relax her body into the reconnection position. Secure in the knowledge Taz would snatch her up before she crashed to the desert floor, Kayla drifted. Taz flitted into view a split second later.

Catch Kayla Taz did, but she was livid, making no effort to hide her displeasure. "We can't afford to lose time. We don't have enough of a lead. Stay on!"

Yes, ma'am, Kayla pouted, her disposition soured by Taz's strident tone. But Taz worried how they would escape the predator when they couldn't rely on the speed that usually bailed them out.

That's the real question. How are *we going to get away?* Kayla scoured the desolate terrain below but spotted nothing that might aid them. The few scrubby bushes and thorny cacti dotting the landscape wouldn't pose much of a threat to the Gaptor's armored hide, and they were too small to slow him down. *How will the cliffs help?*

Kayla didn't have to wait long to find out. They covered the distance from the butte to the cliff edge, where she and Jaden had admired the view that morning, in record time. Crossing over the edge and into the void, Taz tucked her wings and plunged them into the valley.

Kayla's stomach lurched as they dropped twenty feet in a heartbeat. The cliff face surged past in a blur. Terrified, Kayla pinched her knees into the bat's side while feverishly gripping the fur on Taz's neck ridge. It wouldn't do to fall off again. They no longer had sufficient altitude for Taz to catch her. Fear made Kayla tighten her hold on the bat further, and not a moment too soon.

"Prepare for some extreme weaving," Taz warned. "Han and I will try to roll the Gaptor into the cliff face. It's the only way to buy time."

What does that mean? But there was no time to think. Taz rolled so aggressively, Kayla silently thanked her for all the practice runs she'd insisted on in the past few days. Without those, Kayla would've had no hope of staying on. *Is Jaden struggling as much as I am to stay on?*

Risking a glance, she saw Jaden wobble as Han deviated abruptly.

Her breath hitched. Han's every curve, twist, and turn was reflected in Jaden's flexing back and arm muscles as he fought to maintain his position. If she wasn't so worried, she might've enjoyed the view. Regaining his equilibrium, Jaden caught her staring and grinned. Kayla flushed and averted her gaze. *What did my face tell him?*

Trying not to think about it, Kayla searched for the Gaptor. The monster had closed the margin between them. Significantly. Sudden movement under her as Taz swerved again made Kayla forget the revelation. Her focus narrowed to a single task—predicting Taz's movements.

It took only two rocky protrusions to figure out what Taz was up to. She raced along the cliff face, sticking as close as possible and weaving around the irregular outcroppings. This was what caused the violent changes in direction. Proving the point, another bluff loomed, and Taz twisted away. This time, Kayla expected the shift and handled the realignment with ease. Satisfied, she considered how all this weaving around the cliffs would help them, but dropped the thought when she spotted another protrusion in their flight path. Kayla concentrated on keeping her perch as Taz swerved again.

Taz's shout was unexpected. "Han, we're running out of cliff face. Slow down!"

Kayla panicked. *What? Are they insane? Why slow down?* Leaning forward to argue with Taz, the words died when she spotted the Gaptor, terrifyingly close behind. "Hurry!" she screeched in Taz's ear. "He's right behind the boys!"

Taz gloated. "Perfect!"

Her reaction was as unexpected as the abrupt lurch to bypass another gigantic rock. Kayla curled her fingers tighter, her knuckles white with the effort. She was sure she would never walk again, convinced her knees would never unwind from their current locked position. And if she clenched her teeth any harder, she might break her jaw. Striving to forget her discomfort, she sneaked another peek backward and caught Jaden and Han clearing the rocky crag with ease.

But the Gaptor was so close. He lumbered around the ridge, his ungainly form not designed for such precise flying. Before anything happened, Kayla knew he'd made a mistake. His turn was too tight. With a hideous screeching sound, his wing tips scraped the surface of the jutting boulder, the slight nudge affecting his stability. The Gaptor's huge frame pitched awkwardly in the opposite direction as he battled to counteract the fluctuation generated by the impact.

Kayla suddenly understood what the bats were up to. They really meant to roll their tormentor into the cliffs. "Nice thinking," she cooed in Taz's ear as Taz propelled them onward. "It almost worked on that last ridge. Let's not miss on the next one."

Taz rumbled agreement, her wings straining under Kayla when she dived under the next obstacle. Shifting with her glider's motion, Kayla negotiated the rapid change in direction. They cleared the rocky barrier, rolling up and out of the curve, then burst from the valley into the wide, open air. Unnerved, Kayla whipped her head around, scanning for shelter. But there was nothing. *How are we going to protect ourselves now?*

Maybe the ridge we just negotiated will bring the Gaptor down. Kayla swiveled on Taz's back, eager to confirm her theory. Han and Jaden streaked around the ridge. With bated breath, she waited for the Gaptor. She wasn't the only one.

Noticing Kayla's attention was on what was behind him, Jaden likewise turned to look. With their eyes glued to the ridge, they shifted their weight to accommodate the familiar motion of the bats looping up and curling around. The four of them now faced their opponent head on, albeit from a higher elevation.

The Gaptor lurched into view, navigating the outcropping. Distracted by the bats hovering overhead, he lifted his head, making his body tilt infinitesimally. The minute adjustment crashed his wing into the unyielding barrier with a harsh, resounding crack.

Kayla observed the ensuing mayhem with glee. The Gaptor's wing crumpled as it encountered the hurdle, slamming the Gaptor into the cliff face. The impact whipped the Gaptor's stinger over its head, the beast's momentum somersaulting the cumbersome frame over its tail, so it came full circle and bashed into the rocky face again. The Gaptor hung there, suspended for an instant, before dropping straight down.

Jaden whooped. "Yeah!"

"Way to go!" Kayla told the bats.

But Taz's grim face had Kayla reining in her jubilation. Peering down, she found the Gaptor reeling out of its downward spiral, manically flapping its scraggly wings. *Scraggly but powerful*, Kayla thought. The Gaptor dragged himself from the perilous descent and gained altitude. "He's back in business!" Kayla yelled.

The warning was unnecessary. The bats were already reentering the valley for a second run-through in the opposite direction. Jaden and Han led this time, and Kayla watched in admiration as they swooped and curled around the rocky protrusions effortlessly, marveling yet again at their grace and speed.

Despite this, Kayla couldn't quell the gnawing anxiety that it wouldn't be enough. Worse, she hadn't heard the metallic scrape of the Gaptor's wings against the cliffs even once yet. *Was he was getting the hang of this and navigating the tight turns more effectively?* With the end of the valley in sight, they would soon lose the cover of the cliffs, making them vulnerable once again.

Taz must've been thinking the same thing. With a shrill whistle, she signaled Han. "We need to find cover."

"You don't say! Just where would you suggest we find it?" Han barked.

"What about one of the caves in the cliff?" Jaden asked.

The bats cocked their heads, evaluating his proposal. An abundance of openings roomy enough to accommodate them beaded the cliff face. The trick was finding a cave roomy enough for them to squeeze into but too small to allow the Gaptor entry. In addition, it would have to be deep enough to house the four of them while still keeping them beyond the reach of the Gaptor's talons and tail. Assessing each cave's depth was nigh impossible as they sped past the shadowed openings. And yet . . .

"It might work," Taz conceded. "Keep your eyes peeled for something suitable. We'll probably have to pass back to access it—there isn't enough time with the Gaptor so close to us now."

They barreled onward, the bats avoiding the unforgiving outcroppings and the teens peering into every passing cave.

"There's one," Jaden shouted, pointing back at a cave. "Confirm it'll work," he told Kayla.

Kayla eyed the cave as she and Taz drew level with the opening. The mouth was the perfect size, and the small sliver of fading sunshine leaning into it hinted at a deeper passageway. "Yup, I think it'll work!"

"Let's hope it does," Taz muttered, concentrating on skirting the outcropping blocking their path.

As Kayla twisted, accommodating Taz's movement, she spotted the Gaptor behind them and cursed. She should've thought to check on the Gaptor's pursuit earlier. "Taz, we have a problem. The Gaptor's figured out your strategy; he's flying wide of the rocks. He's gaining on us."

Taz bent her head and squinted under her long, graceful body to verify the accuracy of Kayla's statement. "Han, turn! Head back to that cave—right now!"

Han obeyed immediately. He tilted up and curled, executing a perfect roll over Taz and Kayla's heads. But he was too late.

The Gaptor streaked forward, aiming for the narrow gap between the two pairs. The blades on his wingtips were extended and spinning, his ochre eyes blazing as he smelled victory.

Kayla wasn't the only one paying attention. Taz's peripheral vision must've detected the movement. She reflexively twisted into a downward spiral, negating the Gaptor's attempt to take both pairs out with one strike.

Kayla smiled grimly at the Gaptor's momentary distress caused by Taz's unexpected move. But her smile was short-lived. After the briefest pause, the Gaptor swung away from them toward Jaden and Han, now the closer targets.

Barely breathing, Kayla was frantic about the boys. The Gaptor had them in his sights, a mean expression on his ugly mug. She shivered. She didn't want to think about what he would do if he caught them. She couldn't do this without Jaden. He was the one who made all this insanity bearable.

Kayla remembered the last time she and Jaden had been close—when he held her hand at his home before his mother's startling revelations. Contact she had savored because of the lack thereof since he'd reciprocated her withdrawal at his gran's.

Even if she couldn't have him as something more, Kayla still missed him as a friend. Lacking even friendship, there were neither casual hugs nor comforting handholding. No contact of any kind. And now there was a very real chance the contact they'd shared in his room would be her last meaningful moment with him. Kayla shook her head. *No, I can't think like that. Han and Jaden will pull through. They have to.*

CHAPTER SIX

"Hold your breath," Han ordered.

Jaden didn't argue, barely complying before Han accelerated so violently Jaden's head swam. His hands scrambled for purchase as he fought to stay on the hurtling bat. Clenching his knees, trying to flatten himself against Han, Jaden closed his eyes against the wind battering his eyelids shut.

But it was worse with his eyes closed. He could feel both the tremendous speed and his own lack of control more acutely. Losing his sight also meant he couldn't tell how far away the Gaptor was. Blood pounded in his head. His chest was about ready to explode. Wondering how much longer he would have to hold his breath, he felt Han slow.

Gulping air, Jaden opened his eyes, scanning the heavens for the Gaptor. Finding him took only an instant, his bulk impossible to miss. The Gaptor had dropped back a good distance, but to Jaden's chagrin, the monster was closing in again. Rapidly.

"What's the plan?" Jaden wheezed, keen to help in any way he could.

"I truly don't know," Han snapped. "We can't keep up these bursts of speed forever, and unless we find shelter soon, we're toast."

"What about the cave I pointed out earlier?"

"Getting back there is the challenge. In case you hadn't noticed, the Gaptor's between us and that cave."

"Maybe that was his plan."

"Unlikely. He's not too bright—more brawn than brain. Don't give him more credit than he deserves."

Han's comment sparked an idea in Jaden's mind. If what Han said was true, and Jaden had no reason to believe it wasn't, they might escape if they outsmarted the brute. "What about trying to roll under him, toward the cliff face? He might overshoot the mark trying to catch us and crash into the cliff."

"Not the best idea, but better than anything I can think of," Han said. "Get ready to hold your breath again. I must speed up to shoot past him."

Han's tone suggested he wasn't sure if even that would be enough. Jaden scanned the area, searching for Taz and Kayla. They had disappeared. *Where did they go?*

"Here we go," Han warned.

The dive was extreme. Jaden's stomach contents shot into his throat, rebelling against the precipitous drop. Swallowing the bile, Jaden concentrated as Han's muscles bunched under him, preparing for the roll to scoop them under the Gaptor and around the rock that jutted out in front of them. Han started the roll, and their world tipped upside down.

Wham! As something hit them with incredible force, it almost catapulted Jaden off of Han. Desperately grasping at the fur slipping through his fingers, Jaden braced his knees and scrambled to stay on.

Above their inverted position, the colossal, unmistakable shape of the Gaptor loomed. Like some revolting apparition, it hung there, the beast's putrid odor assailing Jaden's nose. The stench made him register the Gaptor was too close.

Jaden tried making sense of it. Abruptly, the Gaptor separated from them. Jaden's eyes latched onto its glinting talons, wickedly curved. And dripping. Thin streams of red blood flowed past Jaden's face as Han flipped out of the roll, bringing appalling comprehension.

"Han, you're hurt!"

Their sickening sway toward the cliff was answer enough. Han had no hold on their direction. They would crash into the very part of the cliff they had planned for the Gaptor if they didn't change course—right now! Frantic, Jaden leaned away from the swiftly approaching rock wall, hoping his weight shift would help Han alter their course. Han groaned in pain.

"Don't pull like that," Han hissed. Nevertheless, they tilted away from the cliff a split second before slamming into it, staggering back out toward the center of the valley.

"Sorry," Jaden murmured, wincing as he thought of Han's injury. Scanning for their foe, Jaden found him above them and to their left, close to the cliffs. Jaden blinked, sure his eyes were deceiving him. The Gaptor was out of control. Han must've managed a swipe at him —either that or the effort of drawing first blood had unbalanced the giant. The Gaptor wheeled closer and closer to the cliff, running out of space to squirm away.

A crashing boom reverberated up and down the valley as the Gaptor collided with the rock. Sparks flew where the massive wings scraped down the rock face, and a terrible, shrill scraping sound drilled into Jaden's brain every time the Gaptor's scaly skin scuffed the cliff.

Han didn't wait for the final scene. He slowly curled back toward the cliff face and picked up speed, aiming for the cave Jaden had pointed out earlier.

Jaden watched the Gaptor until it slipped out of sight behind a curve. Disappointed he hadn't witnessed it smashing into the desert floor, Jaden turned his attention back to their destination. Beneath him, Han's muscles trembled as his glider valiantly strived to maintain a level path.

"Han, will you make the cave? How are those gashes?"

"Scratches." Han shrugged, then hissed at the pain the movement incited. "They'll keep."

Opening his mouth to contradict Han, Jaden halted when Taz and Kayla slipped out of a cave ahead of them. Switching to berating them instead, Jaden shouted, "Nice of you to join us! Han's hurt. Is that cave deep enough for all of us?"

Kayla's face blanched. "Jaden, are you okay?"

"I'm fine," he yelled. "Will that cave work?"

"No, it's not deep enough. We haven't found one yet! While the Gaptor was chasing you, we were checking caves. But it's . . . look out!"

At her shriek, Han angled them sideways. Jaden stayed on. Barely. *Blast! The Gaptor's right behind us again. Why won't he quit?* But that wasn't Jaden's only concern. Through his knees, clamped tightly around Han's chest, he felt a drag on the bat's powerful muscles. Han was fading. *Why can't the monster chase Taz and Kayla for a bit?* The question brought clarity.

When the bats careened in to rescue them from the butte, their first question was what the teens had done to attract the Gaptor to them like a heat-seeking missile. They'd guessed the sonic boom when they "removed" the second relic stone—or was that sound the noise the stones made when bonding together? Whichever, the Gaptor evidently knew what that sound signified. *He's after the relic stones!*

"Kayla," Jaden yelled, "I think the Gaptor's after the relic stones. Han's losing blood. We need a break. Fly past, and I'll toss the rings to you."

Kayla acknowledged with a curt nod. Jaden waited, annoyed when he spotted Taz and Kayla in hurried conversation. He was too far away to hear. About to yell at them to hurry, he sagged in relief when they lifted higher and angled outward. They must've agreed an overhead pass would be best. Jaden tugged the rings off his finger, ready to throw them to the girls as they flew by.

As Jaden waited, he spotted the Gaptor limping back toward them. *Why won't the wretched beast just die?* Judging distances, Jaden worried he and Han wouldn't make it to the safety of a cave. Then he realized that, instead of making a beeline for their position, the Gaptor was curving off to the right, away from the cliff. *What's he up to now?* Han figured it out before he did.

"He's trying to separate us from the girls. Jaden, you need to toss those rings!"

Jaden faltered. The girls were still too far away. "What if I miss? He'll grab them!"

"Jaden, have you ever seen Taz *not* catch something of value? Throw them! Now!"

Jaden wavered only a second before obeying. The girls had closed the distance enough to intercept the rings before the Gaptor. He bent his arm, preparing to pitch the precious artifacts. "Kayla, here they come!"

Jaden hurled the rings. As they left his hand, he feared he'd waited too long. *Will the delay cost us?*

Time slowed like action in a slow-motion replay, except this wasn't a replay. The rings tumbled through the air, and the Gaptor put on a sudden burst of speed. As it passed, its sharp, sword-like beak slashed through Han's left wing. Powerless, sickened, Jaden watched Han's filmy wing membrane shredding, heard his bat's low moan of pain, and felt the abrupt loss of control as Han toppled sideways.

Grabbing at Han's fur as they spiraled earthward, Jaden was aware of the Gaptor above them, racing for the rings. He lifted his head. The girls plummeted down, plucking the relic stones out of the air right from under the Gaptor's beak.

Delight coursed through Jaden as the girls shot past the Gaptor in their almost ninety-degree dive. Taz angled them out of the perilous descent and swooped under Han, slowing as she circled. Then she rose slowly, perhaps intending to support Han and somehow slow the boys' sickening spin toward the desert floor.

Gazing at the girls, Jaden lost his grip and his hand floated in front of his face. He stared dumbly at the ring on his finger. *The ring? Impossible!* He had watched the rings, twisting through the air. But staring at the relic stone, he realized what the difference was. There was only one ring on his finger. *Huh, imagine that,* he thought dully. *I figured out how to separate them.* But Jaden was having trouble concentrating. The dizzying descent was making him nauseous.

A movement between them and the girls snagged his attention.

The Gaptor slid between the two pairs of bats and humans—again. *He's getting in the way. He'll stop the girls from helping us!* Jaden moaned with frustration.

The blast knocked his knees free and lifted the lower half of his body off Han's back. If it hadn't been for his one hand still clinging to Han for dear life, the impact would've knocked Jaden free. Crashing back down, Jaden squinted to see what had happened, but the sky was unbearably bright, blinding him.

The supersonic boom cracking the air was even worse. Jaden didn't know whether to hang onto Han or protect his eardrums. Then he forgot his dilemma when the light dimmed. An electric sizzle of glowing, white current burned between him and Kayla—the rings were emitting some sort of beam.

The Gaptor floated feebly into the current. Brilliant white light briefly outlined the monster's body. Then it stiffened, gave a blood-curdling screech, turned crispy, and disappeared in a puff of ash.

Jaden blinked. *Am I imagining this?* But when his vision cleared, the acrid smell of burned flesh was all that remained of their nemesis.

Opening his mouth for a victory shout, Jaden crashed back to reality—literally. Without the threat of the Gaptor to distract him, events shifted back to real time. No more slow-mo freefall. Instead, the ground rushed up to greet them way too enthusiastically. Jaden registered Kayla's shouting, but he couldn't distinguish her words above the roar of the wind in his ears. No doubt about it; they were going down. And there was nothing he could do.

CHAPTER SEVEN

Jaden fumbled in his fogged brain for a way to help Han, but it was impossible with the world spinning at such a giddy speed. The unexpected jerk as Taz and Kayla bumped up under them knocked the breath from him. Han grunted in agony. Disoriented, Jaden took a moment to realize they'd stopped spiraling and their descent was slowing. Then he heard Kayla.

"Jaden, jump!"

Uncurling his fingers with effort and loosening the death grip his knees had on Han's chest, Jaden lurched rather than jumped. It was only a short drop, but he seemed to hang there, suspended forever. In his state of flux, the wind tossed his body over so he faced Han's underside.

Jaden sucked in a horrified breath when he saw the true extent of the damage. Han's left wing fluttered uselessly, shredded to ribbons. Several long, nasty slashes on Han's stomach trickled bright red blood. Jaden only had time to be thankful that the wound wasn't deep before he crashed into Kayla.

"Hey, watch where you're landing," Kayla objected.

Jaden scrambled aside, so he was no longer squashing her. Unsure where he should be but aware he should find a secure position, he slipped behind Kayla.

"Sorry about this," Jaden muttered, wrapping his arms around her waist and sliding his legs over and around Kayla's. He was too far back to grip Taz with his knees any other way. "I'm not sure how we ride a glider together."

He wriggled, trying to make them both more comfortable, then settled. A moment later, Kayla relaxed against him. He stiffened, and Kayla jerked away. Her movement was so unexpected it had caught him off-guard. Annoyed with himself, Jaden held his breath, waiting to see if she would lean back into him again.

Other than taking his hand on the stairs when they'd left his home, she hadn't touched him since that night at his gran's. And he had tried to emulate the sentiment, so much so that his reaction was a trained response. If only he could take it back. But it was too late.

Kayla sat forward now, her posture rigid. *What is she thinking?* Worry niggled. *Is it possible she relented enough to show me how she felt, and I snubbed her? Or is she comfortable enough with me she leaned back unwittingly?*

Han plunging past them swept aside all thoughts of Kayla. All Jaden's angst for his glider returned. Jaden couldn't help noticing how much easier it was for his glider to compensate for his tattered wing now that Jaden no longer burdened him. *Why didn't Han say something?* Despite Han gaining a measure of control over his descent, Jaden could tell it was too little, too late. He winced as Han smashed into the ground, watching helplessly as his friend flipped over twice and then lay still.

Taz glided in behind Han. "You must jump when we're close to the ground. I can't land with both of you on my back."

It was the first time they'd had to dismount before landing, and Jaden looked at Kayla, not sure how to comply. Kayla's face was blank, her eyes wide. He would have to think of something.

"You go first," Jaden said. "I'll support you while you move. Swing your one leg over to meet the other, then slide down in front of Taz's wing on that side. I'll be right behind you."

Kayla complied without comment when Taz slowed and dropped as low as her wings would allow. When Kayla landed comfortably, Jaden dismounted and followed her down, surprised by how easy it was.

On the ground, Jaden sprinted to Han's crumpled form on the desert floor. "Han, Han, are you alright?" Jaden bent over his glider, searching for signs of life. The slightest movement in Han's chest reassured him his glider was still breathing.

Stripping off his shirt, Jaden pressed the fabric against Han's chest wound. He wasn't sure what to do about the wing. Folded over on itself and twisted at an awkward angle, the silky membrane was ripped in several places. Kayla was the one with medical training. *Surely, she'll know what to do. Where is she?*

Jaden glanced up, ready to shout for her, but Kayla was already there, kneeling next to Han's ragged wing and inspecting it. She gently tweaked the soft membranes, carefully rearranging them so they lay flat. Han's eyes fluttered open, and he murmured his appreciation. Clearly, Kayla unfurling and straightening the flayed pieces had afforded Han a measure of relief.

With the wing laid out to restrict further damage, Kayla turned to the gouges on Han's stomach. Jaden surrendered when she moved his hands and sodden shirt out of the way so she could inspect the area. The wound was still bleeding, although not as profusely. Kayla inspected the edges of the gash, her brow furrowed in thought.

Taz made them both jump when she landed with a soft thump right next to them.

"Sheesh," Kayla complained, "you scared me half to death."

Jaden watched as Kayla resumed working on Han. This girl stayed scared of nothing for long. *Does that include a deeper relationship with me? Will she avoid me forever? Or just until this nightmare ends?*

Peering over Kayla's shoulder at the lacerations, Taz murmured, "Do you remember the dried-up riverbed I pointed out just before we landed?"

"Yes, why?" Kayla asked.

"The mud in that area has excellent medicinal qualities. Mixed with the right herbs, in the right proportions, we can fix Han's wing almost instantly."

Kayla raised her eyebrows. "Instantly? With mud?"

"Yes, instantly."

"But we don't have any herbs," Jaden pointed out.

"We don't have any right now," Taz corrected, "but we should be able to find them in the surrounding vegetation. I'm pretty sure the herbs grow near the mud."

"Pretty sure?" Jaden asked.

Taz huffed. "It's been a long time since our training. We didn't think we'd ever carry voyagers. Believe me, it was a real shock when Zareh summoned us. There wasn't a lot of time to brush up on our knowledge. I remember what the herbs look like, but it's how they're mixed with the mud that'll be tricky. Combine them in the wrong ratios and they'll have the opposite effect . . ." She trailed off.

"Really?" Jaden blustered. "We're just going to experiment with Han's wing and hope you remember the right formula?"

"Oh, stop complaining and go find the mud and herbs already," Taz snapped. Their expressions told her she'd been a little short. "I'm sorry, but we don't have time to waste. The sooner you bring me the mud and herbs, the sooner we get Han back on his feet."

Without waiting for acknowledgement, Taz launched into a detailed description. Once he'd recited it back to her, she dismissed him by returning her attention to Kayla, who had retrieved her med-kit and was repairing the slashed skin on Han's chest.

Jaden turned away in disgust. The only thing he was good for was fumbling around in the dirt, hunting down some obscure plants. He trudged toward the area Kayla had pointed out earlier, hoping her sense of direction was accurate and that it would hold the riverbed he was looking for.

Sure, no pressure. Find the healing mud, find the nebulous herbs, take them back to the girls, and hope Taz miraculously remembers how to mix the magic potion. Jaden kicked at a pebble in his path, finding satisfaction in the way it flew forward. Because it made him feel better, he chased the stone down and kicked it again. Each time it flew forward, his spirits lifted, squelching the desperation threatening to overwhelm him.

Jaden was so committed to the silly little stone that he didn't notice the riverbed until he tripped over the scruffy bushes hugging its parched edge. Toppling down the small embankment, he landed face down at the bottom, chewing on the dusty soil.

More annoyed than hurt, Jaden straightened, spat the gunk out of his mouth, and brushed himself off. He eyed the dust clouds kicked up by his feet, doubting he'd find any mud. But studying the riverbed, he noticed tiny trickles popping up intermittently.

There was so little water, it was almost nonexistent. But water meant mud. Striding over to the tiny bubbles escaping above the surface, he scraped at the edges, elated when more buried water spurted out. Packing the sandwich container with thick, stinky mud didn't take long.

The task complete, he leaned back, recognizing this had been the easy part. Where on earth would he find the plants Taz had taken such pains to describe? Rebuking himself for not paying closer attention to the vegetation on his way to the river, he searched the bank for any signs of greenery—and froze.

CHAPTER EIGHT

A boy stood there. At least, Jaden thought it was a boy. The heat haze shimmering behind the person in the late afternoon glare only allowed a general impression of height and build. The person stood so still, Jaden wondered whether he was seeing things. *Mirages happen in deserts, don't they? But they involve water, not people, right?*

The thought of water made Jaden realize how thirsty he was. In fact, he was a little lightheaded. Standing motionless until the dizziness passed, Jaden stepped to the right, hoping the image would shift, allowing him to see his way clear of it. It didn't move.

Determined to banish the annoying image, Jaden continued angling to his right. But whatever it was, it didn't budge. Puzzled, Jaden shifted closer. When he was within arm's length, the glare disappeared. It was a boy! About his age, dark-skinned, dark-eyed, and with the blackest hair Jaden had ever seen, tied in a neat ponytail.

The boy stared at Jaden, as though wondering what in the world Jaden was up to. "Hello."

Jaden jumped. The boy smiled, conveying he wouldn't bite. "Hello," Jaden offered, still unsure whether what he was seeing was real. *And now I'm talking to my imaginary friend! What next? Flying pigs?*

The boy offered a hand. "My name's Atu. Who are you?"

Convinced he was hallucinating, Jaden decided that whatever this was, he would let it play out. "Jaden," he replied, shaking the proffered hand. "What are you doing out here in the middle of nowhere?"

"I could ask the same thing except I saw your confrontation with the Gaptor. Elite, the way you zapped him. I didn't know you could destroy them like that. I came to help because I saw your glider go down."

Jaden grimaced. *There is no doubt—I am definitely having an episode! The Gaptor and gliders are invisible to everyone except me, Kayla, and Gran. It's impossible the boy could've witnessed anything. Besides, how does he know what a Gaptor and gliders are?* Jaden inspected the phantom, silently considering the situation and speculating what he had to do to get back to reality.

"Hey, bro, you alright?" Atu asked, interrupting Jaden's reverie.

"Yeah, sure, just fine and dandy," Jaden muttered. "I'm daydreaming, and I should be helping Han."

"Who's Han? Is he your glider?"

Inconceivable! How does he know that? What the deuce? Jaden thought, throwing his hands in the air. "Yes, he's my glider, and he's hurt. If you're real, maybe we can stop jawing and you can help me find the herbs we need to mix with this mud to heal him."

Atu beamed, the action lighting his countenance. "I've got you covered, bro. Everything we need is right here," he assured Jaden, patting a bag slung over one shoulder.

"You have the herbs?"

"And the mud, all mixed exactly as they should be."

Jaden shrugged. "Whatever you say." He was too tired to care about working this out. He would escort the boy back to the others, and when they confirmed no one was with him, he might snap out of it. Then he could get back to finding the plants—after drinking about a gallon of water first.

"Follow me," Jaden invited, turning and heading back.

The boy followed, although not without a searching stare, bewildered by Jaden's strange behavior. They accomplished the jog back to Han and the others in silence, Jaden not wanting to talk to what he was sure was fresh air. Nearing their destination, Jaden increased his pace, impatient to find out how Han was doing. Kayla was still tending the injured bat, and Jaden was thankful at least one of them had some medical expertise.

Taz was the first to hear their approach. The hairs on the back of Jaden's neck rose when Taz leaped in front of Han and raised her wings, unmistakably threatening whatever walked beside him. Alarmed, Jaden realized he could've made a mistake bringing the boy back to the camp—surely Taz's response proved he was real?

Jaden hurried to place himself between the boy and Kayla. If he was dangerous, Jaden didn't want her anywhere near the stranger. His tension dissipated when Taz sniffed the air, then lowered her massive wings and cocked her head to one side.

"Who brings the medicine?" Taz asked.

"Says his name's Atu," Jaden replied, shaking his head at the absurdity of the situation. He was sure he had imagined the boy. *Apparently not.*

Taz hopped over to where Atu waited, wonder plastered on his face as he admired the enormous bat.

"Wow! I never expected to meet a glider. I'm honored," Atu said, bowing low.

"You are a seeker?" Taz quizzed, not allowing the boy's impeccable manners to sway her.

"Yes." Atu grinned. "How else could I see you?"

How else indeed? Jaden groaned. Laughing at himself, he realized that not only had they found someone who had the medicine needed to heal Han's wing, but they'd also found another seeker. In the middle of nowhere and when they least expected it.

"Sorry for the cranky reception back there. I convinced myself the magical appearance of a healer was a hallucination," Jaden said.

Atu grinned, understanding Jaden's strange behavior. "I can agree it must've seemed too good to be true. Can I get to work on that wing now?"

He stepped toward Han. But Kayla didn't step aside. "Will you show us your medallion?" she challenged, scratching her birthmark.

Atu smiled, understanding, and reached into his bag. Retrieving his medallion, he held it out for her, allowing its pearly surface to fling light around them. "Satisfied?"

"Yes, thanks. I'm Kayla," she said, stopping scratching long enough to stretch out a hand in greeting. "That's Taz," Kayla said, pointing at her glider, "and Han's our injured friend."

"Nice to meet you all," Atu replied, shaking Kayla's hand. The boy glanced at Han but made no move toward him. Instead, he addressed Kayla. "Will you allow me to repair his wing now?"

Kayla gave him space to work, her eyes never leaving Atu.

Her focused attention on Atu irritated Jaden. *What does she find so intriguing about him? He isn't that interesting!* Jaden sidled up to her. As if sensing his proximity, Kayla turned and gave him one of her dazzling smiles.

Jaden forgot about being jealous. He smiled back, but she fidgeted. Jaden wondered why until he saw her eyes. Uncertainty lingered there. Did she need reassurance? After his reaction when she'd leaned back against him on Taz, he wasn't about to refuse her. Even if his assessment was wrong.

Reaching out, Jaden clasped her hand in his own. He was relieved and pleased when she gripped his hand. She sent him another gorgeous smile, and satisfaction suffused him. He had done the right thing. Hand in hand, Jaden and Kayla watched as Atu leaned over Han, inspecting his tattered wing and speaking in soothing tones.

"Hey. buddy, let's see what I can do for you." Gently lifting the torn sections, Atu examined them, then commended Kayla's work on the wing. "It helps relieve the pain when the wing's allowed to lie flat." Reaching into his bag, Atu extracted a leather pouch secured at the top with a rawhide cord. He opened the bag and dipped his hand inside, scooping out part of the contents.

Kayla dragged Jaden closer, curious to know what was inside. It was a paste of sorts—greenish brown with a mild, pleasant aroma. Atu dabbed the ointment along the tear lines.

Before placing the paste, Atu ensured the two sheared ends met perfectly, joining the jagged edges. Then he applied the healing balm to the join, checking the pieces didn't overlap. He moved methodically, working along each of the four slit sections in order. When he set the last portion to his satisfaction, Atu tipped back onto his haunches.

Han's eyes fluttered open. "What is that? It feels so good."

The absence of pain in Han's voice calmed Jaden. He touched Han's massive shoulder. "Hey, friend, how're you doing?"

Han sighed. "Significantly improved. Where did you find this one?"

"I didn't find him—he found us." When Han eyed him, Jaden elaborated. "He saw our duel with the Gaptor, watched you go down, and came to find us so he could help."

"I think we'll keep him. Thank you," Han said, inclining his head to Atu. "How are you here in the desert?"

"I live here."

Jaden's eyebrows shot up. "Here? What does your family do out here?"

A cloud passed over Atu's face. "My family is no longer with me."

"Man, I'm so sorry! I wouldn't have asked if I had known," Jaden murmured. He regretted asking, but it astounded him that the boy survived out here alone.

Atu brushed off the apology. "You had no way of knowing. Although it would've been nice if my family could've also witnessed what I saw today." He was quiet for a heartbeat. "Our family has waited generations for the gliders to come with their voyagers, by whose hands the fate of the world will be determined."

His unassuming statement jarred Jaden back to reality. He glanced at Kayla, silently questioning how many times they would have to hear their destiny was to redeem their world before they even knew how. Kayla's face reflected his doubt, her shared reservations about their success, and her concern that the expectations of others was too great. But neither interrupted the boy, unwilling to admit that, right now, they felt ridiculously useless.

When several seconds passed and Atu said nothing more, Jaden thought he'd ask. "You don't know how we're supposed to do that, do you?"

Atu blinked, surprised. "You don't know?"

"No," Kayla complained, "but we'd sure like to."

"I'm sorry, but I have no answer for you. All I know is that each seeker has their part to play in bringing the prophecy to pass. My family's role, and thus mine, is to provide healing."

"That's why you have the paste?" Kayla guessed.

"Yes. Amongst other things, it's useful for healing both gliders and voyagers." He studied them. "You really don't know what you're supposed to do?"

"No, we don't." Jaden sighed. "And as much as we've tried to figure it out, we're no closer to getting answers. It's like assembling a puzzle with more than half the pieces missing."

The group contemplated the dilemma until Han flapped his injured wing, stunning them. To Jaden and Kayla's extreme shock, Han rose to his feet and stretched the wing.

"Feels as good as new," Han said, beaming.

Kayla dashed over, verifying his statement. Sure enough, the membranes showed no signs of damage. Astounded, she examined the wing again, confirming she wasn't missing anything. "His wing is perfect. How did you do that?" She whirled around and stared at Atu.

He winked. "Wouldn't you like to know!"

Jaden, doubting Kayla's prognosis, inspected the wing for himself. Thrilled to prove it true, Han flexed and bent his wing. Incredulous, Jaden checked the rip on Han's chest—the area Atu had not yet worked on. It still bore signs of the glue Kayla had used to stem the bleeding and close the wound. Whatever Atu had applied to the wing had healed faster and more effectively than Kayla's glue. Jaden searched the wing for any lingering signs of the muddy paste but found none. For all intents and purposes, the wing was perfect. Jaden marveled. "I'd also like to know how you did that."

Atu smirked. "The magic medicine man never reveals his secrets."

"Thank you," Jaden said, when it was evident Atu wouldn't explain. "It's wonderful to have Han whole again."

"You're welcome. It's been an honor to meet our esteemed guests and to assist with Han's healing."

When Taz stood taller, Kayla smiled. Her glider liked the respectful manner in which their new friend treated the gliders.

The group stood there for a while, watching Han flex and stretch his wings again and again, chuckling at his delight.

That was, until Atu said, "Easy, big guy. It might feel great, but your wing needs time to heal completely. It would be better if you rested for a few hours before flying again. I know a safe place near here where we can spend the night. I'll lead the way."

Jaden considered Atu's words. "Why do we need a safe place? Surely we're okay now that the Gaptor's gone?"

Atu looked at Jaden like he was joking. Realizing Jaden wasn't, he sighed. "When we get to the cave, you'll have your answer."

Jaden glanced at Kayla, but she shrugged. The boy was certainly peculiar. Nonetheless, it seemed he knew something they didn't. They listened while Atu coached Han on which movements were permissible and which he should avoid. Then they followed without question as Atu collected his small pack and led them away from the open valley floor where Han had gone down.

They traipsed toward the base of the cliffs they had been on top of only this morning. The sun was already kissing the horizon goodnight, streaking the creamy clouds with the blushing gold and mauve ribbons of its final embrace.

Jaden was thankful for the little illumination they still had as they crossed the rocky terrain. What had looked flat while flying over it was, in fact, rutted with loose, eroded rock—the kind you needed to pay attention to or you'd end up with an injury.

The going was tough, and after all the exertion earlier in the day, Jaden felt drained. The spike of adrenaline from the battle had long since passed, leaving him devoid of emotion. Although he was running on empty, Jaden stubbornly supported Han under his uninjured wing, aiding the bat as best as he could. He felt dwarfed by the magnificent creature and wished he could be of more help.

Han must've sensed his thoughts because he said, "You're not as puny as you look."

Jaden grinned. "Guess that's a good thing for you."

Han chuckled. "Given time, we'll get you as strong as I am."

"Yeah, wouldn't that be something worth achieving? I could take Markov on physically for a change and come out the victor!"

CHAPTER NINE

Kayla glanced at Han and Jaden as they continued their banter. Or rather, she looked at Jaden. His face had caught the sun, as had his exposed arms and legs, bronzing his skin to a delicious nut brown. His deep blue eyes twinkled, more striking than ever now that they contrasted with his tan, and his laughter was infectious.

If only she wasn't drawn to him like a moth to a flame. The image of a moth going down in smoke had her grimacing. The same thing would happen to her if she ignored his actions, which had made it plain he wanted nothing more than friendship with her.

Earlier, when Jaden had crashed down to ride with her and Taz, her mind had been too scrambled to think. The moment Jaden wrapped his arms around her, the rest of the world faded away. There was no more danger, no more uncertainty, no mission, and no one else. They were all that existed in the world. It was as if she had come home.

Jaden was where he belonged. By her side. Protecting her, keeping her safe. She had forgotten where she was and relaxed back into him, only to lurch away when she felt him tense, cursing her lapse in judgment. *Did I cross a line?* She had waited for him to say something, but he'd kept quiet. His reaction was proof he saw her as only a friend, a

55

partner in this venture. Holding herself erect, she did her best not to touch him again.

But when Atu arrived, tall (although not as tall as Jaden) and with the well-muscled build of a person who spent a lot of time outdoors, she'd watched him make his way toward Han, then flicked a glance Jaden's way. He'd been looking at her with the oddest expression.

Desperate for the comfort having him near always brought, she'd itched to move closer. As if reading her mind, Jaden moved toward her instead. She hadn't dared reach out to him, though. Again, he'd known what she needed and taken her hand. Her gratitude had her smiling up at him. They were in this together. And if friendship was all he offered, she would take it.

Ironic, considering she'd finally figured out her feelings had everything to do with him and nothing to do with medallions or mutants or missions. Atu's arrival allowed her to analyze every nuance of her actions toward the stranger, and she found no sentiments for him other than those of an associate.

She'd gotten what she'd asked for—another male seeker to dispel her qualms about her overemotional state when it came to Jaden. And now it was too late. Much as it irked, Kayla would just have to keep things exclusively friendly with Jaden. She would direct her attention elsewhere. Like Taz, she would focus on the mission and hope that would keep her mind off less fruitful options.

Attempting to break the strand linking her to Jaden, Kayla looked away and realized they'd passed the base of the cliffs and were heading toward a large, elevated, flat exposed area, like some open-air arena. Leading up to it and carved into the side of the cliffs was a set of precise stone stairs.

Kayla gaped. *Who did this and how was it done?* Then she remembered they were in the general area of the cave dwellings this area was renowned for. *But Atu lived here?* That was almost more incredible than the dwellings themselves.

Atu led them up the stairs, across the open space and toward an opening that accommodated the gliders' enormous frames. Once inside, they lost the negligible amount of light they'd used to get this far.

Kayla paused in the dark interior, waiting for her eyes to adjust. She heard a scratching sound. Tensing for some unseen attacker, she relaxed when the match flared to life. Atu coaxed a flame from a torch hidden in a well-disguised wall sconce. Catching, the flame danced on the torch, exuding light and exposing the vastness of the cave.

Atu approached another bulge on the cave wall and removed a second hidden torch. He carried it back to the first and lit it. "This way." He pointed out one of the larger passageways off the main room.

They followed, all the while gazing in awe at the absurd effort it must've taken to carve the home out of the solid cliff rock. But they had barely gone forty paces when they reached a dead end.

"Nice," Jaden commented, making Kayla giggle. "I suppose we're walking through this wall?"

Atu grinned. "We are." He pressed against one of the countless small extrusions high on the lumpy wall. With barely a hiss, a section of the wall slid back, revealing a large tunnel, higher and wider than their passageway. "After you," he offered, laughing at their shocked expressions.

They crossed into the tunnel. When they were all in the hallway, Atu reached behind them, pressing on yet another unseen control. The panel slid back into place, and Jaden extended a hand toward where he knew the panel was, touching the general area. There wasn't even the hint of a seam. "Wow!"

"Thanks," Atu said. "It keeps the tourists out. We normally use one of the other entryways to our home, but since the park's closed, and there's no one around to question where we disappeared to, I thought we'd use this one because it was the closest."

As they wandered down the long hall, Kayla noticed the many smaller passages branching off it. Atu talked as he walked, explaining the purposes of different passages. Several led to storage rooms, three led back to the outside world, and one fed into an underground chamber with water flowing through it for cleaning. The place was a veritable maze.

"Have people ever wandered down here by mistake?" Kayla asked, assessing the odds of outsiders entering the home.

"No," Atu answered, replying to Kayla's unspoken question regarding danger—from humans, at any rate. "The entrances are all well disguised. Even if someone found their way down here, it's unlikely they'd find their way back out without help. So don't get lost down here."

Kayla giggled. "We don't plan to." She didn't doubt the bats could guide themselves out of the underground cavern without breaking a sweat.

Atu nodded. "Good. I'd hate to have to come and find you."

They rounded a bend which abruptly dumped them in an expansive living room. Atu entered and lit the oil lamps dotted around the room. With the room fully revealed, Kayla stared in awe. Comfortable handcrafted chairs with soft, colorful coverings hugged an enormous fireplace. To their left, a well-stocked kitchen invited hungry patrons, although it had no modern conveniences. No refrigerator, stove, or dishwasher, and definitely no droids. To their right, a shorter passage with openings covered by heavy embroidered linens hinted at sleeping quarters.

Jaden gestured toward the fireplace. "You can use this without people on the outside seeing the smoke?"

"Yes. You won't find a breach in the perimeter, if that's what you're looking for."

Jaden chuckled. "Just checking we're secure. Where does the smoke go then?"

"The fireplace has several chimneys leading to the outside. They disperse the smoke so there is only ever the faintest evidence of smoke exiting any one chimney. Since each chimney funnels out some distance from any of the others, and because of both the winds that kick up here and the heat that distorts images, the smoke's practically invisible."

"Wow—again!" Jaden exclaimed.

Atu grinned. "I'm sure my ancestors appreciate the praise." He turned to the gliders. "My home is yours. Please find a place that's comfortable for you to rest."

Taz smiled. "We appreciate your hospitality and your kind aid."

Atu inclined his head. Facing Jaden and Kayla again, he said, "This way. This is what I wanted to show you."

As they trailed Atu to a side wall between the kitchen and the living room, Kayla glanced at Jaden. His face gave no sign of what he might be thinking. *Is he as nervous as I am about what Atu will show us?*

The spot Atu led them to was darker because none of the lamps reached into the shadows covering the walls. Lifting the torch he still carried, Atu angled it so its light spilled over the wall. "This is why I said you weren't safe out there."

Kayla stared, dumbfounded. Jaden's open mouth showed he was just as shocked.

The soft light flickering from the torch illuminated a wall decorated with paintings, faded with age. Against the far left corner of the rocky canvas, a small group of gliders carried tiny stick figures—voyagers. And to their right, outnumbering them and covering most of the rest of the wall, were their pursuers. Hundreds and hundreds of Gaptors.

CHAPTER TEN

Kayla shook her head. "This can't be right."

Jaden agreed. "Impossible! There are way too many Gaptors!"

"Yes, there should only be one," Kayla said.

They continued spouting adamant denials. Atu waited for their objections to fade. "The painting is accurate. My family has taken the utmost care in passing along the stories associated with this picture for generations. Stories which confirm the existence of *many* Gaptors."

Kayla sputtered. "There really are more of those monsters?"

When Jaden moved closer, some misguided response to her reactions, Kayla stiffened. *Can't he see I'm angry and not afraid?* Underlining the point, she scowled. Jaden's brow furrowed. Like he was working out how to comfort her without giving her the wrong idea, then realized she wasn't looking for comfort.

Jaden dropped the arm he'd raised toward her. Kayla deflated. Yet another confirmation they'd reached some unspoken consensus regarding the boundaries of their relationship. Turning to hide her disappointment, Kayla found Atu watching them with interest.

Instead of asking, Atu responded to Kayla's question. "Yes, there are definitely more Gaptors. I'm sorry to be the bearer of grim news, but it's better you know now what you're up against than continue in ignorance."

Atu's words hit home for Jaden. He rounded on the bats. "Were you aware of this?"

To Kayla, his tone was overly harsh. Despite her decision to focus on the mission, Kayla couldn't help wondering about his reaction. *Or is that hope on my part? Am I just wishing he's upset because I rebuffed his attempt at consolation? No, he was the one who jerked away when I leaned into him. He has no right to be upset! With me or anyone else.* However, her perplexity increased when Taz stared at Jaden as though he'd asked a stupid question and Jaden's anger blazed.

"You didn't think this might've been information worth sharing?" Jaden yelled.

Han, understanding his voyager well enough now to sense the coming storm and judging it wouldn't end well, hastened to reason with him. "Jaden, calm yourself. There's no need for anger. There are more Gaptors—just not in your world. Which is why we never mentioned them; there was no need to tell you."

"The others, yeah, they're insignificant, wherever they are! Which is where exactly?" Jaden barked. "Floating out in space somewhere?"

"Don't be silly," Han snapped. "We confine the other Gaptors to our world. The lone Gaptor we destroyed yesterday was the single creature remaining in yours. His sole purpose was retrieving the medallions. Unfortunately, now that you accidentally disposed of him, it's likely things will change. It's possible you've opened the door for more Gaptors to enter."

"Wait, what? Back up a second," Kayla interrupted. "You said you confined the other Gaptors to your world? How come there are so many in the painting then?"

"We have confined all Gaptors—now. But that wasn't always the case," Han explained. "A long time ago, a breach temporarily allowed travel between our world and yours. We believe the Usurper orches-trated the anomaly to send an army of Gaptors into your world, so he might conquer and seize it for himself."

"The Usurper?" Jaden asked.

"One cursed in our world almost since time began and who seeks to regain his earlier, elevated status. His mind is twisted, bent by bitterness, corrupted by cruelty, perverted by power. He is an evil beyond comprehension."

"Sounds like a real gem," Jaden said. "'Usurper' is such an ostentatious name. Maybe we'll call him Slurper. Or better yet, Slurpy, since he's here to suck our world dry, being the harbinger of doom and gloom and all."

Kayla giggled. "I like it."

But Han spoke quietly, his response grave. "Joke all you like, but he's no laughing matter. He's the same one your mother saw in her dream, the one who wants to kill you."

Jaden sobered and grimaced. "So he had plans to conquer our world?"

"Which is what his painting shows?" Kayla asked. "All the Gaptors he sent here? And some kind of battle?"

Atu answered. "Exactly. This painting is a reminder of the overwhelming odds faced by the gliders and their voyagers. And that, despite being totally outnumbered, they still won."

His interest piqued, his anger forgotten, Jaden said, "Won't you go on, please, Atu? We'd love to hear more."

"Why don't we make ourselves comfortable around the fire then?"

Jaden and Kayla chose chairs while Atu kindled the fire and the gliders settled in the large, open area between the living room and kitchen. When the fire crackled and snapped to Atu's satisfaction, he flopped onto a nearby chair and began his narrative. From the way he slipped into a comfortably rehearsed speech, it was obvious he knew the tale well.

Appearing out of nowhere, the Gaptors terrorized all who saw them, their hideous, deformed bodies, immense size, sword-like beaks, and terrible talons invoking pure, paralyzing dread. With good reason because the moment the monsters spotted the humans, they began their vicious onslaught, dealing death to all they encountered.

Carving a deadly and bloody path through the countryside, they killed with impunity. Young, old, male or female, all met the same ferocious and merciless death. Word of the monsters and their lethal mission spread like wildfire, passed along by those close enough to witness the devastation but fortunate enough to escape its effects, sparking widespread pandemonium amidst crippling fear.

Jaden interrupted. "Hold on, the Gaptors were visible to everyone?"

"Yes, as were the gliders when they came. Why that isn't still the case today, I don't know. But I wish you could've heard the way my father told this story. He put you right there, amid it, so you literally experienced the people's horror when the Gaptors appeared, then their panic when the gliders followed. My ancestors were convinced our world was being invaded by giant beasts—one an enormous version of something they were familiar with and the other a total abomination."

Kayla shook her head. "Those poor people."

"You have no idea," Atu said. "Already incapable of fighting off one aberration, my ancestors were horrified when the gliders appeared. I can imagine their conjecturing about what new torment was about to befall them."

"I bet," Kayla agreed.

Atu nodded, then continued. "Rationally, when the gliders landed near their village, my ancestors scattered, convinced they were under attack again. But as they ran, they heard a voice calling them, urging their return. It conveyed the desire to help, assuring them the visitors had not come to harm them."

"What did they do?" Jaden breathed, his eyes bright with excitement.

"Unsure, my ancestors slowed their retreat but remained hidden. Eventually, when the new arrivals still made no move to harm them, they crept back, desperate to believe the herald but still wary of a trap. When they were close enough to identify the one speaking, they doubted the truth of his statements. His size made it doubtful he could do anything, much less help them. He was small with furry ears and the feathered appearance of a giant owl, but he could speak, and he had arms."

"Zareh!" the teens breathed in unison.

It was Atu's turn for surprise. "You know him?"

"In a manner of speaking." Jaden grimaced. "We've met, but to say that we know him would be a gross overstatement. We can tell you more about him later. Please, continue."

"Well, it didn't take the little guy long to persuade our ancestors that he and his companions really were there to help. That objective achieved, he did a strange thing. He called for volunteers to ride on the backs of the giant bats he'd brought with him."

"The first voyagers?" Kayla deduced, a faint smile touching her face. She glanced at Jaden and found him watching her, a grin playing at the corners of his generously curved mouth. His scrutiny seemed more than that of just a casual observer, making her squirm. *Why is he looking at me like that? What is he thinking? No, focus on the mission! Not Jaden!*

Before she could explore the thought, Atu confirmed her assumption, explaining how the people had initially been dubious. That was, until one of their warriors volunteered. Then no one wanted to be left out. Despite this, there were still more bats than people in the tribe, so the remaining unpaired gliders flew away. A few days later, they returned, all bearing voyagers of their own.

With the gliders reassembled, Zareh trained the group, working with both gliders and their voyagers until they satisfied him they could mount an effective offensive. The scene on the wall depicted the few gliders and their voyagers, who volunteered to lure the Gaptors into the valley where they'd set the trap.

The Gaptors, ignorant of the gliders' presence until then, spotted the small volunteer group and snatched at the bait. Chasing maniacally after opponents from their own world, they were of a singular mind—to defeat those who now stood between them and successfully completing their mission. They wanted to crush the opponents who had humiliated them before.

Their hatred of the gliders was their downfall. Not taking time to first consult with their master, they pursued blindly, their loathing driving them beyond reason. Once snared in the valley, it was too late to access their master's wisdom, and they were too busy fighting off their enemies to formulate a plan of any kind.

A brief but bloody battle ensued, and the voyagers slew all the Gaptors. All except one. Somehow, he miraculously escaped the initial attack and concealed himself behind a ridge where he viewed all that transpired from afar. Watching the meticulous execution of Gaptor after Gaptor, he realized his master's plan had failed abysmally, and rather than lose his own life, he slipped away. But Zareh spied his retreating form and sent a few of the gliders and their voyagers after him.

Already battle-weary and their stamina all but gone, the group pursued the fleeing Gaptor. But he had strength to spare, and they lacked the energy and enthusiasm to keep pace with the desperate escapee. When he passed from their sight, they were forced to concede defeat.

They returned to Zareh, bearing the discouraging news. Zareh merely nodded, informed them he needed to consult with others, and assured them he would return. Then he vanished. It was ten days before he reappeared, by which time the people had given up hope of ever seeing him again.

His return sparked wild cheers, and a spontaneous, jubilant celebration marking their victory ensued. During this celebration, Zareh presented the surviving voyagers with medallions. He commanded them to always keep the medallions within their families, so should there ever be a need for the voyagers again, the gliders would know who to seek. When the revelry concluded, Zareh, and the gliders left, promising they would return if the situation demanded it.

CHAPTER ELEVEN

"Where did they go?" Kayla asked.

Atu shrugged. "No one knows. They didn't disappear, the same way they'd arrived, as the people thought they would. Instead, they flew south until they were beyond even the most farsighted villagers' vision. Then they vanished. And no one's laid eyes on a glider since. At least, not until today," he amended, smiling at Han and Taz.

"And the Gaptor that escaped? That's the one we zapped today?" Jaden asked.

"It was," Taz attested.

Jaden sputtered. "But that would make him about a thousand years old!"

"While that may be impossible in your world, it's not uncommon in ours," Taz responded. "Also, we can add something here that Atu's perhaps unaware of. After Zareh left the villagers, he and his companions sealed the breach between our worlds. This cut the communication between the Usurper and his lone remaining Gaptor. Abandoned and isolated, the Gaptor kept to himself, steering clear of humans for a few centuries. We think his philosophy was 'out of sight, out of mind.' Whatever his thinking, it worked. When there were no immediate sightings of the extant Gaptor, rumors abounded that he'd died of injuries sustained in the battle."

"Except we know that wasn't true," Kayla pointed out.

Taz nodded. "But over time, people believed those rumors, ignoring the possibility he was still alive. And while those who'd experienced the battle relayed the stories of the gliders and Gaptors to their children and on to theirs and down through the generations, the stories eventually drifted into the realm of legend. People forgot, and those who heard the tales thought they were just that—tales. Only the seekers knew the truth and remembered to keep it close to their hearts."

"I wonder what happened that prevented our families from passing the truth down," Jaden muttered. His irritation that his own family had not done a better job keeping the story alive was clear.

"Do you remember reuniting with your medallion?" Han interjected before Taz could continue.

"Sure, I found it accidentally when I was clearing out the basement."

"How much of an 'accident' do you think it was that you were the one to find it and not your brother or sister?"

"It was just pure luck—"

"No, Jaden, not luck. Destiny," Han assured him. "Only one family member in each generation receives the medallion. It's that member's responsibility to care for the medallion and pass the stories along."

"Then why didn't my family do that?"

"Unfortunately, as was often the case before this age of modern medicine, the caretaker, or seeker if you will, perished before they could pass the information on to the next generation. In those cases where sudden death occurred, the medallions hid themselves until the next chosen family member was of an age to become their keeper."

Kayla giggled. "They hid? Come on, they're not sentient!"

Han continued like she hadn't interrupted. "Zareh imbued them with this ability. When the family members came of age, the medallions found their way to their guardian as intended."

"What you're saying then, is that when the seeker died unexpectedly, the story died with them?" Jaden asked, pacing the room now.

"Yes. That's why you and Kayla have gaps in your knowledge. While your grandparents did their best to relay the stories, the tales they were told were so garbled and confused, they could only give you snippets of information instead of the complete picture."

Taz picked up where she had left off. "As I was saying, the account of the battle became a legend. The Gaptor faded from memory. Until his master found a way to communicate with him. And that was when the attacks started."

"But how can that be if the doorway was closed?" Kayla asked.

"We don't know. And we're still no closer to an explanation. What we know is that after Zareh and the others returned to our world, the Usurper disappeared to avoid prosecution. We conducted extensive searches because we wanted him found and held accountable. Alas, he eluded all attempts, despite abundant evidence he was still in our world."

"You still haven't found him after all this time?" Kayla's asked.

"No, but our level of concern increased when word filtered back that he'd somehow learned of the medallions' existence. How he got that information, or who relayed his knowledge back to us, remains a mystery. But the theory is that once he found out about the medallions, he devised a way of communicating with the remaining Gaptor. If he could order his agent to retrieve the medallions, he would reduce the chance of resistance when he again returned to conquer your world."

Kayla huffed. "So there's no doubt he's coming back?"

Taz studied her before answering. "All his actions support that theory."

"Bring it on then," Kayla challenged. "Let him do his worst. He must get through us first."

Jaden chuckled. "Whoa, steady, girl! Where's this coming from?"

"I'm tired of being scared. Doesn't the saying go, 'If you can't beat them, join them?' Or in our case, if we can't escape our role, we can make darn sure we win?"

"I like your attitude."

And there it was again. That amazing smile. Kayla had to look away. Her attempts at focusing on the mission, and not Jaden, were failing miserably. When Jaden smiled like that, it took serious effort to resist him. But it was more than the smile. The way he was looking at her had her heart beating faster. His intense gaze made her feel he could see into her very soul. *I sincerely hope that's not possible. Because what will he do about what he sees there?* About to panic, Kayla relaxed when Jaden turned to the gliders.

"That's all good and well to know the history, but we still don't know what we're doing," Jaden grumbled.

Whirling, Jaden faced her again. Kayla swallowed. *Is he looking for a reaction?* But Jaden continued talking without his earlier penetrating gaze.

"Remember when we were floundering around in the storage shed and the Gaptor attacked us? Then we heard that clicking sound, right before he just flew away in the middle of his attack?"

Kayla was amazed her brain could still function enough for her to guess where Jaden was going. "You're thinking that was his master communicating with him?"

"Yeah, I think it was—why else would he have left? He had us down to rights. And only a summons could've made him leave us then."

Taz pounced on the information. "A clicking sound?"

"Yes, like an old rotary telephone would've made if you left it off the hook for too long," Kayla said. "Is that significant?"

"Perhaps," Taz murmured. "I'll pass it along. It might help Zareh figure out how the Usurper is communicating into this world."

Her strange phrase reminded Jaden of something he'd picked up on earlier. "Han, what did you mean before when you said, 'you've opened the door?'"

Han sighed. "If you hadn't killed our attacker, I presume he would've reported back to his master as usual. Because he's dead, he can't. Assuming I'm right, when he misses his check-in, scheduled or otherwise, the Usurper will suspect we have destroyed his agent, or at least compromised him. It might lead him to conclude that whoever his opponents are, they're capable of fighting off a lone Gaptor."

Jaden laughed. "Yeah, because we knew exactly what we were doing."

Han brushed off the sarcasm. "But you *did* kill him. With this thought in mind, the only way the Usurper's likely to still get what he wants is to reopen the door and send more than a single Gaptor through. That's what I meant."

Jaden's pacing picked up. "So, by killing his agent, we've forced the Usurper into finding a way to open the door between our worlds again. Only by doing that can he get more of his minions here and ensure his success."

"But that contradicts your earlier statement about the Gaptors being confined to your world," Kayla pointed out. "So which is it? They're confined or they're not?"

Taz answered this time. "The Usurper entered your world once before. Having since had a few hundred years to mull it over, it's probable he's found a means to enter your world again. And now that he has a reason to, vis-à-vis, no agent apprising him of the situation here, he may well open the door a second time. Especially if it's in line with his timing to invade your world. Therefore, while we currently have the Gaptors confined, it will only take another breach to change things."

Jaden scowled. A few minutes later, he shook his head. Then the rage was back.

Kayla, watching the play of emotions on Jaden's face, asked, "Jaden, what are you thinking?"

"There's a lot of theorizing going on here. And even if the gliders are right, how can anyone blame us? We didn't have a choice killing that Gaptor, did we? Besides, we didn't know the relic stones would do what they did. And even if we did, we would've done the same thing—otherwise, we'd be the corpses instead of that monster."

Jaden paused, and Kayla waited a moment before pressing him. "And?"

"Pursuing this line of reasoning and considering Zareh's expectations that we're supposed to be saviors, more Gaptors entering the world must've been a foregone conclusion somewhere along the line. Why didn't Zareh warn us? Why didn't our gliders mention more Gaptors existed? They had ample opportunity to correct our misconception. I mean, it was glaringly obvious that we believed we only needed to conquer the one predator. So Han's earlier explanation that telling us about the other Gaptors wasn't necessary because they weren't here doesn't hold water."

"Jaden, you're making my head hurt," Kayla complained. "All these questions don't seem to have a point. You're going round in circles."

Jaden gave her a weak smile. "What I'm trying to say is that we aren't being given the tools we need to succeed. There are too many things we don't know and too much we're finding out after the fact." Jaden glared at the bats. "Can you at least tell us why we're being kept in the dark?"

CHAPTER TWELVE

Kayla needed an answer as much as Jaden. "Yes, why *are* we being kept in the dark?"

Taz ruffled her wings, ordering her thoughts. When she replied, her tone lacked its usual haughtiness. It was almost kind. "Contrary to your belief, we don't have all the information either. Regarding the knowledge we do have—and yes, we know more than you—there are limitations on what they permit us to share with you and when. Before you ask, this is because Zareh believes it will compromise the mission if you're told too much, too soon. An assessment I agree with," Taz ended quietly.

Ouch, that's a slap in the face, Kayla thought. *Taz doesn't think we can handle knowing what we're in for? It must be worse than we imagined.* She couldn't help the biting retort. "Nice to know our gliders have such confidence in us."

Taz's gaze was cool. "It's not that we don't believe you're talented. In fact, when we compare you to the other voyagers we learned about in our training, you two are by far the most promising."

"In which case," Kayla shot back, "is there ever a time you think you might trust us with a full report?"

"Like I said, it's not about you. It's entirely related to the information. It's dangerous. If we tell you all we know and you're captured by the Usurper, it'll be worse for all of you. Is this making sense yet?"

Jaden voiced the question plaguing Kayla. "Just to be clear, we only get as much information as we need right now to get to the next step and no more because if we have it all and the enemy captures us, the world will be toast?"

Han nodded. "That's about the gist of it. Barring a life-and-death situation, they prohibit Taz and me from giving you information beyond certain boundaries, despite our feelings on the matter."

Jaden threw his hands up. "Fantastic!" Then something else occurred to him. "Did you two know the relic stones could destroy the Gaptor?"

Han hopped from foot to foot, delighted to have a question he could answer without incurring Jaden's wrath. "No, we didn't. We knew they were a threat, but we didn't know why."

"Gratifying to know we weren't the only ones surprised, then. We can agree that question's answered categorically."

Kayla thought of something. "You mentioned the Gaptor reported to the Usurper. He's the one who ultimately controls them, then?"

Taz's smile conveyed pride, as if Kayla had just worked something out. "Yes. Why do you ask?"

"If that's true, then the Gaptors aren't our actual enemy—their master is. If we beat him, there'll be no need to fight them. We need to find out what he wants and why he wants it."

"Yes!" Taz beamed. "You're getting the big picture now. You already know what he wants. Jaden's mother told you when she shared her visions. He covets your world. Why, only he knows for sure, but my bet is it's got plenty to do with power and very little to do with what will benefit your world."

"That's the reason we need to stop him?" Kayla asked. "Because if we don't, he truly will destroy our world and everything in it?"

"We believe so. Since his first attack here, he's been lurking in the shadows, waiting for an opportunity to strike again—or so we suspect. His actions over the last millennium have increasingly pointed toward the likelihood of a second attempt. He craves a new home, a place to conquer and call his own. Our assumption is that if he succeeds, he will enslave your world, using it to build his army. Then he'll return to ours with that army, where he'll attempt to defeat us again. And if he succeeds, hope truly will perish, and all creation will be forever lost."

Kayla gaped. It was the most Taz had divulged in all their time together about why they couldn't fail. Kayla wasn't aware of reaching out and taking Jaden's hand. She just knew that when she did, she found the solace she sought.

Heat flowed through her hand and up her arm, the warmth relaxing her. When Jaden squeezed her hand in silent understanding, she almost turned into him. Almost. Thankfully, she stopped herself before she repeated her mistake. Keeping her distance was proving more difficult than she'd imagined. But she had managed so far, and she wouldn't break that streak now.

"Not a lot to ask of three teenagers," Atu complained.

Kayla laughed at his dour expression. As unobtrusively as possible, she slipped her hand out of Jaden's and moved away before doing something she would regret. The wounded expression that replaced his amusement stunned her. *He's upset? But why?*

Jaden's behavior had repeatedly implied he only wanted friendship. But this reaction contradicted that belief so strongly Kayla wanted to demand answers. Her heart squeezed in her chest, and she drew in a deep breath.

She couldn't relent now. Especially if her wishful fancies were running away with her, and she was wrong. It wasn't as if she hadn't misread the situation before.

Jaden turned away and she could no longer read his expression. But she heard the undeniable distress in his voice when he spoke, sending fresh doubts through her. "Well, if it's any consolation, Zareh mentioned five seekers when we spoke with him. Maybe the other two won't be teenagers."

Atu had picked up on their tension. He clasped his hands together and mimed begging. "That sounds encouraging. Give me more excellent news."

Grateful for Atu's attempt at levity, Kayla thought food might prove a further distraction. "Can we at least make some dinner while we exchange information?" Kayla asked, hoping the thought of food might distract Jaden. "That is, if you don't mind us raiding your kitchen?"

"Gosh, I'm so sorry. I forgot my manners in all this excitement. Yes, let's eat. I have plenty of food—and lots of fresh fruit for you," Atu said, smiling at the gliders.

Gravitating toward the kitchen, Kayla calmed down as Atu chattered on about inconsequential matters and she caught the hint of a smile on Jaden's face. That heart-melting smile. But his cobalt eyes remained shadowed. She sighed. If things carried on like this, she would have to speak to him about everything they were leaving unsaid. She wasn't ready for that conversation. Not by a mile.

The boys didn't notice Kayla lagging or how quiet she was as they prepared their meal. When the food was ready, they sat at the table, and Jaden filled Atu in between mouthfuls on all that had happened since he'd first glimpsed the Gaptor in the Shadow Mountains.

Atu sat rapt, his food barely touched, amazed by all they had been through. When Jaden finished his account, Atu made Kayla tell him hers, by which time their teacups were cold and the bats had slunk off to find suitable sleeping perches.

"Now you know everything we do," Jaden concluded. "Your turn to share."

Atu shook his head. "Sorry to disappoint, but I really don't have more to contribute. You already heard the story associated with the painting, and you know that healing falls to our family. Beyond that . . ." He trailed off, shrugging.

Frustrated, Jaden pressed. "You're sure you don't know more?"

"No, bro. I wish I did, but I don't. I've often wondered whether there was more to the story, and now I know there is. But apparently, it's something we must work out together."

"You don't think your part in this is over, then?" Kayla asked, speculating where they went from here.

"Far from it. If more Gaptors enter our world, there will undoubtedly be clashes between us and them, which means potential injuries. Without sounding prideful, you'll need me to heal you as quickly as possible. And even if the Gaptors we expect don't materialize, I can be useful in keeping you healthy while you complete your task."

"And what do you think that is?" Jaden prodded.

"Initially, and based on the story I told you, I assumed destroying the remaining Gaptor would solve the problem. But now, knowing someone else was controlling the Gaptor, someone capable of sending more of those beasties into our world, I think it's more in line with Kayla's theory—stopping that person."

Jaden sighed. "That's the second time today we've reached that conclusion. It's the how that remains elusive. Our only guidance is Zareh's insistence we complete the quest, which, if successfully attained, will herald our victory. But what 'completing the quest' means is anyone's guess."

Kayla yawned and rubbed her eyes. "It's late, and I'm bushed. Please, please, please, can we get some rest and work on this again tomorrow?"

The boys laughed at her pitiful request, although Kayla's reference to rest made them realize how the weight of the day was dragging on them too.

"One last thing," Jaden said, raising a finger. "When we met this afternoon, you mentioned your family had been waiting generations for the gliders who would come with their voyagers to save the world. But your family's story ended when Zareh and the gliders left, with his promise that they would return if we needed them again. How are those two connected?"

Atu smiled. "I forgot about that. You must be more awake than you look. The gliders' return was a prophecy made by one of the wise men in our family at least three generations back."

"A wise man?" Kayla ventured.

"Yes, what we call one who can see into the future."

"Similar to the vision my mom had?" Jaden surmised.

"I suppose so, except he never shared his entire vision with us. Or, at least, not that I'm aware of. All he emphasized was that when two gliders returned bearing two voyagers, the time had come for the fate of the world to be decided."

"I wish he'd told you more, dude." Jaden sighed again, then yawned and stretched his arms above his head. "Alright, I agree. I'm too tired to deal with more of this right now. Let's sleep!"

Kayla thankfully retired to the room assigned to her and was asleep within seconds. It didn't seem enough hours had passed before warm shafts of sunshine creeping in through the various natural openings in the cave's roof roused her. Convinced she could sleep another ten hours with ease, she moseyed to the kitchen, trying to wake up.

Jaden and Atu joined her a few minutes later, looking just as sleepy. They had barely assembled when Taz hopped in with an air of urgency. The humans were instantly alert. What was Taz doing up and about and expecting them?

"Is something wrong?" Kayla asked.

"No, but we've tarried long enough. Your journey awaits."

"You know where we're going?" Kayla asked, not daring to hope.

Her answer wasn't what any of them were expecting. "I don't know our next destination. But you should. You're the ones with the map."

As if electrified, Jaden scrambled from his chair and yanked the disc from his pocket, all the while sneaking glances at Taz. Like he suspected Taz knew something he didn't. He twisted the disc until it opened, the map coiling to life around them. Atu exclaimed in wonder.

He wasn't the only one who couldn't believe what he was seeing. Jaden and Kayla gaped. The map had reverted to its original two-dimensional appearance, an "X" once again marking a spot on the map. However, this time, the lines grew both denser and notably fainter toward the "X," which was so dim it was almost invisible.

"How did you know the map would give us another destination?" Kayla asked Taz.

"I didn't. I played a hunch."

"Does this mean what I think it does?" Kayla prompted. "That we have somewhere else to go?"

"Apparently so," Jaden grunted. "And if my guess is right, the lines fading toward the 'X' imply a considerably longer journey."

"Then we should get started," Taz said. "Atu will accompany us."

Jaden raised an eyebrow. In one sentence, she had decided Atu's fate. "And how's that going to happen? Is Zareh planning on sending another glider?"

"No, they permitted only Han and I to cross over. Until we've established the strength of Han's wing, I will carry Kayla and Atu. When we are certain Han's wing is fully functional, we'll switch off carrying two riders instead of one."

Atu's eyes shone. "Wow, I get to fly with you?"

"You do, Healer. But please, assemble your supplies. We leave in one hour." Taz stared meaningfully at Jaden and Kayla, indicating she would brook no argument.

Kayla couldn't resist an eye roll, but she nodded consent, as did Jaden. They helped Atu gather the items he needed, the hour mostly silent while they packed and cleaned and restocked. Ready to leave within the allotted time, Atu led them from the caves using a different route.

Stepping into the already baking early morning sunshine, Kayla squinted until the glare no longer assaulted her eyes. Then she and Atu followed Taz's instructions on how they should climb onto the glider's back. Kayla noticed their takeoff wasn't as quick or easy as usual, but she kept quiet, marveling at Taz's ability to lift two voyagers.

In the air, they hovered over Han as Jaden aerial-connected. Kayla wasn't the only one paying attention to Han's movements as he glided higher, alert for any signs of residual damage to the wing. Atu's keen eyes also followed Han and Jaden, checking for signs of weakness. But there were none.

Kayla raised her eyebrows. *There is definitely more to Atu than he lets on. No way herbs alone can heal that fast.* But it swept away the thought when Han and Jaden joined them, and Atu made a startling comment.

"Not to offend, but from what I observed yesterday, your battle skills need improvement. My family has often spoken of someone trained in these matters who might be of assistance. May I recommend we detour there before following the map further?"

CHAPTER THIRTEEN

Kayla stared at Atu, astonished.

"What?" Atu objected.

"Any more secret people you know who could help with our quest? Or did you forget to mention them too?"

Atu grinned. "Yes, well, there are hosts of behind-the-scenes people who can help us. I'm just bringing them out one by one so as not to overwhelm you."

Kayla giggled. "If this is the only one you bring out of the closet, I won't complain. We could use all the help we can get. It's tricky figuring out how best to attack someone in the air when you've spent your entire life on two legs."

It was Atu's turn to laugh. "Yes, I can see how that's a disadvantage. But I'm sure he can help."

"Does 'he' have a name?" Jaden asked.

"He probably does, but our family always referred to him as the armorer."

Kayla nodded. "He sounds awesome already. Where do we find this armorer?"

"That's the part you won't like. He lives some distance from here."

"How far?" Jaden asked.

"Gotskiena."

"What? You're not serious!" Jaden said. "We can't travel that far. It'll take forever to get there. And I don't think we have time. Do we?" he asked, rounding on the bats.

"No," Taz replied. "And now would be a judicious time to consult that map of yours so we can set our course."

To Kayla's surprise, Jaden dropped the matter. But Taz was right. They had to move on.

Jaden retrieved and released the map. Breathtaking in its beauty, it drifted around them. The group kept a watchful eye on the map as they flew, eager to determine their intended general direction. But today, their movements relative to the map were sluggish compared to two days previously.

Determining the course correction they should make took forever. The latency of noticeable changes on the map relative to their flight time supported Jaden's theory that the faded lines implied a greater distance. Adjusting their course to northerly path set by the map, the gliders settled in for the long flight.

"Ugh," Jaden muttered to Atu, "you might get your wish after all! We're aimed toward Gotskiena. Please, don't let us end up that far north! I loathe chilly weather!"

Kayla smiled. "Wimp!"

Jaden looked indignant. "What? Just because I don't enjoy being cold?"

"Man up!" she said, giggling when Jaden huffed. Studying him, Kayla found his outrage fascinating. His lips pouted, making them decidedly kissable, and he set his jaw in a grim, determined line she would have loved to run her finger along. A little crease crinkled the space between his eyes as he considered an appropriate response. While she thought of leaning over and thumbing the crease away, she sighed and looked away. There was no point trying to focus on the mission instead of the man. He was just too darn appealing. She didn't know how long she'd be able to keep this up.

Unaware of her inner turmoil, Atu laughed and added his own derogatory comment before Jaden came up with a suitable retort.

Then Taz made one of her rare dry remarks, and they all rolled with laughter. Enjoying the repartee, Kayla relaxed, setting aside her earlier momentary quandary. They kept up the lighthearted teasing for a while, with the bats joining in, before lapsing into companionable silence.

As they journeyed northward, the terrain gradually changed. The semi-desert's monotonous reddish-brown sand and stone gave way to more varied hues. The stark rocks lost their rosy flush and became rounded, diminutive, and insipid until they disappeared, replaced by tall, sinuous, golden-toned grasses and scattered, quiet glades of slender emerald trees.

They crossed into more watered regions, sparkling with lakes and peaceful dams. Watching themselves astride their gliders as they skimmed the liquid mirrors, their gliders' graceful forms and that of their tiny voyagers reflecting off the shiny surfaces, was surreal.

When they had flown close on four hours, Taz suggested a break. Descending, they landed on the narrow strip of sandy shore bordering a vast lake, shimmering with the silver forms of careless fish darting just below the surface, fish who had never felt threatened even a day in their short lives.

Wistfully, Kayla watched them, wishing her own existence was as carefree. Then, hearing Jaden laugh, she turned and laughed too when she saw Atu's stiff movements after crawling off Han's back. That was, they laughed until their gliders reminded them this was exactly how they'd looked only a few days before. Shrugging, the teens edged into the shade of a nearby oak and dished out the sandwiches.

Jaden was especially appreciative. "Never knew food could taste this good," he mumbled between mouthfuls.

"Do you feel deprived?" Kayla asked.

"You have no idea." Jaden sighed, taking another enormous bite.

Kayla rolled her eyes before addressing Atu. "Don't tell me you have the same voracious appetite?"

"I enjoy my food—just not as much as Jaden."

But, watching the way Atu helped Jaden demolish the sandwiches, Kayla wasn't convinced. It wasn't apparent the night before when they had eaten dinner. Then again, Kayla was tired and hadn't been paying attention. Now, she realized it was like sitting down to eat with two starving wolves. From now on, she would make sure she secured her share before the boys tucked in.

The bats allowed them an hour's reprieve before insisting they resume their journey. Since Han's wing had proven itself healed, he picked up the extra passenger after lunch. Kayla smiled when Han teased the boys about the enormous quantities of food they'd consumed.

"What *did* you eat for lunch? I feel like I'm carrying a ton of concrete instead of two skinny teenage boys."

Kayla laughed. "Yes, boys, you'd better lay off the food, or you'll be without a ride."

Jaden and Atu chuckled, before Jaden snorted. "Considering that statement, we'd better not wait too long before allowing this weakling a break. I'm sure Taz is more than capable of carrying the load without buckling under our weight."

Han growled at the taunt. "The only part of that speech that bears any semblance of truth is your reference to alternating the load. Taz and I already agreed it's wise to switch off every two hours. That way, at least one of us is better rested and more capable of fending off an attack if we encounter a newly arrived Gaptor."

"You think they might enter our world again so soon?" Kayla asked, disconcerted this was even a possibility.

"Considering the Usurper has been planning another attack for eons, and his longtime agent is no longer responding, it's not inconceivable he'll move his timetable forward," Taz said. "The only thing that would delay him would be his lack of success in finding another way into your world. However, considering the time he's spent working on the problem, I don't think that's an obstacle we can count on. Not for very long, anyway."

As the humans digested her words, gloom at the prospect of more desperate encounters dampened their spirits like a wet blanket on a wintry day. But the afternoon passed peacefully, and by the time they made camp that evening, their usual exuberance had resurfaced.

Plenty of playful bantering around the campfire made for an entertaining and amusing evening before weariness coaxed them into their blissfully warm sleeping shells.

The evening's fun and games faded into obscurity the following morning when, much to their chagrin, Taz insisted they get back to practicing aerial maneuvers.

"We can't slack off just because there's no apparent danger," Taz lectured. "Besides, Atu needs to learn what you already have. It would be most unfortunate if we met another Gaptor, and he fell off during the fight."

Kayla sighed. *There's no faulting her infallible logic. Sadly.* They set to work, taking turns flying solo. Of necessity, this meant they left the third person on the ground while the other two practiced. Although grateful for the downtime they had between sets—Taz was a hard taskmaster—Kayla worried about the time they were losing. When she asked Taz whether they should move on, Taz shrugged.

"This is an unavoidable delay. It's preferable we only travel once we've trained Atu. We need to be ready for battle, should it happen."

That was the end of the discussion. While Jaden still trained with Han and Kayla with Taz, Atu paired with each of the gliders alternately. His flight skills progressed faster than Jaden and Kayla's, thanks to the pointers they could pass along. By midafternoon, Atu had the basic concepts down, although, without question, Jaden and Kayla's mastery still exceeded his own. Taz was relentless in her pursuit of excellence, repeating their drills until they thought they would expire of sheer boredom.

Then, toward evening, Taz switched things up, coaching them on how to do the routines when two of them rode a glider instead of just one. She stipulated Atu pair with one of them and then the other so he could fly with either duo.

Her request proved unexpectedly challenging. Although the teens had no problem understanding her meticulous instructions, surprisingly, they found they lacked the strength for execution. With two of them now fighting for the limited space on the glider, the need for more precise control over their movements and the extended time required for completing each motion taxed their muscles to the extreme. Their strength failed before they had even finished two runs.

"Please," Atu wheezed, "we need a break."

Taz peered at them down her long, pointy nose, contemplating their request. "Yes, I suppose we should stop for the day. No point in training further when you're already worn out. You did well, except for your resilience. Some strength training exercises will solve the problem."

Too exhausted to resent her lack of praise, Kayla was also too weary to point out that all of this was new to them and that a grace period while their muscles adjusted was well within reason. Instead, she hunched on her bat, grateful when the gliders descended at the first sign of a decent resting place.

Almost too weak to walk, Kayla slid off Taz, noticing she wasn't alone. Her arms ached, her legs were jelly, and every other muscle in her body felt entitled to complain too. Kayla and the boys dragged themselves through dinner with a supreme effort before shuffling into their sleeping shells, where deep, dreamless sleep incapacitated them within minutes.

The next two days saw them traveling again, but they brought no respite. Their training ramped up. Taz was inexorable in her requests and Han unmoved by their protests. In fact, the more they complained, the more Taz demanded of them, until this truth filtered through to their fatigued minds, and they stopped whining.

The repetitive, strenuous exercise eventually paid dividends. They became more adept at their routines, learned new moves, more effectively maintained their balance, and even began acclimatizing to increased speeds. Still not enough to satisfy Taz, but they could withstand higher speeds better than a week before. At night, the sensation of flight remained with Kayla, and she curled, rolled, twisted, and dived as she stretched out in her shell, her dreams flooded with the movements.

CHAPTER FOURTEEN

Day four of their journey dawned, and Kayla woke, groaning as her stiff muscles objected to movement. Besides all the new muscles now employed when flying, Kayla was also unaccustomed to sleeping for more than a day on such unyielding surfaces. She ached all over.

"I'm sure there was a rock jabbing my back all night. My ribs are killing me," Kayla moaned, rubbing a tender spot on her right side as she struggled out of her shell.

Jaden, looking the worse for wear, rubbed his hands over his face. "What I wouldn't give for a nice, soft bed and some of my mother's blueberry pancakes."

"Quit mentioning tasty food," Atu grumbled, his hair tousled and his eyes still half-closed as he emerged from his own shell.

As they hobbled over to the area where they'd made their fire the evening before, Atu was the least decrepit of the three. He picked up a stick and poked the still-warm embers, coaxing the fire back to life.

"How are you so much more mobile than Kayla and me?" Jaden demanded, eyeing him.

"I spend a few nights a month outdoors when I'm foraging for the herbs I use in my potions. You get used to it. In a day or two, you'll feel you've slept nowhere other than on rock-hard ground."

"If you say so," Kayla muttered, not believing a word.

They huddled around the freshly stoked fire, leaning in for warmth while they ate their meager breakfast. Their food supply was dwindling, and it was getting progressively colder the further north they traveled, the terrain under them draining of any signs of life.

If they didn't pass over an inhabited area soon, they would have to make a detour to stock up on supplies. *Not only food, but clothing too,* Kayla thought as she tried rubbing warmth into her frozen fingers. But they came across no towns that day. As evening approached, Kayla suggested a supply run, but the bats wouldn't hear of it.

Taz sniffed. "There's plenty of food in this area. What's wrong with catching something?"

Jaden stared, horrified, before admitting, "I wouldn't know how."

Atu grinned. "Providence then that you have someone with you who does. Ever eat roast rabbit?"

Kayla blanched. "No, and I don't want to."

"It's tasty," Atu assured her, laughing. "Wait and try it before making any judgments."

"That's assuming you'll catch any," Kayla mumbled.

"Oh, I will." Atu chuckled, noting her disapproving expression. "Just give me some time once we're back on the ground."

True to his word, when they landed a short while later, Atu disappeared into the overgrown underbrush in search of food. He returned an hour later with two rabbits slung over his shoulder.

Unsure whether she was repulsed or impressed, Kayla watched him skin the rabbits, remove and bury the entrails, and then spear the carcasses for roasting. She glanced around, looking for Jaden, wanting some moral support, but he'd wandered off to find water and hadn't yet returned. *Where is he when I need him?* Dwelling on that thought made her squirrely. He had become way too important to her.

Wanting to take her mind in another direction, she asked, "Where did you learn how to do all that?"

"My father taught me," Atu replied, not looking up, his attention on the spices he was rubbing into the meat. "When you live in the desert, getting to a store for supplies can sometimes be problematic."

Kayla knew he was trying to make light of the situation, but she sensed his deep, underlying sorrow. "You miss him, don't you?"

"Every day. My mom too."

"Do you want to talk about what happened to them?" Kayla asked, not wanting to intrude but offering an opportunity to talk if he needed to.

"There's not much to tell. They went into the desert almost three months ago to the day and never came home. When I realized something was wrong, I tracked them to the riverbed, but their trail disappeared into thin air. It was like they were walking one moment and gone the next."

"Since I'm ignorant about how one person tracks another, did that make any sense? I mean, why would the trail just vanish?"

"I had no feasible answer before meeting you and Jaden. But that day when I glimpsed the Gaptor for the first time, I pieced it together. I suspect their tracks disappeared the way they did because the Gaptor plucked them up into the air. It's the only explanation that makes sense."

His frankness shocked Kayla. *Is he suggesting that the Gaptor took his parents? Why? And if so, what are the chances his parents are still alive?*

He must've read her mind, because he said, "Yes, I do think the Gaptor took them, and it is possible they are dead. But I don't think so. The feeling they're still alive is as real to me as the ground I'm standing on. And if that's fanciful thinking, then so be it. I'll accept they're no longer in the land of the living when I find proof to convince me otherwise."

Now Kayla felt out of her depth. She almost regretted asking. But his quiet conviction tempered her regret, bringing more peace than she'd felt in days. His unwavering confidence that he would establish the fate of his parents, whatever that might be, brought her hope.

"I'm sorry you don't know what happened to your parents; I am. But thank you for inspiring me to believe there can be a happy ending." Kayla took his hand and squeezed it.

Gratitude shone in his eyes. "Thanks. It's nice not to be alone anymore."

"Who's alone?" Jaden asked, picking up on the tail end of their conversation.

"No one." Kayla smiled up at him. "We're all in this together."

"Nice to know." Jaden's face betrayed his awareness he wasn't getting the whole story but was choosing not to pry.

Kayla moved to make space as Jaden sat next to her. His gaze flitted toward her hand, still holding Atu's. The dangerous glint sparking in his eyes had her heart leaping. But the glint disappeared as quickly as it had sprung to life, and Jaden set his face in a congenial mask, leaving Kayla unsure what he was thinking.

Is he jealous? She wished he was. That would make things so much simpler. From the way he ground his teeth before looking away, it wasn't impossible. Resisting the sudden urge to tell Jaden what she and Atu had been discussing so he would understand, Kayla sighed. It would only make things between them awkward again if she was misreading him. Giving Atu an encouraging smile, she released his hand.

To Kayla's relief, Jaden's mask fell away of its own accord as his emotions calmed, and the three of them settled into easy conversation around the campfire while the rabbits cooked. The bats had flown off earlier in search of their own food, and without their critical appraisal, the teens commented on how pleased they were that they weren't as exhausted as they'd been the previous three evenings. The tempting aroma of roasted meat soon made their mouths water. And when the time came to eat, Kayla was first in line.

"Wow, this is delicious," Kayla said, stuffing another bite into her mouth, too hungry to care about table manners and burning her tongue.

"Yeah, dude, amazing," Jaden added, juice running down his chin.

Atu laughed, accepting their compliments. "I told you it would be."

Conversation ceased while they ate, too hungry to interrupt their meal with talking or even greeting their gliders when they returned. The teens demolished the two rabbits in short order, much to the gliders' disgust.

"Carnivores!" Han huffed.

"You were the ones who told us to catch something," Kayla retorted.

"Ugh, don't remind me." Taz groaned. "Ohanzee, let's find a place to sleep. I can't take much more of this."

The gliders took off, and the teens chattered around the fire until the combined effects of the day's exertions, their full stomachs, and the fire's warmth leadened their eyelids. They mumbled goodnights, slid into their sleeping shells, and passed out.

CHAPTER FIFTEEN

A freezing, driving rain woke Kayla the next morning, a most unpleasant way to wake up. She wasn't ready to relinquish sleep, and from the way Jaden and Atu huddled deeper into their shells, pulling the waterproof outer covers over their heads, neither were they.

But the water was everywhere, pounding down and bouncing off of every surface. It pooled around them and trickled over them, somehow finding ways inside their shells, until they conceded defeat. They were all in a foul mood when the gliders arrived back at the camp.

"Where have you been?" Jaden complained, rolling up his sodden shell.

"Bathing." Taz smiled sweetly. "Something I think all of you desperately needed too. At least you don't smell anymore."

Kayla's mouth dropped open. "Really? Of all the things you could say, you insult us?"

"No, I was telling the truth. Would you prefer I didn't?"

Kayla rolled her eyes, too weary to comment.

Jaden, however, took offense, as incensed as a rattled snake. Frustrated, he yelled, "You could at least have said it nicely!"

"I don't think there is a 'nice' way to tell someone their personal hygiene requires attention. Since you're are up and about, shall we fly?"

"No!" Jaden snarled. "We'll be good and ready only after eating breakfast."

Kayla bit back a smile. He was being childish, but it was like he couldn't help himself. Jaden hunched into himself, clearly regretting his rash statement when the icy rain persisted throughout breakfast, pelting them with icy bullets and making the entire experience utterly dreadful.

Kayla soldiered through it, although to her thinking, they would've been better off flying away and eating breakfast when they reached a drier area. Apparently, Jaden wasn't about to admit that to Taz. But it did look like she and Atu would get an apology as soon as Taz was out of earshot.

They took flight as soon as they'd finished breakfast, and Kayla was sure she had never felt so wretched in all her life. She was cold and wet and hungry. The miserly portions divvied up for breakfast hadn't quelled her hunger, and she longed for a hot meal and dry clothes. Glancing over at the boys flying the first stretch with Han, she was shocked to find Atu wearing only a t-shirt. *What's with that? Isn't he cold?*

Before she could ask, the gliders began the day's exercises, as stringent with their mandates as ever. The morning dragged on, the cold never leaving her bones despite the exertion. The longer they flew, the more frigid the air became. Her frozen fingers solidified on Taz's fur, and she was sure her nose would run away if it wasn't attached to her face.

Two hours later, the rain subsided, but the cold persisted. Kayla caught another glimpse of Atu, who still hadn't donned a sweater. Unable to believe it, Kayla said, "Taz, can we get closer to the boys? I want to talk to them."

Wordlessly, Taz closed the gap.

Within earshot, Kayla yelled, "Atu, aren't you freezing?"

Surprise flitted over his face, then something else. *Pain? No, a grimace, but . . . is he embarrassed?* Not expecting this reaction, Kayla was even more baffled when Atu asked the bats if they could land.

On the ground, Atu hopped down and squatted next to his pack. When he straightened, he held a jar. "Sorry, I meant to give this to you last night, but then we got talking, and I forgot."

Kayla sidled over and took the jar. "What is it?"

"A lotion my family and I use to keep the cold at bay."

She studied him, sure he was teasing her. But Atu's earnest gaze confirmed he was serious. "So, what, we apply it just like lotion?"

"Yes, but especially on your hands and face."

Jaden had watched the exchange up to this point. "You're telling us you have a magic potion to keep us warm?"

"Yeah, bro. And dry. Sorry I forgot to hand it out last night—my bad."

Suspicious, Kayla opened the jar and dipped her fingers into the substance, surprised when the texture her fingers found was creamy and smooth. She withdrew a small amount and sniffed it. It smelled of lavender. Not the best fragrance, but better than what she expected. Kayla rubbed the silky lotion over her chapped hands and felt the balm's soothing relief. Then her hands tingled. She jerked them up to study them.

Atu smiled. "Relax, the tingling's part of the process."

Reassured, Kayla yanked her damp sweater off and helped herself to a second round, smearing the lotion over her bare arms and exposed parts of her neck. Despite expecting the tingle, it still felt weird, particularly when she applied it to her ears. At first, she felt nothing. Her ears were so cold that they were numb. Then, abruptly, they prickled and burned. And then they were on fire. With a small shriek, Kayla reached up and grabbed her ears with her hands, trying to scrub the lotion off.

Chuckling, Atu gently pulled her hands away. "Relax. It'll pass."

"When?" Kayla cried, sure the inferno in her ears would set her hair on fire.

Even Jaden was laughing, and Kayla scowled. About to punch him, she realized the fire had died as suddenly as it had started. Her ears felt blessedly warm—and normal. Tossing a devilish grin at Jaden, she said, "Your turn."

He stopped laughing. Jaden reached over and scooped out a small dollop, then gingerly applied the lotion to his hands. When his eyes widened, it told Kayla all she needed to know. He was experiencing the same tingle.

"Wait until you do your ears," Kayla said, smiling when he grimaced.

Still smiling, Kayla took a third helping and disappeared behind Taz's outstretched wings to cover the parts of her skin she didn't want exposed to the boys, while Jaden did the same behind Han. Within five minutes, they were both smothered with the lotion. It was sublime when the tingling passed, and warmth spread, heating Kayla from the inside out.

"Wow, it works," Kayla said, impressed.

"Obviously, it does. I made it. Sorry again for not handing it out earlier. It should make our journey northward more comfortable."

It did. No longer bound by the pervasive cold, Kayla performed her exercises with abandon, freed from the fear her frozen limbs wouldn't support her weight. Her joy soared when she was once again able to revel in the freedom flying brought. Her renewed energy and willingness to do all she asked even impressed Taz.

"We should've thought to warm you up sooner," Taz commented.

"Oh, I'm sorry, are you cold? Do you want lotion too?" It mortified Kayla she hadn't thought to offer some to their gliders.

Taz chuckled, the sound unexpected. "Thank you, but no. Temperatures in our world are far more extreme, so we are unaffected by your weather."

Kayla felt better. "Good to know."

When they landed that evening, Kayla pressed Atu for information about the lotion. "How did you make it?"

"By mixing the right plants together." Atu sat back from the fire he'd just lit. Then witnessing her exasperation, he said, "Explaining the whole process would take too long. And you wouldn't know what I was talking about, anyway. Suffice to say, a solid foundation in botany is essential, but more important is the wisdom passed down by my ancestors for exactly how to combine the various ingredients to craft the desired product. It boils down to how you put the pieces together. If they're combined correctly, they have the power to do amazing things."

The way he delivered his speech had Kayla and Jaden looking at one another speculatively. Was he hiding something? They already suspected there was more to his potions than just mixing a few herbs or plants together, and this speech somehow confirmed it. But it was also obvious Atu would divulge no additional information.

"Magic man," Kayla whispered conspiratorially to Jaden.

"Totally," Jaden whispered back.

The secretive exchange brought a sudden, unexpected intimacy between them, and Kayla wished she hadn't started it. She was closer to Jaden than she'd been in days. And she felt it. Her body yearned to press into his, to feel his arms around her, to . . . *No, no. no!*

Kayla stood so abruptly she almost knocked Jaden over. Apologizing, she dashed away on the pretense of getting water, cursing herself for letting her guard down.

As she left, she heard Atu say, "She'll come around."

"What?" Jaden blurted.

That was as much of the conversation as she allowed herself to hear before bolting away. Kayla pursed her lips, contemplating Atu's statement. One thing she didn't have to wonder about was the boy himself. There was more to Atu than he'd presented to her and Jaden. But he wouldn't reveal more any time soon.

The following day, they continued going north as dictated by the map, the next few days passing much the same as the previous few with some notable exceptions. The voyagers were more adept at performing multiple drills when paired on a glider, having gained the requisite strength. They no longer woke up stiff and sore every morning, accustomed to sleeping on bare ground as Atu had predicted. And they could, albeit clumsily and inconsistently, even catch game of their own now, Atu having taught them a few skills.

The rugged landscape became more hostile. *If we aren't already in*

Gotskiena, we're close, Kayla thought. Perhaps a detour to Atu's friend wouldn't be such a bad idea. He'd be more hospitable than this barren region.

Imposing mountains, dominated by stony ice and glacial snow, pressed down on them from all sides, mute sentries blocking their way. Kayla already missed the open, gently undulating lands with their waving fields and welcoming trees of only a few days before.

The scenery wasn't the only thing changing. As they neared their destination, the map's faded lines brightened and separated, making the "X" visible so they could identify landmarks they could use as guides. But the most obvious sign they were almost there was the arrival of the three-dimensional image with its blinking dot when Jaden pulled up the map late one afternoon.

The day's flight had been long and tiring. When they entered the mountain pass, signposted by the blinking dot's increased tempo, they were in two minds whether to stop and camp there for the evening or press on and perhaps reach their destination.

After a brief discussion, they agreed to fly for another hour while they still had light, then rest for the day. They had not traveled very far down the pass before Kayla noticed Jaden looking around uneasily.

"Han, we need to go back—now!" Jaden's sudden shout startled them all.

Han wobbled in surprise. "Why?"

"I can't explain. I just know we're in for trouble if we keep traversing this pass."

Kayla, trying to reach her birthmark, which felt like it would itch itself right off her arm, couldn't help but hear. Leaning forward, she spoke into Taz's ear while still wriggling to reach the irksome thing. "We should listen to him. I've only known him a short time, but when he gets these feelings, he's usually right."

Taz nodded and lifted her chin to Han. The gliders tilted their wings, intending to curve back around, when something happened. Taz went limp. Unnerved, Kayla scanned the area. They hadn't flown into anything, and Kayla could see, taste, smell, or touch nothing.

But it was like a thick shell crept over Taz, encasing her, dulling her senses and deadening her mind. Kayla slid a glance sideways and noticed Han was equally affected. Without the ability to think or control their limbs, to discern the air currents under their wings, the gliders spiraled out of control, reeling like drunken sailors.

Terrified, Kayla clutched at anything her fingers came into contact with, scrabbling to stay onboard and fleetingly grateful the boys were with Han. It would've tested even her improved strength had she been the one flying with Atu.

Sparing the boys another quick peek, Kayla found them coping with the situation. Then Taz slipped sideways. Kayla snarled, shifting on Taz's shoulders so she wouldn't fall off her glider, now at an alarming ninety-degree angle to the ground.

Kayla bellowed. "Taz, straighten up!"

But Taz was incapable of hearing, like the bat was in a stupor. Taz continued listing to the one side while they lost altitude. The boys rocketed past, and Kayla jolted. Han was completely inverted, the boys hanging on for all they were worth. They were also shouting at Han to no avail.

"Jaden, pull on one of his wings and see if you can turn him," Kayla screamed, panic slipping into her voice when she realized they were running out of time.

If the boys didn't do something drastic soon, they would crash headfirst into the mountain. She watched, not daring to breathe as both boys tugged on Han's left wing. Ever so slowly, Han's weight shifted, but it was inevitable.

"You won't make it. Jump!" Kayla shrieked.

For a few manic moments, she thought they hadn't heard. They continued pouring their strength into pulling Han upright. Then, a split second before they crashed into the snow-covered mountainside, the boys leaped off. Kayla watched, shocked, as the boys tumbled like limp rag dolls through the deep snow, while Han plowed into a colossal drift, carving up the snow as he slowed and came to a complete stop. She frantically searched for signs of movement. All three lay motionless.

Fear crushed air from her lungs. But she had no time to worry about them. Taz jerked forward, righting herself. Then, just as unexpectedly, she dove downward. Kayla screamed at her to stop, but Taz was a slave to some crazy tune in her head only she could hear.

They plummeted down, down, down toward the ice and snow and unforgiving rock. Kayla beat Taz's back, trying anything to get her attention—anything to break the spell she was under. But a few feet from the ground, Kayla knew it was futile. She had only one choice.

Trusting it would benefit Taz as much as her, she jumped. For a second, only the whistling wind assaulted her ears. Then there was blinding, whirling white, followed by a sharp, painful crack as her head hit something. Then inky black. Then nothing at all.

CHAPTER SIXTEEN

"Kayla, wake up!" Jaden commanded. He scanned her face for signs she'd heard him. Nothing. "Can you hear me? Kayla?" She twitched, then winced before scrunching up her eyes like she didn't want to open them. "That's right. It's time to wake up."

The first semblance of consciousness returned. Jaden smiled when Kayla curled into him. *Oh yeah, she likes me, alright. If only she would hurry up and acknowledge it.*

Holding Kayla again was bliss. More so because she wasn't trying to weasel away from him. A temporary accommodation, he was sure, and something she would doubtless rectify when she had her wits about her. Reflexively, sensing the transience of their contact, Jaden tucked her closer. She sighed contentedly, and he released his own long sigh.

Jaden couldn't remember ever being as scared as when he first saw her lying there: limp, ashen, and with dark, sinister blood staining the snow around her head.

His heart had turned to stone, his own life force temporarily draining out of him. If Atu hadn't shoved him out of the way as he ran to Kayla, Jaden would've remained where he'd landed. As it was, the rough thrust unbalanced him, forcing Jaden to move to stay on his feet.

That tiny movement spurred him to take action himself. He raced past Atu, reaching Kayla first and pulling her into his arms before Atu could warn him against it. Now, much as he longed to keep her there, she needed to come back to him. "Kayla, open your eyes." She snuggled closer. But he squeezed her arm, reinforcing the request.

Kayla eased an eye open, moaning at the bright light. She closed the eye again to block the pain.

"That's it. Open your eyes," Jaden said.

"Go away," Kayla grumbled.

Jaden grinned. She was at least talking. "Sorry, I can't do that. Taz needs you."

Her brow furrowed as she tried remembering what happened to Taz. Confusion morphed into fear as the events preceding her blackout stormed back. She bolted up. Her face drained of color as pain spiked her head, and Jaden could almost see the nausea, ripe and bilious, rushing into her throat. Barely twisting her head sideways in time, it gushed out.

"Easy now," Jaden said, drawing her hair to one side and holding it off her face while she emptied the contents of her stomach. He waited until she had finished. "Feeling better?" he asked when she fumbled a handful of fresh snow and smeared it over her mouth with a shaky hand.

"A little." She groaned, lifting a hand. "Ow, my head!" Only mild surprise registered when she found her head bandaged.

"Yeah, you gave it quite a crack. Atu said the cut's superficial and it would bleed like crazy for a while, but he's more worried about a concussion."

"Where is he?" Kayla murmured, remembering to turn her head slowly this time as she gazed around.

"He's with Taz. She took quite a tumble too."

Kayla's face blanched further when she recalled their ghastly descent. She tried standing, but dizziness forced her back down. "I need to get to Taz. Help me, please."

Jaden was kind but firm. "Not yet. Atu gave strict instructions that you stay here until the bleeding stops. Then he wants to check you out before you move." Kayla made an agitated motion with her hands. "Don't worry. He's taking care of Taz."

Kayla gritted her teeth. "Jaden, you can either help me, or I'll crawl over there on my own. What's it going to be?"

Does she have to be so stubborn? Muttering, Jaden slid an arm around her waist and guided her to her feet. Kayla didn't skitter away, and Jaden couldn't decide if it was because she still wasn't in her right mind or because necessity dictated she allowed him to touch her.

When her dizziness flooded back, making her stumble and clutch at his arm, he had his answer. Jaden held her in place until it looked like her head had stopped spinning, before allowing her to take another step. She wobbled, and from the way she swallowed, Jaden guessed she might be sick again.

But Kayla sucked it down, setting her jaw in a familiar line. Jaden sighed. Irrespective of whether this was a good idea, Kayla would get to her glider. Step by agonizing step, they crept up the rocky mountain. After only five paces, sweat slicked Kayla's face. Jaden couldn't take it. Bending, he swept her into his arms, smiling when her lovely eyes widened in surprise.

"Can't have you passing out before you reach Taz." Smiling weakly, she wrapped her arms around his neck and snuggled into him again. *Ah, I could get used to this.* Having her close again, knowing he was keeping her safe, was heaven. Jaden treasured the moment because soon, she would be back to normal and pushing him away again. His hold tightened, as though this would stop the inevitable from happening.

Up ahead, a boulder, huge, fat, and round, blocked their way. Jaden wound around it, feeling Kayla tense when she spotted Taz's wing poking out. She wriggled in his arms.

Kayla whimpered. "Let me get to her."

"I'll get you there. Just be patient. You don't want to black out again, do you?"

Resigned, Kayla settled back against his chest. Rounding the curve,

Kayla gasped at her first unobstructed view of Taz. Her glider lay immobile on the snow, a large gash in her wing. But more alarming was the way her head angled oddly off her body.

"No!" Kayla cried.

"She's alive," Atu assured her, looking up from Taz's side. "But I don't know how to wake her. She's comatose, like Han."

Kayla squeaked. "Oh, Han!" She gazed at Jaden with huge, concerned, apologetic eyes. "He's alright? I mean, other than the comatose thing?"

"Yes, he's fine. Or, rather, he has no other injuries we're aware of."

"And you? And Atu?" Kayla probed, her mind clearing enough to think.

"We're okay too. You and Taz are the ones we're worried about. Come, let's get you to Taz, and then Atu can check you for a concussion."

Jaden carried Kayla to Taz's right side, the side where her wing was still whole. Gently depositing Kayla onto the snow, he stepped back, holding in the sigh threatening escape.

Kayla touched Taz softly on her face. "Wake up, lovely lady," she whispered. When Atu hunkered down beside her, she asked, "Have you checked for neck injuries? Is it possible to reposition her head?"

"I checked her neck, but we can't move her head yet. I'd like to find something to support her head before attempting that. Even then, I'm dubious. I don't know what might shake loose if we do."

Kayla nodded, still caressing Taz's sleek fur. "What do you think their chances are of waking up soon?"

"I can't answer that one either," Atu muttered. "I think this stupor they're in is still part of whatever affected them while we were flying. And before you ask, I have no clue what caused that either. Something environmental is my best guess. For now, let me check you're okay. Let's see how dilated your pupils are."

Jaden remained tense while Atu examined Kayla, running her through several tests before he nodded. "You're lucky it isn't worse." Turning to Jaden, he asked, "Can you get Kayla to talk you through cleaning and rebandaging her wound while I tend Taz's wing?"

"I can do that." He must've looked as uncertain as he felt because Kayla smiled encouragingly.

"I'll help you. Your turn to take care of me."

Jaden liked the sound of that. Except it reminded him of the last time they'd had to take care of a wound: his wound, inflicted by the Gaptor on their way back from the library with the precious book. Kayla had done such a marvelous job. He only hoped he could match her skill. "Yes, time to reciprocate," Jaden said, his businesslike tone betraying none of his emotions. "Where do I start?"

Kayla directed him to her backpack, then talked him through the steps once he had retrieved her med-kit. Although he was as gentle as he could be, she cringed more than once. "Sorry," he apologized. "I'm not as good at this as you are."

Her soft green eyes crinkled into a smile. "I've had a lot more practice."

Jaden grinned. "Let's hope I can never say the same."

His comment sobered them both. Shifting her gaze from him, Kayla moved her hand to stroke Taz's powerful shoulders, well below her twisted neck. She monitored Atu as he tended Taz's wing, no doubt anxious Taz reap the same benefits as Han. It would be a bonus if Taz woke up with a healed wing. That was, if she woke up. From her frown, Jaden could tell Kayla was as worried as he was.

As he packed Kayla's medical supplies back into her kit, Jaden tried working out what had gone wrong. Their trip was perfectly normal, right up to the point when he'd said they should turn back. Then all hell broke loose. *Did something in the valley prevent us from turning back? Or were we just far enough along for someone to attack us? If so, by whom? For what purpose? If an attack was the goal, why didn't our attackers come after us and finish the job? And how were we attacked? What made our gliders lose control?* Jaden's mind went around in circles.

Kayla's voice made him jump. "Jaden, please pass me one of those green pain pills." Kayla pointed at a plastic container.

"Sure, here you go." Jaden removed the pill and offered it with his water bottle, chagrined to find her grimacing again. "Is it hurting a lot?"

"More than I'd like it to be," Kayla admitted, swallowing. "But this will help." A moment later, she added, "It isn't helping that my mind is spiraling trying to figure things out. What do you think happened up there?"

"I don't know. Atu and I discussed it, but there's no plausible explanation. If it was an attack, it was invisible. But if someone attacked us, where are our attackers, and why did they attack us? Without evidence of a foe, the environmental aspect is plausible, but even that has issues. Why did it only affect the gliders?"

"All the same arguments I've been running through." Kayla's face clouded. "You don't think this could've been that EMP thing from a newly arrived Gaptor?"

Jaden's answer was terse. "Atu and I considered that too. If it was, where's the Gaptor?"

"Hmm, good question." Kayla fell silent again.

Movement drew Jaden's attention, and his eyes tracked Atu. The healer had finished with Taz's wing and now darted back and forth between the gliders. Jaden's interest piqued when he realized Atu was comparing them somehow. The increasing rapidity of his movements matched his mounting concern.

Barely containing his own escalating stress, Jaden blurted, "What are you doing?"

"Help me here a minute, would you?" Atu directed, ignoring Jaden's question.

"What do you need me to do?"

"Check Han's chin. See if there's a small cut below his lip."

Mystified, Jaden hustled over to Han and did as asked. "No, no cut."

"How about under his left wing? Is there anything there?"

Jaden inspected the area and shook his head again. "No. What are you looking for?"

"Something I'm not seeing," Atu muttered, moving around Taz and lifting an eyelid. He peered at her exposed eyeball, then ran over to Han and did the same.

"For pity's sake, Atu, tell us what's going on!" Jaden bellowed.

"I'm trying to find some medical reason why our gliders are in this state. Something has to be causing it. And I can't find it."

"That's because there isn't one."

At the voice booming behind them, they spun around and gasped at the sheer size of the man. Human, but so tall and broad and obscured by furs, he could've been mistaken for a small bear. Bounding back to Kayla, the boys assumed defensive positions in front of her and Taz. Jaden hoped the stranger wouldn't question the noticeable gap between Kayla and the boys, a result of Taz's inert body. An invisible creature would be difficult to explain.

CHAPTER SEVENTEEN

"Who are you?" Jaden demanded.

"You're invading my space and you want to know who I am?"

His voice carried the unmistakable accent of a native Gotskienian. When they simultaneously noticed the odd-looking weapon protruding from his hand, the teens sucked in a communal breath. It could've been a gun except for two glaring alterations: the grip resembled a remote control, and the barrel flared outward to a wide mouth instead of the usual short, uniform tube.

Jaden wasn't the only one who heard Kayla's stifled giggle.

"You find this amusing, no?" the man snapped.

"Sorry," Kayla sputtered. "That reminds me of my hair dryer attachment." She frowned when she realized that hadn't sounded rational. "A bump on the head combined with pain medication isn't exactly a recipe for self-control."

The man grunted, studying them for another moment. His next question shocked them. "Are those your beasts?"

He could only be referring to their gliders. *He can see them?* "And what if they are?" Jaden countered.

"Friend or foe?" the man clarified.

Atu answered this time. "They're our friends."

"I thought as much!" the man exclaimed, his face breaking into a broad grin. "I never thought I would ever lay eyes on them."

His reaction was bewildering. Jaden glared at Atu for giving out even this small tidbit of information. *What was he thinking, putting the gliders in jeopardy?* Then Jaden noticed Atu was gazing at the man as though he suspected who he might be.

Tossing Jaden a tight, pacifying smile, Atu reached into his pocket and, to Jaden's dismay, withdrew his medallion, holding it up to the man.

The stranger's reaction was instantaneous. Muttering an oath, he dropped his weapon. Astounded, Jaden watched, wide-eyed, as he patted around inside his heavy jacket. Then, with another face-splitting grin, he produced what he'd been searching for: another medallion.

While Jaden and Kayla gaped, Atu ran to the man, embracing him. "Armorer!"

The man was just as flabbergasted as Jaden and Kayla. Then Atu's salutation registered because the stranger returned the hug, a look of wonder crossing his face. "You're from the desert?"

"Yes. Sava's my father. Do you remember him?"

"How could I forget the masterful storyteller? His tales of the beasts were so real, you experienced their invasion when he spoke of it. How is he?"

Atu's face fell. "I'm not sure. He and my mother went missing three months ago."

"No! What happened?"

"I suspect the Gaptor took them, but to what end, I don't know."

The man cursed unintelligibly. Shaking his head, he gave Atu's shoulder an understanding squeeze. "I am so sorry to hear that."

Atu nodded, then changed the subject. "Come, let me introduce you to my friends," Atu murmured, dragging the man to where Jaden and Kayla still gawked. "Armorer, meet Jaden and Kayla."

"A genuine pleasure," the man said in his strange accent. "Please, call me Sven."

They shook hands, exchanging brief pleasantries before Atu said,

"Armorer, not to be rude, but our gliders are ill. We don't know what ails them. Do you have any idea how we can help them?"

Sven bashed his hand against his forehead, uttering another garbled oath. Without explanation, he hurriedly retrieved his weapon. The teens all stepped back in alarm. He frowned. "This won't hurt you. It's to help them," he explained, pointing at their gliders.

Sven pushed a series of buttons on the flattened grip. There was a soft popping sound, like the seal of a vacuum being broken. The teens' gazes swiveled toward their gliders, expecting movement, but their friends remained motionless.

About to ask Sven what they should observe, Jaden whooped when Han and Taz straightened, albeit stiffly, and assumed their usual resting positions. Jaden dashed to them, Kayla on his heels, both shouting their gliders' names.

Jaden reached Han and put a hand on his fur. "How do you feel?"

Han blinked, still waking up, and surveyed his surroundings. Spying Sven, he struggled to his full height, shielding Jaden with his wings and hissing at the intruder.

"It's alright. He's a friend." Jaden rushed to explain, noticing Taz taking similar steps to protect Kayla. Somewhat mollified, the bats stopped hissing but did not lower their wings.

Atu led a nervous Sven toward the bats. "Taz, Han, I'd like you to meet Sven. He's the armorer I spoke of." When the bats maintained their hostile stances, Atu said. "Sven, show them your medallion."

Trembling, Sven held up his medallion. The sight of the rare artifact finally convinced the bats there was no danger, and they lowered their wings.

"We apologize if we scared you," Han murmured.

Sven gaped. "They speak?"

"We do." Taz sighed, rolling her eyes. She wasted no time getting to the point. "Armorer, do you know what precipitated our disorientation?"

Sven looked uncomfortable. "I'm sorry. I did not know it was you, or I would not have engaged the signal. Please accept my humblest apologies," he offered, bowing to the gliders.

Taz inclined her head, but before she could speak, Jaden charged in.

"What signal?"

Kayla scowled. "You caused all that?"

"But why, Armorer?" Atu asked.

Sven held up a hand to stop the barrage. "The last time something entered my airspace, I got this." Sven tugged his jacket open to reveal a jagged, bright red scar running the length of his collarbone.

Kayla winced. "A Gaptor?"

"Yes. Which is why I made that," Sven said, gesturing toward his strange weapon. "I didn't want that abomination having control if we ever had the misfortune of meeting again."

Jaden nodded, his anger assuaged. "The gun sends out the signal, then? What does the signal do?"

"It disrupts sound waves at an ultrasonic level. I suspected it would affect the sonar the beast uses for navigation, unbalancing it, to the degree it would incapacitate the beast, causing it to fall from the sky. I didn't know whether it would work, but," Sven shrugged, gazing apologetically at the gliders again, "you have proven this will be an effective weapon should that beast ever dare enter my space again."

Jaden whistled. "Impressive! What made you think of disrupting the sound waves?"

Out of the corner of his eye, Jaden caught Kayla's eye roll.

"Boys and their toys!" Kayla chided. "I know all this is terribly fascinating, but should we be standing around here discussing a weapon's design? Sven, do you perhaps have somewhere sheltered our gliders could rest? Considering," she pointed out with some snark, "not all of us escaped unscathed."

Sven barked a laugh. "She has some sputska, no?"

"You could say that," Jaden muttered, reluctant to give up the first bit of tangible information he'd had in days. But Kayla was right. As usual. And now that he examined Kayla's face, he could see the exhaustion drawing her mouth tight and the faint, black smudges under her eyes.

Jaden regretted not thinking of her needs sooner. If he could just scoop her up in his arms and carry her away to a safe place—a place where she could find peace, where no harm could touch her. *Except does such a place exist anymore?* Even if it did, Kayla wasn't one to shirk her responsibilities. *Will she ever let me take care of her?* Jaden sighed, realizing Sven needed a nudge. "She has a point. Our gliders need a sheltered place to recover. As do we." Jaden glanced at Kayla.

Discerning his concern, Kayla smiled, responding to his unspoken request. "Yes, I promise to be a good girl and take it easy when we get there."

Jaden grinned. "I'm glad you're not going to be difficult about it." Turning to Sven, he said, "So how about it? Do you have a place nearby?"

"Yes! You will follow me home. You'll be my guests, yes?"

"Thank you, Armorer. We'd love that," Atu answered.

Sven beamed. "It will be delightful to have company again after all these years alone. Please, come!"

Kayla gave Taz an anxious glance. "How's your wing? Do you need help?"

Taz fluttered her injured wing. "I think I can manage. Did Atu work his magic on it like he did with Han's?"

"Yes, so let's hope it's healed by tomorrow. Are you sure you're alright?"

Taz smiled. Anyone with eyes could see Kayla was growing on her. "Thank you, but it's bearable. How's your head?"

Kayla returned the smile. "It's bearable."

Taz laughed. "You're my kind of girl."

Jaden agreed. She was his kind of girl too. Looking pleased with herself, Kayla took up her position alongside Taz. Then she blinked in surprise and raised a questioning eyebrow when Jaden stepped closer and settled an arm around her waist.

"I don't want you falling over and bashing your head again." Jaden shrugged, as if this was the most sensible explanation in the world. He had wondered how she would react, and that she hadn't drawn back— no, hadn't even flinched—soothed his soul. It was so right to have her snuggled under his arm. If only he could keep her there.

CHAPTER EIGHTEEN

Kayla eyed Jaden as they hobbled after Sven. Something about his flippant response made her believe there was more to the casual contact. Although his touch was light, Jaden's arm was a band of steel, binding her to him as tightly as a vine wrapping around a post. She had to admit—it felt heavenly. Kayla relaxed against Jaden, not in the mood to think about his motivations anymore. Or that she should push him away. She was too tired to keep resisting. All she wanted was to savor his closeness.

As they walked, Kayla wondered where Sven's home was. This was such an isolated region. She couldn't help but speculate on his reasons for living in the middle of nowhere. More than that, she hoped they'd discover other weapons Sven might have developed. Atu *had* said he was the armorer. Maybe Sven could work his magic, the same as Atu, and adapt the contraption he had used to bring them down, so it only worked on the Gaptor and not on their gliders. Wouldn't that be a bonus!

Kayla sighed as they trudged onward, hoping Sven's home wasn't far, even though she didn't want to give up Jaden's arm around her. Much as she was enjoying the contact, she longed for a place to lie down. Glancing at her companions, she found she wasn't the only one in need of a good night's rest. Fatigue weighed heavily on their shoulders as they slogged along.

If everyone's already this tired and we still haven't found what we're looking for, what are our chances of successfully completing the rest of the journey? And what's yet to come? Kayla shuddered as she recalled their last encounter with the Gaptor. *Will more of the monsters be coming our way soon? If so, is our little group really equipped to deal with them effectively?* Frazzled, Kayla jerked a hand through her long blonde hair, flinching and sucking in a sharp breath when the action pulled on her wound. *Why aren't we there already?*

Kayla was so preoccupied with her thoughts, she didn't notice Atu had stopped. Between pressure from Jaden's arm as he held her back and bumping into Atu, it brought her back to reality. "What's up?"

"Sven said he needed to disarm something," Atu muttered, shrugging when she raised an eyebrow.

Kayla looked for Sven, finding he'd stepped off the semblance of a track they'd been using. Kayla frowned when Sven picked an apparently random starting point, then paced forward from that spot in odd, geometrical patterns, until he eased behind a tree to the left of the wide swathe of snow in front of them.

A sparse rash of gray boulders marred the otherwise perfectly smooth surface of the snow, sticking out like ugly, blotchy blemishes. Sven stepped out from behind the tree onto the carpet of white, carefully inching between two boulders. Bending down, he grunted, tugging on something.

There was a sucking sound. Then the serene, snowy slope beyond the boulders disappeared. Kayla blinked as the image slid away, like an enormous canvas being yanked off a wall. It revealed a different landscape: one infinitely more treacherous. A precipice dropped into a vertical abyss a short way ahead of them.

Sven grinned at their stunned expressions. "You like my little deception?"

"Wow, that's unbelievable!" Jaden declared, enamored as always with anything technological. "Explain how you did that! Was that image similar to a holo-screen?"

"Nothing so simple." Sven smiled, pleased with Jaden's appreciation. "When you're dealing with creatures from another realm, it's best not to assume anything, including their ability or inability to detect holo-images. Therefore, I, shall we say, 'adapted' the basic concept of the holo-image, adding some extra sizzle as a surprise for anything trying to cross without first disarming the field."

"Sizzle?" Kayla asked, her own curiosity roused.

Sven smirked. "A hefty electric field with enough voltage to fry anything that touches it, and impervious to EMPs of any kind."

Jaden snorted. "I wouldn't be too sure of that. We've seen an EMP that completely bypassed all the shields on our terraporter. Have you ever come across anything like that?"

"I have," Sven mused, but didn't elaborate. When Jaden pressed, he merely smiled. "We all have our secrets, no? This is one of mine, and I'll not share it willingly. Come, it's getting dark and we have a way to go." Hearing Kayla's groan, he added, "But not too far."

Skirting the icy rim of the cliff, Jaden guided Kayla to the other side, where they waited for Sven as he re-engaged the trap. They marveled as the flawless illusion snapped back into place. Sven reclaimed his position in the lead, and they resumed their journey. Fifteen minutes passed before Sven called another halt. This time, their reason for not going further was obvious. A wide chasm yawned in front of them, stretching without end in either direction.

Kayla peeked at Jaden and Atu, not surprised to find they were equally mystified. Why had Sven brought them to a dead end? There was no way forward.

But, grinning like a loon, Sven reached under the icy ledge curling up at the chasm's edge. A tiny click preceded a soft whirring. Their eyes followed the sound. Two enormous, glittering quarter-circle arches rose, one from each side of the sheer walls, meeting in the middle and forming a perfect bridge over which they could cross.

Kayla chuckled. "Extraordinary!"

Sven laughed. "Yes, I like that one myself. Shall we?"

Making their way toward the bridge, they were delighted when it accommodated the gliders comfortably. And it wasn't at all slippery.

"Okay, how d'you do that?" Jaden asked.

Kayla could almost see those little wheels turning in his head as he tried to figure it out, and she grinned.

Sven's grin was almost as wide as Kayla's. "It's amazing what a little heat and a special coating will do to keep things safe. I can't very well have my guests falling off the walkway to their deaths—that wouldn't be very hospitable."

They all laughed. Reaching the far end of the walkway, they waited while Sven retracted the crystal drawbridge, then tramped after him as he resumed his lead. In under five minutes, they encountered their next seemingly insurmountable barrier: an unscalable cliff, rising immovable and impenetrable before them. The teens and their gliders turned and gazed expectantly at Sven.

"Any guesses where my key is hiding?" Sven teased.

"On the rock face?" Atu suggested.

"Nope."

"Under a ledge somewhere?" Kayla offered.

"No, again. Care to try?" he asked Jaden.

"Well, it's most likely a place you haven't used before. From the little I've seen of your work, you hate being predictable. Since the mountain and any ledges are out, the only other suitable hiding place here would be in those trees." Jaden gestured. "But which tree is the right one?" Jaden pondered, gazing at the proliferation of massive trunks crowding the cliff edge.

"You're smarter than you look. Tell me, which general grouping would you choose?"

Jaden shrugged. "With the way you think, it could be any of them."

"That was what I had hoped to hear." Retracing his steps, Sven navigated the deep snow toward a tight circle of trees, quite some distance from the path. Entering the circle, he disappeared.

"Smart," Jaden murmured. "Even if you were watching from a distance, you could see which group but couldn't identify the exact tree holding the access point. And I'll bet dollars to doughnuts, if you 'bark up the wrong tree' so to speak, you're in for a nasty surprise."

Kayla and Atu giggled. When rumbling sounded behind them, they all turned, Jaden dropping his arm from around Kayla. Too stunned by what she saw, Kayla didn't notice the loss. She gaped as a section of the cliff face slid open, exposing a narrow tunnel. Her first thought was how the bats would fit.

"Amazing!" Jaden crowed, clapping his hands with delight.

Atu was just as fascinated, strolling over to the entrance and poking his head in. "Yup, Armorer has some neat tricks up his sleeve."

Sven returned and accepted their compliments graciously. "Thank you, thank you, you are too kind. But may I suggest we move? I don't enjoy leaving my front door open for too long."

Kayla gazed anxiously at Taz. "Can you and Han fit through there?"

"You'd be surprised at the spaces we can squeeze into when the need arises," Taz said.

And to Kayla's astonishment, Taz slid first one half of her body and then the other through the narrow opening, only barely touching the sides. Kayla was even more impressed when Taz sidled forward, her body sideways. "How do you do that?"

"Twisting in and out of confined spaces is something we learn even before we can fly because not all sleeping areas in your world are as spacious as they are in ours. We were all trained this way in the event we were the ones chosen to carry the next voyagers."

"That's some foresight," Kayla said.

Taz sniffed. "I'm glad you approve."

Kayla spotted Jaden reaching for her—to slide his arm around her again, she supposed. But she was feeling okay now. And she shouldn't delude herself into thinking there was more to the action than he had stated, much as she wished there was. Plastering a smile on her face, Kayla slipped beyond his reach. "I'm feeling much better, thanks. I think I can manage on my own from here."

Kayla almost relented when Jaden froze, forcing himself to back down so he could agree to her request.

Dropping his arm, he attempted a grin. "Alright then. But I'm here if you need me."

"Thank you. I appreciate that."

From his frown, Kayla knew he was confused about what she appreciated: his offer of help or that he hadn't persevered. *Well, I'm not telling him.* As if he knew that, Jaden turned away. Kayla allowed the small sigh its escape.

Ushering Kayla ahead of him, Jaden scooted her further down the tunnel, allowing the others access. They waited for Sven to shut the rocky door, but this time, he urged them ahead. "It's a straight path from here, and it's safe."

"What? No more booby traps?" Jaden asked, disappointment coloring his voice.

Sven's raucous laugh reverberated against the stone walls and echoed down the tunnel. "Even if I couldn't disable them right here at the entrance, I don't think they're things you'd want to experience. None of the conventional knives coming out of nowhere or trapdoors opening under your feet, just some nastier treats."

"Rad!" Jaden shouted. "You must show me sometime."

Kayla rolled her eyes. "More toys! Talk about a man-cave haven."

"Now, now, no stereotyping," Jaden chided, his good humor restored as they negotiated the tunnel. Glancing at Kayla and confirming she was coping, he loped ahead, his curiosity stirred.

Kayla watched, amused, as he rushed down the corridor, inspecting it and trying to find the hidden traps. She giggled. He was incorrigible. Taz gritting her teeth wrecked Kayla's carefree moment. Even though they were ambling, progressing through the cramped space was taking a toll on her glider.

About to suggest a break, Kayla smothered the words when the tunnel widened into a spacious hallway. A relief because Taz was too stubborn to admit to her pain. As they pressed on, Kayla kept a watchful eye on her bat, but Taz appeared to get stronger by the second. Whether this was because of the added space or Atu's medicine taking effect, Kayla didn't care. She was grateful either way. No longer distracted by Taz's health, her own pain and fatigue resurfaced, and Kayla stumbled.

"You alright?" Atu murmured behind her.

"Just wasted. And my head is aching again."

"Armorer, how much further?" Atu called back.

"About five minutes," Sven replied.

Kayla groaned. "Is that until we get to the next obstacle or your home?"

"Home," Sven's worried voice returned. "Is everything alright up there?"

"I'll let you know if it isn't," Atu replied. He studied Kayla. "Think you can make it?"

Kayla nodded gingerly but wasn't at all sure she could last even another step. It felt like they'd spent half the day just reaching this spot. But her PAL refuted that notion—their journey had taken under thirty minutes. *So what are another five? I can make it. If Taz can tough it out, so can I.* But every step sent sharp stabs of pain skittering through her skull, and by the time the stone hallway emptied into a wide valley, Kayla was fighting back nausea.

She stretched a shaky hand out to Atu. "Can we stop for a bit?"

One look at her ashen face and Atu instantly understood the problem. "You need to throw up again?"

"I would if there was anything left in there."

Atu scowled. "We should've stopped in the tunnel. You've been pushing yourself too hard. Why didn't you say something? You should know better with your medical training."

Kayla glared. "Sure, that really would have helped us reach a safe place quickly."

"Nice to see you still have to have the last word," Atu remarked, the tightness around his eyes easing. He waited, his tension ebbing when he saw slight traces of color filtering back into her face as they rested. "Feeling better?"

"A little, but can we give it a few more minutes before we move again?"

"What's wrong?" Sven asked, catching up to them.

"Kayla needs a break. We can move again soon."

"No, we're there," Sven declared, pointing ahead.

And when Kayla looked, there it was. The organic building materials blended seamlessly with the surrounding vegetation, camouflaging the building perfectly. "I wouldn't have known it was there if you hadn't pointed it out."

"Let's catch the geek before he walks right into a wall," Sven said, referring to Jaden, who was blundering ahead. Scooping Kayla into his burly arms without effort or preamble, Sven carried her the remaining distance.

Too startled to protest, Kayla huddled there, thankful she didn't have to take another step and closing her eyes in relief. Aware of Taz hovering, Kayla opened one eye to smile reassuringly at her glider, letting her know with one look she would be fine and that she was safe with Sven. When Sven slowed, Kayla opened her eyes. In time to witness Jaden catching himself just short of crashing into the wall of the house.

"Some craftsmanship," Jaden said when he heard their approach, not turning to face them but analyzing the house with interest. Taking a few steps back, Jaden squinted at the house, verifying it was invisible until he'd almost walked into it. He was such a geek.

"Thank you, thank you!" Sven beamed. "Let's get indoors where it's warm."

Jaden turned then and found Kayla in Sven's arms. Emotions flashed across his face: concern she wasn't on her own two feet; regret he had left her; and then guilt he had. He was by her side in an instant.

Jaden stroked a hand across her forehead. "Hey, what happened?"

Kayla managed a smile. His hand felt so warm and soothing against her head. "I almost made it. Sven just helped without asking first."

Sven grinned sheepishly. "Sorry, I thought—"

"No, don't apologize," Kayla hurried to reassure him. "It really was nice to not have to walk that last part. Thank you."

Glancing at Jaden, Kayla's pulse skipped when she saw the fire in his deep blue eyes. They sparked, and for a moment, Kayla feared the sparks would fly out and burn Sven's hands. The way Jaden was eyeing Sven's arms around her . . . he wasn't happy. Kayla suddenly felt much better.

Jaden gritted his teeth and smiled tightly. "Yes, Sven, thank you for helping her."

Kayla was happier than she'd been in a long time. Even though Jaden's reactions weren't making sense. She was too tired to care. One thing she was sure of, though: next time, he would make sure he was the one by her side. *And wasn't that a lovely thing to know.*

CHAPTER NINETEEN

Peering around Sven's arms at the entrance to his home, Kayla frowned. This time, their gliders couldn't possibly fit inside. "Um, I thought you said you had somewhere our gliders could rest?"

"I do," Sven said. "They have their own entrance. Here, let me take you inside and set you down. Then I'll show them where they can enter."

Kayla smiled her thanks as Sven took her indoors and settled her on a soft, overstuffed sofa in what looked like the living room. Jaden and Atu followed Sven in, examining their surroundings.

"Please, make yourselves comfortable," Sven said. "I'll be back shortly with your gliders. Look for us over there." Sven gestured toward the far wall.

"More magic tricks?" Atu teased.

"You'll see," Sven answered, disappearing out the door.

In seconds, the whirring had even Kayla scrutinizing every inch of the wall for the first sign of something unexpected. And unexpected it was when the roof over their heads shifted instead of the wall. They watched, fascinated, as the walls grew taller and the roof lifted higher, and then an opening appeared in the wall they'd been told to watch. On the other side, their gliders waited behind a beaming Sven.

"You like?"

Jaden grinned. "That has to be the best conversion we've seen today!"

"Yes!" Atu whooped, making them all jump and then laugh at his outburst. "Didn't I tell you Armorer could help us?"

"You did," Jaden answered.

Han and Taz stepped cautiously into the room, showing their lack of confidence in the newly created space.

"Are you sure the roof won't fall back down?" Taz questioned, glancing up at it.

Sven chuckled. "No chance, I assure you."

"If you say so," Taz muttered, stepping further into the room.

Han trailed her. "You have made a striking home here, Armorer."

"I tried to account for any eventuality. It was a little difficult guessing your size, but I'm pleased I allowed enough space. I'm honored you and Taz can use my home for shelter."

Han dipped his head toward Sven, then hopped closer to Jaden, where he assumed his usual resting position. Taz did likewise, taking up her position behind Kayla.

Jaden gawked. "You suspected you might have to house gliders?"

"'Fortune favors the prepared mind.'" Sven smiled, quoting Louis Pasteur. "I've had time to work on the house and my many other inventions. I went big, and if I didn't get to use all this," he said, gesturing expansively toward the house and general area around them, "it wouldn't have mattered because I hoped it might help future seekers. I never dreamed I'd meet the seekers who'd be the next voyagers or their gliders."

Digesting this, Jaden asked, "When was the last time you saw a Gaptor?"

"When that beast attacked me more than a month ago. Why?" Sven returned, interest gleaming in his eyes.

Jaden's smile was tight. "According to the stories Atu's father passed down, only one Gaptor remained in our world. And that abomination won't be bothering us again. It's the possibility of more Gaptors coming through that concerns us now. Since you've seen none in the last week, we can tentatively assume that hasn't happened yet."

Sven held up a hand. "Whoa, steady! That was a terabyte. What do you mean the one that attacked me won't be back? You defeated it?"

"We did—although quite by accident."

"How?" Sven's barely contained excitement made them all smile.

Jaden displayed the ring on his finger, as did Kayla. Sven rushed forward, pulling their hands together as he examined the rings, his eyes glittering. "What are these? I've never seen such jewelry before."

"They're called 'relic stones,'" Jaden replied.

"Where did you get them? And how do they work?" Sven's enthusiasm bubbled over. "What are they made of? Did they kill the beast or send him back to his own world?"

Jaden paused. "That's an excellent question. We thought the rings killed him because he turned to ash before our very eyes, disappearing as though he'd never existed. But it could've been the aftereffect of sending him back to where he came from." Jaden frowned. "I suppose the real answer, then, is we don't know for sure whether he was obliterated or transported. I wonder if Zareh would know—"

"Who's Zareh?" Sven asked, his head snapping up at the unfamiliar name.

"I hate to be the party crasher here," Kayla ventured, "but I need food to settle my stomach. Jaden, I'm shocked you haven't asked for any yet."

On cue, Jaden's stomach growled.

"Yes, yes, where are my manners? We need to get you and your steeds fed. Please, don't give me any more information until we have eaten and slept, no? Or I will keep you awake all night," Sven confessed, bustling off toward the kitchen. "Come, let us speak of other things while I prepare dinner. I'll do the talking—then I can't get distracted, no? Fresh information is too tempting for me, I'm afraid." He shrugged apologetically. "So, do you have questions for an old man like me?"

Kayla snorted. "You're not old!"

Sven grinned at her, then winked at Atu. "I like this girl. You can bring her around anytime."

They all laughed. Kayla voiced the question uppermost on her mind. "I have a question. How did you end up living out here in the middle of nowhere?"

Sven stopped what he was doing, gazing off into the distance.

"If that's too personal, you don't have to answer," Kayla hurriedly added. "I'm sorry. I'm just being nosy."

"No, not too personal. I'm just deciding where I should begin." Sven brooded. "Maybe with what made me choose this location. It was a place safe from those hunting me."

Kayla blanched. That didn't sound good. Maybe he meant the Gaptor? "You mean the beast?"

"No, my dear, humans. The people I used to work for."

Stunned silence followed his revelation. The teens looked at one another, unsure whether they should ask more questions or leave things as they were.

Sven decided for them. "I used to work for a highly covert branch of Gotskiena's intelligence division."

The room could not have been more still if a yet-to-be-invented atomizer vaporized them. *Way to drop a bombshell,* Kayla thought. *Weren't people who worked for those sorts of organizations not supposed to mention that?*

Gripping his paring knife more firmly, Sven frowned and resumed chopping vegetables. "It began long ago when I was still a boy. I would spend hours in my father's workshop, tinkering with the odds and ends he left lying around. Growing up on a farm meant there were always plenty of those, from steel pipes, to gears, to wheels, to pulleys, to scrap metal, and a thousand screws, nuts, and bolts, circuit boards, and chip sets."

"Sounds like my kind of odds and ends too," Jaden said.

Sven nodded. "I would find alternative ways of combining them, inventing things useful to both my parents. I grew older, and my interest in weapons manifested. I devised ways to modify weapons so they would be more powerful, more effective, and more accurate. Not exactly the thing an adolescent mind should dwell on."

"Was that when my father met you?" Atu interrupted. "He mentioned you lived in a rural area and had developed some unbelievable weapons."

"It was. I'm surprised your father ever mentioned me to you."

"You must've made an impression. He always told me that if I was ever in trouble and in need of weapons, you were the person I should reach out to. That's why he called you the armorer."

Sven chuckled. "Well, yes, now that I think of our first meeting, I suppose I made quite an impression."

"It sounds like there's a story there," Atu said.

"Someone dared your father to sneak up on me. Not knowing any better, he agreed and hid behind a cow. So I made the cow disappear."

"What?" Jaden and Atu exclaimed, and Kayla giggled.

"Yes, it was rather funny watching your father's face," Sven said, chuckling more.

"Wait, you're saying you invented something that could disintegrate matter?" Jaden asked, wide-eyed.

Sven gave him a shrewd glance. "You're definitely smart."

"But isn't that what all the hullaballoo is about with force weapons?" Jaden probed.

Kayla rolled her eyes at the interest flaring anew in Jaden's eyes. Then again, his mind enjoyed solving puzzles and thrived on information. *This quest must drive him nuts*, she thought with a smile. *One heck of a problem and not a lot of information. Am I a problem for him to solve too? Or does logic even enter the equation?*

Considering the day's events, Kayla realized his actions were bewildering and contradicted her conclusion he only wanted her as a friend. She closed her eyes. Her head was pounding. Now was not the time to get her hopes up.

Sven paused before he answered Jaden's question. "It is."

Jaden gave a shout and leaped up from his chair, pacing. "Well, if you've already designed a force weapon that can do that, why not sell your design to the highest bidder? Overnight, you'd be wealthy beyond your wildest imagination!"

"Because money is not what this is about." Sven sighed. At Jaden's quizzical expression, he elaborated. "Technology like that is far too dangerous to pass along. Think for a moment. Someone could commit murder, and there would be no evidence to show they had ever committed a crime. No blood, no body to find, no evidence, just missing people. How do you think they could maintain law and order after that?"

Kayla hadn't considered this, and apparently, neither Jaden nor Atu had either.

Sven continued. "The perpetrators could be anyone, including quadrant military or sector regulators. They could eliminate those who threatened them with no repercussions at all. No, that weapon is far too dangerous. For that reason, I adapted it, developing the first ever pulse weapon, the one they have reverse engineered all others from."

The three teens whistled as one.

"*You* invented pulse weapons?" Jaden sputtered.

"Yes. An achievement I now regret because our quadrant's military defense and intelligence division noticed it. They wasted no time recruiting me, and I joined their ranks shortly after selling them the plans. That was the beginning of the end for me."

"Why? I would've expected it would be a dream job, access to unlimited resources and labs to die for," Jaden said.

Kayla debated telling Jaden to stop his inquisition. Perhaps they were intruding on areas Sven didn't want to discuss. But Sven showed no signs of discomfort, so she let it ride. Besides, her head was hurting too much to get into it with Jaden.

"I thought the same thing," Sven said. "And for a while, it was true. But everything changed overnight when they discovered my prowess in accurately predicting certain, shall we say, behavioral patterns. They took away my labs, confined me to a secure, isolated environment, and had me running statistical analysis for them, wasting my days identifying potential threats." He fell silent, lost in thought.

Kayla stared. *What is he talking about? Behavioral patterns?*

"You mean intelligence work instead of weapons design?" Jaden suggested.

"Yes."

Kayla considered Sven's brusque response, and it crystallized for her. "Uh, intelligence work like profiling?"

Sven didn't answer immediately, confirming Kayla's guess. Then he sighed. "Exactly. But the work I was doing didn't focus on crimes already committed. I conducted my analysis for the purpose of designing a system that could forecast which citizens were likely to fall prone to certain kinds of behavior."

"But wouldn't that be helpful, to recognize potential threats so they could be monitored?" Atu asked.

"It would, if that's all they were planning on using it for—monitoring. But it wasn't. I realized something was terribly wrong when they asked me to change certain parameters. To set my mind at ease, I bugged my supervisor's office."

Sven paused, and the teens held their collective breath. It was clear how much even thinking of these things distressed Sven.

"Sven, you don't have to tell us," Kayla said, her earlier concerns resurfacing.

"No, I do." Sven hissed. "You need to understand the people I was working for. Not even a day after placing the devices, I heard their conversation. My results were helping them eliminate people who posed even a hint of a threat—*before* they had actually committed any crime. There were so smug, thinking they were so smart and that *they* were the righteous ones. It made me sick."

Sven paced now, and Kayla wished she could ease the grief emanating from him.

"I couldn't live with myself. All those conceivably innocent lives, now subject to execution. All because of my work. What if my logic was flawed? I had warned them about that repeatedly, begging them for someone I could consult with, someone who could validate my reasoning. But they provided no one and acted as though the results were infallible. They could've been murdering innocent people. So I changed things."

"What did you do?" Kayla breathed, too caught up now to want him to stop.

"I destroyed all versions of my program, blew up their offsite backup facility, and escaped from the hellhole they had confined me to."

Jaden whistled. "Talk about a radical solution!"

Sven bristled. "What would you have done?"

"You misunderstand. I'm not saying what you did was wrong," Jaden hurriedly clarified. "Just extreme. I totally get why. If I was in the same situation, I'd have done something similar."

Sven grunted. "At least we agree."

"What happened next?" Kayla prompted, impatient to hear the rest of the story.

Sven smiled sardonically, returning to the counter and tossing cut vegetables into a heated pan where they sizzled and popped when they hit the hot oil. "I was 'persona non grata' after those stunts. With those people, resignation is not an option. Termination is more their style. Between my access to sensitive information because of my high security clearance and the knowledge I possessed concerning their murderous, preemptive actions, sending an assassination squad after me was a foregone conclusion."

"Assassins?" Kayla felt like she was in a spy novel.

Sven grinned, waving away her horror. "I had planned well. I eluded their traps and escaped their facility, then the complex, and finally the sector. After two weeks on the run, I arrived here, in the middle of a blizzard, too worn out and too cold to travel further. I probably would've died, if the deep-seated betrayal I felt had not pushed me to find shelter so I could seek revenge. A sentiment which you'll be happy to know I am rid of." He stirred the vegetables and added some cooked chicken.

"Revenge leads no one down a righteous path," Kayla agreed.

Sven nodded and continued. "Much of that last day is hazy, but I remember falling in the snow, too fatigued to rise again. I knew I needed to find shelter, or I would die. In a brief reprieve from the wind and snow, I spotted the entrance to the tunnel we traveled through to get here. It was a sign."

"Then what?" Atu asked, his eyes wide.

"I clawed through that seemingly endless stretch of snow to the tunnel, taking refuge there. How long I lay there, I don't know. I collapsed from sheer exhaustion. When my thirst drove me to wakefulness, the storm had passed. I would not go back, so moving forward was my only option. It's impossible to describe how overcome I was when I emerged from that tunnel into this beautiful valley. The moment I set foot outside, I knew I had found my home. Reaching into my pocket for something to wipe my nose, my fingers touched something warm."

"Let me guess," Jaden interjected, "your medallion?"

"How did you know?" Sven puffed, his bushy eyebrows shooting up.

"Let's just say I've also had mine burn a hole in my pocket before." Jaden remembered the evening of the day he'd found the medallion and the way it had felt like it was searing into his flesh when his thoughts strayed from it.

"It was the strangest thing," Sven went on. "During my flight, I must've reached into my pocket countless times, and not once before had I found it. After everything they forced me to leave behind, with all the betrayals and disappointments haunting my heart, it cheered me to hold our family heirloom. And it served as confirmation that this was where I should make my new home. I began building, but to this day, I truly don't understand how the medallion got into my pocket."

"Jaden and I know—Zareh explained," Kayla commented.

"There's that name again. Who is this Zareh? And what did he tell you?" Sven demanded.

"We'll tell you about Zareh later. Suffice to say, he imbued the medallions with some ability to ensure those he gave them to never lost them. That was how your medallion magically found its way into your pocket," Kayla replied. Then she paused, abruptly changing the subject. "But, please can we eat? That smells delicious, and now that my head's not hurting so much, I'm starved!"

"Certainly. We'll eat and then sleep and talk more in the morning, no?"

"That sounds wonderful," Jaden replied for all of them. "Where do I find the plates?"

CHAPTER TWENTY

The thunderous explosion crashed through the thick walls of Sven's home, jerking Jaden awake. Bleary, he blinked, noting the commotion woke the others too. Dazed, they jolted up when a second deafening detonation followed the first. Leaping from sleeping shells strewn across the living room floor, they sprinted outside. Sven stood there, an enormous grin plastered over his face. He wore one relic stone on the index finger of each hand.

"Good morning! Sorry to wake you. These are most impressive. Such fun to play with." Sven raised his hands again, about to repeat the process.

Comprehension hit the teens simultaneously.

"Stop!" Kayla shouted, waving her hands in the air.

"Armorer, don't! You'll bring more beasts!" Atu yelled, his words falling over Kayla's.

Jaden ran, tackling a startled Sven to the ground before he could bash the stones together again. Sven went down hard, grunting in shocked admiration.

"Humph, didn't expect someone your size could put me down so easily."

"That's what happens when you have friends like Markov," Jaden muttered, standing up and brushing himself off. "You get used to thinking you can do anything."

Sven pushed himself up from where he lay. "Do things like that often, do you?"

"Only when I have to," Jaden said, pausing for a moment before addressing the sticky issue at hand. "Sven, those stones are dangerous. Don't use them again until we've told you more about them, please!" The anger brewing just below the surface since he'd realized his ring was no longer in his possession bubbled to the surface. "And would you mind explaining how the deuce you got our rings?"

Sven had the grace to look embarrassed. "I apologize. Removing them wasn't deliberate. After waiting and waiting and waiting for all of you to wake up, my curiosity got the better of me. I snuck over to where you slept, meaning to just get a closer look at your ring. But then, when I picked your hand up, the ring just *poof*—jumped from your finger to mine. It was extraordinary. I couldn't help wondering whether Kayla's ring would do the same . . ."

"And let me guess—it did," Jaden offered dryly, his anger moderated by Sven's sheepish expression and his own desire to get more information on this whole blasted subject.

Sven looked hopeful. "You understand then? I didn't intend taking them from you. When they were on my fingers, I couldn't resist going outside where the light is better so I could inspect them more closely. And, well, I just had the overpowering urge to clap my hands together."

Kayla grinned. "That was the first crash we heard?"

"Yes."

Kayla rolled her eyes. "And then you just had to try it again?"

Sven grinned. "Ah, you understand me. These stones are astounding. Such power! So tiny and yet they hold so much destruction. Where did you get them?"

Jaden's need to have his ring back got the better of him. "That's a lengthy story for another time. Could Kayla and I have our rings?" The words were more a demand than a request.

"I'm so sorry." Sven faltered, hastily reaching for the closest ring.

Then, rethinking the matter, he left the ring where it was and scurried over to Kayla, lifting her hand. Nothing marked the moment the ring transferred itself from Sven's finger back onto hers. It was exactly as Sven had described it.

It fascinated Jaden. "Hmm, do that again with mine."

Sven laughed. "Intriguing, aren't they?"

Marching back to Jaden, Sven reached for Jaden's hand. When the stone leaped from Sven's finger to Jaden's, the movement so imperceptible as to be invisible, Jaden knew his mind was incapable of unraveling the forces of work.

"I can see why you wanted to do it again," Jaden admitted grudgingly, grinning.

"Yes, amazing, aren't they? Tell me, how did they get rid of the beast?"

Jaden scratched his head. "We're not sure. We think it was because the Gaptor flew between Kayla and I, making the rings send out a beam that fried him."

Sven nodded. "And you were each wearing a ring at the time?"

"Yes," Jaden replied, wondering where this was going.

"Excellent! That is what I wanted to hear. Based on my limited observations, I believe I can make a weapon that will duplicate the rings' effect. Without the necessity for two people! That just adds an unnecessary complication and is far too restrictive. I must test the weapon, to compare results, but I think I can do it!"

"Can you build it without using the relic stones again?" Jaden asked.

"Now why would I need to do that?" Sven grimaced, unhappy at the thought.

Kayla answered. "Because we think the downside of using the relic stones is that they act as homing beacons for the beasts. And if our theory about more Gaptors coming through holds true, using the relic stones will direct any new arrivals right toward us."

"More beasts are coming?" Sven asked, eyes round.

"We think so," Kayla said. "Jaden mentioned that last night. Remember?"

Sven rubbed his chin thoughtfully. "Yes, now that you remind me, I recall. The news about your rings' ability to destroy those monsters eclipsed all else. But didn't Jaden also say he thought no more had entered yet?"

"I made a tentative assumption," Jaden corrected. "That's quite different from knowing for sure. Until we do, it's best if we avoid using the relic stones."

"Pity." Sven sighed, and they laughed at the longing in his voice. "But speaking of items that could help win this battle, I have something for you—especially after observing your lack of skill when my device affected your gliders."

"You try staying in the air when your ride is flying sideways," Jaden retorted. "You saw what your device did to them. It was pretty miraculous we stayed on for as long as we did, considering our gliders' lack of control. No offense," he said to the gliders, who had snuck up on the group while they talked.

"None taken," Han replied. "The Armorer's device was effective. Did I hear correctly that you have something which might help our voyagers?"

"You did." Sven beamed. "Wait here and I'll fetch it."

He disappeared inside the house and reappeared a few minutes later, carrying something that looked familiar.

Kayla giggled. "A wetsuit?"

"But one that is probably more than it looks." Atu winked.

"You *are* getting to know me. I call it a 'smart suit.'"

"What does it do?" Jaden asked, eyeing the suit. Kayla would look amazing wearing it. Her long, blonde hair flowing loose over her shoulders, her sage green eyes sparkling, weapons strapped to her waist and perhaps her thigh, resembling some ancient warrior princess. He grinned. She really didn't need any props. She was attractive enough without them. And if he was having a tough time keeping away from her until she showed him she was ready to take the next step, how much more difficult would the suit make it? He sighed. He wasn't sure he was up to the challenge.

Sven held the suit out for Jaden's inspection. "The suit has thousands of microscopic wires embedded in the fibers. They remain inactive until someone dons the suit. Then the wires monitor the wearer: breathing, movement, muscle tone, et cetera."

Jaden asked, "To what end?"

"While there are many things the suit can do, its primary purpose is training muscle memory. This was the last project I had the pleasure of working on in my lab before they moved me to that other unmentionable division. Our quadrant's military wanted something that would give our soldiers an edge—to help them learn how to fight more quickly, teach them how to move better, and show them how best to incapacitate their adversaries."

"But I still don't see how the wires help if they're just monitoring your movements," Kayla said.

"I think I do," Jaden ventured. "Are the wires programmed so they control your body movements instead of your brain?"

"Again, you figured it out! Inspired, isn't it?" Sven chuckled. "The wires intercept signals between the nerves and the brain, interpreting them and sending impulses back to the nerves more quickly than the brain can. Since these impulses reach the nerve endings faster than the signals sent by the brain, the body responds to them, allowing the person to act more swiftly and accurately than would normally be possible."

"Okay, then—a suit that tells your body what to do?" Atu confirmed.

"Precisely. But come, try it on," Sven said, pulling the suit from Jaden's hands and handing it to Atu. "It's easier to understand when you wear it."

Atu took the suit, eager to try it, darting back into the house to change. When he returned, he was wearing only the suit.

Kayla shivered, fingering the soft collar on her thermal jacket. "Aren't you cold?"

Atu grinned. "Nope, nice and toasty."

"Ah, I forgot to mention the suits regulate the surrounding air so you don't get too hot or too cold," Sven murmured.

Jaden hooted. "Is there anything the suits don't do?"

"Well, yes, quite a lot in fact—" Sven began, before stopping himself. "But they will serve their purpose as they are now."

Atu chuckled. "Okay, genius, so I'm suited up. What do I need to do?"

Without warning, Sven swung one of his massive arms toward Atu. Jaden was too shocked to react. But Atu did. Before Sven's meaty palm even neared his face, he stepped backward, out of harm's way.

"Whoa!" Atu chortled. "Do that again!"

"What?" Kayla squawked, horrified.

But Sven swung again, this time not only aiming a fist at Atu's face but following it with a quick kick at Atu's stomach. Atu nimbly danced out of reach of both strikes.

"Yeah! I could do this all day!" Atu whooped. "Give me more."

And before Kayla could protest, Sven reached out, faster this time, and tried to knock Atu over. But Atu's body reshaped itself like an elastic band, curving out and then back upright. He didn't fall.

Jaden put it together. "The suit made you do that?"

"You bet it did." Atu grinned.

"Why do you get to have all the fun?" Jaden grumbled. "Sven, do you have more suits?"

Sven chortled. "I have an entire rack."

"You do?" Kayla asked, her face still ashen from the shock of the moments before.

"I do. When I worked on this project, I created a slew of prototypes. It was a project I regretted not finishing. So, after my rather sudden and unexpected departure, I had a trusted friend steal them for me. Since it was safer for both of us if he didn't know where I lived, I met him at a place far away from here, where I took delivery. Then I brought them home, perfected the suit design, and now have all of them at my disposal."

Kayla smiled. "Another case of fortune favoring the prepared mind or whatever that quote was?"

Sven laughed. "No. Here, I must confess I just wanted what was mine. I didn't want those felons using what I had created against me."

Nodding understanding, Jaden asked, "What now?"

"Now, I get to play in my workshop while you three learn hand-to-hand combat, courtesy of the suits."

"Uh, I don't think we'll beat the Gaptor that way," Jaden pointed out.

"No, but the exercises will hone your perception, agility, and balance, all skills that *will* help you should you have to fight another beast," Sven answered. "After you and Kayla get your suits, I'll load the training programs and show you how to toggle the controls so you can turn the training program on and off or change the routines. You need this knowledge so you can train without me. Because you're doing that while I work on a weapon that will duplicate the relic stones' effects."

CHAPTER TWENTY-ONE

An hour later, familiar with the program controls and kitted out in their suits, the teens were ready for the suits to run them through the drills they had programmed.

Jaden had been right. Kayla looked spectacular. He hoped his suit was as effective as Atu's at doing all the work because Jaden doubted he could drag his eyes away from Kayla long enough to take evasive action of his own. His concerns were unwarranted. The program kicked in, and in minutes, he was having too much fun to focus on her.

It didn't take long to work up a good sweat. The routines were physically demanding, and the teens soon learned it worked better if only two of them practiced while the third took a breather.

Muffled thumping, pounding sounds hammered out from Sven's workshop, but he remained sequestered there for the rest of the morning. When their stomachs told them it was time to eat, they took a break, clustering around the counter in the kitchen as they made sandwiches.

"Do you think we should take Sven lunch?" Jaden asked when they were halfway through their meal and it became apparent Sven wouldn't be joining them.

Atu and Kayla grinned at one another, knowingly.

"What?" Jaden asked, affronted.

"You only want to get inside his workshop," Atu said.

"Well," Jaden huffed, "even genius inventors need to eat."

"Yes, they do," Kayla agreed, laughing. "But it doesn't hurt that it would also get you inside his workshop, or do you disagree?"

"Okay, I admit. It crossed my mind."

He looked so deflated that Atu and Kayla laughed even more.

"Bro, you're pitiful! Just take him the sandwiches," Atu sputtered.

"Really?"

Atu and Kayla shook their heads and continued sniggering.

Scowling, Jaden grabbed an empty plate and slapped a few sandwiches on it. He stomped outside, but his eagerness to get a glimpse of the workshop's interior soon put a grin on his face. Arriving at the workshop door, he found it locked. Using the intercom on one side of the door, he pressed the buzzer. No reply. He waited a few minutes, then pressed the buzzer a second time. This time the door opened so abruptly, Jaden stepped back in surprise.

Sven peered out, looking annoyed. "Yes?"

"Uh, I brought you some lunch."

"Thank you." Sven grunted, grabbing the plate of sandwiches. "Next time, please don't trouble yourself. I have food here." He slammed and locked the door.

Jaden stared. Was this the same person who had welcomed them into his home yesterday? His only conclusion was Sven resented being disturbed when working. *Something I can identify with*, Jaden mused, slinking back to the house.

"What wonders did Sven's workshop hold?" Atu asked, when Jaden entered the kitchen.

"I didn't even get to sneak a peek inside, let alone set foot in there. He locks the workshop doors with an invisible mechanism, and there's no door handle!"

"What did you do with his food, then?" Kayla asked, her eyebrow lifting in surprise.

"Oh, I gave it to him, but I had to use the intercom to get his attention. Had to buzz him twice before he opened the door, and then he said about two sentences and shut the door in my face."

"That's a little bizarre," Kayla murmured.

"Was he angry?" Atu asked.

"Perhaps, but I think it's more likely he doesn't want anyone to disturb him because he said not to worry about meals. He has food there."

"Well, alrighty then," Kayla responded, so dryly the boys burst into laughter.

They cleared the lunch dishes and then relaxed on the comfortable sofas in the living room while they drank tea.

"Why don't we go flying this afternoon?" Kayla suggested. "I think our gliders are getting bored watching us fight on the ground. And I could do with fresh air in my face."

"Yes!" Atu agreed enthusiastically.

Jaden grinned, and they finished their tea before strolling outside to give their gliders the good news.

"Finally." Taz sniffed. "I was wondering when we'd be useful again."

"They're just too full of food to bounce around on the ground like they did this morning," Han teased the boys. "How much lunch did you two consume?"

"Enough to give you a workout this afternoon," Jaden snorted.

Han chuckled. "I seriously doubt that."

Jaden reveled in the glorious sense of freedom flowing over him minutes later as he breezed through the air with Han. When he and the others discovered the suits helped them correct their balance more quickly and fluidly, his exhilaration only increased. So much so they began urging their gliders to try increasingly difficult routines, elated to find they could now execute these impeccably.

It wasn't the same for Taz. "You need to practice without the suits —they're making the exercises seem simpler than they are. And you can't rely on having time to suit up before engaging a Gaptor."

She was right, but the teens didn't exactly relish suffering through her critical assessments for the afternoon.

It was Atu who came up with an idea that appealed to them all.

"Didn't Sven say he designed the suits to build muscle memory?" When Jaden and Kayla nodded, he said, "Well, let's test that theory. Taz, would you be content if we kept the suits on for now but practiced the more difficult runs repeatedly? And then, when we're nearly done for the day, we'll take the suits off and see if our muscles really have retained what we practiced?"

Taz considered his request. "Well, if they'll help you learn faster, then by all means. Han?"

"Anything to help our voyagers."

Time became meaningless as they ran through the exercises, the gliders and teens equally impressed with how quickly they mastered techniques they had been grappling with for days. Over and over they practiced until even Taz had nothing but praise. It was still surprising when Taz pronounced them competent enough to try without the suits.

"There goes any positive feedback for the rest of the afternoon," Jaden muttered to Kayla and Atu.

Without the suit, Jaden felt vulnerable. It had made him feel invincible.

"Who's going first?" Han asked when they emerged from the house.

"I will," Kayla said, astonishing them all. "What?" she shot back when they gaped. "Better to get it over and done with; at least we'll know one way or another whether the suits work."

Kayla aerial connected with Taz, clearly feeling the weight of her own muscles again. But as the girls lifted higher, Jaden noticed her body moving more intuitively with Taz's than it ever had before. And when Taz flipped upside down and began the long and complicated series of rolls, twists, and spirals, Kayla didn't falter in her movements —not even once.

Jaden grimaced. Flying with Taz, she was in her element. Unlike yesterday, when she had pushed him away as soon as she felt she could walk unaided, making it clear she had resumed her earlier defensive attitude toward his affections. She wasn't ready for more between them. Or rather, she wasn't ready to admit she wanted more.

Jaden was growing weary of giving her time to reach the conclusion on her own. He only hoped his patience would last to give her the space she needed.

Kayla loosed an ecstatic whoop, startling Taz if the slight wobble in her flight was anything to go by. Jaden could hear Taz protesting even from this distance.

"What was that for?"

Jaden heard Kayla's reply just as clearly. "Celebrating the fact that you won't be yelling at me anymore when we learn new routines."

Jaden and Atu cracked up. Even Han joined in.

"Humph," Taz responded, but her smile showed how delighted she was that her voyager was carrying out the exercise more than acceptably.

When they landed, Han and the boys cheered.

"The suits really do live up to Sven's promise!" Jaden said. "Atu, are you ready?"

"You bet!"

The four of them took off, and Kayla watched from the ground as they too executed the program without error. By the time they landed, the sun had already slipped behind the steep, craggy cliffs forming the valley, sending shadows creeping along the ground.

"Time for dinner," Jaden said when his stomach grumbled.

"Food, food, food," Han moaned. "Does the boy ever think of anything else?"

Jaden smiled but was too tired for any repartee. The gliders took off again in search of their own dinner, and the teens trudged indoors, feeling the strenuous effects of the day's training.

Jaden hadn't felt this wasted in days. He wasn't as strong or as fit as he thought their training had made them. Glancing at Kayla, he could see she was just as worn out. Her lovely green eyes had lost their sparkle and were dull with fatigue. Her limbs dragged. Despite this, she retained her graceful movements, lethargic though they were. He wished he had the strength to pick her up and carry her inside, then grinned as he imagined her response. Just as well he lacked the energy.

CHAPTER TWENTY-TWO

It disappointed Jaden when they didn't see Sven that evening or the next day or the following evening.

"Do you think we should check on him?" Kayla asked over dinner that second night.

"No, I think he wanted us to leave him alone," Jaden answered. "If his mind works like I suspect it does, he won't leave that workshop until he has a functional weapon."

"That could take a while," Kayla mumbled.

She was right. But Sven didn't need as long as she thought he would. It was only a few days later when Sven surprised them by bounding in when they were eating lunch.

"I think I have it!" Sven boomed. "Come, let us test it!"

Jaden leaped up, eager to see the weapon. Only Sven didn't reveal his invention immediately. Instead, he put them to work, setting up the various objects he planned to test the weapon on. It surprised Jaden when the gliders even pitched in, their own curiosity piqued by the potential weapon.

When they had arranged the testing area to Sven's satisfaction, he retrieved the much-anticipated weapon from his workshop.

It was nothing more than a carving knife. Keen disappointment lanced Jaden. He looked at the others finding them just as dubious as he was. *This will kill Gaptors? How can we even get within striking distance with such a short blade?*

Sven grinned, aware of what they were thinking. Then, deliberately, he held the knife out in front of him and pressed on the hilt. An elegantly long, brilliantly white, sizzling blade of light slid out, curving as it did.

"Rad!" Jaden shouted, joined by Atu and Kayla's exclamations of approval.

Even the gliders cooed their admiration. It was like nothing they had ever seen before. The blade crackled with electricity—or at least, a charge of some sort. It flashed and sparked, begging to unleash its energy.

As if answering the blade's unspoken request, Sven raised his hand over his head and slashed toward a rock thirty feet away. A ray of energy separated itself from the blade and hurtled toward the rock. It fell short of the target, landing in the snow and searing its way down to bare earth before dissipating. Sven cursed under this breath, moving ten feet closer to the target. This time, the beam did not miss. It struck the rock with a resounding crack, splitting it in half and sending sharp echoes up and down the valley.

"Wow!" Jaden breathed.

"Well done, Armorer!" Taz murmured.

Sven grinned and bowed. "Thank you. But can this weapon do what the relic stones can? That is the million-dollar question, as they used to say. Let's test its powers against other mediums before we get too excited, no?"

In quick succession, Sven lashed out at the various objects they had set up, determining the beam's effectiveness against wood, glass, ceramic, various metals, and a host of other materials. Most of the items fragmented immediately, some even disappearing in a puff of black smoke. But a specialized ceramic jar and two metal cubes proved impervious.

"I understand the need for limiting the use of your relic stones, but it would help enormously if we could eliminate some variables. Any chance we could apply the power of your stones to those items?" Sven begged.

His expression was so hopeful, his tone so beseeching, Jaden reconsidered their earlier ban on the use of the stones. Besides, he reasoned, it would be an excellent opportunity to establish exactly how the stones worked. That way, if they encountered another Gaptor, they would know what they were doing instead of leaving it to chance.

Jaden submitted his thoughts to the gliders, who agreed this would be a wise use. Asking Kayla and Atu, Jaden confirmed they felt the same way. Sven whooped when they consented. Jaden chuckled. Then he and Kayla strolled over to the remaining objects, stopping when the ceramic jar separated them.

"Okay, let's work on our operation manual for these rings," Jaden said.

"Yup, we need to get the hang of how to control them before we meet another Gaptor."

"Yeah. Best that we figure that out now. Ready?"

"I've always enjoyed playing with fire," Kayla confessed, grinning.

They raised their hands. Anticipating some process for adjusting the angles of the rings and the placement of the object between them, they both flinched when lightning flashed. An almighty clap rent the air, and the ceramic jar vaporized into a fine mist of ash. Euphoric shouts followed shocked silence.

"No skill involved at all!" Kayla hollered.

"Yeah, just point and shoot in the general direction, and the rings take care of the rest," Jaden said.

Sven and Atu sprinted over to where the two of them danced gleefully, ignoring them as they darted about, trapping the drifting ash in glass jars.

Kayla giggled, observing Sven and Atu's hurried movements. "What are you doing?"

Jaden ceased dancing as his mind engaged on another level. "I'm guessing Sven will analyze how the object's chemical composition changed. That's how you're working out what force the rings deploy?"

"Maybe I'll let you into my workshop," Sven said. "You might prove useful."

Jaden tried suppressing his excitement. "Really?"

Sven chuckled. "Yes, really. You think I don't know that was what you were angling for when you brought me that meal the other day?"

Jaden grinned. "That obvious, huh?"

"You're not too hard to read when it comes to technology," Sven said as he labeled jars. "Now, we test the stones on those metal blocks, no?"

Sven and Atu stepped back, giving Jaden and Kayla space. They assumed positions on either side of the first metal cube. They expected the sudden blazing light this time. Eclipsed by it for an instant, the block reappeared only momentarily before melting into a pool of gray, bubbling liquid. As they watched, fascinated, it seeped into the snow.

"Catch what you can!" Sven yelled, tossing each of them a glass jar with a spatula inside, rushing forward himself and scooping up as much of the disappearing fluid as he could.

Atu was already on his hands and knees, ladling the snow and molten metal into his own jar. Jaden and Kayla scrambled to assist, each salvaging at least some gooey liquid before it disappeared.

"Well, that was unexpected." Sven muttered, labeling the new jars. Motioning toward the last block, he said, "I expect that one will turn to ash too. Here's a pre-marked jar for each of you. You know the drill."

And, as expected, the block turned into a pile of ash just as Sven had predicted. Only none of them had expected the ash to be red.

"I've never seen red ash before," Atu said. "What does the color mean, Armorer?"

"Another variation I didn't expect, but when I consider what happened to the first block of metal . . ." Sven drifted off, his mind puzzling through the problem. Reaching a conclusion, he addressed Jaden and Kayla. "Would you be averse to confirming the rings' powers on a second boulder and a second wooden object? I have a theory I'd like to test, and this would be the quickest way of proving my hypothesis." When they hesitated, he hurriedly added, "Please, I understand your concerns about using the stones, but if I can just see the results, and if they're what I now expect them to be, we'll get a functional weapon substantially faster."

Kayla looked to Jaden for confirmation.

Jaden cocked his head to one side and raised the corresponding shoulder in resignation. "I guess we're going all in. If more Gaptors have come through, we're already in trouble. If not, hopefully, Sven's right."

Jaden paced, Atu fidgeted, and Kayla picked at her fingernails while Sven went back to his workshop for another rock and a piece of wood with the same general chemical composition as the originals. Their gliders, sensing their tension, took to the air, informing their voyagers they would be scouting. If Gaptors were inbound, they would find them.

Sven hurried back, put the pieces in place, and then requested they turn the rings on the boulder first. Jaden and Kayla obliged, startled when it imploded on itself, crumbling to dust, which Sven and Atu slipped into yet more glass jars. But that was nothing compared to their shock when the rings had no visible effect on the wood.

"How can the rings destroy so many things, yet not even scar a piece of wood?" Jaden wondered, running his hand over the unmarked surface in amazement.

Sven smiled. "My theory is the rings apply differing levels of energy to their target based on how that target was formed. The wood grew from the earth, not shaped by anything other than sun, wind, and water. The rings did not perceive these gentle forces as a threat, so they sent forth a beam with little or no energy, leaving the wood untouched. On the other hand, the application of immense heat and pressure formed the rock. The rings somehow detected these extreme forces, viewed them as a threat, and accordingly dispensed a beam with enough energy to destroy it."

"Whoa! Hold up!" Jaden exclaimed. "You're implying the rings are intelligent? That they have some way of sensing how the object we direct them against was formed?"

"As unbelievable as that sounds, that's exactly what I'm suggesting. If this is true, should you direct the rings against a human or animal, I would expect the person or animal to remain unharmed too."

"So the rings destroy anything that's been altered or formed under pressure?" Atu asked.

"Correct."

"But that means—" Jaden began.

Sven sighed. "Yes, the Gaptor isn't natural. Someone created it through the use of intense force."

"You mean like engineered or created in a laboratory?" Kayla blurted, appalled at the idea.

"Or something along those lines," Sven said. "But that is a question for another time. I need to refine this weapon. I can't create a differential ray such as that dispensed by the stones, but I'm certain I can at least generate an equivalent force."

"Maybe the ray's differential or 'intelligent' power signals the beasts," Atu speculated.

"Hmm, a plausible theory," Sven acknowledged. "My preliminary deduction was the stones' power being harnessed in our world as opposed to the other world, is what drew the beasts. However, your hypothesis is equally valid." Sven remained adrift in his thoughts for a while before shaking his head. "Either way, as long as the weapon I create destroys as completely as the rings without giving off a signal, we will have accomplished our goal. If you will excuse me?"

They nodded, and Sven stacked the labeled glass bottles back in the box they had come from before hustling to his workshop.

"I guess we're on our own again," Jaden said.

Atu grinned. "Just as well we can feed and clothe and look after ourselves."

Kayla's face soured. "Too bad our gliders don't feel the same way. Wouldn't it be glorious to decide for ourselves how we spend our time?"

It was a rhetorical question, given their situation and the fact that their gliders demanded daily training in their hand-to-hand combat and aerial skills. The days dragged by, blending into one another, the teens too exhausted by day's end to care how long Sven was taking. But the intense training began paying dividends, and their proficiency improved radically, until even the gliders had to admit there was no more they could teach them.

"What? We're up to your supreme standard of excellence?" Kayla teased when she heard this.

"Well, if you'd prefer to keep training today instead of taking the rest of the afternoon off, we'd be pleased to oblige."

Taz's imperious answer had them all laughing.

"No, no, we accept your generous offer," Jaden said.

At that, their gliders dropped them off at Sven's home, then flew off to only they knew where.

CHAPTER TWENTY-THREE

Despite being a short training day, it had still been strenuous, and the three soon lazed on loungers set out in the snow, taking in the welcome, languid warmth of the afternoon sun.

Jaden and Atu flanked Kayla on either side, their shirts off so they could work on their tans. As they relaxed, Kayla covertly eyed Jaden from behind her sunglasses. His physique had changed remarkably. His once narrow shoulders had widened and broadened, his chest muscles were now deliciously defined, and his incredible abs were impossibly even more toned. His arms and legs were sinewy with corded muscles. His handsome face, bronzed by days of working out under the sun against the backdrop of reflective snow, creased in an enticing smile, following something Atu said.

Kayla held back a dreamy sigh. *Yup, he's gorgeous. And not only on the outside.* His personality and character had first drawn her to him. But Kayla felt increasingly powerless to fight her growing attraction to him.

If Jaden put his arms around her again, Kayla didn't think she'd be able to pull back this time. Contemplating his interactions with her when they'd first arrived in Sven's valley, Kayla considered whether it was possible Jaden saw her as more than a friend. But if so, why hadn't he acted on it? Abruptly, Kayla slammed the brakes on her rambling thoughts. This could lead nowhere. But her half-closed eyes flicked irresistibly back to Jaden again. *Oh my, he has certainly changed!*

"It's finished!"

Sven's shout sliced through Kayla's contemplations. *Just as well.* Her thoughts had definitely been going down the wrong path. Again. And that way of thinking would get her into trouble sooner rather than later.

Bounding over to where they lay, Sven beamed and held out the innocuously disguised weapon. "Who wants to try it first?"

"Me!" Kayla shouted, eager to leave errant thoughts about Jaden behind.

The boys' equally enthusiastic shouts drowned her reply. They glanced at one another, then laughed.

"Kayla, why don't you go first?" Jaden said.

"Thanks, I'd love to!"

Jaden snorted. "You were supposed to say you appreciated the offer but that I could go first!"

"Or that you don't subscribe to the notion that girls go first," Atu added.

Kayla grinned. "Nice try, boys. I get the first turn, regardless!"

They chuckled, then jostled Sven with them to the makeshift test range they'd set up for the first trials. They were pleased when they found Sven had already set up several targets, ranging from the metal blocks used in the first set of tests to chunks of wood and glass bottles, amongst other items.

Kayla laughed, shaking her head in amazement. "Where on earth do you get these things, living out here in the middle of nowhere?"

"Just because I live away from the populated areas doesn't mean that I don't travel there. It also doesn't hurt to have friends in the right places."

"Aren't you worried someone will betray you to the people looking for you?" Atu asked.

"They can't share what they don't know. And none of them know where I live. I never set up meetings in advance. To protect all parties, I take every precaution. I know who I can approach for what supplies, and they all have code words to use if they think I have compromised them. They're not foolish enough to expose me, even if someone promised no retribution if they did. They know that if the people looking for me found them, they won't survive any longer than I would."

"That's a sad way to live," Kayla said.

Sven shrugged. "It is what it is. I don't dwell on what cannot be. Instead, I focus on what's possible—and right now, that's this weapon."

Since he was the only one who had handled the weapon when he'd introduced it, Sven launched into a detailed description of how to aim, showing the various components and what they should know when handling it to avoid carving a piece out of themselves. His lecture over, he handed the weapon to Kayla.

"Let's see what you can do."

Kayla latched onto the hilt of the small knife, careful to face the blade facing away from her as Sven had stressed. Now that she held it, Kayla noted it was a thing of beauty, the craftsmanship outstanding. Sven had put a lot of thought and care into his construction. *How did the quadrant decide he was more adept at something else?*

"Wait!" Jaden shouted, making her jump.

She glared. "What?"

"Tell us which object you're aiming at."

Kayla smirked. "So you can gauge how accurate my aim is?"

"Of course. Where's the fun without a target?"

Her competitive spirit couldn't resist. "Green bottle, third from the left."

"That's a small target for your first attempt—" Atu began but stopped when Jaden shook his head.

"Her aim's seriously wicked. Play a round with her on an arrowball court and tell me if I'm wrong."

Kayla smiled at his compliment. *Well, let's make it real*, she thought, focusing on the target. Kayla flipped the safety, and the sizzling extension slithered out, hissing and crackling with latent energy. Drawing a slow, steadying breath, Kayla lifted her arm and aimed. As she breathed out, she flicked her wrist like Sven had described.

A blazing arc of light peeled off the shimmering wand and hurtled toward the target area. It smacked into the metal block to the left of the bottle with an almighty bang, giving off a blinding light and leaving nothing but ash where the cube had been.

Sven punched his fist in the air. "Yes! It works!"

"Close," Jaden sympathized, understanding Kayla's disappointment.

"But not close enough. Same target again," Kayla said, gritting her teeth.

This time, she didn't miss. The bottle exploded into a million glittering shards before disintegrating into a powdery black smoke. Kayla grunted, satisfied. "That'll do."

Sven danced around behind her. "Where did you learn to shoot like that? I expected it would take you all day to even get close to the targets."

"It still might," Atu muttered under his breath.

"The arrowball court, as Jaden pointed out," Kayla answered, grinning at Jaden while she re-engaged the safety, then watched the extension slide back out of sight. "Your turn—and don't forget to identify your target."

Jaden grinned, taking the weapon. He tipped the safety, and the extension slid out. Awe showed on his face.

"Yup, it's light for something so deadly, isn't it?" Kayla commented.

Jaden nodded, then took careful aim.

Kayla interrupted. "Uh, when I said to identify your target, that means pointing it out before you shoot anything."

"It has to be the only other green bottle. That way, when I hit the target first time around, you can't say my object was larger than yours."

Sven roared with laughter, delighted by their competitiveness. "And you?" he asked Atu. "Are you planning on the smallest target?"

"No, the biggest." Atu grumbled. "I can't say aim is anything I ever excelled at."

"What about your hunting?" Sven said, surprised.

"Snares." Atu shrugged. "The bow was never my forte."

"Don't worry, my friend. We'll get you there," Sven reassured. "Maybe you can learn a few tricks from these two, no?"

"Perhaps." Atu responded, doubtful Jaden or Kayla could improve on his father's instruction. Despite this, he studied Jaden's every move.

Like Kayla, Jaden took his time preparing for the shot. Then he flicked his wrist, enthralled when the shaft of light glided off the extension toward the target. He didn't miss. The second glass bottle disappeared in the same impressive fashion.

"Yahtzee!" Jaden exalted.

"You learned from my mistakes," Kayla groused.

"You bet I did." Jaden grinned. "When you flicked your wrist the first time, you adjusted its angle. I think that's what threw you off. I just made sure I didn't repeat your mistake."

His grin was infectious, and Kayla had to giggle. "Nicely done!"

Jaden faced Atu. "You're up."

"Don't expect any miracles," Atu grumbled. "It'll take me the rest of the day to even get close, let alone hit anything. You'd be wise to kick back and relax for a bit."

"Don't be so hard on yourself," Kayla said.

"We'll help you," Jaden added.

"Thanks, but know that I don't do well at this."

Jaden smirked. "That's because you haven't had us as teachers."

"Let's not get ahead of ourselves," Kayla said. "At least not before we have Atu hitting the targets."

When Atu felt inclined to try his luck, Jaden and Kayla stepped back. They didn't pressure him into declaring his intended target. Instead, they waited quietly with Sven.

Atu took a deep, steadying breath as Kayla had suggested. Then he lifted his arm, checking the angle of his wrist as Jaden had shown him.

He snapped his wrist. Nothing happened. He tried again, still falling short of the desired result.

"Try flicking with more snap; the beam requires some force to separate from the blade," Sven suggested.

"Yeah, yeah," Atu snapped, his annoyance at himself coloring his tone.

"Focus," Kayla ordered.

Atu straightened his back. Concentrating, he lifted his arm again, cocked his wrist, and then flicked it firmly. His relief showed when the beam separated and zoomed toward the objects.

Kayla held her breath. With an earsplitting clap, the beam liquefied one of the metal blocks.

"Fantastic! I did it!" Atu howled, bouncing up and down like a pogo stick. That was, until the beam almost sliced his foot off. Swiftly retracting the beam, he placed the knife on the ground and then skipped to the others, giving them fist bumps. "Did you see?"

Laughing, they assured him they had, congratulating him and slapping him on the back, all sharing his triumph.

"Where were you two when I was learning to use a bow and arrow? That shot would've made my father proud," Atu said, sobering.

The others, sensing his melancholy, sobered too.

"I'm sure your father is still alive just as you believe he is," Kayla said. "And your mother too."

Atu nodded. His throat worked as he struggled to hold back the tears. But the first tear trickled out. "I'm sorry," Atu whispered. "I didn't cry when I realized my parents were missing. I haven't cried in all the months I've searched for them. And I didn't cry when I saw the Gaptor and figured out the monster had taken them. I just pushed all my energy into finding them, believing they were still alive. And now, here, far away from the red rocks of my home, in this crisp mountain air and among friends, I'm feeling my loss for the first time." Another tear traced a watery path down his cheek. Then more followed, rolling down his face, one after another, gathering momentum.

"It's okay. Let it all out," Kayla said, pulling him into a hug.

That was all it took for the floodgates to open. He sobbed, deep, racking sounds wrenched from his innermost parts, tearing away the worry that must've been crushing him all this time. Kayla held him, rubbing his back and comforting him. When she assured him his parents would get to see how true his aim was, it lifted the last of Atu's burden, and he smiled.

"Trust you to think of saying something like that."

Kayla smiled as his deluge subsided.

When he drew back, Atu was at peace. "Thanks," he murmured.

"Any time."

Kayla glanced at Jaden, seeing his gratitude that she had been there for Atu. For a moment, Jaden's lack of jealousy over her physical contact with Atu surprised Kayla. The last time she'd touched Atu, Kayla suspected Jaden was envious.

Then Kayla realized what the difference was. Jaden understood their friend needed solace, and he wouldn't begrudge him that. Kayla shook her head at her own lack of faith in Jaden. What would it have said about his character if he had wanted her to allow their friend to suffer alone? If anything, it spoke volumes about his own compassion. And it just increased his appeal. *Ugh, not what I planned on getting out of consoling Atu.*

Kayla looked away, noticing the light seeping from the wide, blue sky. Dusk slunk in, drawing its black cloak behind it. Soon it would suffocate the remaining light and surround them with darkness, choking any chance of continued practice.

She wasn't the only one to notice. Squeezing Atu's shoulder, Jaden said, "Why don't we call it a day and go have dinner?"

Atu nodded so hard, he looked like one of those bobblehead figurines in an antiquated car when it hit an unexpected bump. Kayla grinned. She was decidedly hungry herself.

Jaden fell in next to Kayla while Sven put a strong, supportive arm across Atu's shoulders, and they trudged back to the house. Only when they were halfway there did Atu remember the abandoned weapon.

"The weapon—I left it back there—" Atu began.

"Don't worry; I got you," Jaden said, displaying the weapon in his hand.

"Excellent!" Atu declared. "We'll need it to get my parents back."

And just like that, Atu regained control. Kayla had to admire him for it. Then again, they had a weapon, they had a mission, and they would help him find his parents along the way. It was as simple as that.

Atu smiled at Sven. "Armorer, thank you for helping us. Your aid has been invaluable."

"Yes, it has. Thank you!" Kayla echoed.

"We could never have gone forward without you," Jaden said. "From your unstinting hospitality, to your astounding smart suits, to the design and construction of this extraordinary weapon—you are a blessing, and we appreciate your help."

Sven flushed, unaccustomed to such praise. "My pleasure. What else was I going to do?" he said, his voice gruff with emotion.

They reached the house and entered, dropping their shoes and accessories at the door.

Studying the weapon he still held, Jaden motioned to Sven. "Now that we have a weapon, do you have a name for it?"

Sven's eyebrows shot up. "I hadn't considered that."

"Well, you named the smart suits, and it was likely you who came up with the label for the pulse weapon—both of which are your inventions. You must have some inkling of a name for this one?" Kayla prompted.

"Yes, I did, and do, name my inventions. But this one . . ." Sven drifted into silence.

The others gave him room to think. They wandered into the kitchen and began putting dinner together. They were halfway through their meal before Sven spoke again.

"I will call this one the 'Dog Decimator' or 'DD' for short."

"DD for a blade instead of BB for a gun?" Jaden snorted, amused.

Sven grinned. "You have a quick wit."

"I don't get the dog part." Kayla frowned. "Dogs are cute, lovable creatures."

"Not all of them. You've obviously never met mongrels like those they had guarding the complex they sequestered me in. Vicious monsters, trained to rip you to shreds. And that hideous aberration vividly reminded me of them when it did this to me." Sven pulled his shirt to one side and displayed his scar again.

Kayla winced. "Who am I to argue? DD it is."

CHAPTER TWENTY-FOUR

They woke the next morning to find their gliders had returned during the night. Eager to show off the impressive weapon, the teens donned their smart suits and dashed outside. Explaining the weapon's functionality, Kayla wondered about the meaningful glance the gliders exchanged when the teens mentioned Sven's name for his invention. But the boys' torrent of enthusiasm as they showed the gliders what the weapon could do swept her along. Concluding their mini presentation, they grinned when the gliders were suitably impressed.

"Congratulations, Armorer. You have done well." Taz smiled, inclining her head.

"We are most fortunate to have you with us," Han added.

More than tickled about coaxing a smile from the typically stern Taz, Sven beamed. "All part of teamwork. Now, why don't you show me what the five of you have been working on? I'm eager to see the results of my smart suits."

They obliged, taking to the air, the boys with Han and Kayla with Taz. The longer Sven watched, the more agitated he became, until he was dancing from foot to foot. *What has him so worked up?*

When they swooped past again, Sven bellowed, "Come down, would you?"

That doesn't sound promising, Kayla thought as their gliders descended. The voyagers dismounted, landing next to Sven. He waited until the gliders had floated graceful turns and made landings of their own before speaking.

"If you think you will win a battle with strategies like that, you're mistaken!"

Taz's lips thinned. "I beg your pardon?"

"Forgive me!" Sven said, raising his arms in a gesture of apology. "I do not mean to offend. But all I've observed this morning are aerial movements—no strategies." When they looked perplexed, he explained. "I noticed no sequences designed to place the beast within range of the DD, nor any that would entice the beast into moving between you so you can harness the stones' power to eliminate him."

"I think I understand what you're driving at," Jaden said. "Instead of just learning how to stay on our gliders irrespective of their movements, we should've also focused on how we could use those movements to our advantage. Setting them up in sequences to make the Gaptor the hunted instead of the hunter?"

As he spoke, understanding filled Jaden's incredible blue eyes with light. If only that light would come into his eyes when he looked at her. But only anything logic-related seemed to stoke that fire. It never ceased to amaze Kayla he was such a geek. He had this innate desire to understand how things worked, to see if he could improve them or find more efficient ways to do things. If there was ever a person who should be on this quest, it was him.

How she fit into that picture, Kayla didn't know. There must be a reason they selected her family. Sure, she had a little medical training. But Atu surpassed her in that area. And there was no contest with tech. Jaden was the winner, hands down.

So what's my role? Am I just Robin to Jaden's Batman? If I mention that to him, will he even know what I'm talking about? The anime captivating most of her generation had long since usurped superhero comics. Kayla sighed. *Am I just old-fashioned? Is that how Jaden sees me? Not interesting enough to be more than a friend?* Realizing she was diving into a place she shouldn't, Kayla tried concentrating on Sven.

"Exactly. You need to work on both offensive and defensive flying. Your focus has been defense. If you don't come up with some offensive routines to trap those beasts, you'll be the ones in trouble. Speaking of which," Sven said, turning to the gliders, "from the stories I heard, you could streak through the sky like meteors. Were those stories of your speed exaggerated?"

"No, Armorer, they are true. But we can't reach our potential with our voyagers on our backs. They fall unconsciousness before we've even attained a fraction of that speed."

Kayla squirmed at the unwelcome memory. "We are getting better at traveling faster," she muttered.

Sven frowned. "But you're still struggling?"

"Correct, Armorer," Han answered. "Do you have a solution?"

"I do," Sven said, darting away.

"More toys!" Kayla sighed, rolling her eyes.

But that soon changed. When Sven returned from his workshop, bearing molded rubber hoods and thin silver miniature harmonica-shaped instruments, Kayla was intrigued.

"What are those?" Kayla asked, pointing at the shiny tubes.

"Aerolators," Sven replied without elaborating.

When Kayla pressed him for more information, her questions and those of the boys went unanswered. Sven smugly told them to wait and see. He motioned them into the house where he demonstrated how the hoods used AI to self-connect to the suits. Using a mirror, they followed his instructions and attached their hoods, after which Sven hooked an aerolator onto the outside flap of each hood. Then he ordered them back outside.

When the teens strode out, their gliders peered at them. Then Han guffawed, the rich, rollicking sound washing over them. "Aliens!"

Kayla, a little miffed, had to admit he was right. With their hair tucked under the hoods so they now resembled skinheads, the silver tubes on the hood flaps forming garish, unnatural horizontal bars across their throats, and their figures streamlined into similitude by the smart suits, they did resemble beings from another planet.

"Thanks, Han, way to make us feel at peace with these suits," Kayla griped.

Han erupted into more peals of laughter.

"Are you going to join him?" Kayla snapped, noticing the corners of Taz's mouth twitching as the bat tried not to burst into delicious laughter herself.

With a supreme effort, Taz managed a somewhat regal reply. "Not yet."

That just made Han flap his wings about as he dissolved into hysterics. They watched, open-mouthed in amazement. Then it was too much, and they joined Han. Even Taz let her iron control slip, subsiding into irrepressible giggles.

With their mirth spent, they wiped the tears from their eyes, leaning on one another as they pushed themselves upright again.

"Whew! That felt great!" Jaden declared.

"Yes, just what we needed," Atu agreed.

"And now, to business," Sven directed, composing himself. "Atu, you will need to remain on the ground for this test. Jaden, Kayla, up and on your gliders. Taz, Han, once you're airborne, fly as fast as you can."

All movement around Sven ceased. They stared at him.

"You can't be serious?" Kayla objected. "We don't stay conscious when they go at less than half their top speed. Now you want them flying full tilt?"

"If they pass out, you can catch them, no?" Sven asked the gliders, ignoring Kayla's comment.

"We can," Taz murmured, "but is it wise to run such a test?"

"A little trust?" Sven begged, his face pained.

Kayla balked at the idea. She didn't want to pass out again. There was nothing worse than being out of control. But studying Sven's face, she found gleeful anticipation lurking behind the feigned outrage. He thought they could do it. Kayla fingered the silver bar across her throat and then the hood of the smart suit. Somehow, these two things would stop them from passing out? Only one way to find out.

Kayla glanced at Taz, raising her eyebrows. Understanding, Taz vaulted into the air. Han watched Taz with a bemused expression, as if trying to fathom what she was up to. Comprehension suddenly brightened his countenance, and he also took to the air. Too late. Taz was already whipping back toward them.

"Beat you to the end of the valley and back," Kayla shouted at Jaden as she aerial connected with Taz. Chortling at Jaden's stunned expression, she and Taz sped away.

Kayla's exhilaration rose as Taz increased her speed. The wind blasted her face, whooshed in her ears, forced her eyelids shut and pressing the skin on her cheeks flat against the underlying bone. Kayla's grip on Taz weakened, and she strained to stay aloft. As fear replaced pleasure, adrenaline spiked her veins. Her heart raced, and blood drummed through her head. Panic swelled within her.

Kayla gasped when the smart suit forced her flush against Taz's neck. The wind speed diminished. Relieved, Kayla opened her eyes a little. Her gaze fell on the ground beneath them, streaking by so fast she couldn't even identify what they were passing over.

Kayla's breath snagged. *Not enough air*, she realized, when the familiar lightheadedness came on. The silver bar pressing against her lips startled her. Even more bizarre was the creeping sensation as the hood crawled over her face, masking it. When the flat goggles spread over her eyes, forming protective covers, Kayla lost it.

Why didn't Sven warn us? It was like walking through a spiderweb in the dark. Tendrils of unseen silk brushing ever so lightly across your skin, prickling the flesh as you frantically wondered where the spider was and whether it was poisonous. Kayla shivered. With a snapping sound, the mask completed its upward circuit and latched onto the crest of the hood.

The rubbery compound now encased her face—and her breathing was normal. Hazarding a quick downward glance, she verified the ground still whizzed beneath them at terrifying speed. She glanced up again.

Kayla no longer had trouble staying on Taz. The wind wasn't roaring in her ears, and she could see through the convex shells over her eyes. And her breathing . . . oh, her breathing. It was so normal. It had to be the silver tube. *What does it do and how does it do it?*

"Slowpokes!" Jaden yelled, as he and Han sped past.

"Not for long," Taz trilled, accelerating with a glorious burst of speed.

The suit smeared Kayla against Taz's neck again as it adjusted for the change in momentum. After her initial distress, Kayla relaxed. She was still in control. In fact, she felt fantastic.

Hunkering over Taz's neck, Kayla settled in for the thrill ride of a lifetime. By the time they reached the end of the valley, she was comfortable enough to assume her usual flying position. Even the blurred landscape under them no longer scared her. Kayla watched it race by, then blinked. *What's wrong with my eyes?*

"Are we slowing down?" Kayla asked Taz, puzzled.

"No, why?"

"I can see what's under us."

"So?"

"I couldn't see anything before. But now . . . it's like everything is clear again."

"Could it be the suit?"

"Duh! It must be the goggles compensating for the speed and slowing things down. Imagine that!" Enchanted by the discovery, Kayla spurred Taz on. "Let's beat those boys!"

Taz laughed, surging ahead. Kayla knew things would never be the same. It was akin to being launched in a rocket. She and Jaden were finally experiencing the true speed and power of their gliders. And it was phenomenal!

Kayla spotted Sven and Atu, jumping up and down on the ground and waving as they cheered. They were coming up fast. Kayla figured their chances of winning. The boys were still ahead. But where Han had strength, Taz had speed. They closed on the boys, and Kayla wailed like a banshee when they clipped the imaginary finish line over Sven and Atu's heads a fraction of a second before the boys.

"Cheaters!" Jaden yelled. "You had a head start!"

"Sore losers!" Kayla shouted back.

They grinned at each other, the adrenaline rush from the race buoying their spirits as their gliders slowed, lowered, and then allowed them to dismount some distance from Sven and Atu.

Kayla rose from her landing crouch and found Jaden standing in front of her. Uncomfortably close. Before she could back away, he grabbed her, pulling her to him and lifting her as he swung her around and around, whooping with sheer delight.

Kayla giggled. Impulsiveness was so like him. Glancing up at his angular face as she locked her arms around his neck, her breath caught. His face was alight with the thrill of the ride, his eyes twinkling with repressed mischief and a much deeper shade of blue than usual. *Yup, too darn handsome by far.* When his mouth tilted in that gorgeous smile as he searched her face, her breath hitched again.

"What are you thinking?" Jaden asked, setting her back on her feet.

Still breathless, Kayla turned away, pretending to tuck a stray hair back into her hood as she scrambled for an explanation. She couldn't tell him what she'd really been thinking. "You're in a good mood."

"Aren't you? That was incredible! I've never felt so alive before."

Neither have I. And not from the extreme flying. His back muscles straining and flexing under her hands as he lifted and lowered her while they twirled was exhilarating. Combined with knowing he was vibrant and valiant and with her only increased the heady sensation. His joy, flowing to her as they celebrated, added to the intoxication. As did his body pressing against hers, wound tight with the thrill of the race still running through him.

That moment, right then, with no one else intruding, with no mission complicating matters, with nothing to think of other than the pure wonder of sharing such an amazing experience with him—that had been the real thrill.

Their gliders landed with a soft thump, startling Kayla. She smiled at Taz when her glider sent her a questioning glance, thankful Taz grasped that she shouldn't ask until they were alone. The four of them turned to meet Sven and Atu, who were racing toward them. This time, Taz was the first to praise Sven.

"Armorer, you are astounding! I never dared hope we might rely on our speed to avoid the Gaptors, but you have given us all a more certain future!"

Sven beamed, turning bright pink for the second time in as many hours. "Thank you!"

"Atu, you up for a turn?" Jaden asked.

Without hesitation, Atu loped over to Taz. "Ready to beat those two again?"

Taz chuckled and took to the air. This time she waited for Han before they raced back to the waiting voyagers, picking them up simultaneously. Kayla couldn't believe what she was seeing. The gliders were above them one moment, then gone the next. *So that's how they always seemed to just vanish!* She grinned at Sven. "You really are amazing, you know that?"

Sven smiled. "Your appreciation makes for a pleasant change."

"You deserve it," Kayla said, squeezing his arm.

They waited only a few minutes before the gliders zoomed back toward them. They did indeed resemble streaking meteors. *Was I really going that fast?* Kayla joined Sven as they vocally drove the two teams on.

Atu and Taz were the victors, much to Han's chagrin. "There'll be no living with her after this!" he muttered.

The humans couldn't contain their laughter.

"Cheer up," Jaden said. "You're stronger than her any day of the week. Speaking of which, my strength could use some bolstering. Where's breakfast?"

CHAPTER TWENTY-FIVE

For Jaden, life became an endless blur of constants. Blistering cold, blinding sunshine, blustering winds. Aching muscles, acute fatigue, accumulating tension. Constantly expecting some horrible, unforeseen event. Never knowing what Sven would demand of them next. Living in dread of more Gaptors arriving before they'd fully prepared themselves. Unsure of their endgame.

He wasn't the only one who grew numb. Kayla and Atu shared his disposition. All three of them could only center their attention on what was right in front of them, pouring their energy into conquering that single specter, not permitting their focus to waver for even a second. Then they turned to the next item demanding their attention. Jaden lost count of the number of days they spent with Sven, irrelevant anyway since time had no meaning when they were with their gliders.

Following their successful test flight of the hoods and aerolators, Sven programmed the suits with various routines designed to train them in offensive aerial strategies. Each day, a new combination of movements. Each night, a reconstruction of the day's exercises and how they could've improved.

And when they improved, Sven acted on Taz's earlier observations and added random flying objects, designed to come at them out of nowhere to teach the teens how to maintain disciplined flying principles while distracted. If this wasn't enough, Sven added commands to the suits, teaching them how to handle their weapons while flying.

"We can't have you chopping your gliders' heads off because you forgot where your blade was or misjudged its length," Sven joked.

Han and Taz didn't find this amusing. That was, until Sven's programming saved them on more than one occasion, compelling the voyager careless enough to bring the blade too close to flip the safety on. This retracted the blade before it did any harm, a failsafe reassuring the voyagers as much as their gliders.

Sven also insisted they continue with their hand-to-hand combat practice and with the strength and fitness regimes he had implemented, despite their protests they were unlikely to be of use in a fight against a Gaptor.

"And how do you know that? What if your gliders are injured, and this is the only way you can defend yourselves against that brute?" Sven barked.

"But Sven, the Gaptor's about five times our size! And no doubt five times as strong or more. And have you seen his hide? Even a tank would have trouble blasting through that," Jaden complained.

"You can never be too prepared," Sven said. "Would you rather you had no clue how to land a blow or avoid one?"

Jaden eventually gave up arguing.

Then there were the wake-up calls at all hours of the night, sometimes multiple times. All part of Sven's plan to shorten the time it took them to get battle-ready. It was exhausting. And finally, the piece that almost broke Jaden was Sven withholding their food, testing their retention of the rudimentary elements of edible plant and insect identification Atu taught them.

"Lack of food will sap you of your energy and drive to continue more than anything else," Sven warned. "You must be capable of feeding yourselves wherever this journey may take you."

Kayla rolled her eyes wearily. "Sven, there's practically a store in every town. And with our enhanced speed, I'm sure we'll always be within reach of food."

"Again, what if your gliders are injured? Do you know how to feed them? And how will you survive if there's no store nearby and you have no inkling of how to find food and water? It comes down to basics—you have to know them."

"We know." Atu sighed. "'Fortune favors the prepared mind.'"

That was the last time they'd tried convincing Sven he was going overboard. They just did their best to cope with whatever he threw at them at that particular second of that particular day.

Jaden, in a rare moment of clarity one morning, realized this was Sven's intention from the start: to teach them to react without thinking, so their responses would be reflexive. If they could achieve this, their chances of success improved exponentially. Sven reminded Jaden of this when, after what seemed like endless, intense training, Sven made an announcement.

"Today, you'll be pitting your skills against an actual opponent," Sven informed the bleary-eyed teens as they slouched on the table, plowing through breakfast.

Jaden perked up, as did Kayla and Atu. *Finally! Something to break the tedium. Something to fight against.* Jaden observed Kayla as she straightened in her chair, looking more alive than she had in weeks. Their grueling schedule had taken its toll.

Her green eyes were more striking than ever, their color accentuated by the dark smudges of exhaustion underlining them. Her hair was tousled, as though all the time under the face mask had left a permanent kink in some places. And although her muscles had gained definition, Jaden could tell she had lost weight.

Her smart suit, once a snug fit, hung loose in places. If only he could protect her. But that was beyond his control. Despite his concern over her wellbeing, this training was perhaps the only way to keep her safe. He would do what he could to help her excel. She had to be better than the rest of them. She had to survive.

"What sort of opponent?" Atu asked.

Sven grinned. "One that will test whether you're ready for those beasts."

They didn't bother asking more questions, convinced it would be an exercise in futility. Instead, they raced through the remnants of their breakfast, eager to discover what awaited them. Bounding outside, they shared the good news with their gliders. Sven emerged from the house in time to see Han and Taz taking to the air. Seconds later, the gliders breezed back, picking up their voyagers via aerial connection and then rapidly gaining altitude.

Jaden smiled as Han quivered under him. Although they wouldn't admit it, their gliders seemed almost as curious as the teens about their mysterious opponent. And when it came at them, as unexpectedly as the Gaptor always had, it didn't disappoint.

A smaller version of the real thing—a drone shaped into a Gaptor-like clone—darted in front of them. Shooting out a mechanical arm, it swiped at Han's wing as it passed. Han tipped his wing and dipped downward as he nimbly dodged the attempt.

Jaden realized he wasn't the only one staring when he caught sight of Kayla and Atu's shocked faces. Sven's miniature beast momentarily confused them. But it didn't take long to figure out this was intentional. By giving them a scaled-down target, Sven was guaranteeing their success in taking down a larger, more cumbersome version. Because as they engaged the diminutive clone, assessing its abilities, Jaden found it more agile than its real-life counterpart. It executed tighter turns, responded more rapidly to attacks, and provided quicker comebacks than the Gaptor they'd faced only a few weeks before. They had their work cut out for them. The time for observation was over.

Jaden signaled Kayla and Atu, paired on Taz, expressing the play he thought would be most effective against the clone. They signaled acceptance. Their gliders maneuvered them into the correct positions. Then they attacked.

Han and Jaden lunged past, drawing its attention. The clone immediately dashed after them. While it honed its attention on the duo, Kayla, Atu, and Taz curved downward from a higher altitude, arcing like a scimitar through the empty sky.

Carving a path at the rear of the hunt, they ended up behind and underneath the racing duelers, catching the clone squarely between them and the boys. A nanosecond before the relic stones flashed, the clone dropped at an alarming rate.

"Unbelievable!" Jaden yelled.

"Not fair!" Kayla shrieked.

The real Gaptor could never lose altitude that fast. As their gliders held their positions, Jaden glanced at the others. They were all thinking the same thing: Sven had programmed the drone to avoid the specific attacks they'd learned. *Is he testing whether we can improvise and how skillful we'll be at it?*

As the drone dropped from sight, Jaden signaled he wanted to speak with the others. Taz winged her team upward until they hovered alongside Han and Jaden.

"Sven did that deliberately—" Jaden began.

"You think?" Atu grunted. "It's the only way his clone will win!"

"Or so he thinks!" Jaden said. "We will put his adaptive programming skills to the test."

"How?" Kayla asked.

Jaden grinned ghoulishly. "I suggest beginning our next offensive with play one, but when the roll comes, we switch to play seven, picking it up where the roll ends. That should scramble its little tin brain."

Kayla's eyes slanted in a sly smile. "Especially if we add play four between the lift and the curve."

"Love it!" Atu crowed.

"Me too," Jaden said. Then he yelled, "Watch out—here it comes again!"

They broke apart, flying in opposite directions as they had been taught. Dividing the clone's focus served two purposes: it gave them a slight time advantage while the hunter selected its target, and it minimized the risk of both gliders being injured in one attack. As expected, the drone faltered, then took off after Taz.

"Looks like we're the bait," Kayla shouted above the rushing wind.

Jaden watched them streak away, just catching Atu's reply.

"I don't think it liked our surprise first attack. It's hoping that if it destroys us, there won't be further unpleasant shocks."

"How wrong that logic is . . ." Kayla's words drifted away as she passed out of range of Jaden's hearing.

He could see her laughing, though, as Taz began a long, slow spiral upward. The drone, sensing its prey's reduced speed, accelerated. Its trajectory would place it smack in the middle of Taz's spiral, where it could do the most damage with the least effort. But a fraction of a second after it sped up, Taz tucked her wings and flipped into a roll.

Their timing was perfect—long enough after the drone expended energy to negate deceleration and close enough to prevent the drone from changing direction without ripping one of its artificial wings off. The drone rocketed past Taz, inadvertently increasing the distance between them. But Taz's team had no time to gloat. Registering the play, the drone slowed and corrected its path, aiming for where its prey would arrive if they completed the routine.

Jaden grinned. Tin Can was in for a rude awakening. He held his breath as Kayla and Atu gripped Taz's fur, readying for the switch in play. The extreme sideways force of the change knocked them off-balance for a second, but their smart suits adjusted their postures, compensating for the sudden torque. They came out of the roll and streaked across the sky horizontally, faster than a shooting star. Jaden whooped, ecstatic.

The drone hovered, muddled, at a loss what to do. Then it lurched after Taz again. But it had taken too long. Han and Jaden had raced in from behind, within striking distance. Jaden activated his DD, careful where he directed the blade.

Before the drone could dart away, Jaden lifted his arm and flicked his wrist. A thin sliver of energy separated from the wand, crackling and popping as it sliced through the air. Jaden held his breath. His aim was true. He waited for contact, but it never came.

As if responding to an unheard external command, the drone boosted upward, powered by hidden rocket thrusters. When Jaden spotted the telltale trail of flames, he groaned. *Sven, the swindler! He's cheating again!* The drone could've only moved so fast if Sven had overridden its command center.

So Sven could control the clone from the ground—he could see what was going on. That was only possible if the drone had cameras sending Sven feedback. They would have to take care of that, assuming the drone escaped the remaining play aimed at placing it between the relic stones.

Han bitterly lambasted Sven's less-than-sportsmanlike behavior before growling, "If it chases us, we can still complete the play and destroy it."

"I agree. Let's go!"

Han surged upward, catching the air under his wings in powerful gusts. They closed in on the drone. Curiously, it didn't duck away. Jaden debated the meaning but diverted his attention to holding on when Han collided with the drone, raking his tough talons across the shiny shell forming the main body.

The drone bounced sideways, away from the vicious nails, bobbing aimlessly for a split second before recovering. It zipped left, then rotated its gangly frame as it dropped below them. Instantly, Jaden understood. The drone hadn't moved earlier because heat from the rocket thrusters must have compromised at least one of its cameras. Sven was blind to attacks from below. *Useful information.* Jaden softly communicated this to Han, who gave a satisfied, toothy grin in acknowledgement.

"Hah, Sven's lost some of his advantage," Han gloated. "Now, if only that clone would chase us! What's it waiting for?"

Jaden was thinking the same thing. Up to this point, the drone had decided rapidly. In a flash, it came to him. *Because the heat damaged more than just the cameras. It must've fried some wiring. It's probably running some diagnostic or rebooting. Either way, it's a golden opportunity.*

"Han, we need to attack—now!"

CHAPTER TWENTY-SIX

Han didn't argue or demand an explanation. Tucking his wings, he dove toward the still-motionless drone. With one sinuous movement, Jaden flipped the safety off the DD, moved the blade upward, and waited for the right moment. *Just a little closer.*

The drone came within range. Jaden flicked his wrist, and with an explosive crack, the DD's sizzling beam smashed into the drone. In a brilliant shower of sparks, the drone vaporized into a harmless cloud of gray ash. The nebulous cloud disintegrated as the breeze caught the particles, leaving no evidence anything had ever been there.

"Great shooting!" Kayla hooted as they caught up to Jaden and Han.

Excitement flushed Kayla's face. Some of her long blonde hair had escaped her mask and whipped around her impish smile. Jaden laughed. Her exuberance was infectious. Just as well they were still perched on their gliders, or Jaden would've drawn her into his arms and kissed that remarkably mobile mouth of hers.

He caught himself. Had he really just contemplated that? He sighed. Controlling his thoughts and emotions around her was becoming almost impossible. It wouldn't be long before he slipped up, and then he would have to pay the piper.

As much to get his mind running on a different track as to tease her, Jaden said, "What took you so long? We had to have all the fun without you!"

"Sure you did!" Atu grinned. "What was the point of sharing the glory?"

Jaden laughed. "Next time, get here faster, and I'll let you take the first shot! What say you we go rub our victory in?"

Chuckling as their gliders descended, they coasted back to where Sven waited. Alighting with ease, the trio strode over to Sven. Their gliders landed behind them a second later.

"You don't exactly look pleased about our success," Jaden said.

"Do you know how long it took me to build that drone? And you demolished it without a second thought!" Sven shook his head in disbelief. "Thankful that I am that those monsters haven't reappeared, at least it wouldn't have mattered if you had terminated them. But destroying my drone, and while it was defenseless because it was rebooting? It's untenable!"

"I thought that was the point of the exercise," Atu cooed sweetly. "To take advantage of our enemy when he was at his weakest?"

"But that wasn't the case here. You should've waited and faced it like soldiers, or at least tried capturing it instead of destroying it!"

"Why? So you could cheat another way and take us out instead? I think not!" Jaden shot back.

"I didn't even get to deploy the distraction drones. You shouldn't have won," Sven lamented.

"Oh, so there were more drones. Talk about stacking the odds against us! Not to mention all those sneaky enhancements—like knowing our plays," Kayla remarked sourly.

"And making the drone quicker and more agile than the real thing," Jaden added.

"All necessary for an accurate test of your abilities," Sven said.

"And yet, when we prove ourselves, you're not happy about it," Jaden asserted, bringing the conversation full circle.

Sven sighed heavily. "No. you did well. My regret is that it was over so quickly. I was hoping for a more comprehensive test."

Taz fluttered her wings, rearranging them. "I doubt you would've succeeded even if you had more time."

Jaden smiled. "Spoken like a true champion."

"You have no idea," Han murmured, making the teens eye him questioningly. He huffed. "Ask me about it another time."

The teens turned to Taz and caught her smirking.

"What?" Jaden demanded.

"He's right," Taz said. "It will have to wait for another time. Armorer, I believe in our voyagers, but I'd like to hear your thoughts on our performance."

"Formidable!" Sven divulged. "Especially the way you mixed up the plays. I confess, it took me a while to work that out. Tell me, what was the complete idea? Had you planned on incorporating another play, or was it only the two I saw?"

Jaden picked up the thread, taking pleasure in enlightening Sven as to their strategy.

"Ah, excellent!" Sven said. "I didn't think you could combine the plays like that. It seems my error was underestimating you. You did well—all of you," Sven said, acknowledging the gliders' part in their victory.

The teens grinned while their gliders inclined their heads as they accepted Sven's compliment.

"Can we have a snack now?" Jaden asked.

"Afraid I am, all for which there is time, that is."

The voice behind had them leaping back, and assuming offensive positions, but it was unnecessary.

"Zareh!" Jaden and Kayla breathed.

He dipped his head, greeting them and their gliders. "To all of you, salutations! My congratulations, for two more seekers reclaiming!"

"Thank you, Zareh," the gliders replied, their heads bowed.

But Jaden's anger flared. He lashed out. "We wouldn't have if we hadn't found the map. Thanks for the help with that, by the way. So good of you to vanish before you could give us any information that would be genuinely helpful."

"Ahem, yes," Zareh grunted, clearing his throat. "Me to spot, Kayla's mother, permitted was not."

"Like she would've been able to." Jaden snorted. "She's not a seeker. Nice try, but no banana! Care to try again?"

Zareh fixed him with a beady stare. "Accept I do, that upset you are. But know also do I, that explained to you the reasons for that lack of information, your gliders have. Understand, please try."

"Why?" Jaden fumed.

"The only one affected, you are not. Saving people by too little knowing, you are. Think upon them, you should."

"As if that makes any sense!"

"Tried it yet, you have not," Zareh replied, "or of introducing me to your friends, you might have thought."

Somewhat chastened, Jaden corrected his error, more to pacify the gliders glaring at him than out of courtesy to Zareh. Atu and Sven stretched out hands in greeting toward their much talked-about visitor.

"Welcome to my home," Sven gushed, his massive frame towering over the pint-sized protector.

"I thank you," Zareh said.

"Very nice to meet you," Atu said, shaking Zareh's hand.

"To meet you, a pleasure likewise it is, Healer."

Atu's eyebrows shot up in surprise.

"Yeah, don't let that shock you," Jaden snarked. "He apparently knows everything about everyone."

Zareh ignored Jaden. "For your services, to both of you, my deepest thanks. Fear do I, that lost our gliders would have been, if your healing powers they had not benefitted from," Zareh said, looking directly at Atu before turning his gaze on Sven. "And surely, no hope without your invaluable battle strategies and remarkable inventions, would we have had."

Sven and Atu beamed.

"I'm happy to be of service," Atu said.

"A personal joy it is, a generation to find to whom our original journey to this world I can trace," Zareh purred. "But regret do I, that time for reminiscing we do not have. At an end, your time with the Armorer is. No longer delay, can you. At once, leave you must. Fear do I, that already too much time here have I allowed you."

"Why? What's happened?" Kayla asked, alarmed by the urgency in Zareh's tone.

"As yet, nothing. But not long will it be before that changes."

"There you go, talking in riddles again!" Jaden exploded. "Could you be more specific about what will happen? Or will we just have to find out on our own again?"

"Jaden!" Kayla hissed. "Simmer down. Losing your temper won't help, and it will just reduce the time Zareh has to tell us anything worthwhile."

"Wisely she speaks." Zareh nodded, eyeing Kayla appreciatively. "Limited with you, my time is. Summoned elsewhere, already have I been. But, this once, endeavor to answer your question I will, before leave I must. To the extent I can, that is."

Jaden glared at him, but Zareh waved a pacifying arm.

"Obtuse to be, my desire it is not. Elaborate I do not, because exactly what comes, even I cannot see. To a momentous event, all the signs point. But hidden remains, what that event is. The future many outcomes presents, depending on which paths are taken or avoided."

"If that's true, how can you say with any confidence that this 'momentous event' will actually happen?" Jaden countered, sneering as he quoted Zareh's phrase.

"Because, on rare occasions, converge all the paths do, meaning no matter what action we take, changed cannot be the event that at their union occurs."

"And this is one?" Kayla guessed.

"Correct, you are. So while warn you, I would like, about what coming your way is, the knowledge to do so, I lack. Only inform you, can I, that coming something is, and soon. Therefore, resume your quest, you must. Your departure, delayed I have, as long as was permissible because this time you needed. Learned much, you have, and in good stead, it will stand for what is coming. But farewell, bid you I must. The map, follow—your guide, it is."

And he disappeared as unexpectedly as he had arrived.

Jaden seethed. "There he goes again!"

"Now I understand what you meant when you said he arrives and leaves at will." Sven whistled, looking dazed.

"Atu, you're awfully quiet," Kayla said.

"What he said is true," Atu murmured. "Even my people marked this time period as the end many generations ago."

Jaden groaned. "You didn't think to mention that earlier?"

"The marking of time, particularly when done so long ago and using a different calendar, has meant the exact time period on the calendar we are familiar with was an educated guess. When my parents disappeared, I wondered. My suspicions grew when I saw the Gaptor and then met all of you. Today is confirmation."

"Do your legends say what event causes this end?" Kayla asked.

"No, only what our visionaries perceived as happening after the event."

"Which was?" Jaden pressed.

Atu sighed unhappily. "Something you won't like. They visually depicted the time following the event as black blotches."

Kayla shivered. "You're right. I don't like the sound of that."

"Nothing other than those ominous black marks to show what occurs after?" Sven asked.

"Correct. The absence of pictures made my people believe this event would mark the end of our world."

The group considered the implications.

Then Sven said, "But it could also just as easily signify their inability to see past this event?"

"Well, yes. Considering what Zareh explained, that is a possibility," Atu allowed.

Kayla relaxed. "I'm opting for that line of thinking. It's far more optimistic."

"Zareh did stress the future is unwritten," Jaden reflected. "So, it's up to us to ensure it's written in our favor. And how can we possibly fail, considering how easily we knocked Sven's cheating drone out of the sky?"

The rest of them smiled, but no one was given to laughing.

Sven cleared his throat. "I commend you for your positive outlook, but I fear it won't be so simple. Keep my warnings about being realistic in your expectations at the forefront of your minds. That will do much to keep you alive."

The teens nodded, their faces earnest.

"We'll keep Jaden in check," Kayla promised, giving Jaden a playful shove.

Jaden grinned, gently shoving back, grateful for the umpteenth time she was in this with him. With Kayla on their team, their chances were better than average. She had become a fearsome fighter besides being an excellent strategist, was protective of her friends, and firm in her belief they would succeed.

Jaden would keep her safe; he would protect that which was most precious to him. Somehow, they would make it through this. They had to. The world was counting on them. And when they had completed this mission, he would be free to pursue her.

"Yes, Jaden's ours to tame," Atu said, joining in the fun and tousling Jaden's hair.

"You'd better," Sven said. "I'm expecting a victory lap back here when you've completed this journey—not only so I can reclaim my equipment but also so you can regale an old man with more glorious tales."

Soberly, they nodded, aware Sven was avoiding their imminent departure. But Jaden knew they all felt it—their dread at having to part ways. Sven was their mentor, and now they were being kicked out of the proverbial nest, to fly or die without him.

"We will miss you," Kayla said, flinging her arms around Sven and hugging him while ineffectually keeping tears at bay.

Sven returned the hug with a ferocity betraying his own emotion at their separation. Without loosening his grip on Kayla, he reached out and pulled both boys into his massive arms too.

"Come back to me," Sven said gruffly.

"We will," Jaden answered. "We've had an exceptional teacher. Now we'll make you proud."

They embraced for only a moment longer before drawing back. No words were necessary as the teens headed indoors and grabbed their go bags provided by Sven only two days previously, already packed with the provisions Sven deemed necessary.

Sneaking one last long look around the place that had become a home to them, Jaden stiffened his spine and marched outside, his strides sure and confident, his face set with determination. Kayla and Atu wore similar expressions.

Their gliders had already expressed their own thanks and farewells and now hovered overhead, waiting for the sign their voyagers were ready to leave. Each teen solemnly shook Sven's hand and gave him another quick hug before stepping back. Then they signaled their gliders. As they completed their aerial connections and took to the heavens, they waved to Sven one last time.

Then Jaden's voice rang out, loud enough for Sven to hear as they tore down the valley. "Let the adventure begin!"

CHAPTER TWENTY-SEVEN

With difficulty, Kayla cleared the valley without a backward glance. Staring dead ahead, the boys' rigid postures as they sat astride Han showed they regretted leaving as much as she did. They too avoided what was behind, facing their destiny instead.

Unwilling to think of what was coming, Kayla dropped her gaze. The glistening snow slipping away beneath her was another reminder of what they were leaving behind. But its alluring prismatic effect was both calming and mesmerizing, and when they exited the secluded sector sheltering Sven's home from the outside world, she wasn't nearly as broody.

Nearing the spot where Sven's device had downed their gliders, Jaden tossed the map out. It unfolded around them, glowing softly. Kayla smiled as she remembered Sven's wriggling body when he'd gallantly resisted the urge to snatch the map away from Jaden so he could pick it apart.

Although desperate to unravel the map's "inner workings," Sven quashed the temptation considering the map's importance. Kayla's grin widened. *Would Sven have had willpower to resist if the blinking dot or mysterious "X" had made an appearance?* Since neither had, it was a moot point. The map had been annoyingly bland that day, showing only their current location as a static two-dimensional representation, the absent "X" a blatant, blaring message they weren't going anywhere.

Today's map was a stark contrast. Their guiding "X," amidst its constantly shifting lines, had magically materialized, although it was virtually hidden at the center of the lines fading toward it. But it was undeniably there, providing them with a dynamic, continually updating, two-dimensional image as it guided them onward.

Jaden grunted.

"What?" Kayla asked.

"You don't think it's strange the 'X' has magically re-appeared?"

"Not really. Isn't that what it's supposed to do?"

"Yeah, but think about the changes to the map in conjunction with what Zareh said about us staying at Sven's 'for as long as he could allow.' Do you think Zareh somehow controls the map?"

"Interesting question," Atu said.

Kayla nodded at the map. "Looks like we're heading south again."

"Yay! Where the sun has heat attached to its light," Jaden said.

"What? You didn't like my lotion?" Atu teased.

"No, dude. No offense—it's great. But give me warmth any day over the cold!"

Kayla grinned. "Wimp!"

"Yeah, he's not a man for lotion," Atu commented.

Their playful banter picked up as their spirits lifted. Even the ground under them relented, thawing to greener pastures when the craggy mountains dourly gave way to steep, earthy mounds. They flattened into marshy fields with waving reedy grasses, interspersed by exuberant, colorful wildflowers.

Since their gliders were no longer hindered by slow speeds, the amount of terrain they crossed increased exponentially. The soft, sodden ground literally dried before their eyes as they sped over it, replaced by endless cultivated land.

When they stopped for a late lunch in an untenured field, far from any signs of civilization, the faded lines on the map were already separating out, and both the lines and "X" were notably brighter.

"We should be there by tomorrow at this rate," Atu ventured.

"I agree," Jaden said, taking another enormous bite out of his sandwich.

Kayla sighed. "I wonder what we'll find."

"Nothing that'll surprise you, I'm sure," Taz said. "Your training is far more comprehensive than any of the previous voyagers. Because of that, you're more prepared than any of them ever were."

Kayla sent Taz an appreciative smile. Their initial prickliness had transformed into a deep respect and mutual understanding. The more time they spent together, the fonder Kayla grew of Taz. Kayla no longer worried about their mission; they would either succeed, or they would not. Instead, she worried about Taz's safety.

She, Jaden, and Atu had the gliders to protect them while they flew. But the gliders had no such luxury. They were at the forefront of any attack. Kayla could only hope all the hours they had spent practicing their routines were enough to keep their gliders safe.

With lunch over, they resumed their journey, only stopping again in another remote field when the light drained from the sky. As they descended, Jaden stowed the map, a simplified version of the morning's map. Most of the dense lines had fallen away, leaving something akin to an enlarged section of the original central area.

None of them wasted time obsessing over the changes. Immediately after dinner, Kayla and the boys crept into their sleeping shells, resolute and unanimous in their desire to get a decent rest. They were all certain they would face another challenge before the sun went down the following day.

The next morning, Kayla rose, refreshed and ready for whatever they might encounter. Her enthusiasm soon dwindled with the morning's monotonous flight. The increasingly boring landscape exacerbated the uneventful hours in the air. The farms and well-tended acreages thinned out, replaced by bare earth and scattered fragmented rocks. Small at first and in erratically clumped groups, the rocks became larger and more prolific the further south they flew. Adding to the tedium was the unbearable heat. Unlike the cold, crisp air of the mountains, this air was dead and dry, sucking the life from them. Even their gliders grew lethargic as the sun reached its zenith.

Spotting a patch of shade beyond a large rock, Kayla begged for a break. "Please, can we stop there? I need food and a siesta!"

"Hear, hear!" Atu agreed.

"Yes, that sounds rather pleasant," Taz murmured, surprising them all.

Kayla caught the weariness in her voice and felt guilty she hadn't suggested they stop earlier. Without a doubt, their gliders must be tired. They were doing all the work!

The gliders descended, circling the rare shady area for signs of danger. Observing nothing amiss, the teens dismounted and moved aside, allowing their gliders space to land as they assessed the shade. It was sorely inadequate for a party their size.

Determined to make it work, Jaden proposed letting the gliders use the shade from the rock whilst the teens created a second shaded area by stringing their sleeping shells from another side of the rock. The teens soon sat cross-legged under the makeshift shelter's protection, greedily slurping water after having first offered some to their gliders. Their thirst quenched, the teens attacked the dried fruit, nuts, and hard biscuits constituting their lunch.

"While these snacks may be nutritious, they don't feel like real food," Jaden said.

Kayla sent him a sidelong glance. "Missing your sandwiches and pizza?"

"If only you knew," Jaden grumbled.

Lunch dispensed with, Kayla flopped onto her back, the boys following her example. With the sun baking down and the air so still, it felt hotter than it really was. Kayla wriggled, trying to find a spot that wasn't so stony.

"Settle," Jaden murmured, his voice heavy with impending sleep.

"I can't find a comfortable place for my head."

Jaden opened one eye and looked at her. "Here, turn this way," he said, motioning with his hand for her to lie perpendicular to him.

Kayla did, startled when he inched closer and eased her head onto his stomach. But she didn't complain, and she wasn't about to back away either. Lying there felt so right. In fact, it was sublime. Much better than the hard ground. And the contact with Jaden calmed her jittery senses. Kayla finally relaxed and lay still.

They dozed, the heat making lazy waves over them. They must've slept because when they finally roused themselves, the sun was midway across the afternoon sky, only a few hours from its own bed.

Rising, the teens stretched, working the worst of the kinks from their necks and shoulders. The heat remained suffocating, but the bats had adjusted. They were bouncing around like jumping beans, eager to be on their way.

"Seems we needed the rest more than you did," Kayla remarked as she and Taz took to the air.

Taz smiled back over her shoulder at Kayla. "We prefer the heat. It just took a while to adjust after all that cold mountain air."

At her mention of cold air, Kayla realized the air up here was blissfully cooler than on the baked desert floor, and she sucked down deep lungfuls, her energy levels rising with each breath. Glancing at the boys, Kayla found them savoring the cooler breeze too.

"Feels great, doesn't it?" Kayla called to them.

"It sure does!" Jaden shouted back.

Circling their resting spot, their gliders checked their course against the map before shooting away like rockets. The sudden burst of speed sent a boost of adrenaline pumping through Kayla's veins. If she hadn't been awake before, she was now. Even the gliders exuded a restless energy, as if pulled forward by some unseen force.

The land beneath them lost all trace of dirt, the floor turning into a gravelly layer of pebbles peeking out from gaps between the rocks. The rocks themselves merged into thick, co-joined slabs of uneven, toothed rock, rearing higher and higher. A corroded effect was the visual result when the canyons gouging the stony floor between these ragged giants plunged progressively deeper.

Strange conical rock formations with hollow centers soon appeared on the sides of the jagged slabs, like popped pimples on rough skin. Barely two feet high at first, they rapidly grew in stature until they overcame their hosts and towered over the group, sending their gliders weaving between them to avoid crashing into the mini volcanic-shaped vents. The bizarre landscape reminded Kayla of an underwater ocean trench, except there was no water here.

Before long, the conical formations surrounded them so completely that their effect was smothering. The bats, tired of veering between them, rose so they could fly over the pockmarked land rather than through it. Lifting high enough for the raw beauty of the land to reveal itself, Taz emitted a low whistle.

"What?" Kayla demanded, aware Taz wasn't admiring the view when she caught Taz staring at a grouping of cones ahead, arranged in the shape of an octagon.

Taz didn't answer. Instead, she launched into a series of rapid squeaks and squeals Kayla had never heard before, presumably conversing with Han in what must be their native tongue. When Han replied the same way, Kayla looked at Jaden and Atu, alarmed.

"What's happening?" Kayla mouthed.

Jaden and Atu shrugged their shoulders, just as perplexed.

"They're excited about something," Atu murmured.

That much was obvious. Their gliders abruptly slowed when they reached the octagonal formation. Caught off guard, Kayla scrambled to grab any available fur to stop herself from tumbling over Taz's head. Regaining her balance, Kayla stared at the boys, dumbfounded, as their bats slowly circled the curious conical arrangement.

The gliders' twittery conversation picked up, their pitch rising as they became more animated. They gestured markedly with their heads at the tallest of the towers, their chattering continuing unabated.

"My guess is they recognize this place," Kayla said.

The boys nodded. But it was several minutes before the bats concluded their lively exchange and deigned to confirm the teens' suspicions.

"This place is familiar to us," Taz said when their jabbering ceased.

"But we aren't sure how or why," Han babbled. "Jaden, will you pull up your map, please? It may hold some clue."

Jaden obliged, the map springing up around them. But, to the glider's supreme disappointment, it was unchanged. Their gliders continued circling as they pondered the area's significance.

Kayla glanced at Jaden, but he seemed as helpless as she felt. Miserably, she waited while Taz circled until Kayla could take it no more.

"Do something!" Kayla mouthed at Jaden.

CHAPTER TWENTY-EIGHT

Jaden shrugged. He wasn't sure there was anything he *could* do. But after several minutes passed and they still hadn't left, he said, "I don't think we'll get any closer to an answer by staying. And the sun travels its path. Shouldn't we move on?"

Reluctantly, the gliders agreed. There was no doubt their failure to identify the reason for their attraction to the area unsettled them. Quiet and withdrawn as they resumed their journey, they didn't fly as fast as before. In fact, their pace was downright sedentary. Jaden considered saying something but vetoed the idea. The area had made an impression on them, and they appeared absorbed in their own thoughts and memories as they tried unraveling the mystery.

The strange formation was scarcely behind them when Jaden felt the telltale chill at the back of his neck. His head whipped around, his eyes meeting Kayla's. She felt it too. *Bam!* A Gaptor cut across their path. Jaden inhaled sharply. Instinctively, he backed away from the threat, bashing his head on Atu's cheekbone.

"Ow! Steady on!" Atu warned.

Jaden ignored him. He eyed the Gaptor as it blasted past, disappearing off to his right. Then he blinked. The Gaptor was heading back to them. *How did it change direction so fast?* His brain churned sluggishly, computing the conflicting variables. His eyes, scanning the skies, picked up on the anomaly. There was a second Gaptor! And before he comprehended that fact, a third sliced up in front of them. *Blast! Slurpy's found a way to send more Gaptors through.*

"Two!" Jaden yelled, hoping Taz and Kayla understood.

They did. Jaden breathed again when the girls shot off laterally. The gliders snapped out of their slump. Han responded to Jaden's command as quickly as Taz, tucking his wings and plunging them downward. A cone speared up, threatening to impale them, and Han unfurled his wings, taking evasive action. They skimmed past the vent, missing it by less than an eighth of an inch, then straightened out. Han wasted no time increasing their speed. Jaden scanned for the girls.

"They're ahead of us," Atu said, pointing to them, racing on a parallel course above.

"Perfect! Could you tell how many Gaptors there were?"

"I only saw three, but that doesn't mean there aren't more."

"Let's hope there aren't. Han, can we outrun these beasts?"

"Yes, provided we don't have to outpace them for long. If they persist in pursuit and we can't lose them in the canyons or find a suitable hiding place, we might be in trouble."

Jaden swiveled, wanting to assess how far back the Gaptors were. He couldn't find them. But that didn't mean they weren't there. Something hurtled up from below. Teeth snapped, snatching his attention. Jaden gasped, horrified.

Dropping back down from its leap was a rat gigantic enough to be mistaken for a horse. Its hind legs were exaggerated—long limbs with powerful haunches designed for jumping. *What sort of abomination is this?* It hopped behind them disturbingly fast, sniffing the air, verifying their position. When it lifted its head, it bared its six-inch, spear-like, yellowed teeth in a snarl.

Jaden gagged. "What is that thing?"

"A kangaroo rat?" Han supplied, chuckling at his own joke.

"Hilarious! Kangaroo rats don't look like that, and they aren't that size!"

"Not where I'm from either." Atu dug his fingers into Jaden's arm as they veered wildly around another obstacle.

Before Jaden could revive his line of questioning, something else caught his eye. Slinking around the vent they had just avoided was a mechanical snake, the size of a giant anaconda. But, instead of millions of tiny scales, this one had singular, hefty, c-shaped scales, each one twice the size of his hand. Their surfaces shimmered with a polished, steely brilliance, the scaly partitions lifting, flattening, and then dropping as the serpent slithered forward. Sickened, Jaden watched as the snake rounded on the unsuspecting rat and gobbled him up in one bite.

"Ugh, that's gross!" Jaden exclaimed.

"At least it ate the rat and wasn't after us," Atu said. "What's with this place and these grossly oversized, unnatural creatures?"

Jaden wished Atu hadn't asked. An unbelievably hairy, fire-engine red spider clung to the side of an upcoming vent. It would've been fine if the spider's hair was actually hair and not sparking, electrified wires sticking out of its body, or if it wasn't the size of a beach umbrella!

Its bulbous body hugged the steep shaft effortlessly, and the silvery liquid filling its abdomen glinted portentously. The monster lifted its abdomen and spewed a thin strand of silk from its spinnerets. Only it wasn't silk. It was high-tensile steel, thicker and stronger than any cable. It whipped in front of them, cracking the air as it attached to a cone opposite the spider. If Han hadn't reacted so swiftly, it would've sliced their heads off.

"Better watch out for webs," Atu said. "We wouldn't want to fly into one of those."

"Maybe lifting out of this valley is a better option?" Jaden asked.

Han obliged. Up here, catching up to the girls was easier. Drawing alongside, Jaden glanced back again, hoping to spot the Gaptors. But there was still no sign of them.

"Are you alright?" Kayla squeaked, her lips drawn in a thin, tight line. "We saw those mutant creatures down there—what were they?" Kayla asked when Jaden didn't answer her first question.

"We're fine, thanks," Jaden answered, eager to smooth the worry from her face. "And mutants about sums up what I can say about those creatures."

"They're deformed versions of themselves, like something's corrupted them," Atu remarked thoughtfully.

Jaden caught the meaningful glance passing between their gliders. Neither Kayla nor Atu noticed, apparently too preoccupied with thoughts of the mutants to pay attention to much else. That changed when a mammoth structure sprang up on the horizon, rising suddenly and noticeably above the rest of the landscape, clearly not part of the natural environment. It was impossible to ignore.

"What is that?" Jaden marveled, forgetting to ask the bats about what he'd witnessed.

"I don't know," Kayla said.

"I have a feeling that's where the map's leading us." Jaden threw the map out and proved himself right.

Their two-dimensional map with its compass-like "X" was gone, replaced by a three-dimensional image of the area they were flying over. The blinking dot was back, its position corresponding to the structure. Jaden twisted the map back into its compartment as they surged forward.

Before they could celebrate, a Gaptor blocked their path. Automatically falling into rolls that separated them, the gliders dove toward the canyon floor. The uneven landscape was advantageous. The Gaptor faltered for an instant as it chose its prey, then it darted after the boys.

With one eye on the beast and one eye on the girls, Jaden gave the signal. Kayla flashed a thumbs-up, accepting the play, and the game was on. This configuration relied on the Gaptor maintaining its lower altitude while chasing the boys, allowing the girls to take up a position above and behind, placing the Gaptor within range of the relic stones' power.

The play took less than a minute to execute. The girls were overhead and lined up before the boys felt any pressure. Jaden waited, sure the Gaptor would sense their offensive and curl away, but it continued its dogged pursuit. The girls dropped, and Kayla lifted her arm. Jaden did likewise. In a brilliant flash and with a thunderous sound, the Gaptor disintegrated.

"That was almost too easy," Jaden muttered.

"Take the win, bro—" Atu began.

Three more Gaptors materialized in front of them, cutting off the rest of his sentence.

"You were saying?" Jaden said.

"Never mind! How do they keep doing that? They're not there, then they are!" Atu seethed.

"That's irrelevant," Han snarled, frustration coloring his tone. "We need to find cover!"

The girls must've reached the same conclusion.

"Head for the ruins!" Kayla yelled, as she and Taz nimbly ducked under the imposing barrier of Gaptors ahead of them.

Han, guessing the Gaptors would expect him to make the same move, went over instead of under. The monsters' wings faltered as they passed, confirming they had been ready to drop. The creatures struggled to realign themselves so they could give chase. Jaden smiled. Although fearsome adversaries for strength, they lacked mental acuity.

Drawing level with the girls, who had held back in case the boys ran into trouble, Han and Taz put on the speed necessary to outpace the Gaptors.

The structure loomed larger, the ruined remnants of a once magnificent edifice, some finer details now visible. What Jaden had initially taken to be smooth sides were in fact stepped ridges, reminding him of the ancient pyramids.

Unlike those fabled structures, though, these ruins displayed two major variations: most notably, the structure did not rise to a triangular apex, and there were many openings along the vertical sides, serving as multiple entry points.

Shaped like a crescent moon, the structure rose in both height and width from each of the two pointed ends until it reached its apex at the center of the outer curve. Here, tapered edges rose, forming a thin ridge that climbed to a lone lanky tower. Stretching up into the sky like a skinny finger, the tower beckoned.

"What's the bet that whatever we have to find, it's in the tower?" Jaden predicted.

Atu grinned. "A wager I'd be willing to take if I were a betting man."

But there was no time to validate their theory. With the Gaptors still pursuing, their small group raced toward the tower, the distance between the two groups gradually increasing. Closing in on the tower, Jaden was dismayed to discover no obvious shelter. For one thing, the tower was too narrow to accommodate their gliders. For another, the entrances, although many, would barely allow the voyagers to pass through, let alone their massive companions.

"We must find another way in," Jaden thundered, stating the obvious.

"There might be a wider entrance lower down where there's more space," Kayla hollered back.

Without questioning the suggestion, their gliders tucked their wings and dropped on the far side of the crescent, along its inner curve, away from the pursuing Gaptors. Skirting the lower levels, they reduced their speed.

"There!" Jaden pointed at an entrance considerably larger than the others, about two floors off the ground in the middle of the structure with a ramp leading up to it.

Han and Taz adjusted their course. To their surprise, the entrance allowed them to coast right in without having to dismount or land beforehand. As the gliders settled on the stone floor, the teens leaped off and turned back toward the entrance, ready to face any pursuing Gaptors. But there were none. In fact, when Jaden cautiously poked his head outside and scanned the sky above, they weren't there either.

"Where are they?" Jaden muttered. His brain ran probabilities on the most likely strategies the Gaptors would use. "Do you think they entered on the other side?"

"It's possible, but why would they? They have the advantage in the air," Kayla pointed out.

"That's what we've always assumed," Jaden said. "We've never seen them fight on the ground before. Maybe they're just as dangerous."

"No, Kayla's right. The air is their preferred battleground," Taz confirmed. "They avoid ground combat. Their cumbersome frames are too large a target."

"Great! So where are they then?" Jaden repeated.

Atu and Kayla stepped up beside him, craning their necks. Atu spotted them.

"There!" Atu said, pointing out three specks in the distance.

"Why are they so far away? I didn't think we had that much of a head start," Jaden said, worried.

"We didn't," Han replied.

Eyeing the Gaptors warily, Jaden noticed the beasts came no closer.

"Something's keeping them back," Taz eventually decided. "Watch —there's some line they can't cross. As soon as they fly into it, they're thrown upward by some vertical force."

Kayla scrunched up her eyes. "Must be your bat vision. I can't see that!"

Han chuckled. "I thought bats were supposedly blind in your world."

"Well, you're not exactly from our world, now are you?" Kayla countered. "It's possible super-sized bats have super-enhanced vision!"

Han laughed out loud, the sounds rumbling through the air melodically.

But Kayla's words reminded Jaden of something. He snapped his fingers. "Hey, remember Sven added magnification and night vision capabilities to our goggles? Try that!"

The teens quickly engaged their goggles manually, pressing on the tiny magnification button the moment it covered their eyes. The Gaptors' frames invaded their view, larger than life. The teens could finally see for themselves.

Using varying tactics, the Gaptors stormed the invisible barrier, only to be thwarted the moment they reached it. Usually, they were tossed upward, but occasionally, they nose-dived—much to the teens' delight.

"Well, we're safe for now," Jaden decreed after a few minutes. "Let's not waste the advantage. Time to find our treasure!"

CHAPTER TWENTY-NINE

The entrance kept its roomy dimensions as the gliders and teens moved deeper into the structure. Kayla marveled at the elegant proportions, the intricately carved stone sculptures adorning the entryway, and the unbelievable scale of the building.

Unable to contain her amazement, she voiced her thoughts. "How on earth did they build something like this so long ago without modern engineering or heavy equipment?"

"Pyramids give you a clue?" Atu grinned.

Kayla rolled her eyes. "Smart aleck! That doesn't answer the question. Doesn't it fry your brain thinking about how they accomplished this? It must've taken decades to complete. How did they keep the dimensions straight? I mean, you saw how perfectly shaped it was from the air . . ."

"Come and look at this," Jaden interrupted.

Kayla and Atu strode to him, a short way from the entrance. Late afternoon sunlight slanted in, illuminating the walls. Jaden directed their attention to the faded symbols and badly eroded markings etched on one of the side walls. "What do you make of these?"

Kayla studied them, then shimmied over to the opposite wall in what was turning out to be a long, rectangular tunnel leading away from the entrance. "I don't know, but someone painted pictures over here."

"Maybe a history?" Atu suggested, staring at the symbols and carvings as Jaden passed Kayla and disappeared further down the tunnel.

"Mmm, could be," Kayla agreed, crossing back to Atu. "But I think they're more than that." She ran her fingers over the worn carvings and symbols. "There seems to something missing here," Kayla murmured, half to herself.

Jaden's sharp cry had them jerking their heads. They ran toward the sound but couldn't locate him in the growing gloom.

"Jaden, are you okay?" Kayla blurted, her heart in her mouth, anxiety curling through her gut. *Where is he? Why is it so dark in here?* She had to find him. Before her growing concerns could spiral, Jaden grunted.

"Yeah, I'm alright, but watch out for the yawning hole in the floor as you exit the tunnel. I almost fell in. You'd think they'd have some warning if the floor was going to just open up under you!"

"Maybe that's what those markings on the wall were," Han suggested as the rest of them crept forward.

"Yeah, yeah, funny boy," Jaden said. "Fine for you—you can see in the dark."

"There are stairs going up as well," Atu commented, ignoring Han and Jaden.

Jaden huffed. "And how would you know that? I can't even see my hand in front of my face."

"Uh, weren't you the one who reminded us not five minutes ago of our night vision goggles?" Atu chuckled.

Kayla heard Jaden's goggles click just as hers did. She wasn't the only one who hadn't thought to engage the feature.

"Ah, much better!" Kayla sighed, even more relieved when she saw Jaden in front of her, whole and healthy with no apparent signs of injury. Unable to resist, she gripped his hand, not daring speech for fear her voice would betray her emotions. Jaden turned and looked at her, smiling faintly as he squeezed her hand. *Oh, I'm so happy to see that smile!*

Not releasing her hand, Jaden lifted his head and admired the room they found themselves in. If that was even a term they could use. "Wow! Magnificent!"

Awestruck, they gawked at the impressive reception area. The tunnel had opened into an enormous, round rotunda. On the far side, a long, imposing hallway marched off into the distance, crafted by the skilled placement of two parallel lines of elegant Grecian-style pillars.

At the far end of this hallway, barely visible, were two enormous stone chairs resembling thrones. Exits dotted the length of the hallway at regular intervals, hinting at other, lesser rooms off to the sides.

Above them, a domed ceiling capped the rotunda. It was staggeringly high, centered over a wide stone staircase winding upward, its broad, sturdy handrails impossibly set on dainty, curled posts. Walkways drifted off the central staircase in several directions on each level above, creating a crisscross effect. Stone-carved handrails protected the illusionary floating pathways on either side.

In stark contrast, the stairs leading down, at the base of those leading up and directly in front of them, had no such restrictive barriers. They plunged into a hefty square cut deep into the thick, polished floor, giving no warning of impending disaster to the inattentive visitor.

"You're lucky you didn't break your neck!" Kayla scolded when she spotted the gaping hole.

"Tell me about it!" Jaden grinned, squeezing her hand a second time.

Taz was far from amused. "Voyager, this is no time for recklessness. Exercise more care! We can't lose you to something as innocuous as a hole in the floor."

Jaden had the grace to look sheepish. "Sorry. I really didn't plan on making my exit so ignominiously."

"Planned or not, you should not have moved ahead without assessing the dangers first," Taz said.

"Okay, I get it! I'll exercise more care," Jaden said, mimicking Taz. She glared at him, and Jaden squirmed under her intense gaze. "Well, now that that's settled, shall we move along?" When everyone nodded but made no move, Jaden asked, "Up or down?"

"Treasure's always buried," Atu answered. "I say we go down."

Kayla shook her head. "I don't know about that. Isn't the basement where the dungeons are in a fortress like this?"

They all laughed, but it turned out she was right. Unlike the stairs leading up which branched off to several higher levels, those descending had no such distinction. They stretched deep into the bowels of the structure, excessively far from the levels above, giving credence to Kayla's theory. Those attempting escape would've had so far to go to reach the main level, it would've drastically reduced their chances of success.

"I'm glad we left the gliders up there to watch our backs," Kayla muttered when it became clear she was right.

The air grew rank and thick, and the dank chill rising from the stone stairs crawled up her jeans. Whatever was down here was long gone or long dead. She shivered, grateful for the warmth of Jaden's hand in hers, for his body heat pulsing next to her, assuring her they were, in fact, still alive. She gripped his hand tighter, eliciting a curious glance. When she gave a wan smile and lifted a shoulder, indicating there was no actual cause for alarm, Jaden returned the smile and resumed concentrating on the descent.

Finally reaching the bottom, the stairs delivered them into a small, round room which looked like it might've been a guardroom. Neither the smashed table occupying one corner nor the several broken chairs strewn around the room gave this impression. Rather, it was the broken, barred metal gates blocking several tunnels leading off from the room.

The tunnels, arranged at regular intervals, would've resembled the spokes on a wheel if they had viewed them on a map. Interestingly, they found no sign of people, either living or dead, nor weapons of any kind.

Picking a tunnel at random, Jaden tugged Kayla behind him, then pushed on the ruined, rusted gate, cringing as it squealed open.

Gingerly, all three of them crept into the tunnel beyond until they found the first of several cells.

Rusted metal bands that had once encased solid three-inch thick doors were almost all that remained of what had once been the cell door. The remaining moldy wood crumbled away from the restraining bars of the partially open door. Glancing at one another, the teens paused before Jaden took the plunge and stepped into the room beyond, letting go of Kayla's hand.

That Jaden motioned for her to stay behind him, that he demonstrated his concern for her, took most of the bite out of Kayla's loss of contact. When he exited the room a second later, gagging, Kayla was glad she'd made no move to follow him.

"Is it as bad in there as you're making it look?" Atu asked.

"Worse." Jaden squeezed out between gritted teeth.

Atu frowned. "Surely, whoever's in there is just a skeleton?"

"It's not who's in there," Jaden clarified. "It's what."

When he didn't elaborate, Kayla had to know. "What?"

"Believe me, it's better you don't know. These people were barbaric."

Her morbid curiosity piqued, Kayla snuck past Jaden and peeked into the room. What she saw made her breath stutter.

Tarnished knives, brown with long-dried blood, lined the right wall, arranged by size and shape. Below them, a selection of menacing manacles hung, their meaty chains dangling deviously free.

Above the knives was an assortment of tools Kayla didn't recognize—some shaped like corkscrews, others wide on one end and tapering at the other. Yet others were reed-like tubes, some with curious barbed edges, others thin metal wands with ominously curved hooks at the end.

Along the left wall was an antiquated contraption: a rack with its pulleys and gears and tattered ropes. Nervously, her eyes swiveled away from the device, landing on the stone table in the middle of the room. The brittle, dried-out bones of some poor soul still covered it, the long-coagulated rivers of his blood still staining the sides of the table. Much as Kayla rarely minded blood, the implication of how it had gotten there had her backing out of the room quickly.

"It's really that terrible?" Atu asked, steadying Kayla as she bumped into him.

"Yeah, take our word for it," Kayla managed.

"That being the case, let's move on. We might find something more useful further down," Atu said.

Kayla grimaced. "Sure, but you're taking the first look at what's in the next room."

Atu paled at the thought but bravely stepped over the threshold of the following cell. When he walked back out looking puzzled, Jaden and Kayla stared, astounded.

"That didn't turn your stomach?" Jaden asked, raising his eyebrows.

"Nope. This room has 'who's and not 'what's, a few skeletons that have been there for ages. Nothing in there to turn you into a squeamish mess."

Jaden and Kayla poked their heads into the room. He was telling the truth. Although the occupants had been prisoners, their bones had long since fallen from the shackles binding them while their owners were still alive.

"Okay, so can we go now?" Kayla demanded. "I think we've established this was the hall of horrors. I doubt there's any treasure here."

Jaden sighed. "Yeah, I think you're right."

They retraced their steps, moving back up the tunnel to the base of the stairs. Taz peered at them from the opening far above.

"Find anything noteworthy?" Taz asked, her voice echoing thinly as it deflected its way down to them.

"Unless you'd call substantiating these people were irrationally cruel something worth knowing, then no, nothing noteworthy," Kayla replied.

Han's face appeared next to Taz's as he stepped in beside her. "Do you know what you're looking for?"

The teens hesitated. It was a valid question. Truthfully, they didn't know exactly what they had to find, so how would they know when they found it? It could've been down there, staring them in the face the whole time.

Correctly interpreting their perplexed expressions, Taz offered advice. "Have you consulted your map?"

"Uh, duh! No!" Jaden scowled, slapping his forehead with his hand before he hastily opened the disc.

The dot was definitely blinking much faster. And its three-dimensional placement made it abundantly clear they were headed for the tower.

"Hey, we were right," Atu said, thumping Jaden on the back.

"Told you we wouldn't find the treasure in the dungeons," Kayla groused.

"And you were right," Jaden said. "We shouldn't have taken you to the 'Hall of Horrors!'" Satisfied when a slight smile tugged at the corners of her mouth, Jaden addressed the gliders. "Are you coming up with us?"

"No, we'll follow on the outside," Taz said. "We've already ascertained the lack of suitable entrances higher up. If we find trouble, it's better if we're not trapped inside."

"But you'll be close by, right?" Kayla asked.

"Yes, we'll keep circling. We should be able to spot you at any of the openings. Just make sure you look for us from there at regular intervals, so we know where you are."

"We will. Ready?" Jaden asked Kayla and Atu.

As Kayla wound up the magnificent staircase, she saw the gliders hopping back to the entrance. When they reached the large stone landing outside, they stopped and monitored their enemies' progress. Apparently, the invisible barrier still held the Gaptors back because their gliders launched themselves into the air.

A moment later, Kayla spotted them out of one of the side openings as they circled the structure, close enough to spot the teens when they waved from the opening but not close enough to limit their flight options should they come under attack.

Inside the structure, Kayla, Jaden, and Atu traversed the levels quickly, eager to reach the tower. Unfortunately, they had to take a few detours along the way so they could keep their promise to check in with their gliders. Although the diversions were a nuisance, it gave them a sense of the structure's layout.

On the level immediately above the imposing reception room and to the immediate left and right of the stairs were what the teens initially thought were meeting rooms. What were once ornately carved chairs surrounded massive, dusty wooden tables dominating spacious rooms, alternating with rooms lined with rows of long stone benches facing a podium on one end.

However, when they moved further down the hallway and found the broken pieces of a spinning wheel and then part of a stringed musical instrument, they adjusted their thinking. Entertainment and leisure activities had apparently also happened on this level, which meant the first rooms could've been dining rooms. In the absence of other items, it was impossible to tell, and they didn't bother wasting time figuring it out.

Reaching an opening at the end of the hallway, they signaled their gliders and moved up to the second level. Smashed bed frames, hefty wooden chests that stood open where they weren't disintegrating, and an assortment of smaller pieces of wood no longer identifiable as anything recognizable amidst grotesque statues that had served some dark, decorative purpose didn't make this level too hard to figure out.

"Sleeping quarters," Jaden muttered.

"Although how they ever slept with these hideous images around them, I can't fathom." Kayla shuddered. Peeking into a squalid, tiny room alongside one of the larger rooms, she noted a rusty iron grate in the center and an almost perfectly round hole in the floor at one corner. "And this would be the bathroom!" Kayla gagged. "Thank heavens for modern plumbing!"

With that delightful thought, they crossed to the window, signaled their gliders, and pressed upward again. But the higher they went, the more uneasy Kayla felt. A slithering sense of discomfort settled over her when the functionality of the rooms changed abruptly.

Gone were the cavernous areas of the lower levels, presumably used by the nobility for meeting, greeting, entertaining, living, and sleeping. In their stead, tiny, chilly rooms crowded the upper levels. The outside light was restricted, although the setting sun's rays were practically perpendicular to the vertical slits serving as openings.

Kayla shivered. She didn't want to imagine how dark it could get in here at night. Musty air, so thick it was suffocating, blanketed them. These areas were purely for work. A ribbed iron washboard in one room, rusted iron buckets in another, and a vast, grimy kitchen taking up an entire level all supported this idea.

Then they reached the levels which must've housed the servants. The slits serving as openings to the outside were narrower, allowing even less light in. The teens re-engaged their night vision goggles. That was a mistake. Row upon row of alcoves pitted the bare stone walls lining the narrow hallway, each one scarcely large enough to accommodate a person.

The teens stared at one another, aghast, as they put it together. These tiny alcoves were where the servants had lived. Not only had their owners crammed these people in here tighter than sardines in a can—they had left them no space to call their own, deprived them of any privacy, any humanity.

Without thinking, Kayla moved, backing into Jaden. But she didn't step away from him. Rather, she leaned into him. Just having him there, pressed against her back, calmed her. Relief coursed through her when his arms wrapped around her. His hands slid down her arms to cover her own; his touch brought warmth that chased away the chill invading her bones. They stayed touching for only a moment, taking comfort from each other before Jaden sighed and stepped back. They had to move on.

Eschewing the ranks of berths taking up three full levels, the teens scurried upward, fleeing like rats from a sinking ship, not pausing even once to signal their gliders. Escaping the horror, they reached a level devoid of interior walls. The floor was a wide, open space with multiple slitted openings lining the exterior walls.

Although the sun had almost set, the sudden light after all the gloom was almost blinding. Groping for the nearest opening, they reached out and waved to their gliders, then sagged against the wall, breathing hard. As their eyes adjusted, they faced a new puzzle. The bones of long-dead animals littered the floor, carcasses of differing sizes and shapes.

"Why would they have animals up here?" Atu wondered, pushing himself up so he could inspect the bones. "It makes no sense. How would they have fed them?"

Jaden and Kayla similarly rose to their feet, all three teens inspecting the room for feeding troughs. But they found none. Not wanting to linger, they moved up. A shoulder-high wall that didn't quite reach the sides separated the next room into two spacious halves. On this wall, they found the markings. And this time, they were legible.

Kayla rushed over and examined the markings. Loosing an excited squeal, she dropped to the floor, flung her backpack open, and scratched around for a piece of paper and a pen, never taking her eyes from the wall. The boys watched her curiously, wondering what she was up to. But she plunked herself down on the floor and began scribbling, too excited to give them an explanation.

CHAPTER THIRTY

Jaden glanced at Atu, perplexed.

"What's she doing?" Atu asked.

"Not the foggiest," Jaden responded.

Sauntering over to where Kayla sat cross-legged, Jaden peeked over her shoulder. As best he could figure, she was copying the symbols from the wall into her notebook. More confusing was the way she was underlining some symbols and crossing others out.

Jaden cleared his throat. "Care to tell us what you're doing?"

"Shh, I almost have it!"

Annoyed by Kayla's shushing, Jaden frowned. He glanced at Atu, but his friend shrugged, just as mystified. Eager to get going again, Jaden waited impatiently before he began pacing. A sense of urgency rose in him like a tidal wave. Nervous energy surged through him. When he couldn't contain it any longer, he spat it out. "Kayla, we have to go! I feel like we're running out of time."

Kayla stopped her frantic scratching and studied him. "A *feeling* feeling or just a feeling?"

"A *feeling* feeling," Jaden hissed. "It's these walls, the carvings, those statues we passed on the way up. Something's wrong with this place."

Kayla nodded. "You're right."

"Why do you say that?" Atu asked.

"Well, these markings for one," Kayla replied. "I know what they mean."

"What?" Jaden and Atu exclaimed.

"No need to get so excited." Kayla smirked.

Jaden rounded on her. "How do you know what they mean?"

"Did you forget my talent is linguistics?" Kayla sighed, before steadying herself and explaining. "This is an old language. In fact, it's so archaic it's almost extinct. It's difficult to learn because, frankly, the materials available for learning it are rare. Now that I say that aloud, that should've given me a clue because my grandmother was one of the few people who had books teaching it."

"Your grandmother?" Jaden was more confused than ever.

Kayla waved a dismissive hand. "But that was all so long ago, and I was still so young . . . how was I to know? Regardless, the moment Grammy heard my talent was linguistics, she insisted I study it. I remember being mad with my mom because I couldn't believe she backed up Grammy's demand. But Grammy must've somehow known I would need it someday," Kayla murmured pensively.

"Okay, that's creepy," Atu admitted.

"Yeah, weird and all, but are you almost done?" Jaden demanded.

"Almost. I'll hurry. I'd say we could go, except, from what I have so far, I think the message is important."

Jaden shrugged. "If you say so. Just be quick about it. I'll sneak a peek outside and let the gliders know we're still okay."

Hurrying to the nearest opening, Jaden didn't spot the gliders. He skimmed the darkening skies. *Where are they?* They had to be on the other side of the structure. Aggravated, Jaden waited, giving the gliders a few moments to finish their circuit and make their way back around. Five minutes later, he got worried. Sprinting over to the openings on the far side of the room, he peered into the deepening gloom. They weren't there either.

Atu, noticing Jaden's barely concealed tension, asked, "What's wrong?"

"I can't find the gliders."

"You sure you didn't just catch them on the other side?"

"Yes! They should've come around by now."

"Chill, bro." Atu raised both hands and let them drop in a calming motion. "Stay there on the east side. I'll take the west. I'm sure we'll find them."

But they didn't. The gliders were gone. Apprehensive, Jaden risked stepping out onto the tiny balcony of the strange room. Craning his neck around the curve as far as he could, he still couldn't locate the gliders. Just as he was considering going back down, he spotted them, streaking toward him like their lives depended on it. Jaden's eyes darted past them, searching for pursuing Gaptors. But he saw none.

"Hurry!" Taz yelled as soon as they were within earshot.

"Why?" Jaden shouted, his sense of urgency spiraling out of control.

"No time to explain—just get to the tower as fast as you can. Don't waste time checking in on each level. We'll meet you there!"

Then she and Han dashed away. Jaden spun around. Kayla and Atu were staring. "You two get that?"

"Sure did." Atu loped back to where Kayla squatted.

"Packing up," Kayla muttered, stuffing her pen and notebook into her backpack.

"Did you finish?" Jaden asked as he joined them.

"I wrote it all down but didn't have time to finish decoding."

Jaden nodded, then took the lead as they raced up the stairs.

They barely registered the next level, split into tiny rooms with barred gates blocking each entrance, eerily reminiscent of the dismal cells they'd seen in the dungeons. Or that the next level had more rooms, larger and missing the iron gates, with more plentiful openings along the sides which granted more air and light.

But as they hurtled up, Jaden realized two things: first, the openings to the outside were becoming more plentiful; second, the number of rooms on each level was diminishing. In fact, the level they had just passed only had three rooms, all opening into each other.

Even though the openings along the sides were too small to allow the Gaptors access into the tower, they could still reach into the room with their stingers if they clung onto the walls outside. Jaden shuddered, remembering the terrible talons at both Horatio's store and the storage unit.

Jaden was so absorbed in the memories, he came up short when the stairs dumped them in a triangular room at the very top of the tower. They had arrived.

Jaden glanced out the large opening directly in front of them, perfectly situated in the center of one side of the triangle. The sun was just leaning down to kiss the horizon. Almost twilight, prime time for Gaptor attacks. His spirits dropped with the sun as he confirmed his fears. The Gaptors had multiplied while they were inside the tower. Although still restrained by the invisible barrier, Jaden now understood their gliders' concern.

"So that's why we had to hurry," Kayla commented, coming up behind him and following his gaze.

"No doubt. Let's find what we have to find and get out of here."

They scrambled over to an ostentatious table. But when they got there and spotted the blood dried in lines down the fluted pillars supporting the flat stone top, the long-congealed black pools on the floor, and the blackened, dried blood spatter on the walls closest to the table, they recognized it for what it was. An altar. Not just any altar—an altar used for sacrifice.

Jaden immediately turned to Kayla. She looked like she was trying to convince herself they had only sacrificed the animals occupying the floor a few levels down. But the barred gates on the rooms in the level above the animals told her otherwise. They had also sacrificed humans here. She heaved.

Grabbing her hand to give her moral support, Jaden tried joking. "Ugh! You'd think they would've cleaned up their mess!"

Kayla only stared. His attempt at humor wasn't helping. She gulped, swaying where she stood.

Can she handle the gruesome truth? Concerned for her wellbeing, Jaden steadied her by holding her arms, gratified when she sent him a weak smile. Sensing her rising agitation, he murmured, "What do you need?"

"Fresh air."

Her voice was barely recognizable. Kayla all but fell against him when Jaden pulled her closer and helped her to the opening in the wall near the altar. For the third time since they entered the temple, Kayla had not backed away from physical contact. *Maybe she's finally coming around.*

Kayla sucked in deep, refreshing breaths of air. Gradually, her serenity returned, and Jaden saw her eyes focus, allowing her to assimilate what she was seeing. He followed her gaze.

The altar, somehow half-in and half-out of the room, was strategically placed in full view of the extensive courtyard nestled far below, between the points of the crescent. Baffled why he still felt like he was inside, Jaden looked up and took in the generous overhang protecting the altar.

Kayla swayed next to him, giddy again from looking up too. Lowering her head, she pressed into Jaden more closely.

Perhaps I shouldn't be too quick to make assumptions. Maybe she just needs my support. It's a pretty scary place after all. Sighing, Jaden continued studying his surroundings. To the right and left of the altar, a balcony circled the tower like a widow's walk. Tucked away and half hidden in the shadows between the overhang and the outer corners of the triangle on the far side of the altar was a ladder, disappearing upward through a hole in the overhang.

Kayla glanced back at Atu, still standing in the room. She stiffened beside him.

"Boys, look!" Kayla whispered, gesturing with the hand that wasn't scratching her arm.

They did. And they saw it, too. Carved into the gray flagstone floor was the unmistakable semblance of the medallion.

CHAPTER THIRTY-ONE

Jaden whistled. "Well, if that doesn't validate we're in the right place, I don't know what will. Should we confirm it?"

Kayla allowed Jaden to lead her back to the medallion, smiling when he only let go of her once he was sure she could stand unaided. Then Jaden hurriedly retrieved the disc, his fingers flying as he worked the opening sequence.

Sure enough, when the map bounced up, the dot was blinking so rapidly it confirmed they were practically on top of whatever the map was leading them to. Taking their cues from the dot's altered tempo depending on the direction in which they traveled, they ended up on the image of the medallion itself. No big surprise.

There, the dot stopped flashing and started glowing. Kayla glanced down expectantly. But she found only the engraved feather, albeit a magnified version of the one on their medallions. Convinced she was missing something, Kayla fell to her knees, the boys joining her as they frenetically ran their hands over the carving.

"There has to be a lever or button or something!" Kayla mumbled. "Perhaps hidden in the dips and dents?"

But search as they might, they came up empty handed.

"Maybe we have to dig again like we did to find the relic stone?" Kayla offered.

Jaden frowned. "How would we dig through two feet of stone? Unless you have a pickax or laser or perhaps some explosives hidden in your backpack I'm unaware of?"

"No need to get snippy." Kayla bristled. "There must be something here that can help us. The shovel was there on top of the hill. The only reason we didn't find it sooner was because we didn't know to look for it. So, let's look for something. Perhaps whatever will get us under the stone is somewhere close."

Jaden scowled. "Have you looked outside? The number of Gaptors is only increasing. We don't have time!"

"Calm down," Kayla hissed, her own temper rising. "We won't make any progress if we run around in circles shouting the sky is falling!"

Atu stepped in. "Bro, Kayla's right. Walk it off. Take a breath. Then open your mind. Kayla's always talking about those feelings of yours —use them. What are those feelings telling you to do?"

From the glare Jaden gave Atu, Kayla could tell he wasn't in the mood for anything except ranting. She watched as he stomped back and forth between the altar and his friends and then the altar and the entry to the room, from one opening to the next, trying to calm himself enough to focus.

Jaden's temper was barely contained when he stalked back to the medallion. His foot skidded on the rim outlining the shape, and his fretful movements stilled. He stared at the medallion.

"What?" Kayla breathed, sure he had figured something out.

Instead of answering, Jaden lifted a finger in the air and then leaned down and inspected the outline. His fingers traced something running around the thin rim: the faint line of runes, remarkably similar to those on the walls earlier. He grinned up at her. "Kayla, you need to decode that message!"

Relieved he seemed to have come to his senses, Kayla smacked her fingers to her head in a mock salute. "Yes, sir!"

Dropping her backpack, Kayla snatched up her notebook and

pencil. Trying to ignore her surroundings, she sat on the floor and worked on the translation. Within seconds, she forgot where she was, her entire being concentrated on applying what she had learned under duress all those years ago.

Jaden stalked back to the opening that overlooked the courtyard, muttering, "Well, doesn't this just give an excellent view of that growing crowd of Gaptors lurking beyond the barrier?"

"More and more," Atu mumbled. "The Usurper must've found a way to get them back here."

"Unfortunately, I have to agree with you. On the bright side, it seems they're only coming through one at a time."

"More like a few at a time," Atu corrected, "judging by their numbers."

"No, I think it's only one at a time. I count ten now, which means at least six have come through in the last thirty minutes, so about one every five minutes."

"Why would they only come through one at a time?"

"Perhaps Slurpy can't get the door open wide enough or long enough for more than one Gaptor."

Atu chuckled. "You're really going to keep calling him that even though the gliders warned you not to?"

"It made you laugh, didn't it? Come up with a better name and I'll use it."

"How about Terminator?" Atu suggested, warming up to the game.

"Nah, too cliché."

"Hitler?"

"Nope. We need something that describes him better."

"You sure it's a him? Maybe it's a her, and we can call her Damianca or something like that!"

Jaden laughed. "Since we don't know if Slurpy's male or female, maybe we should go with something more generic, like Doom."

Atu tilted his head to the side, considering. Then he grinned. "I like it. Especially if it means we can call the Gaptors the 'Dogs of Doom.'"

Jaden guffawed. "As in *dog* decimator," he sputtered.

"Yeah." Atu snickered. "You got it!"

Kayla scowled. "I know you're having fun and all, but can you keep it down?"

"Sorry," Atu mumbled, doing his best to control his mirth with little success.

Jaden was having the same problem. Kayla tossed her hair. They were like two naughty schoolboys! The more they tried to rein it in, the more they laughed. It *was* good to hear Jaden laughing, though. It felt like an age since they'd truly had something to laugh about.

Much as Kayla wanted to soak in the view and watch his face relaxing into that amazing smile, she had work to do. She shut the sound out and continued translating. It seemed only a second later when Jaden marched back to her.

"Anything Atu and I can do to help?"

"Hmm, just a moment. I almost have it," Kayla mumbled through the pencil clutched between her teeth. "Yes!" Her shout of triumph startled both boys. She beamed. "Ready to hear what it says?"

"Well, don't keep us guessing." Atu smiled as he joined them.

Kayla handed them the notebook. On it she had written:

Light the sacrificial fire
Hide the object of desire
Up the side and out
Do not act in doubt
Not what you see with your eyes
Your heart will not tell you lies
Not if you believe
But when you believe
Stop the world from turning
Stop the boy from burning

"Stop the boy from burning?" Jaden repeated, reading the last sentence aloud. "That definitely doesn't sound good."

"As usual, you have a talent for stating the obvious," Kayla said, rolling her eyes. "What do you think the whole thing means?"

"That this is a temple, and they hid something valuable here?" Atu speculated.

"Yes, and?" Kayla prompted.

"That we need to believe?" Jaden guessed.

Kayla blew out an exasperated sigh. "How about the third sentence?" When they still looked confused, she said, "That maybe this time we should go up instead of down?"

The boys gazed at her finger, pointing upward. Then they understood. Immediately above the spot where the dot glowed was the pinnacle of the tower.

"Oh, 'Up the side and out,'" Jaden mouthed. "You think we should climb that ladder up through the overhang?"

"Finally! The boy gets it." Kayla applauded. "And since you're the best climber I know, I vote you go."

"But what am I supposed to do when I get up there?"

"I don't know. The message gives no clues. You'll have to make it up as you go along."

"Well, I'm not climbing up there without air support. I'll get Han to cover me."

Kayla couldn't hide her relief, extinguishing the trepidation she instantly felt about him being out there, all alone, so high up. Trying to cover it, Kayla teased, "Ah, heeding Taz's advice about caution? She will be pleased." Jaden's mouth smiled at her, but were his eyes telling her he knew she was saying something different? Kayla turned away. They couldn't deal with this now. They had to find what they had come for. "Well, what are we waiting for?"

The trio scuttled over to the ladder. Before they reached it, they spotted their gliders racing toward them. Not far behind, the horde of Gaptors previously assembled at the barrier now pursued them—a black, seething, impenetrable mass.

Kayla wailed. "How did they get through the barrier?"

"Who cares?" Atu yelled. "We have to get out of here!"

"No," Jaden said, so softly Kayla thought she'd misheard him.

Kayla and Atu gaped, not comprehending.

"What?" Kayla asked.

"We're not leaving. Not before we've recovered whatever we came for."

"Are you insane?" Atu asked "The Gaptors outnumber us five to one!"

"Unfavorable odds, I agree. But we won't get another shot at this. We either recover the item now, or they do. Decide quickly. Han and Taz are almost here."

Kayla stared at him wildly. There was no reasoning with him when he was like this. It was like he became someone else. Much as she hated to admit it, he was right. If they didn't get whatever was hidden here, they might as well pack up, go home, and admit defeat. And that was something she absolutely loathed. "I'm in."

Jaden gave her a tight, grateful smile, telling her he understood what they were up against. But who said it would be easy? He glanced at Atu.

"Who am I to back out?"

"Good man. Here's the plan."

Barely a minute later, Kayla and Atu stepped up to the edge of the balcony. Turning to face Jaden, still standing where they'd had their impromptu meeting, Kayla plastered on a brave smile. She couldn't think about things going wrong. She had to focus on the plan working. She had to get this right. His life depended on it.

CHAPTER THIRTY-TWO

Looking at Kayla standing there, so alone and vulnerable, Jaden broke out in a cold sweat. Sudden panic compressed his chest. She shouldn't be going. He should've refused. What was he thinking, letting her go out there?

But before Jaden could move to stop her, Han and Taz swooped in, and Kayla and Atu were leaping into open air. *Too late!* Jaden groaned. There was only one way to make it right—he had to fulfill his part of the plan. And he had better be quick about it.

Long, traveling strides took him to where Kayla and Atu had stood only seconds earlier. Scanning the black skies, Jaden waited apprehensively for the sign their plan was working. His spirits plunged when he noticed nothing had changed. The Gaptors were closing in on the tower at an alarming rate.

Just then, they veered away from the tower. *Kayla and Atu are initiating their part of the plan.* Unsure whether he was relieved or worried, Jaden peered past the lip of the overhang as far as he could, confirming no Gaptors lingered overhead. *Clear.*

Grabbing the ladder, Jaden felt the loss of his ring. They had agreed the relic stone would be useless on its own, so he had entrusted it to Atu. Ruefully rubbing his bare finger, Jaden hoped their assumption the Gaptors would leave once the voyagers recovered the item had not been foolish.

A loud crack shocked him. His hand slipped off the rung he'd been holding. Shaken, Jaden took a second to recover. The relic stones had hit a Gaptor. Or a DD had. Jaden whirled, hoping to witness the efficacy of the weapon. But he could see nothing from here. He needed altitude. Warning himself to not let go because of sudden, deafening sounds, Jaden hauled himself up, hand over hand.

A smile creased his face when he recalled Kayla's adamant claim that he was so much better at climbing. Although going up a ladder hardly counted as climbing. That hill now . . . yes, he had scaled it much faster, but he had wanted to be sure nothing lurked at the top that could harm her. Or had he wanted to impress her?

Movement to his right. The Gaptor dropped and arced toward Jaden. Snatching his DD off his belt, Jaden wrapped an arm through a strut on the ladder, securing his grip. He flipped the safety, swinging the DD just as the blade began sliding out. The unexpected contact with the Gaptor surprised him.

With a sizzle, a wing separated from the Gaptor's body like butter sliding off a hot knife. Jaden watched, dazed, as the wing twirled away in one direction and the Gaptor spiraled away in the other, leaving a fat, black trail of blood like the thick smoke of a downed World War II airplane.

Jaden hadn't known the blade would work like a sword. Whether Sven failed to mention this by design or ignorance, Jaden didn't care. He was just grateful it had worked. The Gaptor had come in so fast he'd almost been unprepared. He had to adjust for that next time. Stuffing his DD back into his belt, Jaden resumed climbing. He did his best to block out the intermittent, distracting, thunderous cracks, heralding the demise of yet another foe at Kayla and Atu's hands.

As Jaden reached for the next rung, his fingers slipped. Cool air washed over him, warning of the impending night as it slicked the metal with condensation. *Concentrate!* Kayla and Atu had enough to worry about without him adding to their burden. Tightening his grip,

Jaden boosted himself toward the ladder's apex as rapidly as he could. The top reached, Jaden stole a moment to check on his companions.

The Gaptors had swallowed the bait, hook, line, and sinker. They hunted his friends with an intensity born of insanity.

Atu and Han, drawing a pursuing group into a play, swerved past a large, rectangular block jutting out from the side of the structure. The two closest Gaptors, lacking agility, smashed into the stone with such force the structure literally shuddered from the impact all the way up here. Both Gaptors tumbled to the ground, senseless.

Meanwhile, Kayla and Taz simultaneously executed a roll out of their parallel flight with the boys, perfectly positioning themselves above the remaining group.

Curiously, the Gaptors all raised their heads and lifted their antennas. It was the first time Jaden had ever seen them do something so strange, made even stranger because nothing happened. The Gaptors cast confused glances at one another a split second before Kayla and Taz raced over them, Kayla cutting a swathe through their ranks with her DD.

Jaden grinned. She'd figured it out, too. They were doing okay. If they could just keep it up.

Jaden faced his next obstacle. The ladder ended abruptly less than halfway up the needle, its rusted metal ends suggesting it had gone higher at one time. Weirdly, this exact spot was also where the tower's needle morphed from a triangular shape into a rectangular one. What the significance of that was, Jaden couldn't tell.

But is this where they hid the object I'm searching for? Jaden had to be sure. Unlocking the map, it glowed softly all around him, confirming the item was indeed at the very top of this tower and not here. Jaden sighed and put the map away. He would be climbing.

Studying the stony, rectangular walls rising steeply above him, Jaden was glad now that he had told Kayla to leave. He would've been even more worried if she had to climb this without Han or Taz around. This could be a difficult ascent, even for him.

Jaden ran his fingers over the surface overhead. Countless tiny ledges riddled the area where the stones of the rectangular section of the tower overlapped. He grinned. Not so difficult. Plenty of hand-holds. Selecting one, Jaden pulled down on it, confirming it would support his weight. It would.

Firmly keeping his weight over his feet, Jaden gripped the ledge with his fingers and pulled himself up, using only the one limb. Then he lifted the opposite foot to the hand he had just used, and, pressing himself against the tower, he inched up further. Alternating his hands and feet, Jaden clawed upward, all the while alert for more Gaptors.

Another beast took a run at him when he was about halfway to the top. Wedging himself into a more secure position, Jaden loosed his DD's blade. This time he didn't wait for the Gaptor to close the distance. He flicked his wrist, and the light beam flew off, hitting the Gaptor square in the face.

With an almighty boom, the Gaptor disintegrated. Only black smoke filled the area. *Impressive! Sven will be pleased.* Although Jaden didn't recall the sound being so loud. He jiggled a finger in each ear, thinking he must've tuned the sounds of battle from Kayla and Atu out. *Or had it just been quiet?* Panicked, Jaden searched for his companions.

There! Taz and Kayla, closely followed by Han and Atu, led a group of three Gaptors. But Taz's flight was not the thing of beauty it typi-cally was. She was favoring her left side. Jaden scowled. Han and Atu were far too close to the girls—almost protectively so.

Put some distance between you, he wanted to shout. Hadn't they learned anything from their drills with Sven? The two pairs rolled away from the three Gaptors gaining on them. His breath caught. A long, wide wound split Taz's side, running crosswise over her ribs. Kayla had swung both her legs over to Taz's other side and flew side-ways. The smart suit must be working overtime to keep Kayla balanced. Suddenly feeling sick, Jaden scanned Kayla for signs of injury, but he was too far away to make an accurate assessment.

Why was she chosen for this? What will I do if something happens to her? If only I could see better. Jaden considered engaging the magnification lenses on his goggles, but that would take too much time. Besides, he had to be wary of more Gaptors coming his way, and the goggles wouldn't allow that. He just had to believe Kayla wasn't hurt. That she would make it through this.

Sighing, Jaden looked around, searching for more Gaptors but found none. The three chasing his friends were all that remained of the group that had made it through the barrier. To have killed so many Gaptors in such a short time, they must've been fighting like loons. No wonder Taz was injured.

Jaden continued watching, helpless, as his friends executed a play to place the Gaptors in a straight line between them. Sven had theorized the relic stones were potentially far more powerful than they could comprehend, conceivably able to kill more than one Gaptor at a time. Is this what his friends were aiming for? It was quite a gamble.

Jaden bit his lip, hoping they had already put Sven's theory to the test and this wasn't a last-ditch effort to kill their remaining enemies with one fell swoop.

Taz was decidedly slower than usual. Han was continually adjusting his flight path to accommodate her. Getting into position took far longer than it had in practice, but they finally succeeded. Jaden stopped breathing. Light suddenly flashed between the two pairs of gliders and voyagers, more than blinding. Jaden whipped his head away from the brilliance, spots dancing in front of his eyes.

When he chanced turning back, thick black smoke billowed in gigantic waves over the area the Gaptors had occupied, but no Gaptors remained. The relic stones really were more powerful than they could've imagined.

Jaden peered into the thick smoke, trying to find his friends. *Where are they?* A second later, they emerged from the cloud. Taz wobbled in her flight. Han was right beside her, almost supporting her. Away from the smoke, Han dropped below Taz. Atu stood up on Han's back, rubbing something over Taz's wound.

Yes! They'll make it. Jaden whooped, giving an enthusiastic fist pump when they glanced in his direction. Their grim smiles reminded him he still had a task of his own to complete.

Checking his position, Jaden found the peak wasn't much further. He set out with a vigor born of desperation. Stabbing pain in his leg momentarily loosened his grip. Scrambling for purchase, Jaden clamped down on a handhold and peeked at his leg—in time to glimpse the scaly tail disappearing around the tower. *Where did the Gaptor come from? Was I stung? If so, is the sting venomous?* Jaden laughed bitterly. *How could I think it isn't?*

But Jaden couldn't dwell on it. The Gaptor was already curling up and around the other side of the tower, its massive body not concealed by the skinny structure. Shakily withdrawing his DD, Jaden flipped the safety. Through the waves of pain now crashing over his entire body, Jaden fumbled for the best course of action.

With the Gaptor so close, the sword would be more effective—though that risked him being knocked off the tower. The safer option would be to wait for his blade to lengthen, but that would take time. Time he might not have. His eyes tracked the blade's extension. *Come on, come on!*

Perspiration beaded his forehead. Jaden swiped it away. The Gaptor was closing in. The last inch of the blade slipped into position. *Finally!* A nanosecond before the Gaptor rammed into him, Jaden snapped his wrist. Sparks showered him as the beam of light collided with the Gaptor. Amidst glittering light and thunderous sound, the Gaptor vanished. Jaden's ears rang. He hazily wondered whether he still had eardrums left. The acrid smoke denoting decimation drifted into his mouth, tasting like death. *Too close.*

Still clutching the tower, Jaden searched the skies for more Gaptors. His earlier assumption they had destroyed all the Gaptors was no longer true.

A shadow grew on the horizon, pulsing toward them with unwavering conviction. Before Jaden could distinguish the individual shapes, he understood a whole new fleet of Gaptors were winging their way toward them.

He roared at his friends. "Kayla! Atu! Move! More Gaptors!"

They glanced in his direction, puzzled. They'd heard his shout but were too far away to perceive the words. Jaden frantically pointed at the sky behind them. They turned. Jaden knew they understood when they abruptly picked up their pace. Atu plopped back down on Han,

Kayla swung her legs behind her so she lay flat on Taz's back, and they rocketed off, away from the tower.

Jaden regarded their retreating forms. *Where are they going?* The only explanation didn't bolster his spirits; they could give him more time if they battled the Gaptors further away from the tower. Which meant they didn't think they stood a chance. Nausea was a lump of fiery clay in the pit of his stomach, churning, burning. The thought of something happening to Kayla was intolerable. Jaden had vowed to protect her. He had to get this done. Now.

Daring a glance at his injured leg, Jaden assessed the damage. Blood oozed through his smart suit, smearing it with sticky red gunk. The pain was excruciating. Gritting his teeth, Jaden fumbled for the next handhold unsteadily. He dragged his body upward.

The movement intensified the pain, and Jaden almost blacked out. Only sheer force of will kept him conscious. *One hand, one foot, one hand, one foot.* That mantra became the essence of Jaden's being. His throbbing leg and aching body spun each minute into an hour.

The needle's pinnacle beckoned. Only two feet to go. Jaden felt like a chameleon, rocking forward and backward several times before committing himself to any forward momentum. But move upward he did. Then he was there. Blankly, Jaden stared at the four-sided pyramid topping the tower. *Now what?*

CHAPTER THIRTY-THREE

Kayla wished she could've explained to Jaden they weren't deserting him. When they left, his shock had reverberated in every stiff line of his body. If only she hadn't seen his slumped shoulders, hinting at the betrayal he surely felt. Like she was leaving him. But she had no way to communicate the truth to him. *Spittlebugs! Sven should've built comm systems into our suits. Why didn't he think of that?* An oversight she'd insist he rectify when they saw him again. Because no way she, Atu, and their gliders would fail and leave Jaden to finish this mission on his own.

When Han recommended their departure, it was a shock, Taz more surprised than any of them. She sputtered, incredulous. "We can't leave Jaden here alone!"

"We can, and we will," Han shot back. "It's the only way we'll give Jaden, and ourselves, a fighting chance."

Taz snarled. "Explain!"

"Facing our enemies as far from the tower as possible will increase Jaden's chances of success. No matter how many Gaptors we dispatch, there'll be stragglers who get past us. And the further we are from the tower, the more time Jaden will have to deal with them—assuming they don't group together and attack Jaden all at once. Which, considering their mental fortitude, is unlikely."

Kayla nodded. "You're right. Distance provides a tactical advantage."

"Hopefully, that won't be our only advantage. I remembered why the place we passed over after lunch was so familiar." Han grinned.

Taz pounced on the revelation. "Why?"

But Han had refused to elaborate. "No point getting your hopes up. I might be wrong. If so, we must beat the Gaptors there. Tazanna, are you up for some speed?"

"Yes, Atu's salve is already helping. There's no longer a tearing sensation every time I move my wing."

Although it didn't negate the quantifiable amount of blood she'd lost, it was also true only rest and time would remedy that. So the decision was made, and they'd sped away in hopes of better odds.

Now, with the sun almost lost in the horizon's embrace, providence wouldn't favor them much longer. Arguably, the onset of twilight had broken the barrier's hold on the Gaptors, but Kayla's mind still picked at what else could've let them through.

It wasn't the only conundrum occupying her mind. Taz hadn't said a word since they'd agreed to follow Han's lead. Was it because Taz had nothing to say or because Taz needed more effort than she would admit to for her to keep pace with Han?

Mentally tallying the diminishing distance between them and their approaching enemies, Kayla doubted they'd reach their destination before the two groups clashed. Chewing on her lip, she contemplated their options as they pressed on, silent, each bound by their own thoughts.

Then the tops of the octagonal formation of rocks appeared. Hope fluttered. Kayla was tentatively revising her assessment when the single Gaptor appeared without warning, yet again. It was unnerving.

Kayla balanced her weight as Taz rolled, avoiding the waiting Gaptor. Taz's smoother movements soothed Kayla. Atu's salve was working its magic. With the threat behind them, Kayla swiveled on Taz's back, checking on the boys. Deftly dipping past the Gaptor, they took off to the right instead of the left. *Oh, so this is how we're playing it.* Kayla scanned the rapidly dimming skies ahead. This Gaptor seemed the lone attacker. *Not that I should put any stock in not seeing others!*

Atu called the play. "Three!"

Kayla flashed a thumbs-up sign, and Taz spiraled lower, losing altitude but maintaining their same general position. As expected, the Gaptor focused on them. Kayla couldn't believe the plays were still working. Han and Taz's assertion about the Gaptors being "dumb brutes" was proving true in spades.

Taz held their position as the Gaptor approached, raising its antennae toward them. *What's that about? Or is that just what they do before attacking?* Another group had done the same thing back at the tower. But there was no time for idle thoughts. The boys were almost in position.

The Gaptor leered at them, thinking it had the easy kill. Han and Atu zoomed overhead. Kayla raised her arm, and the relic stones flashed. Light and sound rent the air, and the Gaptor was history.

Kayla smirked as the boys settled next to them. "Nice work!"

Atu grinned. "Thanks."

"Let's not waste time gloating. We need the high ground," Han said.

Kayla rolled her eyes at Atu over the gliders' heads, and he chuckled.

"Whatever you say," Atu replied.

Their gliders used the heat still drifting up from the stony floor to both elevate the group and drive them onward. Activating their goggles' magnification lenses, Kayla and Atu observed the now not-so-distant group of Gaptors. Close enough now, the teens verified the group wasn't a jumbled mass. Rather, the Gaptors fanned out in a jagged V. Two Gaptors followed the lead Gaptor, not quite in line, and then three further back created another squiggly line. Small clumps of Gaptors formed in similarly arranged groups at intervals. The groups toward the back had greater numbers.

Studying the strange formation, Kayla understood. "He's found a way to send multiple Gaptors through simultaneously!"

"I agree," Atu said. "You heard my discussion with Jaden in the tower then?"

"Even though I was working on the translation, it was almost impossible to ignore you. You were so loud!"

Atu ignored her veiled complaint. "How did the Usurper solve the problem?"

"What matters isn't how he did it. It's what we will do about it."

Atu nodded. "Any ideas?" he asked the gliders.

"Make it to the haven before they reach us," Han snapped.

Their gliders surged forward. Apprehensive about the effect of the increased speed on Taz's injury, Kayla kept sneaking glances downward. But whatever Atu had done, it was holding. Grateful and relieved, Kayla considered what lay ahead of them. The advancing Gaptors were still some distance away. Meanwhile, the peaks of the conical formations were within reach.

Bam! The Gaptor slammed into Taz, ramming her head squarely with his armored chest. The impact knocked Kayla free, her grip already compromised by lying prone to minimize Taz's pain. Tumbling off, Kayla caught the glint of the whirring blade at the end of one scraggly wing the instant before it bit into her shoulder. She screamed. Then the blade disappeared, and she was plummeting in the open sky, pain lancing through her.

With difficulty, Kayla orientated herself for Taz's pickup. Only then did Kayla notice Taz was falling too. A split second later, Taz fluttered past, unconscious.

"Han!" Kayla yelled.

"I have you!"

His deep voice rumbled from somewhere nearby. "No, get Taz!" Kayla ordered, the rest of her words cut off when she landed with a thunk on Han's broad back.

"I can't help her—you have to," Han explained. "Atu has something to bring her to her senses."

Even as he said the words, Atu pressed something into Kayla's hands. Her fingers closed reflexively around the slim tube.

"Just pour it out in front of Taz's nose," Atu directed.

Then Han tipped her off. Kayla gasped, stunned. The shock of landing on Taz's back juddered through her, rattling every vertebra in her spine and spearing a white-hot poker into her shoulder. Kayla groaned, digging her fingers into Taz's soft fur and securing her grip on the still-somersaulting glider. Jaw clenched, Kayla blocked the pain and swung her legs into position around Taz's chest, then scooted up Taz's neck until she could reach Taz's nose. Without ceremony, Kayla dumped the tube's contents.

Jerked alert, Taz instinctively tucked her wings close against her sides until she had the measure of the surrounding air. Then, at the precise moment she leveled out, Taz extended her wings. The movement jarred, but they stopped spinning. Unfortunately, they didn't slow down.

To reduce the stress on her wings, Taz remained angled downward. Kayla tensed. The rocks below were awfully close. *Pull up, pull up!* Tempted to close her eyes, Kayla didn't. If they crashed, it would limit both their injuries if she dismounted before they hit. Kayla waited, hoping against hope she wouldn't have to. When it became clear Taz was losing the battle, Kayla prepared to leap.

Taz, perceiving Kayla's movement, gasped, "No, wait, I think I have it."

Kayla hesitated, eager to feel the muscle movement lifting them away from danger. But it didn't come. It was now or never. Kayla vaulted off Taz.

Touching down, Kayla found the ground rockier than she'd thought. She rolled, distributing the force of the impact. As sky and earth merged in a wild cartwheel of swirling color, her elbow crashed painfully into one rock, then her thigh and uninjured shoulder into another. *Maybe rolling wasn't the best approach.* Kayla lifted her arms to protect her head. A passing rock punched her shoulder. Then the world went black.

CHAPTER THIRTY-FOUR

An acrid smell had Kayla averting her head. She opened her eyes to find Atu bending over her. "How am I doing, Doc?"

"You'll survive."

Kayla eased up. Her shoulder still ached, but it no longer felt like someone stoked a fire in there. Glancing down, she found greenish goop covering the gaping hole. "Your handiwork?"

"Yes—you can thank me later. We need to move."

Kayla accepted Atu's hand as he helped her up. While she steadied herself, Atu signaled their gliders, and the pair charged down to collect them. When Taz dropped lower, Kayla saw the rough scrapes along Taz's abdomen. But they weren't deep or serious.

Aerial-connecting with Taz, Taz didn't wait to say, "You bailed too soon!"

Kayla smiled. "And I suppose you would've still been able to lift with my weight had I stayed on?"

"Naturally."

"Oh, so that's why your belly looks like that gritty desert floor sandpapered it?"

"Fine, I confess! Maybe I wouldn't have been able to pull it off." Taz sighed.

It was quite something for Taz to admit that. "No worries. I'm just glad you're okay."

"You didn't look it, all bloodied and unconscious on the desert floor," Taz whispered. "I'm sorry I couldn't lift us before you had to jump."

Now Kayla felt bad. She hadn't intended to make Taz feel guilty. Running her arms down and around Taz's neck, she gave a gentle squeeze, hugging her glider. "Really, Taz, it's not a problem. I'm alright. And so are you. And that's all that matters."

The air went out of Taz as she relaxed. Good. Kayla couldn't have Taz niggling about that when they had foes to face.

The gliders accelerated toward the octagonally arranged cones while Kayla and Atu monitored the Gaptors pursuing them. Their unexpected collision had allowed their enemies to gain on them. Kayla's heart sank. They wouldn't evade the group for much longer. But she had to do what she could to give Jaden more time. How was his part of the mission was going? If only they lived through this. She had a few things she needed to say to him, whether or not he wanted to hear them. He better survive. She wouldn't forgive him if he didn't.

"Okay, so I know no one wants to admit this, but we're in for a fight. Let's figure out a strategy," Kayla said.

Taz's eyes glittered. "Way to not back down! We take the fight to them and, if losing is mandatory, we kill as many of them as we can."

"That goes without saying."

"Have I told you I like your competitive spirit? Yes, I like it very much! And I know how we can increase our chances."

Kayla rubbed Taz's neck. "Thanks. I like yours too."

"How do we increase our chances?" Han interjected.

"See those cones coming up?" Taz asked. When her companions nodded, Taz said, "We're going to find some allies."

Han grinned. "The kangaroo rat?"

Atu, picking up on what they were thinking, added, "And the spider?"

"You bet," Taz confirmed.

By the time they set the trap, their enemies were almost upon them. They hovered over the area, waiting for their foes to reach them.

Atu spoke. "If I don't get to say this later, it's been . . ."

"None of that," Kayla snapped, cutting him off. "You only get to say those things when the battle's over and we're the victors."

Atu nodded curtly. "I suppose we'd better win then."

The lead Gaptor was within range. "It's time," Kayla declared.

Han and Taz dropped like weighted stones into the maze of cones. The first Gaptor, stunned by their swift movement, lunged after them. His companions followed suit. Consumed by their prey, they didn't register their predicament until it was too late.

Han and Taz dodged the cone suddenly in front of them, adroitly skirting the obstacle. The lead Gaptor, too close and flying too fast, smacked right into it. He plummeted to the desert floor, wings shredded by the sharp stones peppering the cone all the way down. The second Gaptor avoided the same fate, but the third Gaptor went down in the same impressive fashion.

The lone escapee slewed awkwardly past the obstacle, only to stop between a pair of cones when he found his prey missing. His cohorts caught up, and the group hovered, unsure of their direction. As they hesitated, the relic stones flashed from between the two adjacent cones.

Kayla and Atu squinted against the bright light, almost impossibly intensified when it destroyed multiple targets. Their goggles protected their eyes to a degree while the special inserts in their hoods likewise cushioned their ears from the sonic boom. When the smoke cleared, no Gaptors remained.

"That takes care of the first group," Kayla crowed, rubbing her hands together gleefully. When she noticed her shoulder no longer hurt, she was even more delighted. "Time for the next lot."

Their gliders lifted above the cones and sped back to their starting spot. But the next group was already there. They were quicker than Kayla had bargained for. And now the gliders were squarely above the newcomers.

"Six," Kayla bellowed, and the gliders split, Han and Atu soaring over the group while the girls ducked under them. Their DDs were already fully extended. Lifting her arm, Kayla sliced through the rigid, metallic cases protecting the monsters' soft innards. Three Gaptors dropped before those behind them figured out where the threat was coming from. Screeching, they flapped upward, trying to put distance between themselves and the girls.

But Han and Atu were ready and waiting. It was like taking candy from gullible kids. Han weaved between the Gaptors who bobbed up, and Atu swung his DD with impunity, separating wings from bodies, heads from shoulders, and tails from abdomens. Thick black blood gushed from the wounds he inflicted, coating him and splashing down to Kayla and Taz.

Ugh, it stinks! Kayla tried keeping it off her to no avail.

Atu slashed left and right while Han's talons sparked as they too exacted a toll on their enemies. Then the air cleared. Darting quick glances, Kayla and Atu readied for attack from any direction. But they'd smoked this group.

Kayla beamed. "Not bad."

Atu chuckled, taking in her disheveled appearance. "Do I look as awful as you?"

Kayla glanced down. Slicked with the beasts' black gore, it looked like someone had dipped her in a vat of crude oil. She imagined that, like Atu, only her teeth shone white against the blackness. She grinned. "You sure do!"

It wasn't long before the next group arrived. Kayla swallowed. They would pose a problem. Where the previous two groups had numbered under ten, this group hit double digits. And if that wasn't daunting enough, the group after, already visible and not too far off, was even more prolific. It was all Kayla could do not to groan aloud. Sucking down her apprehension, she waited. When the next group was within range, she said, "Time to use our unwitting ally."

And into the fray they went. Sinking between two Gaptors who were farther apart than the rest, they successfully split the group in half. As expected, one half chased after the boys, while the others followed the girls. This time, each choosing a different direction and trailing a line of Gaptors, Han and Taz raced past the cones used in their first attack. Leading the two groups to another cluster further away, they expertly dodging the many obstacles speckling the path to their goal. The precision required for negotiating the pitted landscape paid off, and they lost a few of their pursuers to cone collisions along the way. But at least nine monsters still chased them as they closed in on their target. Kayla hoped the spider was ready and waiting.

Evidently, he was. Kayla glimpsed him as Han and Taz converged on the narrow opening between two cones, flipping vertically to traverse the narrow gap. High-pitched shrieks sounded behind them when the first pair of Gaptors in each of the lines had neither the time nor space to implement the same evasive tactic. The closer Gaptor crashed into the cone where the spider lurked. The impact ricocheted him into his teammate, plunging both beasts down in a tangle of wings and tails.

The spider, ire spiked by the rude intrusion, wasted no time on pleasantries. Raising his abdomen, he jetted a thin tendril of wire across the opening to the cone opposite his home. It landed and stuck with a thwack. The second pair of Gaptors in each line had already passed him, but the third set, oblivious, slammed into the wire. Heads separated from bodies, as though their armored outer shells were no more resilient than tissue paper. For an instant, the decapitated heads hung suspended before following their heftier body parts toward the desert floor, the bizarre headless anomalies sparking pandemonium amongst the others.

As they tracked the pair of Gaptors who had slipped past, the teens and gliders beheld the ensuing chaos from their elevated position. A few Gaptors tried forcing their way through the gap, now slung with even more wires and deadlier than ever. Their attempts were fatal. Others tried turning back, crashing into those who still followed, intertwining themselves and hurling the knotted groups to the canyon floor. And the spider lanced one when it passed too close, its demise a matter of time.

"Wow, that worked considerably better than I thought it would," Kayla murmured.

"Now that's what I call an effective attack!" Atu hooted. Pointing toward the lone survivors of the group who were winging their way toward them, he said, "We just have to deal with those two."

"V split and hit them between the angle?" Kayla suggested.

Atu nodded, interpreting her intent. They held their position, watching the approaching Gaptors, who lifted their heads and raised their antennae.

"What's that all about?" Kayla asked Atu.

"I don't know. They did it back at the tower as well."

"Whatever it is, it's not very practical."

"How so?"

"They reduce their visual range when they angle their heads like that. When I'm in a fight, I want to see as much as possible."

Atu shrugged. "Probably why they look totally bamboozled every time they do it."

The Gaptors reached the sweet spot on the imaginary line opposite the V, angling out from where Kayla and Atu waited. As soon as they did, Taz and Han sped outward along the imaginary V, the girls to the right and the boys to the left of the oncoming beasts.

The Gaptors immediately slowed, confused by the sudden offensive move. Meanwhile, the gliders continued forward, their flight tangent putting distance between them and their enemies but keeping them on the same plane. Then the Gaptors were lined up between them, and the teens lifted their arms in unison. The relic stones sparked. Thunderous sound and dazzling light affirmed their enemies' demise.

"Ready for the next onslaught?" Kayla lifted her chin toward the fresh group of Gaptors, already far closer than she would've liked.

"Do we have a choice?" Atu retorted.

Kayla grinned. "Same again, you think?"

Atu looked down. The spider was drooling over his loot, running his spinnerets over his victims, both alive and dead, preserving them for future feasts. "I think our friend is too preoccupied to be of much help this time around."

"Our original attack then?"

"It's the only one we have. Unless we find another anomalous rat or snake."

Kayla grimaced. "If only!"

In the brief time available to plan their attacks, they'd been unable to find either a rat or a snake in addition to the spider. *More's the pity,* Kayla reflected, as they raced back to hover above their starting position. Abruptly, Kayla grasped the enormity of the advancing group. Their recent victories paled.

If only they had more time! They could've come up with another viable idea. But they were fresh out of luck on that front. Considering the group's size, she doubted they'd make it through this skirmish unscathed. *Ah well, only one way to find out.*

And hopefully, whatever the outcome, they would at least give Jaden the time he needed. Her heart contracted at the thought of not seeing him again. *No, that thinking will* not *do! There's no place for it.* They would succeed. She would see Jaden again. And when she did, he would find out how she truly felt.

CHAPTER THIRTY-FIVE

Han and Taz spun them to face the Gaptors closing in on them. In an almost comical moment, the lead Gaptor slowed, as if unaccustomed to such blatant confrontation. Regrettably, his hesitation was only momentary. Baring his teeth, he sped forward and renewed his attack.

Han and Taz held their positions. At the exact moment the lead Gaptor came within striking range, they dropped under him and curved down toward the cones sticking up from the desert floor like tall buoys offering safe harbor amidst a rocky sea. Reducing their speed so they managed to only just stay ahead of their pursuers, their gliders aimed for the spires used so successfully before. Except, this time, when Kayla glanced back, she was dismayed to find not all the Gaptors had dropped behind them. A small group remained overhead.

"Stay below the deck," Kayla shouted to Atu. "Some are still above us."

Atu glanced up, noted the danger, and nodded. Sparing no words, he concentrated on what they had to accomplish. Once more, the gliders slid through the treacherous landscape with agility while their clumsy opponents lost several of their own attempting the same feat.

Nearing the twin cones they'd hidden behind the last time, Han and Taz accelerated, putting distance between them and their pursuers. They dodged a single cone in the center of a group, then disappeared behind the adjacent pair behind it. Pulling up on the other side of the cones, they waited for their assailants to catch up.

Kayla checked on the group overhead. They were still too far back to have noticed their ploy. When the first Gaptor hit the single cone, it jolted her attention back. Almost without delay, a second pursuer crashed into it too. Then came the agitated shrieks. Kayla signaled Atu, and he raised his arm.

The Gaptors dribbled into the long, narrow space between the adjacent cones, slowed by the preceding obstacles. Kayla and Atu waited for as long as they could. By the time they had to act or lose their advantage, they had five Gaptors lined up. They released the power of the relic stones.

This time, the sound was so overpowering, even their auditory inserts were useless. Kayla slapped her hands over her ears, stunned by the volume. Raising her head to check on the Gaptors that had been overhead, she suddenly understood the reason for the racket.

"Han. Move!" Kayla screamed.

But he didn't hear. Atu didn't acknowledge her either. Desperate, Kayla pressed her legs into Taz's sides. Taz turned, her gaze quizzical, but Kayla saw her question only as a mouthed response. Their hearing was definitely affected. When Taz's eyes suddenly widened as she saw what was happening over Kayla's shoulder—where the boys hovered —Kayla knew explanations weren't necessary.

Surging forward, Taz annihilated the scant distance between them and the boys, brazenly bumping into Han before streaking away. He turned to glare at her, the slight movement giving him full view of the imminent danger. Without hesitation, he pitched forward using huge, powerful thrusts of his wings.

Atu grabbed on. He turned his head to find the girls. And finally, he saw it too.

Repeated blows sustained during their last foray must've weakened the cone the boys had been hiding behind. Either the massive sound wave or an errant Gaptor sent off course by the blast had crashed into it and cracked the top. It was now tumbling off the base in colossal chunks and careening downward. Han's efforts to skirt the falling pieces of rock were not swift enough. A large, jagged chunk clipped one of his hind legs. He yelped, tucking his injured leg under his body and lurching away from the rest of the debris.

When they caught up to the girls, Kayla eyed him. "How's the leg?"

"A nick—no broken bones. Thanks for the assist."

"Sorry it wasn't sooner," Kayla murmured, digging a finger in her ear and shaking it. "We need a comm system in these suits!"

They watched as the rest of the cone came down, exultant when its destructive descent eliminated two more foes. With an almighty crash, the rocks hit the ground, and an enormous dust cloud fluffed over them. Zero visibility.

"Five!" Kayla cried.

Digging in, Kayla leaned the right way to counter Taz's movements. Grateful her goggles protected her eyes from the dust, she was nonetheless disappointed she still couldn't see a thing. *So this is how it feels to fly blind.* Her play demanded that the boys go lower, which meant they were moving further into the dust cloud rather than away from it. She would have to let them know when to lift so they could help her and Taz. And she would have to pray they heard her. A second later, she yelled, "Now!"

Kayla breathed when the boys shot up, popping above the cloud just in time to catch sight of the three Gaptors trailing the girls. They were almost in the perfect position for lining up the relic stones. Taz adjusted their course, putting them right on target. Kayla lifted her arm, as did Atu, and the Gaptors disintegrated.

But there was no time to savor their victory. Not only were four more Gaptors rising from the dust cloud, but the relic stones must have alerted the monsters above to their position. They descended on the girls, pinning them between the two groups.

"What's the play?" Taz barked.

Kayla flipped through options. They'd never formulated a strategy for this scenario. They would have to work independently of the boys and hope they could somehow split the groups—or would it be better to work together and combine the groups?

Where is Jaden when I need him? He's better at working these things out than I am. If the aerial strategy game they'd played together one afternoon hadn't told her that, all the hours spent training at Sven's had. Time and again, Jaden was the one who came up with new and varied combinations.

How is he doing? Has he found what we're looking for? Is he safe? Kayla just wanted him with her. She needed him and his big brain. He would know how to approach this. She was still thinking when the first Gaptor made its move.

Swerving in from above, it clipped Taz's wing, sending her off-kilter. Taz spiraled for a moment before correcting her flight and dropping. Their attacker dived after them, his blades spinning. Kayla tore her DD free of its holster. The blade was still sliding out when the beast's talons tipped down onto her arm.

The pain, oh, the pain! Kayla screamed as her flesh split, almost dropping her DD. Snatching at the falling weapon with her other hand, she snagged it before it fell free. With one awkward movement, she swung the DD toward the monster who had refused to back off, cackling when her blade made contact. The Gaptor screeched as Kayla ripped into his exposed underbelly. Black blood spurted over her before the Gaptor dropped away, spilling what remained of his life force.

"Are you okay?" Taz's worried voice penetrated the haze of pain.

"Yes. You?"

"Same. Where's Ohanzee?"

Clutching her injured arm and attempting to stem the blood flow, Kayla searched for the boys. The other Gaptors were keeping their distance. *Good.* That little display of the DD's effectiveness had dampened their enthusiasm. A second later, Kayla found the boys.

They must've been waiting for her to call the play because only now were they sinking down to aid the girls. Transfixed, horrified, Kayla could only stare as another Gaptor intercepted them, whipping its stinger under its belly and catching Atu full in the face. He toppled off Han.

Taz moved toward the boys, but Han was faster.

Sensing his voyager's peril, Han flipped onto his back. Before his enemy could react, Han barreled up and sank his fangs into the Gaptor's long neck. With a vicious twist, he ripped the brute's head from its body. As ash rained down, Han lowered his head and chased after Atu, desperate to catch him before he reached the group of Gaptors waiting below.

When Han caught him, Atu's graceless landing revealed how out of it he was. Han shuddered as the impact jarred his injured leg, making blood drip.

Taz tensed under her. While the drip was a minor distraction, it wasn't what had them worried. How would Han avoid the enemy below if Atu didn't snap out of his funk? Then Atu fumbled in Han's fur, and Kayla and Taz relaxed—marginally.

Taking a hot second to bind her cut arm, Kayla studied Atu. Blood ran down his face where the stinger had inflicted its damage. He still looked dazed. They wouldn't have much time before the rest of the group decided they could attack. "Atu, get with it!"

Hearing her, Atu lifted his head and shook it as though to rid himself of the effects of the impact. It didn't help. Atu reached a shaking hand into the pack and withdrew a vial. Without hesitation, he put it to his lips and downed the contents. The effect was instantaneous. His eyes cleared.

"What are you waiting for?" Atu cried, dashing blood away from his eyes. "We need to attack before they hit us again."

Kayla smiled. *Yup, he's fine.* She studied their enemies. The Gaptors bore down on them in two parallel lines, one above and one below, leering grins on their faces as they anticipated conquest. While the relic stones were powerful, Kayla didn't want to put too much stock in their ability to take out that many Gaptors. The plan simmering in the back of her mind came fully to her awareness. They only stood a chance if they worked together.

"Eight—girls on the top," Kayla called.

Atu grinned. Time for payback. Signaling he understood, he and Han took off between the parallel lines. The sudden challenge gave their enemies pause. The lines faltered, all the time the boys needed to begin their assault.

Atu raised his arm as Han zoomed forward, Atu's DD slicing the Gaptors above them while Han's talons raked across the backs of those below. At the same time, Kayla and Taz weaved across the top line of attackers, hitting every foe they could with their own weapons.

Kayla wasn't as accurate as normal. Using her left arm was maddening! Despite this, she still landed a few fatal blows. Blood and gore spurted around them as the two pairs hit their marks. But when they reached the end of the line, they hadn't thinned the enemy ranks nearly enough.

"Again," Kayla ordered as they circled on the far end.

Their gliders tilted their wings, arcing them back to face their foes. What Kayla saw agitated her. The two groups of Gaptors, expecting a fresh attack, were also wheeling around, destroying their earlier neat lines. Which meant their relic stones were still useless. Their enemies' scattered positions would make the upcoming run nigh impossible.

"Loop and roll," Kayla called.

There was no other option. They would have to take out the Gaptors one at a time. They rolled around the first Gaptor together, catching him between the stones. Zap! He disappeared. They approached the next. But he veered away, and they had to let him go. The third, fourth, and fifth Gaptors bunched together. They looped, Taz taking the high road while the boys curled under.

Kayla was too close to let loose with her DD, so she slashed at the nearest Gaptor. With her less-than-reliable arm, her movements were clumsy, and she only sheared off its wing. It careened into her foot, and she let out a sharp cry as its weight smacked into her ankle. Tucking her throbbing ankle under her body for protection, Kayla watched, aghast. The one-winged beast plummeted uncontrollably right into Han and then into another Gaptor, the two brutes spiraling downward. Han howled with pain as the beast knocked him sideways.

"Han, I'm sorry!" Kayla cried. "Are you alright?"

Han wheezed. "You mean apart from my bruised ribs?"

Mortified, Kayla ordered herself to be more careful. She couldn't be taking out members of her own team! Especially when they were all they had. As they looped over the next Gaptor, destroying it with the stones, Han's labored breathing evidenced the gravity of his injury. Before Kayla could comment, two more Gaptors crossed their path.

Still checking on Han, Atu was a tad slow off the mark. His DD swung through the air, dispatching the first. But the second bashed into his wrist, and his DD tilted sideways, the shiny blade glancing off his left arm.

Horrified, Kayla expected Atu's limb to fall off. But it flopped to his side, dangling limp and useless. She and Taz caught up to the boys. "What can I do?" Kayla called.

"Nothing. It's paralyzed. Hopefully temporarily, but we can't worry about that now." Atu lifted his chin to Kayla's left, and she saw the next wave of Gaptors closing in on them.

CHAPTER THIRTY-SIX

How can we fight so many? They hadn't been able to use the relic stones as effectively this last time. Maybe the Gaptors were learning. Hefting her DD in her less-than-reliable left hand, Kayla decided they would just have to do their best. "Ready?"

Atu nodded. They resumed the looping and rolling routine they had practiced so many times at Sven's. The memory tinged Kayla with momentary sadness when she realized those wonderfully carefree days were over. Then they were curling around their next opponent, and things sped up.

Although she and Atu took out their first two attackers, one Gaptor nicked Taz's tail before they dispatched it. Blood flowed freely from the wound when Taz's continued flight widened the tear. Then a stray Gaptor talon tore Han's side as he rolled away from the next group of beasts banded together to face them. Luckily, the wound wasn't deep, but that didn't stop it from bleeding profusely either.

Cursing, Kayla stabbed the Gaptor who had wounded Han, gratified when it dropped away, trailing its abominable black blood. But another Gaptor was ready and waiting to take its place. Maniacally hacking to her right and left as the Gaptors fell on them like carrion, Kayla's arm trembled. Fatigue crept through her weakening limb.

Sneaking a peek at the boys to see if they could help, she found them equally swamped.

Then it happened. Something plucked the Gaptor in front of them from the air. Stunned, Kayla and Taz watched it disappear. When Taz identified their unexpected rescuers, black shapes leaping up from the gloom below, she thrust them upward.

The Gaptors overhead, not as attuned to their surroundings, squawked shrilly when Taz suddenly barreled into them. Their scraggly wings flapped wildly as, comically, they veered out of the way. The Gaptors below didn't escape. They disappeared in rapid succession, the pack of mutant rats on the desert floor picking them off one by one.

"Where did they come from?" Kayla babbled.

Taz shrugged. "Perhaps the scent of so much fresh blood drew them?"

Kayla grinned. "Well, they couldn't have chosen a better time to appear."

"Whatever the reason, it's our chance for escape," Taz said. "Han!"

But Han must've read her mind. He was already streaking toward them. Close enough for the girls to hear, he bellowed, "Time to make a run for it!"

"We need altitude," Taz insisted, even as she surged ahead to keep pace with Han, their greater speed whisking them away from the remains of their enemies.

"Why?" Kayla demanded, not understanding where Taz was going.

"The Gaptors can't match our altitudes. Not only will height allow us some battle-free time to reach that formation, it'll also provide an excellent view of what's waiting for us once we get there," Taz explained.

"Simple, yet effective." Han grinned toothily.

The teens flattened themselves on their gliders, and their aerolators slipped into place when their gliders rocketed upward. The bloody battle scene below shrank away. Kayla was rather glad. The rats were ruthless, taking down anything that moved above them. She shivered thinking about their long, yellow teeth. Then she realized it wasn't just that making her shiver. She was suddenly freezing. And utterly drained.

Apparently, she wasn't the only one. Taz wobbled under her as they raced toward the octagon of conical towers, their refuge. After what felt like an eon, they were high above their destination. Circling warily, their gliders approached the cones, assessing which would offer the best protection.

"The cones have side vents," Han observed.

"That's no guarantee tunnels lead off from them. Access to a main vent would be preferable—maybe the largest cone, over there?" Taz asked, lifting her chin toward one tower in the octagon rising higher than the others.

Kayla studied it. No sign of Gaptors. And unless she was mistaken, those pursuing them had dropped back. They must be flying faster than she'd realized. Then again, it was also almost night. The sun had already dipped past the horizon but wasn't so far gone yet as to blanket everything in obscurity. Still, the black Gaptors would be tough to spot.

"That vent seems a suitable option," Han said.

Since their eyesight was so much better, Kayla had to trust their gliders' assessment. They drifted toward the vent, preparing for descent. Just as they dropped into the gaping mouth of the main vent, a black mass swarmed up to meet them.

Kayla squealed. "Taz, lift!"

But Taz ignored her. In fact, Taz seemed bound and determined to go head to head with the unknown threat. About to point out her folly, Kayla jumped when Han loosed a piercing shriek. She swiveled on Taz's back, glaring at him. If he'd been within reach, she would've clocked him. "What are you doing? Why don't you just announce our arrival?"

Her annoyance rose a notch when Taz made the same shrill sound. *What is* wrong *with them?* She looked to Atu, hoping he might have an answer, but he was just as flummoxed. Kayla's tired mind churned, too befuddled to work it out.

Panic welled when Taz acted on her initial impulse and, instead of flying away from the inky cloud, dashed toward it. Kayla peered into the gloom, trying to make out the individual black shapes. She was tempted to lean away from what she had convinced herself would be a gruesome death. *But . . . wait.* In a flash, it all became clear. *Gliders! They're gliders!* Kayla laughed out loud, relieved and delighted. "Taz, allies! Did you know they were here?"

Taz grinned. "No, I didn't. But I suspect Han did."

"So *that* was what he meant when he said we might have more of an advantage!"

Taz chuckled, and the girls gazed at Han. He looked extremely pleased with himself. Winding through the newcomers like they were long-lost friends, he appeared to be doing an aerial dance with them.

When Taz dived, copying his movements, Kayla assumed it was their way of greeting the others. Silently, she admired the gliders circling them, surrounding them, saluting them. Then Kayla blinked. Was she imagining things? Every glider passing Taz seemed to bow. That was ridiculous! How could a glider bow while in flight? But the more Kayla studied their movements, the more convinced she was. *What is that about?*

One glider, seemingly older than the others, wafted closer. "Welcome! I am Pallaton. We've awaited your arrival eagerly."

Taz inclined her head. "Thank you, Elder." She made the introductions, then said, "You can't imagine how comforting your presence is. We are more than relieved to make your acquaintance. As I'm sure you can tell," she said, tipping her head toward the approaching Gaptors, "we would appreciate your aid."

Pallaton beamed. "I think that's something we can help with."

Emitting a low, slow whistle, climbing in scale the longer it continued, the other gliders answered his call, moving away and fanning out above Taz and Han. In seconds, they'd arranged themselves in groups which immediately began attacking the incoming Gaptors.

Kayla, Taz, Han, and Atu remained where they were, raptly observing the precision and deadliness with which their new friends attacked the Gaptors. The backdrop of fading light before the sun's total descent into oblivion formed an excellent canvas against which the scene played out. It didn't take their allies long to annihilate the already decimated ranks of Gaptors. With the skies empty of threat, their friends again surrounded them, whistling and chirping as they communicated with Han and Taz.

"Alright!" Atu whooped, raising his arm and pumping his fist into the air. "That was inspiring!"

Taz smiled. "They are incredible, aren't they?"

But Kayla was staring at Atu. "Atu, your arm!"

Atu frowned. "What about it?"

"Isn't that the arm your DD touched?"

Atu inspected his arm, then grinned. "So it is. The effects of the DD must be temporary on humans. Another feather in Sven's cap. He'll be ecstatic."

Pallaton separated from the group and drew near.

"Well done, Elder!" Taz said. "The accounts of your prowess weren't exaggerated in our histories."

"Thank you, Tazanna," he answered before a worried expression settled on his elderly face. "Pardon me if I am being indelicate, but we were expecting three seekers. Could you enlighten me as to the whereabouts of the third?"

Han stopped chirping and answered. "We left him at the temple. Our departure gave him his best chance at success."

Pallaton nodded. "Not to alarm you, but he will need you, Ohanzee. You should make haste and return to him."

Kayla's heart rate spiked. Why did Han have to get back to Jaden? Was he in trouble? They shouldn't have left him. But it had been the only way to give him more time to retrieve the item unhindered.

Kayla's thoughts and emotions were at war, neither giving way to the other, both building the wave of anxiety rising within her to a tsunami. Sensing her agitation, Taz turned and stared at her curiously. Kayla knew she had to get a grip, or there would be some explaining to do—if there wasn't already. Taz was no fool. Kayla sucked in a deep, calming breath. Then another. Then a third. As her stress levels dropped, her mind snapped back to action. She had to get back to him. As if in tune with what she was thinking, Han asked the obvious question.

"He's in danger?"

Pallaton cocked his head to the side. "Not yet. But he soon will be."

"How does he know that?" Kayla whispered to Taz.

Her glider shrugged. "How did he know it was time for them to wake up and help us?"

Kayla opened her mouth to ask another question, but Taz stopped her. "Now is not the moment for questions. Later."

"Yes," Kayla murmured.

"Do I have a moment to heal Han before he leaves?" Atu interjected.

"You do, Healer," Pallaton said. "In fact, it would be best if you did."

"Uh, would you be willing to let me use your back so I can work more quickly?" Atu asked Pallaton hesitantly.

"It would be my honor." Pallaton smiled, moving closer. "Jump when you're ready."

Atu wasted no time. Even as he uttered his thanks, he slipped off Han and landed lightly on Pallaton. Rising to his feet as soon as he had his balance, he worked rapidly, applying potions to Han's bleeding leg and side. Almost at once, the blood stopped flowing.

"Could you lift just a little higher?" Atu asked.

Pallaton obliged, and Atu stretched his arm out, placing his hand over Han's ribs. A small popping sound was audible, and then Han's face brightened as his breathing returned to normal.

Kayla gaped at Atu. "You healed his ribs. How did you do that?"

Atu smiled. "Don't focus on how I did it, just be thankful that I can." Addressing Han, he said, "Any other injuries I should attend to before you leave?"

"Healer, you have truly lived up to your name today. I thank you! And no, I have no other injuries that need tending. It's time for me to reunite with my voyager."

"It is," Pallaton agreed. "Swiftness is key; return to your voyager without delay. Avoid unnecessary confrontations. We will follow you as soon as possible and clean up any laggards."

Dipping his head in farewell, Han sped away. He took Kayla's heart with him. *Please, Jaden, be alright. Please, Han, get to him before he comes to harm.*

In a split second, Han was a speck on the horizon. Atu faced the others. "Alright, who's next?"

CHAPTER THIRTY-SEVEN

Jaden clung to the needle, the inferno in his leg creeping inexorably higher. The pain was muddling his thinking. Making a concerted effort, he gathered his scattered thoughts and focused on the four-sided pyramid in front of him. Constructed the same way as the tower, the only difference was these stones were far more delicate, a petite version.

Leaning closer, Jaden examined the join connecting the pyramid to the needle. Demarcated by a thick, gritty line and darker than the other material cementing the stones together, it circumvented the base. An idea flitted across Jaden's consciousness. Tapping the stones immediately below the pyramid, he worked his way lower until he heard it, a hollow section right under the pyramid. Pushing softly on the pyramid, Jaden tried sliding it. It didn't budge. Shoving harder had no effect either.

A welcome gust of wind lifted his hair from his sweaty forehead. *Duh! Whoever had designed the pyramid must have factored in the wind speed up here. There must be a switch or lever preventing the top from being blown away.* Running his fingers over each layer of rock, Jaden poked and prodded at anything resembling a switch. Although he jiggled several stones, he couldn't dislodge them or release the pyramid from whatever glued it to the needle. Five minutes later, Jaden had exhausted his options. He stared at the pyramid, perplexed.

Detecting movement far beyond the tower, Jaden squinted into the dark sky. The inky blackness was getting denser by the second. He activated his magnification lenses, then cursed inwardly when he identified two Gaptors. Were his friends alright? Choosing to believe these Gaptors were just lucky enough to have slipped past them, he drew his DD and waited.

When the Gaptors were in range, Jaden flicked his wrist. The first Gaptor disintegrated amidst the usual light and sound show, made more spectacular by nightfall's backsplash. By the time Jaden's eyes readjusted, the second Gaptor was almost upon him. Hastily, he flicked his wrist. But the shard of sizzling light slid harmlessly past as the Gaptor dodged it. *Huh, they're getting smarter. Does it also know we can use the DD as a sword?*

Apparently, it did. The Gaptor swept in at an angle, tilting its huge frame so it exposed only a tiny fraction of its extensive body. Swatting at the beast, Jaden only nicked the minuscule target. But the beast, curling away from his DD, was more successful.

Jaden howled as talons raked across his back, sending tongues of fire racing up and down the ragged incisions. Momentarily faltering as he absorbed the pain, Jaden gripped the pyramid. Taking a moment to steady himself, he rotated his arms carefully. Although the tears along his back screamed, he could move without mind-numbing pain incapacitating him. The cuts couldn't be that deep. *Not so lucky, you brute!*

Turning, Jaden searched for the Gaptor. There it was, amping up for another run at him. Twisting his wrist, Jaden tucked his DD behind his arm, hoping his body somewhat hid the glow. This time, the brute wouldn't see his death until it was too late.

Jaden hunched over, pretending his injury was worse as he waited impatiently for the Gaptor to close the distance. It lumbered forward, unsuspecting. When it was only two yards away, Jaden suddenly straightened, lifted his arm, and cracked his wrist. The sliver of glowing death only had to travel a short way. With no time to react, the Gaptor was toast. Jaden smiled, satisfied.

At shrieks behind him, he whirled defensively. Another Gaptor closed in from the opposite direction. *Blast! I should've known there would be more than just two.* Using the pyramid as leverage, Jaden pitched his body around the tower, wincing at the pull on his back. He couldn't feel his leg anymore. It dangled uselessly off to one side. He didn't know if that was bad. Squarely facing his attacker and not waiting to fortify his position, Jaden snapped his DD. But the atrocity expected this. It veered sideways, avoiding the electric sizzler. Provoked, the beast sped up. Jaden readied his DD.

The Gaptor maintained his course until a fraction of a second before he would've been within reach. Then he abruptly swerved sideways, away from the blade, deliberately whipping his tail under him at the last moment.

Jaden, too focused on sinking his DD into the beast's belly, didn't see the move coming. The tail smashed into his injured leg first, sending agonizing rivers of pain through his veins and weakening his hold on the tower. When the stinger connected with his other leg, the impact knocked him loose. Jaden fell.

He thought of Kayla. Had she and Atu survived their encounter with that horde of Gaptors? If only he could see her one last time. He had things to tell her. Why hadn't he been more proactive? Now she would never know. And she would have to complete this terrible mission without him. All because he couldn't keep his hold on the tower. His only consolation was that Atu was with her. And the gliders. They would have to protect her. He had failed. That thought galvanized him into action.

Clawing at the tower rushing past, Jaden desperately tried to find something, anything, to latch on to. But he was too far away. Spinning head over heels, he thought he saw Han torpedoing in at an untenable speed. *What is Han doing back here? And why aren't the others with him?* Jaden stretched his arms, hoping to steady himself long enough to authenticate what he thought he had seen. But human arms weren't made for flying, and he continued somersaulting toward the ground. Then he hit something. Hard.

Pain erupted in every bone, muscle, tendon, and tissue. His leg went numb. His back ran with fresh streams of blood. His vision blurred as he blinked back tears. Struggling to breathe, the wind knocked out of him, Jaden wriggled up, ready to defend himself—and found himself on Han's broad back.

"Ow!" Han muttered.

"Han! You're alive! You came! You saved me!" Jaden wheezed.

"Of course I came. We're a team."

Jaden leaned down, stretching his arms around his glider's neck as far as his injured back would allow. "Thank you!" His heart cringed as he debated asking. Hope tempered his trepidation. "And the others?"

"They're safe. Just as you are," Han assured him.

Jaden laughed, unable to hold back the relief. She was alive! His spirits soared. "Yes, I am. Thanks again for catching me and sorry for the crash landing!"

"You're welcome." Han smirked. "But if you land like that next time, I'll let you fall."

"Sure you will." Jaden grinned. "Now, let's finish that freak."

"Aren't you forgetting something?" Han asked, cocking his head and raising an eyebrow.

Under the lighthearted comment, Jaden recognized his concern. Han must've noticed his injuries. Jaden could almost see Han calculating how much blood he'd lost. But neither of them could do anything about it. Considering Han's question, Jaden chuckled, trying to ease some of Han's concern. "I'm guessing we won't get very far without my DD?"

Han's laugh rumbled out. "I guess not. Lucky for you I know where it fell. Are you able to jump down and retrieve it?"

"Absolutely," Jaden said, although he wasn't sure if his injured leg would take the landing.

Han dipped toward a ledge sticking out further than the others. "It's over there, just behind that ridge. Do you see it?"

Jaden nodded. "Yes. Ready when you are."

Han angled closer, and Jaden slithered off. He landed awkwardly, favoring his injured leg, which refused to cooperate and hurt more than ever. But he could put weight on it without falling over. He limped over to his DD. Snatching it, he turned, ready for Han's pickup. Han swung past, and they were back in business. It was bliss having his weight off his leg again. They gained altitude. To Jaden's dismay, he noticed two more Gaptors had joined the Gaptor who had knocked him off the tower.

"Have you recovered what they hid at the top of the tower?" Han asked.

"No, there wasn't time before I fell. But I'm almost certain it's under the pyramid. I just couldn't figure out how to pry the pyramid off the needle."

"We have to go back there then?"

"Yes, but we must deal with these Gaptors first."

"I agree."

Han inclined them toward their enemies, then barreled down on the monsters at high speed. They obliterated the first Gaptor before the others could react, the beast disintegrating when the sliver of light peeled into him. Screeching raucously, the remaining two arced away in opposite directions. Han instantly chased after one. Within seconds, it too was gone. That only left the third.

Han circled upward, seeking the height that would give them the advantage. Unfortunately, the third Gaptor found it first, and he had backup in the form of a new arrival. The rapacious pair fell on Han and Jaden in a frenzy, beaks gnashing, wing-blades spinning, and tails crackling.

Jaden's smart suit, able to react now that he saw the danger, snapped him away from each new attack while Han's teeth and talons ripped chunks off the Gaptors' bodies. Jaden lashed out at the closest Gaptor with his DD. The blade shattered the beast's hard exoskeleton, and it fell.

Jaden whipped his head about, searching. "Where's the other one?"

"The coward ran back to his mates." Han snorted in disgust, lifting his chin to point out a rapidly retreating shape.

Jaden fumed as the Gaptor scurried toward a dark cloud growing in the distance. More Gaptors.

"There's no point wasting valuable time chasing him," Han said. "Our priority is finding the object the map led us to. The others will settle that weakling's fate."

"Others?" Even as Jaden voiced the question, he spotted another mass to the right of the Gaptors and headed their way. This group was substantially larger. It was also somehow different, but he couldn't readily ascertain why.

"Did Kayla ever mention the prophecy Taz told her about?" When Jaden nodded, Han continued. "Turns out it was true. We found the lost legion of gliders Zareh kept on your world."

Jaden practically bounced on Han's back with excitement. It suddenly made sense. "That second group—they're gliders?"

Han grinned. "Every last one of them."

"Alright! Where were they?"

"Hidden in that place we flew over earlier today—the one Taz and I thought was familiar but couldn't establish why."

"You've been there before?"

"No, but I don't doubt Zareh put a picture of that place in our minds, signifying its importance, yet not giving any sign why. It came together when we were fighting the Gaptors just before we left you. It wasn't like I worked it out. The knowledge was mysteriously just there."

"Sounds like Zareh," Jaden muttered. He glanced over Han's shoulder. They were suspended over the needle. "Question now is how do we get that wretched pyramid off the tower?"

Han grinned. "Thanks to Zareh, I know exactly what we have to do."

Jaden stared. "You do?"

"Yes. Have your medallion handy?"

Jaden pulled it from the zippered pocket inside his smart suit. "What now?"

"Place it in my arcachoa."

"What?" Jaden blurted.

"You heard me," Han answered softly.

"You said that was dangerous and to never do that."

"It is dangerous. And that's why Taz and I gave you the dire warnings we did. But now *is* the time to use it." When Jaden hesitated, Han growled. "Jaden! Time is against us."

Jaden still wavered. "What will happen when I do?"

"There's no time to explain!" Han barked, exasperated. "Don't be afraid. We'll need the illusion it generates to solve this puzzle."

"But you said we could get stuck there—"

"Jaden Jameson, put your medallion in my arcachoa. Now!"

With trepidation, Jaden did as ordered, placing his medallion in its holding space between Han's ears. Instantly, light blazed, settling into a gaping, glowing circle ahead of them. Wind swished past Jaden's ears as the dark tunnel encapsulated by a light tube sucked them in.

Crossing the threshold of the radiant circle, all sound vanished. Air still raced over Jaden's skin, cooling it, but no sound accompanied it. As it thrust them downward, the dark space of the tunnel swirled with the light of the tube, accosting Jaden's eyes and making him dizzy. Just when Jaden thought he couldn't handle another second, the light became all-consuming, swallowing the black tunnel and becoming a second circle of light, marking the exit. With a whoosh, the tube spat them out. Sound rushed back. No longer under the tube's driving influence, they stopped abruptly. Jaden yelped as his wounds protested the painful end to their journey. They had arrived.

CHAPTER THIRTY-EIGHT

Staring wide-eyed at the scene laid out before them, Jaden tried making sense of it. They were almost precisely where they had been before he'd put his medallion in Han's arcachoa, but it was all different. It was day again. Or perhaps late afternoon? Way down below, an immense crowd assembled in the courtyard at the base of the temple. Almost directly ahead of them was the triangular room at the top of the tower. A tall, bony man stood on the balcony. Dressed in long, elaborately decorated robes, his face covered by a grotesque mask, he addressed the throng in a strange language.

Comprehension filtered through Jaden's sluggish mind. They had most definitely been transported back in time. There was no sign of anything modern anywhere. Fiery torches burned in the triangular room. The people gathered in the courtyard wore simple clothing made from rough cloth, lacking color. The land surrounding the tower wasn't the rocky wasteland of the future. Instead, fields lush with crops stretched away from the temple. Rudimentary farm implements lay scattered where the people had left them when they went to gather. Herds of cows, sheep, goats, and donkeys grazed lazily within the confines of crude wooden fences in expansive open areas between the fields. These people were a civilization unto themselves. They appeared wholly self-sufficient.

Jaden turned back to the room at the top of the tower when the man, presumably some form of priest, suddenly stopped talking. What they were witnessing was some ancient ceremony.

"Take heed, Voyager," Han commanded, "and you will see what it is you have to do."

Jaden nodded, observing as the man walked back into the center of the room and knelt. This basic act highlighted a glaring omission.

"Han, there's no medallion on the floor!" Jaden hissed.

"Hmm, so I see," Han answered, making no effort to keep his voice down.

"Shh, they'll hear us!"

"Seeker, they are oblivious to our presence. The arcachoa makes us invisible to those in the alternate timeline."

"Great, something else I didn't know," Jaden mumbled.

"Pardon me?"

"Nothing. We should pay attention."

The man appeared to be pressing something into the stones, but they were too far away for Jaden to be sure. "Can we get closer?"

Han obliged, but it didn't help. The man had his back to them, obscuring his actions. The only way to establish exactly what the man was doing was if they were on the other side of the room. And there was no opening on that side.

Movement near the stairs leading into the room drew Jaden's eyes like a magnet. Two men herded a prisoner into the room like an animal. They dragged him forward by the rope tied around his neck, making him stumble, his movements further hindered by the shackles binding his hands and feet.

Jaden's gaze flitted back to the altar, piled high with wood. Next to the altar, buckets brimmed with a dark, viscous liquid. And on a small side table, beside a perfectly folded, silky, jet black cloth, a jeweled dagger sat prominently displayed in its holder. There was no doubt. This was a human sacrifice. Jaden's stomach turned.

"Han, do we really have to watch this part too?"

"Possibly."

Jaden focused on the prisoner. He blinked. Now he *was* imagining things. "Han, tell me you're seeing what I am?"

"I am, and I have no explanation," Han breathed.

There was no mistake then. The prisoner Jaden had so blithely ignored upon first glance was unmistakably himself. His mind clicked through options furiously as he considered the implications. They towed his doppelgänger to the altar. With more illumination in that part of the room, Jaden could now see the multitude of cuts and bruises all over the young man's body. *What did they do to him?*

The guards yanked their prisoner toward them, pulling away bits of raw skin at his wrists and ankles as they removed his shackles. The man slumped vertically. Either the process had been painful, or the young man was very weak—or both. The guards caught the falling man, tossing him onto the unlit pyre. Working quickly, they tied him down. *Get up! Fight!* But the young man did not move. He just lay there, either unconscious or resigned to his fate.

The priest straightened, drawing Jaden's attention. He stalked toward them, past the bound prisoner, holding an oddly shaped stone in front of him. When he reached the balcony, he stepped forward ceremoniously. As soon as he was within sight of the people in the courtyard, a hush descended. The hideous mask whipped from left to right and right to left as the priest inspected his audience. Evidently pleased with what he saw, he lifted the rock above his head and launched into some long incantation.

"What's he saying?" Jaden asked Han.

"I wish I knew."

Jaden sighed. "Obviously, an interpreter is too much to ask for. Where's Kayla when we need her?"

He missed her. He wished she was here. But if wishes were stars, and stars were within reach, anything would be possible. He would have to trust Han's word that she was safe. Unbidden, memories flashed through Jaden's mind. Kayla's feisty attitude, her zest for life. Her lovely face and lively green eyes, sparkling with mischief. A yearning for Kayla such as he'd never known before filled him.

And shocked him into a realization. This was no mere teen fling. His feelings for Kayla were serious. Far deeper than he'd realized. She was *The One*. Regret pummeled him. If they ever got out of here, he would tell her how much she meant to him. He should've already. All his excuses for waiting now showed as what they were: the skins of reasons stuffed with lies. But it wasn't the time for regrets. If Jaden had any hope of making good on his resolution, he had work to do.

Han smiled. "Yes, she may well have been able to help. But there's no guarantee. And I'm sure if we needed to understand, that would've happened."

"The arcachoa can do that too?"

"No, but Zareh could."

Jaden grunted. "No surprise."

"I think the important thing here is not that we understand what that abhorrent man is saying, but that we remember what he does."

"If you say so."

They lapsed into silence. The priest droned on. When he finally quieted, he reached behind him and plucked the black cloth off the nearby side table. Carefully, he wrapped the fragment of rock in the cloth, coating it several times. Then he secured the bundle in a leather pouch on the gold girdle around his waist. With measured steps, he made for the ladder. Then he began climbing. The man disappeared between the two levels for a moment, then appeared above the overhang.

Jaden noticed something he hadn't before. "The ladder goes all the way to the top of the tower."

"Yes, it does," Han murmured, keeping his bright eyes on the priest.

For someone with skin crinkled enough to be ancient, the priest climbed fast. In minutes, he reached the top.

Figuring this was what they'd been waiting for, Jaden leaned forward on Han as they hovered over the scene.

The priest's quick, furtive glances all around made it plain he intended whatever happened next to be covert. Jaden glanced down. The overhang hid the priest from the crowd in the courtyard. No one would know what he did up here. Except them.

Deciding it was safe, the priest hooked his feet around the rungs and behind the rails of the ladder, gripping the ladder with his feet so he could free his arms. Positioned on the west side of the tower as the ladder was, the man reached around the pyramid with his arms and simultaneously pressed the pyramid's north and south sides in their very center, about six inches from the top. Then he pressed the east side, followed by the side he was resting against in the same general position. The man repeated the pattern in reverse, this time on the line of stones immediately above those he had just touched, followed by another circuit, another level higher.

Huh, he's pressing the stones in a sequence, like the code on a keypad. Ingenious! Jaden memorized the pattern as the man worked his way to the highest level, another three circuits.

Pressing the final stone, the priest waited as the top part of the pyramid disappeared down on itself, each of the four sides sliding back into the lower section of the tower. A small, rimmed ledge was all that remained. The priest, uttering more unintelligible words, placed the cloth-wrapped stone on the ledge. As though the act had relieved him of a great burden, his shoulders drooped. Then he pressed a small indentation on the northern side of the tower, just below the ridge. The capstone rose back into position, covering the compartment. And the man descended.

"Han, we need to get that rock," Jaden said.

"We must be in our own timeline to accomplish that."

"How do we get back there?"

"Remove your medallion from the arcachoa."

Jaden stretched out his hand. A commotion in the tower distracted him. Someone, a girl, had run into the tower room. She arrowed for the priest who had just stepped down from the ladder. Her long, blonde hair, dirty and disheveled, hung limply, disguising her face but not her distress.

Wailing, she latched onto the priest's arm. With a brutality that shocked Jaden, the man lashed out, striking her face so hard she fell down. Whimpering, she curled up, running a hand along her bruised face, pushing her hair back. Kayla!

Jaden's heart twisted. His mind told him this wasn't his Kayla, as the prisoner down there wasn't really him. But emotions overrode logic, every inch of him clamoring to save this girl. "Han, we have to help her!"

"That's not our Kayla. Our Kayla is back in our own time." When Jaden opened his mouth, Han cut him off. "No, I have no explanation for why these people look like you and Kayla. It's quite unsettling."

"How do you know it's not really us?" Jaden pressed, his mind refuting Han's words.

"Because we can't physically enter or be a part of an alternate timeline. The arcachoa only allows a view of the events transpiring at that time. It does not allow for physical interaction."

"So it's impossible to mix the two worlds?"

"Mostly," Han replied. "But we'll discuss another time. We must get back."

Jaden leaned forward again. With his hand floating over his medallion, he glanced back toward the triangular room, spotting the priest's raised arm. He was about to strike the girl again. But he never got the chance. Ebony smoke curled into the room, thin and wispy at first but growing in density and volume until it filled the room. The priest went rigid and collapsed face down on the floor.

Across the space of time, Jaden watched, transfixed, when the smoke coalesced into the shape of a man, his features refining by the millisecond. Then he was whole. Devilishly handsome, his jet-black hair fell in waves to just below his neck. His sculpted physique—enviably so—stood over six feet. But when Jaden gazed into his cruel, coal-black eyes, he saw an evil so rampant it was paralyzing. Beyond doubt, this was the person who had appeared in his mother's dreams. This was who the gliders called "Usurper." Jaden understood why. Wickedness washed off the man in waves, chilling Jaden's bones to their very core.

The new arrival acknowledged neither Han nor Jaden. All his attention was centered on Jaden's twin, lying helpless like a trussed-up chicken on the altar. Grabbing a flaming torch, he strutted toward the Kayla and Jaden replicas. Reaching the altar, he drew a long, brutally twisted blade from his dark cloak.

"Jaden, we cannot tarry any longer!"

Han's warning rang in Jaden's ears, but his eyes remained glued on the embodiment of evil. His fingers touched the medallion just as his nemesis stepped forward, standing over Jaden's replica, the torch in one raised hand and his blade in the other.

With an anguished cry, Kayla's twin leaped between the other Jaden and the blade just as it plunged downward. Jaden watched, aghast, as the blade sank into her chest. All the way to the hilt. An agonized, involuntary scream erupted from his throat.

At that precise moment, his fingers, fumbling around the medallion's edge, finally found the way to wrench it free. As the time tunnel pulled on them, Jaden's adversary jerked his head toward him, pinning him with deep, impenetrable black eyes.

CHAPTER THIRTY-NINE

"I thought you said we were invisible in that timeline," Jaden shouted as the circle of light sucked them in.

"Typically, we are," Han yelled back. "But then, the Usurper's not just anyone."

The absolute silence of the tunnel muted further conversation. This time, Jaden didn't feel the tunnel's discomfort as it blasted them back to their own time. Because, suffocating him, the evil soaking the apparition's presence pursued him back through time, its oppressive weight squeezing air from his lungs, chasing even thoughts of what had happened to Kayla's twin from his mind. By the time they crossed the threshold marking the end of the tube, Jaden gasped for air.

Han's voice reached him from a distance. "Jaden! Are you alright?"

Incapable of speech, Jaden nodded, gulping air into his starved lungs. It felt like an elephant had taken up residence on his chest. The feeling eased as his lungs filled, and his breathing returned to normal. Shaking his head to clear his clouded mind, Jaden struggled to return to reality.

Did that really happen? Or is it just an omen of what's coming? Did Kayla's twin die? The torch the Usurper held over my twin—is that the "burn" in the riddle? Or is this just all some cruel coincidence? Maybe all this has happened before. How many times has Slurpy tried to conquer our world, and how many times have we already stopped him? Does all that even have anything to do with what I must do now—recover that cloth-wrapped stone at the top of the tower?

The questions buzzed like angry hornets trapped in his head. Everything was a fuzzy mess as Jaden clawed free of the past's swampy haze. He vaguely registered Han was shouting at him. "Okay, I hear you. Settle down."

"Jaden, you can't dwell on that past. I need your full attention here, centered on the task at hand!"

"I know, I know," Jaden muttered. "Give me a minute."

His head felt like it would explode. Jaden snapped his water bottle off his belt and took a long draught. Water gushed down his throat, soothing and refreshing. Breathing, Jaden drank more. His hands were shaking. Was this because of what he'd seen happen to the "other" Kayla? He couldn't clear his mind of that image—the knife plunging into her chest. Why had she placed herself in harm's way? Was that destined to be her fate this time too? He felt sick. Jaden took another sip of water, trying to quench the dryness in his throat that wouldn't leave. Blocking the disturbing image, his head finally cleared. Jaden focused on what was in front of him, surprised to find Han had positioned them alongside the needle.

"Are you ready yet?" Han pushed, tension weaving a steel timbre into his deep voice.

"I am."

Han moved them closer, keeping his wings clear of the tower while placing Jaden within easy reach of the pyramid. Meticulously, Jaden counted the levels from the top. When he was sure he had the correct layer, he began the sequence.

Pressing the various stones in order, his fingers worked their way to the top. To Jaden's surprise, the stones moved with ease, considering how much time must've passed since the priest hid the parcel there. Jaden had expected to find the tiny slits allowing for movement gritted up, but evidently, the wind up here swept debris away, as opposed to depositing it. Jaden's fingers touched the last stone.

Pushing it, he waited. A shrill grating abraded his ears. Then the sides of the pyramid slid down on themselves, as they had in the other timeline.

Jaden stared at the bundle. The fabric covering the stone had not survived the centuries intact. Its tattered remains flapped in the breeze. Jaden retrieved the bundle, separating the cloth from the stone. He dropped the rags onto the ledge, where the wind picked them up and tossed them away.

Inspecting the stone, Jaden found it didn't look like anything special. Just a piece of rock. *But it must be important, or there wouldn't be such a fuss associated with it, right?* Sighing, Jaden secured the rock in the zippered pocket of his smart suit alongside the map. Then he pressed the switch and closed the pyramid.

"You have the rock?" Han asked, squinting back at him.

"Yes, but I have no clue what we're supposed to do with it."

"The others might know. They're in the tower room."

"You mean Kayla?" Jaden asked, daring to hope.

Han rolled his eyes. "Yes. And Atu."

"Naturally." Jaden grinned, his soul singing. Not that he didn't care about the others. Kayla was simply so much more important to him than anyone else. It was only then that Jaden noticed the hundreds of gliders forming a protective barrier around them, filling the sky on all sides. "Wow! You really found them," he breathed, enthralled.

"We did. They've been here, keeping us safe while you recovered the stone."

"They killed the other Gaptors?"

"I assume that was their goal. Whether they succeeded, I don't know, but I'm sure Tazanna won't pass up the opportunity to gloat."

"She's here?"

"She is, with Kayla and Atu. They're waiting for us in the tower," Han reiterated.

"What are we waiting for then?" Jaden hollered, his heart leaping at the thought of seeing Kayla again.

With a throaty chuckle, Han arced them away from the pinnacle. Only, he didn't aim straight for the triangular room. Taking a detour, he winged them through the mob of gliders looping, curling and rolling around the tower. Jaden spotted Taz in their midst, carousing with newfound friends. He grinned. This was Taz as he had never expected to see her. She spotted him and assumed a more ladylike demeanor. He waved, delighted she was safe. Then she disappeared in the throng, and they were in the middle of a whole new group. Shouted greetings floated their way, and Jaden was astonished to hear his own name more than once. "Your friends know who I am?"

"Yes, Seeker. They've waited for you for a very long time."

Jaden swallowed the lump in his throat. *All these gliders. Here. For us.* "How can we ever thank them for their help?"

"Thanks are unnecessary. In fact, if you understood our language, you would know they were thanking you."

Jaden snorted. "What for? They're the ones taking all the heat, confronting that horde of Gaptors."

"Are they?" Han answered quietly.

His mild question had Jaden reconsidering. Looking at it from another angle, he could understand that the gliders were thankful their little band had taken up the gauntlet. But the gliders were taking out the Gaptors in one-on-one combat. They didn't have DDs or relic stones. "I still don't get why they're grateful," Jaden decided.

"You will, one day. Prepared for your reunion?"

Jaden was. But his somber mood had returned. There was still so much he didn't know. Mainly whether the events he'd seen in the alternate timeline were things that had happened to him and Kayla or two people who just resembled them. The thought was disturbing.

At the tower, Han tipped him toward the balcony, then took off to join the other circling gliders as soon as he was free. Jaden tried to soften his landing, taking as much weight off his injured leg as he could. Nevertheless, the landing hurt, and he drew in a sharp breath as he came to a stop and stood.

Turning, Jaden faced the room. His breathing hitched when he saw Kayla running toward him, the most magnificent thing he had ever seen. Without a word, he moved toward her, going as fast as his injured leg would allow. All he could think about was having her in his arms again and never letting go.

"Jaden, what's wrong?" Kayla slowed as she neared, her smile faltering when she noticed his grim expression and pronounced limp.

He went to her, wrapping her in his arms. The relief, oh the blessed relief that she was alright. Jaden never wanted to be separated from her again. She melted into his arms, showing no signs of reserve. Jaden hugged her closer, thrilled. He hadn't been sure how she would react, but if the hug she was giving him was any sign, she was at least glad to have him back too. Jaden held the embrace longer than he knew he should've. But he couldn't help himself. What if he'd really seen their fate? He squeezed her tighter.

"Jaden, ease up. You're squashing me," Kayla gasped.

"Sorry," Jaden mumbled, dropping his arms, abashed.

Kayla studied him. "You still haven't told me what's wrong."

"I'm just relieved you're alright."

"Why wouldn't I be?" Kayla half-laughed, mystified by his behavior.

Jaden shrugged. "Life and death situations and all that." He couldn't stop staring at her. Kayla was here, and she was safe. And even if he couldn't tell her how he felt right now because there were so many others around, he could at least be with her.

Kayla eyed him. "Aren't we all in the same boat?"

"We are. And for that reason, we should appreciate our friends when we have the chance." Breaking the almost hypnotic effect she had on him, Jaden turned to Atu and dragged his surprised friend into a heartfelt hug. "Thanks for being there for us."

"Sure, bro. Like Kayla said, we're all in this together."

They stood there for a moment, grinning at each other.

Then Atu rubbed his fingers together, noticing the sticky blood. His eyes went to Jaden, picking out his injured leg. Gripping Jaden's shoulders, Atu turned him around. "Jaden, your back!"

Jaden grimaced. "It's not as bad as it looks. My leg hurts more. The Gaptor's tail stung me."

Atu plucked his pouch from his belt. Rummaging in it, he

produced a vial of purplish liquid. "Drink this. It will counteract the venom."

Jaden took the vial, swallowing the liquid in one gulp. At once, the fire in his leg died down. "Ah, that feels much better!"

"Doesn't it?" Atu grinned, but his attention was on Jaden's back. Extracting a different container from his pouch, he dipped his fingers into the gel. "This will hurt."

"Can't be worse than what I'm feeling now," Jaden muttered, waving Atu's concern away.

"Actually, it will be."

"If making it worse will make it better, I'll take it."

"Take a seat, then, and unzip the top part of your suit."

Jaden sat, and Atu used one hand to pull the smart suit away before smearing the gel onto the first of the serrated wounds running down Jaden's back. Jaden jerked away, gasping.

"Want a breather before the next one?"

Jaden gritted his teeth. "No, just get on with it."

"As you wish," Atu answered, starting on the next jagged line.

Jaden thought the fire in his leg had been bad, but this was far worse. Whenever Atu applied the gel, the pain intensified. Just when his vision began alternating between streaks of light and black spots, Atu leaned back.

"All done."

"Thanks," Jaden managed, breathing hard.

"Give it time," Atu cautioned when Jaden made to stand after a few minutes.

"Oh goody," Jaden muttered, but he was secretly pleased he didn't have to exert himself just yet. Obedient, he remained where he was.

Aiming for distraction, Kayla said, "Tell us what you found at the top of the tower."

"A rock."

"A rock?"

"Yes, a boring old piece of stone. No markings, no engravings, no coded message. No clues for what we should do with it." Jaden pulled the rock from inside his smart suit.

As soon as Kayla laid eyes on it, she squealed. Reaching forward, she snatched the rock from him.

Jaden blinked, nonplussed. "It means something?"

"Only because Atu and I were there when it happened," Kayla replied.

Jaden waited for an explanation. When none was forthcoming, he moaned, "Really? I have to ask?"

Kayla, studying the rock, raised her eyes. "Oh, sorry! A few minutes before you joined us, Atu and I heard this almighty crack. We thought a Gaptor had crashed into the tower or that part of the tower was coming down. But no Gaptor and no falling rock. Then we figured out the noise had come from inside the room."

"Could you just spit it out already?"

Kayla grinned, pointing at the medallion etched on the floor. "Turns out it was that."

Jaden studied the spot. An irregular indentation marred the previously level surface of the medallion, the exact shape and size of the rock in Kayla's hands. "A key!"

"I believe so." Kayla beamed.

"What are you waiting for? Try it already!"

"Before we do, shouldn't we at least confirm this is where the map was leading us?" Kayla asked.

It was Jaden's turn to roll his eyes. "Really? Like there's any probability the map will lead us somewhere else?"

"I agree the likelihood is low, but I want to be sure we're not missing something here."

Shrugging, Jaden retrieved the map, running through the twists and turns that unlocked it. When it floated free, there was no doubt. The glowing dot pulsed directly above the depression in the floor. "Now can we try it?"

Kayla laughed. "Oh, alright, if we must."

Jaden paused mid-way through moving his hand to put the map away. Hearing her laugh again was liberating. He would never tire of the sound. Chuckling with Atu at Kayla's glee, he completed the motion he had started, covering and closing the map with his palm.

Not bothering to return the map to his pocket, Jaden shuffled closer to Kayla, and Atu followed. When they surrounded the depression, Kayla bent and slotted the stone into the hollow. With a soft sucking sound, the indentation absorbed the stone, seamlessly melding it with the surrounding rock. In an instant, it was impossible to tell where the stone key had been.

Jaden stared, wondering what it meant. Then a scraping sound signified something else was happening. Astounded, they watched as a thick slab of rock, about a square foot, dropped and slid sideways, exposing a shallow compartment.

Three heads bent forward. Peering into the hole, Jaden was close enough to Kayla to feel her rubbing her birthmark. "You okay?"

"Yup, my arm just feels like it's on fire," Kayla complained. "But it'll be alright."

Kayla stopped the soothing motion a moment later. Jaden, hands wrapped around their map, and Atu, hands curled around his medical pouch, both looked to her. Kayla frowned and then grinned, realizing they were allowing her the honor.

Reaching in, Kayla withdrew the contents. Lifting them into the light, she revealed three items: a long, slender, pure white feather; a soft scrap of thin, irregularly shaped leather with clear markings and a glossy, paneled wooden cube.

Fire, brilliant blue and blisteringly hot, bulleted into Jaden's hand. He yelped. Yanking his hand back from the source, he inadvertently flung the disc housing their map back over his shoulder. It soared through the air, trailing a flaming blue streak of liquid lava. Then the light disappeared, and the blazing blue cooled to a dull, lifeless gray as a fine mist of ash fell to the floor. Jaden stared, rooted to the spot. *What just happened?*

"Was that our map?" Kayla whispered.

"Yeah, bro, please tell me that wasn't our map," Atu echoed.

CHAPTER FORTY

"It was," Jaden babbled, confused. "But I don't know what happened. It just burst into flames. I did nothing to it."

"Entirely true, that is not," a familiar voice squeaked.

The teens spun. Zareh stood there, his head cocked to one side, observing the trio with his bright, beady eyes. "Well, all at once, welcome me do not!"

Jaden glared. "Why should we? You'll just deliver your cryptic messages, then disappear again before we can get any proper answers!"

Zareh clucked. "Ah, that temper of yours, tamed you have not."

"What are you doing here?" Jaden demanded.

"Jaden!" Kayla warned. "We won't get anywhere if you're so aggressive."

Zareh smiled. "Kayla, thank you I do. His voice of reason, you still are." Facing Atu, he said, "For your invaluable services in the battle today, my sincere thanks."

Atu smiled and, to Jaden's annoyance, gave a slight bow. "A worthy task considering the gift you gave our family."

Biting back irritation, Jaden repeated his question. "What are you doing here? And you might as well start by explaining how I was wrong about doing nothing to our map."

Zareh sighed. "Come I did, your success to congratulate. Our highest expectations surpassed you have. For your commitment to this mission, grateful we are."

"You're welcome," Kayla and Atu chimed in unison.

His statement just made Jaden's temper soar. "Fine, we've exceeded your expectations. But that only raises more questions—again. Like the 'we' you referred to in that last sentence. How many of you are there? And do the three of us answer to all of you? And lest you forget, I'm still waiting for that explanation."

Zareh studied him, choosing his words. "Technically, wrong you were about your map not affecting. Initiated, its destruction was, when into the light the cube you brought. Know your map did, that complete its task was."

"An inanimate object had a brain that could tell it to terminate itself when another object revealed itself?" Jaden mocked. "Yeah, right!"

Zareh gazed at Jaden, no hint of what he felt expressed either on his ancient face or in his body language. "Better, perhaps, communicated I should have. Correct, you are—a brain, the map had not. But a sensor, it had. React to the cube's proximity, programmed it was."

Jaden felt like an idiot. It could've had something like that. Annoyed with himself for the oversight and to cover his embarrassment, he asked, "Why?"

"Because achieved its objective, it had." Zareh raised a hand, waving away Jaden's unvoiced question. "Lead you to the first of three artifacts and another map, that was. Need these, you will, if this quest successfully to complete, you are."

"So which one's the map? The cube?" Kayla guessed, cutting Jaden off before he could continue his tirade.

"Thinking as always." Zareh smiled.

Taking the feather from Kayla, Atu studied it. "How does a feather help us save the world?"

"Become clear at the opportune time, it will. Of the utmost importance now, safe you keep it, at all costs. To your victory, essential it is."

"More so than the book?" Jaden asked, his mind working overtime.

Tilting his head, Zareh scratched his chin with a long, curved, black claw. "A tough question to answer, that be. Almost equally valuable, they are."

"But if it comes down to the wire, and we have to make a choice?" Jaden pressed.

"The feather, it would have to be. Around the loss of the book, work we can, if we must, but impossible this is, if lost the feather were."

"Alright then—the feather it is. Before you disappear, can you explain what I saw when I was in the alternate timeline?" Jaden appealed.

"A picture of the past, was that not?" Zareh answered. When Jaden opened his mouth again, Zareh interrupted. "And, the important thing there, was it not, the manner in which the stone key to retrieve, it was?"

Jaden considered Zareh's words. His tone had carried an unmistakable warning. What Jaden couldn't fathom was what Zareh was trying to warn him about.

Zareh didn't wait for Jaden to figure it out. "Expired, my time here has. Leave, I must. The next seeker find. Before long, require her aid, you will."

And then he vanished. Jaden cursed. "Didn't I say he brings more questions than answers?" he complained, looking to Atu for confirmation.

But Atu just shook his head in amazement. Jaden threw his hands up, exasperated. He turned to Kayla.

She laughed, shaking her head. "You're preaching to the choir here."

"Why does he do that? It's the most annoying thing on the planet!" Jaden seethed.

Kayla thought. "I can't answer that. But I can tell you there's no point getting upset about it. We already know we will only get enough information to get us to the next point in our journey."

"And that doesn't bother you?"

"It does! I loathe not controlling my destiny as much as you. But sometimes, we must accept the only option is to move forward in faith. And this would be one of those times. Have you always had all the answers when you ventured into unknown territory?"

"Obviously not."

"Proving my point. Sometimes, you only have an idea about what you want to achieve, without knowing how you'll get there. And because you want that predetermined result, you press on regardless, trusting you'll figure it out along the way. That's my take on this. We've been chosen. And we can either act to keep those we love safe, or we can effectively opt out of our responsibilities by wasting time ranting and raving about the details." Jaden remained quiet, and Kayla moved closer, adding, "Sometimes we have to trust someone other than ourselves."

Her last sentence brought that horrid image of the blade sinking into her chest crashing back to screaming life. Jaden wouldn't survive if her trust in him led to her death. But what she had said was true. They would have to exercise more than a little trust to succeed. He already trusted her implicitly. He trusted Atu. And their gliders. Was it really that crucial he knew every minuscule part of the plan? "You're right. If we don't move forward in faith, we may as well quit now."

Kayla beamed, that smile lighting her beautiful face. Jaden ached at her nearness. He longed to enfold her in his arms again, draw her close. Inhale her delicate, sweet scent, run his hands through her long hair, touch his mouth to hers. But he wasn't sure if she was ready to acknowledge her feelings for him. Maybe the hug earlier meant she was getting closer to a commitment—but was she there yet?

Regardless of her position, Jaden had resolved to discuss things with her, and he would. Just not right now. They had work to do. Suppressing his emotions with difficulty, he returned his attention to Atu. "Are you back on our planet yet?"

"Yes," Atu said, although he still looked a little awestruck by Zareh's appearance.

"Well, you can pull Zareh down from that golden pedestal you've put him on. He's more likely to disappoint you than give you answers."

"It is his way," Atu accepted. Then with more conviction, he said, "Followers do not question where they are led. They simply follow, trusting the path is the right one."

Jaden glanced at Kayla, amused to find her giving exaggerated hand signs showing Atu had lost it. He leaned in and whispered, "I'm with you."

Kayla giggled, the delightful sound bubbling out of her. Her heady scent filled his senses, and Jaden pulled back before he did anything rash.

Atu gazed at them, a superior, knowing expression on his face, as though he knew something they didn't. When he spoke, his tone was aloof. "Think what you will. Zareh is leading us on the right path."

"So you say," Jaden grumbled. "Did either of you notice his little speech only mentioned two of the three things we found?"

The others considered, and Kayla nodded. "So he did. He implied the cube held the map, but he didn't confirm it, did he?"

Jaden scowled. "He didn't. But assuming the map *is* in the cube, and the feather *is* the artifact, then what is the piece of leather for?"

"An excellent question," Kayla murmured, unfurling the curiously shaped scrap of leather. "It's still in excellent condition, and . . . ow!" Dropping the piece in Jaden's surprised hands, Kayla yanked up her shirt sleeve, inspecting her birthmark.

"Kayla, what's wrong?" Jaden was instantly alert when pain scrunched up her face.

"Wretched birthmark! It feels like it's on fire."

Jaden touched her birthmark, then jerked his hand away. "Yeah, that's toasty."

Atu stepped forward to offer his aid, but Kayla's face abruptly cleared. "Don't worry, the sensation's gone."

Not ready to leave anything to chance, Jaden touched her arm again. "Yeah, it's back to normal."

"See, all good," Kayla muttered. Eager to focus their attention on something else, Kayla said, "Why don't you spread that leather out so I can see what it says?"

Still casting dubious glances her way, Jaden did as asked, spreading the leather on the floor and revealing the markings.

Kayla frowned at them for a moment.

"What?" Jaden asked. "Can you read what it says?"

"Yes, it's the same language as that on the wall. But it makes no sense."

"Tell us what it says already!" Jaden exclaimed.

Kayla grinned, an impish expression on her face. "I wondered how long you could hold out." When Jaden made a move toward her, she danced away, giggling. "Alright, alright! But don't say I didn't warn you. Roughly translated, it reads, 'Believing with faith.'"

Jaden groaned. "Now what's that supposed to mean?"

Atu smiled. "I think it means what it says. Weren't you two just talking about this, albeit with a lot more words?"

Jaden and Kayla glanced at one another. So they had. Were the words there as confirmation for them to press on?

It was Jaden who said it. "Do you think that's what the symbols said before we started talking, or do you think they rearranged themselves after we spoke?"

Atu chuckled. "We'll never know, will we?"

"Perhaps," Kayla mused. "If the words change again, we'll know it's possible they changed before we saw them the first time." Shaking her head, Kayla said, "But Atu's right. We shouldn't get hung up on it. What we should focus on is that it seems we still have two more artifacts to find."

"And the last seeker," Jaden added. "Does anyone have any bright ideas on how we find her?"

"The map led us to both last time. Think this one will do the same?" Kayla asked.

"I hope so," Jaden replied. "If not, perhaps Han and Taz will have some suggestions."

The mention of their gliders had all three teens turning toward the opening off the balcony. Hundreds of gliders weaved and swirled around the tower.

"I think they're getting a kick out of being with their own kind," Kayla said, a smile on her face.

Jaden nodded. "Yes, they are. But what will we do with all those gliders when we leave?"

"I assumed they would come with us," Atu answered. "No one can see them."

"I suppose that's one solution," Jaden conceded. "But it would be like traveling with an entourage. We'd be announcing our position, giving away any tactical advantage a small group provides."

"He speaks with wisdom," a deep, gravelly voice asserted.

The teens found Pallaton floated at the opening to the left of the balcony.

"It is a genuine pleasure to meet you, Jaden. I am Pallaton, leader of the Lost Legion."

Jaden dipped his head toward the distinguished-looking, older bat. "Trust me, the honor's all mine. I can't thank you for helping us defeat our enemies—or for keeping my friends safe."

Pallaton grinned wickedly, showing teeth even longer and sharper than Han's. "It was our pleasure. And one I am sure we will relish repeating before your mission is over."

Jaden laughed. "With that threatening tone and those wicked teeth, I'm glad you're on our side!"

The others laughed, and Pallaton's grin spread, revealing more of his ferocious teeth. He looked positively deadly.

Jaden said, "I agree we'll encounter more Gaptors before we finish this. You've fought them before—with Atu's ancestors?"

"We have," Pallaton confirmed.

"In that case, you're the best person to make recommendations on how we should proceed. Do you mind weighing in?"

"Thank you, I'd like that."

"Do you agree that traveling with a sizeable group could be a liability?"

"I do. Such a convergence would draw every Gaptor to us, like rats to rot. Far better the Legion sends scouts to gather information than acting as your escorts."

"But what if we get into trouble? What if we need help?" Atu blurted. "Or if you need healing?"

Pallaton smiled. "Healer, it is touching you would think of us. But we are here to help you—not the other way around. It is our duty to provide you with your best chance at success. There may not be another opportunity, and we are all willing to do whatever it takes to guarantee a favorable outcome. If you need our aid, all you need do is blow on this."

Pallaton pulled a delicate, short pipe made of reed from under his wing and gave it to Atu. The teens peered at where he'd taken it from, wondering where he'd hidden it. But they couldn't tell.

Atu took the pipe, awe stamped on his face. "How close do we have to be for you to hear it?"

Pallaton laughed, the throaty, rumbling sound rebounding off the walls of the compact room, filling it with a rich resonance. "Distance is not an issue with the reed. Just blow, and we will find you wherever you are."

"I guess that means this is goodbye then?" Jaden asked.

"It is, Seeker. But I will leave Aren, my best warrior, here for the Healer's personal use."

Atu's face glowed. "Really? I get my own glider?"

Pallaton chuckled. "You do, Healer. We can't have you embarking on this quest as the only voyager without one!"

Atu grinned. "Yes, how would that look to your kin back home?"

Still chuckling, Pallaton gave a long, low whistle, similar to the one he'd used before to command his troops, and a huge glider, young and muscular, drifted closer to the tower.

"Aren, I have paired you with Healer," Pallaton informed him.

"Thank you for the honor, Pallaton," Aren hummed. "I will protect him with my life."

"See that you do. You know what is at stake."

Aren inclined his head and looked at Atu. "Healer, I am delighted to make your acquaintance."

Atu nodded, running closer to the enormous bat. "I am likewise pleased to meet you. I look forward to traveling with you."

"Ah, no, not this again," Jaden motioned, rolling his eyes theatrically. "Enough of the formality! Atu, give him a nickname already."

Kayla's laughter bubbled out at the affronted expression on Atu's face.

"I will not," Atu declared.

"We'll see." Jaden smirked, shaking his head knowingly.

"Seeker, it is time we left. The longer we linger, the more attention we draw to this place," Pallaton counseled.

"Yes, we have what we came for. It's time to go." Jaden scooped the scrap of leather off the floor. Wrapping it together with the feather and cube inside a piece of clothing, he secured the three items in his backpack.

As if he had heard Jaden, Han appeared at the opening near the balcony. A second later, Taz popped up alongside Han.

"Ready to leave?" Taz asked Kayla.

"Am I ever! Something about this place gives me the creeps."

Without another second's hesitation, Kayla sprinted forward and flung herself off the balcony. Taz grinned and dove to collect her.

"Your turn," Jaden said to Atu.

Atu loped to the edge of the balcony. His relationship with Aren would require time to reach the same level of mental communication the other voyagers shared with their gliders. "May I do the same as Kayla?"

"Oh, I like him!" Aren beamed at Pallaton. Then addressing Atu, he said, "Go for it."

With a whoop, Atu leaped off the balcony, and Aren darted after him. Jaden shook his head, smiling. What was the world coming to when teenagers wanted to hurl themselves off high balconies? He turned to Pallaton, still waiting at the other opening. "Take care of your Legion."

"I will, Seeker. We will meet again."

"We'd better. See you on the other side."

Pallaton nodded, then arced away. Jaden glanced at the opening where Han was waiting, grinning at him.

"So, how will we outdo the others?" Han teased.

"Oh, I'm sure I can come up with something," Jaden sniggered. He thought for a moment. Then he snapped his fingers. "Okay, I have it."

He ran toward the balcony the same way the others had. But at the last moment, he twisted around so he was facing the room when he sprang. Going out backwards and doing a flip while in the air was more innovative than simply going out facing forward.

But the moment his feet left the ground, he wished he hadn't seen the room again. Leering back at him was the abysmal face from the past, its terrible beauty accentuated by the cruel smile playing at the corners of his too-beautiful mouth.

His words came to Jaden as if spoken across a great chasm. They were hollow and echoed eerily in the empty room. "Don't think you've escaped. We will meet again, Gatekeeper. And when we do, it will be the last time."

CHAPTER FORTY-ONE

Soul troubled and mind reeling, Jaden was unprepared when Han snatched him up. Landing hard, he almost bounced right off before correcting his balance and scooting to his usual flying position.

Han grunted. "Set on breaking my bones today, are you?"

"Sorry, I was distracted."

"By what?" Han asked, scanning for Gaptors.

"You didn't see the Usurper in the room just before I jumped?"

Han started. "Most certainly not! I watched you so I could time my pickup. If he'd been there, I couldn't have missed him."

Jaden said nothing. Just because Han hadn't seen him didn't mean the tyrant hadn't been there. Because, as he was learning, nothing was beyond the realm of possibility on this journey. "Never mind," Jaden muttered, too weary to dwell on it. "Where are the others?"

Relieved Jaden wasn't arguing, Han pointed them out. They had moved away from the temple and now waited with Pallaton in the middle of his Legion. Han glided them through the outer ranks until he aligned them with their friends. Jaden caught snatches of farewells as they passed the other gliders. Drawing level with Pallaton, the elder grinned at Jaden, showing off his fearsome teeth again.

"As you said, see you on the other side."

"You bet! I expect our next meeting will be sooner rather than later."

Pallaton inclined his head. Then, with a soft whistle to summon his troops, he streaked away, leading the Legion.

"What did he mean?" Kayla asked.

Jaden chuckled. "Nothing sinister, just something he was teasing me about."

When he didn't elaborate, Kayla didn't press. She seemed as tired as him. But that didn't stop her from asking, "So, where to now?"

"Yeah, bro, open the map!" Atu urged.

But Jaden shook his head. "I don't know about you, but I could do with a hot shower, some decent food, and a good night's rest before hitting the road again."

"Ooh, that sounds divine!" Kayla squealed. "Can we please, pretty please?" She fluttered her eyelashes at Taz.

Jaden grinned. He'd never seen her do that. It was a good look on her—although one he doubted he'd see too often.

Taz looked to Han and Aren, who both nodded. "It seems we agree. A short time for recuperation would be beneficial for all."

Atu still seemed hesitant. "We're splitting up? You're going to Daxsos, and I'm returning home?"

Jaden was quick to refute the notion. "I was hoping you'd come back to Daxsos with us. I know my mom would love to meet you. And she's always up for houseguests."

Atu beamed. "Really?"

"Absolutely. And since she knows who we are and what we're about, you won't have to answer awkward questions either."

"Alright!" Atu crowed. Then, thinking about it, he fidgeted nervously. "If you're sure she won't mind? I mean, I wouldn't want to impose. I can make out okay without my folks at home."

It was Kayla who assured him this time. "We wouldn't want you anywhere except with us. Don't lose hope, Atu. We'll find your parents. I'm sure of it."

Atu smiled. "Thanks. It's a blessing to have friends I can rely on."

"Home it is, then," Jaden announced.

Aren, who hadn't said a word up to this point, fell in behind Han and Taz as they headed for the horizon. Five minutes later, his voice registered surprise when he spoke. "We can travel at our usual speeds without our voyagers falling off? You have trained them well."

"We had help," Taz admitted. "The Armorer's insights and gadgets are effective."

"I take it the masks and those silver tubes covering their mouths are his doing?" Aren surmised.

Han flashed a smile. "They are. And the suits they're wearing help our voyagers maintain their balance. Although," he said, giving Jaden a sidelong glance, "they do well without them too."

Jaden grinned. "Thanks, Han. I suppose I owe you one now?"

Han chuckled, jiggling Jaden where he sat. "Try not to crush my bones on your next landing, and we'll call it good."

Aren smiled. "It sounds like there's a story there?"

Still chuckling, Han explained, then launched into a more detailed report of all that had transpired since they had met the three seekers. Conversation was lively as the others chipped in, adding their thoughts, comments, and the inevitable jibes. It would've been abnormal if Taz hadn't insisted they teach Aren their plays when the conversation slowed. So they did, adding new moves as they thought of them and giving Aren and Atu time to become attuned to one another's moods and thoughts.

It took another three days to reach Daxsos, thoughts of what he'd seen in the alternate timeline tormenting Jaden all the way there. When the Shadow Mountains eventually rose to greet them, as imperial and imposing as ever, Jaden's shoulders sagged with relief. It had been an exhausting trip, longer than he'd thought, although curiously, but mercifully, free of encounters with Gaptors. Feeling like he'd been away from home for years, Jaden was so revved about seeing his family again he could barely focus on anything else.

So when Han led them to the Jameson's rooftop landing site and the dark shroud of the approaching evening lifted to reveal the piercing glare of the noonday sun, Jaden was shocked to spot his mother's dejected figure turning to leave the deck. He had forgotten that while it had been weeks for them, no time had passed for her at all. He glanced at Kayla.

Her green eyes searched his, concern etching little furrows on her lovely features. "You okay?"

Jaden took a breath. "Yeah, thanks. I forgot about the time thing. It threw me."

Oblivious to Jaden's emotions, Atu asked, "What time thing? Is that why it's suddenly the middle of the day?"

Sensing Jaden was still out of sorts, Kayla answered. "Yes. The simple answer is when we're with our gliders, time stops for the rest of the world. If it makes any sense, even though we've been gone for weeks, we're arriving back at Jaden's home almost right after we left."

Atu whistled. "Talk about mind-blowing! That's something my ancestors never passed along."

"Perhaps it wasn't true back then—you know, like how everyone could see the Gaptors and gliders back then, but now they can't? Maybe the same principle?" Kayla theorized while studying Jaden.

"I suppose," Atu granted.

Jaden was aware of Kayla's searching gaze, but his mind couldn't focus on that. All the grief he'd felt when they left his mother was flooding back, compounding the loss he still felt every time he thought of Kayla's ancient twin falling. Was he doomed to lose them both?

The insidious undercurrent flowing beneath the surface of his calm exterior threatened to drown him. Jaden gulped air. He was home. His mother was here. And Kayla was right next to him. Nothing had happened to either of them. They were safe—for now. He should be grateful for the time he had with them and not agonize about the past or future.

Unable to help himself, Jaden called out. "Mom!" Clara Jameson stopped mid-stride. She faltered, then resumed her unsteady gait toward the exterior door. Jaden called out again, more urgently. This time, his mother turned. She waited, staring anxiously at the empty air before her.

It baffled Jaden. She couldn't possibly have heard him. How had she known he was calling out to her? He grinned. It didn't matter. He was keen to find out whether his idea would work. Han maneuvered for the landing. Not waiting, Jaden leaped off and ran to his mother.

Clara Jameson jolted, shocked when Jaden materialized as quickly as he had disappeared. Before she could utter a word, Jaden grabbed her hand. She cocked her head as he grinned mischievously. He could see her wondering what he was plotting. Easing the relic stone from his finger, he slid it onto hers. Jaden knew he had succeeded when she gasped, and wonder widened her eyes, her mouth popping open in astonishment.

His mother squealed. "Ooh, they're magnificent!"

Jaden grinned. "It's nice to see you too, Mom."

She laughed, the tinkling sound soothing Jaden's frayed nerves. Forcing her eyes away from the compelling creatures, his mother tugged him into her arms. Hugging him fiercely, she pulled back almost immediately. Squeezing his arms and then studying his face, she murmured, "Jaden, you've . . . changed."

"Uh, thanks?" Jaden mumbled, unsure what she meant.

"No, I mean it in a good way. You've filled out. Wow, look at you! I never thought I'd see the day you'd grow into your limbs. And you've caught some sun." A worried frown creased her brow. "How long were you gone?"

Jaden sighed. *Here it comes. The worried rhetoric of a parent. Best I get her focused on something else. Like my awe-inspiring friend.* "We'll fill you in later. Let me introduce Han, my glider."

Han, hovering nearby, dipped his head toward Clara. "It is an honor to meet you."

Distracted, Clara dropped into a quick, graceful curtsy. "No, the honor is mine. I can't ever thank you enough for keeping my son safe."

Han smiled. "I think you'll find he can hold his own."

Jaden chuckled. "I'm only one half of a spectacular team. Zareh did well pairing us."

"Zareh's the peculiar one your grandmother told me about?" his mother quizzed, eager for details.

"Later, Mom—have you forgotten your manners?" Jaden teased.

"You haven't said hello to Kayla or met her glider, Taz. And we brought more friends. Meet Atu. He's flying with Aren."

His mother giggled, too overcome by having her son home to worry about much else. She faced the others, still astride their gliders. "Excuse my lack of decorum. It's just such a relief having Jaden home again. Kayla, I'm so thrilled to see you home safely too. As I am to meet the rest of you."

Kayla returned the smile. "Hi, Mrs. Jameson. You don't know how nice it is to see you again."

The genuine relief in Kayla's tone had Jaden studying her more closely. Did something happen while they were apart? Although he'd spent every spare moment on their way home gazing at Kayla, drinking her in, rejoicing in her survival, his constant search for Gaptors had distracted him. He had wanted no surprise attacks. Kayla was far too precious for him to lose a second time.

But he'd been more distracted than he realized. Now that his joy at having her by his side again no longer blinded him, Jaden could see the worry pulling on her mouth, the clouds in her eyes. Guilt pricked him. How hadn't he seen this before? They'd spent days traveling home together, and he'd missed the signs. True, they hadn't had a moment alone since being reunited at the tower, but it didn't excuse his lack of attentiveness. Why didn't she dismount from Taz already? Then he could go to her, comfort her. His mother's voice reminded him where he was. *Uh, maybe now isn't the right time.* He held back the sigh, desperate to escape. Would there ever be a "right time" for them?

"Hello, Atu, it's nice to meet you," his mother said, giving her characteristic finger wave.

Waving shyly, Atu said, "You too."

It reminded Jaden of a second thing. "Mom, okay if Atu stays with us for a while?"

Clara Jameson didn't skip a beat as she answered, but Jaden saw her burying her curiosity. "Of course. You're most welcome to stay for as long as you want."

Atu beamed. "Thank you. You don't know how much that means to me."

From the look on his mother's face, Jaden thought she did.

Clara smiled. "It's always wonderful having Jaden's friends spend time with us. I'm glad you're here." Addressing the gliders, she said, "It's unexpected and quite a privilege to meet you. I never thought I'd ever see a glider in my lifetime, let alone three. You truly are the most spectacular creatures. Will you be staying too?"

Her hopeful tone made Jaden smile.

As one, the gliders grinned, showing off their perfectly pointy teeth. Han cocked his head at Jaden. "You didn't tell us your mother was so charming."

Clara giggled. "It seems I'm not the only one."

Han laughed, the throaty sound washing over them in mellow waves. "Like mother, like daughter."

"Yes, she warned me to watch you. She's very fond of you both."

"Please pass our regards on to the Wise One," Taz purred. "Thank you for your generous offer, but we won't be imposing on your hospitality. We have a place nearby where we can rest comfortably."

Ever the mother, Clara offered them food, but again, the bats declined graciously.

"There are fruit orchards near to here," Taz explained. "And we have healthy appetites."

"If you're sure then?" Clara checked. When Taz nodded, Clara said, "Well then, I'd best get to feeding the human part of this posse."

CHAPTER FORTY-TWO

Kayla nuzzled Taz, putting her cheek against the soft down behind Taz's ear. "You'll be close, right?"

"We will, Interpreter. Close enough to be here in seconds should you need us."

"Be safe then," Kayla said, giving her glider's neck a soft rub before dismounting.

After his own brief conversation with Aren, Atu followed her lead. They strolled to Jaden and Mrs. Jameson and watched as the gliders circled once before streaking away.

"Wow! They are incredible," Mrs. Jameson breathed.

"Do we get food now?" Jaden asked.

"You!" Mrs. Jameson laughed as she gave him a friendly swat. "It's reassuring to know some things haven't changed. Atu, do you eat as much as Jaden?"

Atu smiled, looking like he already felt at home.

Kayla interjected. "He'll tell you he doesn't, but don't believe him."

"Look who's talking," Atu sputtered, making them all laugh.

Mrs. Jameson led the way downstairs. "So, what'll it be?"

"Pizza," Jaden answered without hesitation.

Mrs. Jameson snorted. "Some things definitely haven't changed."

The teens made themselves useful, helping Mrs. Jameson in the kitchen. They talked as they prepared the pizza, then ate, starting the lengthy task of catching her up on all that had transpired since their departure.

When the late afternoon sun curled around her where she sat on the couch, Kayla yawned and stretched her arms above her head. "I'd better get home. I'm sure my mom will call soon to find out where I am."

On cue, her PAL chimed. Jaden smiled. "Now that's a sound I haven't heard in a while."

Kayla grinned, tapping her CC. "Hey, Mom. Your ears must be burning." She listened, then replied, "Yes, sorry, I meant to tell you I'd be hanging out with Jaden today. I'll be home soon." Kayla noticed Jaden studying her as she nodded a few times and murmured more responses before saying goodbye and clicking off.

Jaden eyed her. "Have you considered how you'll explain your tan? Or those perfectly toned muscles?"

That last question threw Kayla. He sounded like he admired them. Flustered, she wondered what else he had noticed. He was paying more attention than she'd given him credit for. But was that all there was to his attentiveness? Then the meaning behind his question filtered through, and she grimaced. "Not the faintest idea."

Mrs. Jameson cleared her throat. "We'll have to come up with a plausible reason for Atu being here too."

Kayla wrung her hands. "I had forgotten about all the lying—I hate it!"

Mrs. Jameson smiled in sympathy, the living room quiet as they contemplated the dilemma.

What else will I have to explain? Speaking of which, Jaden had some explaining of his own to do. Ever since they had left the tower, Jaden had been subdued. His mind was elsewhere, and Kayla wanted to know where. She hadn't had a moment alone with him to make good on her resolution and straighten things out regarding her feelings for him. But she had sensed his depression lurking just below the surface. It had worried her all the way home. What exactly had happened between the time she and Atu left him and their return?

That thought prompted another. Until this exact moment, she hadn't registered Jaden wouldn't be with her tonight. Neither would Atu. *But truthfully, it's Jaden I'll miss.* It would be the first night they had spent apart in weeks. After all their time together, she couldn't imagine spending even one moment without him.

Ziggety! I should've appreciated our time together on the trip home a little more. She smiled bitterly, knowing why she hadn't. They were all too preoccupied with avoiding Gaptors. She wouldn't make that mistake twice. Kayla glanced at Jaden, noting his glum expression. *What now?*

"Maybe Kayla could stay here tonight?" Jaden suggested.

Kayla almost fell off her chair. It was like he'd been reading her mind. She wasn't the only one shocked.

Mrs. Jameson turned surprised eyes on Jaden, and he added, "Just until tomorrow—until we figure out a cover story, I mean."

Kayla studied Mrs. Jameson's thoughtful gaze as she observed her son. *Yup, I know that look. When my mother looks at me like that, it's like she knows what I'm thinking.*

Jaden fidgeted under his mother's gaze. Mrs. Jameson turned that stare on Kayla and then Atu. Clearing her throat, Mrs. Jameson said, "Now don't shoot me down before you've heard me out."

Now she wasn't the focus of that stare anymore, Kayla relaxed.

Jaden was just as relieved. "You have an idea?"

"I do. But I don't think you will like it."

"Anything besides more lies, please," Kayla begged.

"Well . . . don't you think we should bring the rest of the parents into this?"

Shocked silence greeted Mrs. Jameson's proposal.

"You mean tell them the truth?" Jaden croaked. When she nodded, he said, "Mom, you realize they'll all think we've lost it?"

"It's the reason we didn't tell you at first," Kayla expounded. "And when all the lies began. I mean, who would believe stories about hideous otherworldly aberrations, ginormous bats, and teenagers on a mission to save the world?"

Clara smiled. "There is actually a simple solution." When they frowned, she hinted, "Jaden, you gave it to me today."

Jaden considered her words, then grinned. "The ring! It let you see the gliders."

"Yes, and if I can see them, then I'm sure your father and Kayla's parents can too."

Kayla looked doubtful. "Do you really think it's a good idea to tell them?"

Measuring her words, Clara replied, "Do you think it's a good idea not to? This last journey, you came home, so no problem. But what about next time?"

She didn't have to fill in the blanks. Kayla could, all too easily. What if she came home injured? Or not at all? She nodded. "You're right. They deserve to know."

Clara looked at her son. "You're quiet. What are you thinking?"

"I agree. Dad should know what's going on."

Gazing at Atu, Clara hesitated a moment before speaking. "How about your parents?"

Atu shrugged. "They already know."

Clara floundered until Jaden placed a hand on her arm. She looked at the hand and then Jaden, then understood Jaden's implication. She didn't press Atu for an explanation, especially when it was clear the mention of his parents had Atu struggling with powerful emotions.

"Alright," Mrs. Jameson said, "The sooner we tell the others, the better. Who knows when you must leave again—or whether there'll be time to explain then." Her face soured at the thought. But the negative emotion vanished, replaced by resolution. "I'm calling Sadie and inviting them over for dinner."

On impulse, Kayla asked, "Is it alright then if I just stay until dinner?"

Kayla almost regretted asking when Mrs. Jameson scrutinized her again, then flicked her gaze to Jaden, and then Atu. She must know a bond had been forged between the three of them. But did she know Kayla's bond with Jaden was stronger than any Kayla had ever felt? Desperation welled in Kayla when she thought of separating from him. And from his expression, he wasn't too keen on her leaving for even a short while, either. *Now what does all that tell Mrs. Jameson?*

"Sure, I'll let your mother know," Mrs. Jameson replied, before leaving the room to make the call.

Jaden watched his mother leave, then swiveled around. "Anyone as nervous as I am about how this will go down?"

"Yup," Kayla confessed. "But I'll be much happier when I don't have to lie anymore. Especially with all that could happen."

"I hear you," Jaden murmured, squeezing her hand.

Kayla smiled when peace settled. His touch always made everything seem so much better. Easier than it was, more bearable than it should be, more conceivable than could be hoped for. She squeezed his hand in return, hoping her touch gave him as much comfort. She really needed to have that talk with him.

The evening went better than expected. They agreed Mrs. Jameson would be their spokesperson, and she waited until dessert to drop the bomb. After their predictable shocked disbelief and vehement denials, reluctant acceptance won through, and the other adults asked Mrs. Jameson to produce the proof she'd offered. Mrs. Jameson led the entire group upstairs.

Kayla studied her parents, but they still seemed in a stupor. She knew the questions and comments would rain down as soon as their daze lifted.

Mrs. Jameson snuck a glance at Jaden. "Will they be there?"

"Probably, but it's possible they only sense it when we're in danger. I guess we'll find out."

Kayla saw her parents exchange looks when they overheard the conversation. *We'll all find out soon enough.*

The group fanned out onto the Jameson's rooftop landing site. A pleased sigh escaped Jaden when he found their gliders hovering near the edge of the roof. Then he spotted his mother's face. "Mom, what's wrong?"

Clara almost wailed. "I can't see them!"

Jaden frowned. "They're right there. You should . . ." His voice trailed off as he thought of something.

Sliding the relic stone his mother had returned off his finger and onto hers, it confirmed his suspicion when his mother's face brightened. Jaden's didn't.

"Something wrong?" Kayla asked.

Jaden shrugged. "No—just another puzzle. While my Gran only had to wear the ring once for the gliders to remain visible to her, it seems my mom has to be wearing the ring to see them."

"Could it be because Ruby's the chosen one in your family and your mom's not?" Kayla theorized, more concerned with Taz's distress.

"Perhaps," Jaden mused.

Taz interrupted. "Are you in danger?"

"No," Kayla answered, eager to calm her glider now that she understood Taz's concern.

Taz relaxed. "We sensed you needed us."

"We do." Jaden outlined the discussion that afternoon, culminating in the evening dinner and why the gliders had sensed their voyagers' need for them. He pointed out the other adults in the party, and the gliders eyed them with curiosity.

"You look like your mother," Taz commented, zipping her gaze between Kayla and Sadie.

"So everyone keeps telling me." Kayla studied her mother, squinting as she tried to find the resemblance. All the adults except Mrs. Jameson were whipping their heads around, peering into the surrounding air, their expressions a mixture of dread and anticipation. They'd figured out the teens were talking to their gliders. However, their inability to see them with their own eyes was making them edgy. It was time to break the ice.

Kayla strolled over to her mother. "Here, Mom, why don't you go first? Let me introduce you to Taz, my glider." Taking her mother's hand, Kayla transferred the relic stone from her finger onto her mother's. She wondered why the ring hadn't jumped as it had with Sven but dismissed it as a question she could rationalize later. She knew exactly when Taz and the others became visible to her mother.

Sadie Melmique took an involuntary step backwards. "Oh, my! They're huge!"

The teens cackled. Mrs. Melmique's stunned countenance was priceless. And the mixture of emotions playing on the dads' faces was just as comical.

"What were you expecting?" Kayla teased. "We travel on their backs, and we're not toddlers anymore."

If her mother heard, she didn't respond. Enthralled by the splendid creatures floating in front of her, Sadie Melmique ogled them, not bothering to hide her awe. When she realized they were waiting for her, she cleared her throat. "Uh, hello, I'm Kayla's mother, Sadie."

Taz smiled. "I'm Tazanna. They paired me with your daughter. It's a pleasure to meet you. You've raised quite a fighter."

Her mother's eyes filled with tears, and Kayla understood her mom had been hoping all that Clara Jameson had shared with them was a horrible hoax. But the proof was irrefutable.

Composing herself, Sadie replied, "Thank you. It's comforting to hear that." After a moment's hesitation, she asked, "It means your chances of success are higher, doesn't it?"

Taz, discerning Sadie's need for reassurance, gave it willingly. "These young people are the finest voyagers we could've asked for. They surpass all those who came before and about whom we learned before coming to your world. If there was ever a chance of success, it rests with them."

Kayla sent Taz a grateful smile. She could tell how much Taz's faith in them meant to her mother.

"Okay, okay, my turn already," Kayla's dad grumbled. He had been watching his wife and looked tired of only hearing half the conversation.

Sadie turned to him, a slight smile tugging at the corner of her lips. "Don't get a fright."

He grinned. "You mean like you did?"

Sadie laughed, taking his jesting in the spirit he'd intended. Holding Vicken's hand, she slid the ring off her finger, suspending it between them. "Ready?"

"Yes."

Although he didn't step back in alarm, his wonder was identical to his wife's. Vicken Melmique whistled. "Now I know what all the fuss was about. Wow!"

Taz smiled. "Thank you. I am Tazanna, your daughter's glider."

"And I am most relieved to meet you. Those teeth and claws look like very effective weapons."

Taz laughed in delight. "They are. But your daughter has a few weapons of her own that are just as fatal."

They talked for a few minutes, Taz reassuring Vicken of his daughter's abilities and Vicken passing out compliments like candy. He realized Ty was still waiting for his turn. Turning to him, Vicken said, "Ty, put the ring on. You've got to see this!"

Ty Jameson smiled at his wife, who was eyeing him. "It'll be alright. What's scarier than hearing your son and his friends are tagged to save the world?"

Clara Jameson nodded. "You have a point."

"So are you going to hand the ring over or not?"

"Sorry," Clara said, surrendering the ring. The moment it left her finger, she looked like a child who'd had her favorite toy confiscated.

Sadie gave her friend an understanding nod. "I'd never guess we'd want to keep looking at such terrifyingly wonderful creatures."

Clara chuckled. "Yes, once you get past your initial shock, you don't want to stop looking at them."

They all laughed when Ty responded in much the same way. When he began conversing with the gliders, Sadie said to Clara, "Who would've thought so much could happen in the brief time since we met?"

Clara shook her head. "Indeed. It's been quite the unforgettable few weeks since we did."

Sadie giggled. "At least we like each other. Can you imagine living through this nightmare with other parents you couldn't communicate or commiserate with?"

"Inconceivable! It's a bonus our husbands get along too."

The women turned to watch their men. They were not only exchanging banter with each other, but with the gliders too.

"Yes, a nice, tidy support group," Sadie said.

Clara didn't comment, looking like she didn't want to think about the implications.

"Sorry," Sadie grimaced, realizing what she had just inferred. "Poor wording."

"Maybe we could call ourselves a fan club instead," Clara offered. "I mean, the mascots are out of this world!"

That sent them both into uncontrollable fits of laughter, the sound drawing their husbands' attention.

"Having your own party without us?" Ty jibed.

"Well, we can't let you boys have all the fun," his wife giggled.

Kayla observed the adults joking with one another, aware Jaden was doing the same. Then his gaze swept over the deck as he searched for Atu. Jaden looked guilty when he realized their friend had disappeared back into the house at some point. All this time with someone else's parents when your own were MIA had to be tough on the guy.

"You think Atu will be alright?" Jaden asked.

"Yes. He just needs some space."

Jaden gestured toward their parents. "Unlike them. Considering the size of the download they took tonight, they're all coping pretty well."

Kayla gazed at them. "I think it's bothering them a lot more than they're showing. They're putting on a front is for our benefit. Because I don't think they want us distracted by worrying about them."

Jaden accepted the assessment. "Let's not disappoint them then."

Kayla gave a vehement nod. "Yes, let's not!"

CHAPTER FORTY-THREE

Jaden stared into the flames, curling around and licking the dead wood, shooting tiny showers of sparks into the air every time they hit a sap vein. But he was blind to what was right in front of him. His mind writhed with questions. Why had the Usurper called him Gatekeeper? What did that even mean—was it significant? What had Slurpy meant when he said the next time he saw Jaden would be the last time? Was he implying the person Jaden saw in the past timeline had, in fact, been Jaden and not just his doppelgänger? On and on the questions boiled, plaguing him. A quiet rustling made him lurch around. It was only Markov. Jaden returned to brooding.

"Dude, what are you doing here all by yourself?" Markov chided. "You're missing the game."

"I'm not up for it. That doesn't mean you should miss out. Get back there and enjoy it."

But Markov didn't budge. Instead, he considered Jaden's answer, then plopped down beside him on the log they'd dragged in front of the fire earlier. "What's up?"

"Nothing."

"Dude, don't think I don't know when you are neck deep in something. Tell me."

Jaden shook his head. Where would he even start? He couldn't tell Markov. Could he? What would Markov think if he suddenly spouted nonsense about invisible alien creatures invading with the sole aim of world domination? Jaden would sound like a total loon—unless he showed Markov their gliders, who were within easy reach should danger present itself. Jaden toyed with the idea before dismissing it. He wouldn't endanger his friend. "It's complicated."

Markov snorted. "Nothing's ever that complicated. Start with the simple stuff."

"Like what?" Jaden muttered. *Why won't Markov just leave me alone?*

"How about explaining your sudden trip to your Gran's—disappearing for a week and telling no one! Unlike you, dude. You always invite us. Then when you get home, you're even weirder, not calling us for another week. When you do deign to reach out, it's not even so much as a 'How do you do?' It's just, 'Want to do a group hike?' Don't tell me nothing's wrong. It's insulting."

If only you knew.

Upon their return, the teens and gliders agreed they needed more than a day to rest and recuperate. Atu used the opportunity to go scavenging for herbs and roots for his potions, while Jaden and Kayla spent precious moments making the most of the time with their families. With every day threatening imminent departure, they were ever cognizant of the fact they might never see their families again.

Then the day Jaden had dreaded arrived. Their gliders, completely healed, became restless and insisted they leave.

Before resigning himself to his fate, Jaden wrangled permission from the fidgety bats for one last trip to the Shadow Mountains with his closest friends and their families. Not only did he want to see them again before they left, but it was an excellent opportunity for Atu, Kayla, and Kayla's parents to meet everyone.

When he pinged Markov to float the idea almost a week after they got back, his friend had ragged him about the lack of comms. Jaden fumbled through an explanation about visiting his gran, then muddled on to invite Markov and his family on the hike. *Yeah, I have to agree. I'm not acting like myself at all.*

Markov watched the play of emotions on Jaden's face before leaning toward him conspiratorially. "Is this about Kayla?"

The question was so unexpected, Jaden laughed out loud. And of course, she had everything to do with this. But not in the way he knew Markov meant. Although it gave him an easy way out of all the questions. He shoved Markov playfully. "So what if it is?"

Markov almost fell off the log. He stared at Jaden. "Dude, have you been working out on the sly?"

Jaden mentally cursed himself. He hadn't meant to exercise any of his newfound strength. But that boat had sailed. "Sorry. Guess the training we've been doing with Atu is paying off."

Markov eyed him. "Yes, then there's that."

"What's that supposed to mean?"

"Are you abandoning your childhood friends for strays? You go incommunicado for days, and then, when you touch base, you not only have a girlfriend but also some new trainer in tow?"

"It's not like that. Atu is Kayla's friend, visiting from the Dedorian sector. Besides, if I was abandoning you, you think I would've asked you on this hike?"

Markov grinned, a wicked gleam in his eyes. "They say actions speak louder than words. And you *are* just sitting here, *all alone*. You haven't joined us in a game yet." He gave it a second. "Afraid of losing in front of your girlfriend? And yeah, I noticed you didn't deny that."

This time Jaden did shove Markov off the log, chuckling as he did. "Oh, so it's like that, is it?"

"He giving you a hard time?"

Kayla's voice surprised them both. Jaden pivoted, assessing. How much had she heard? "Nothing I can't handle," Jaden said as evenly as he could with his heart racing.

"You sure about that?" Kayla asked, stepping up beside him and deliberately slipping her tiny hand into his.

Jaden spotted the smile tugging at the corner of her lips when his eyes widened.

Without missing a beat, Kayla said, "Markov seems like a guy you have to keep an eye on."

Markov smirked. "I was right then. You two lovebirds going to join us or skulk here by yourselves?"

Still reeling from Kayla's unexpected move, Jaden had no ready reply.

But Kayla took it in stride. "We might."

Markov chuckled. "Well, don't wait too long."

Still chuckling, he strolled back to the game the others had started as soon as they had arrived. Kayla watched him leave, then faced Jaden. "I thought you could do with some help."

"Is that what this is?" Jaden asked, quirking an eyebrow as he raised their joined hands.

Kayla smiled. "It's exactly what you think it is."

Jaden returned the smile cautiously. "And what would that be?"

Her smile turned impish. Rising onto her toes, Kayla planted a soft, brief kiss on his lips. "Does that help clarify things?"

Jaden laughed, his heart soaring. "It does." Confident of exactly where he stood now, he slowly drew her toward him until she was nestled in his arms. "Let's try that again, shall we?"

Bending his head, he kissed her, savoring her sweetness. She sighed and melted into him, and his arms tightened around her protectively. Awestruck, Jaden realized that as much as he'd wondered about kissing her, the reality far surpassed his wildest imaginings. She, quite simply, took his breath away. Needing to get his feet back under him, Jaden reluctantly lifted his mouth from hers. Opening his eyes, he gazed down at her. She was grinning like a Cheshire cat.

When she spoke, her voice was a whisper. "Jameson, you sure know how to knock a girl off her feet."

Jaden chuckled. "Relieved to hear I'm not the only one feeling that way right now."

Kayla laughed. "Glad I could oblige."

Leaning forward, Jaden kissed the top of her head, running his hands through her silky hair as he had longed to do so often. She barely reached his shoulders. But what she lacked in height, she surpassed in everything else. Running his hands down the underside of her arms, his fingers glided over her birthmark. "Are you ever going to tell me more about this?"

"Someday," Kayla murmured, nuzzling into his shoulder.

Hearing someone approaching, Jaden reluctantly dropped his arms and took her hand. "Ready to go kick Markov's butt now?"

She giggled. "That sounds perfect."

Meandering back to where the others played their game of grid, they didn't meet anyone on the forested path. Debating whether he had been hearing things, Jaden forgot all about it as soon as they stepped from the shelter of the trees onto the open area where the game was in progress.

"Took you long enough," Markov teased.

"Is that any way to encourage someone to join in, or is it meant to chase them away?" Jaden retorted.

Stovan jogged up, grinning. "I'm claiming both of you for our team while he's running his mouth."

"You have us," Kayla said, giggling.

Soon, the game absorbed them, and they ran and laughed with the others. The teams competed fiercely, with the lead swinging between them, victory an elusive imp. When the parents hollered lunch was ready, Markov's team had just squeaked past Stovan's.

"Didn't think you had it in you!" Markov grinned, slapping Jaden on the back as they walked off their improvised field.

Jaden smirked. "What, the ability to kick your sorry butt?"

"That and other things," Markov said, glancing meaningfully at Kayla. When she joined them, Markov said, "You're quite the sportswoman. If a short one."

"Thanks. And I'm not short—just vertically challenged."

Jaden snorted. "That doesn't stop her, believe me! Just wait until you get her on an arrowball court. Then you're in for it—and don't say I didn't warn you."

Markov laughed. "I'll consider myself warned."

The players trooped over to the picnic tables where Jaden spotted an elaborate cake adorning the closest table. He couldn't contain his delight. "Bree, is that your doing?"

"How did you guess?" Bree puffed, still out of breath from the game.

"Yum," Stovan murmured, rubbing his hands gleefully. "Can we start with cake?"

Bree chuckled. "I won't stop you."

With a grin that almost split his face in two, Stovan grabbed a plate and headed for the cake. The other famished teens swarmed the tables, collected their own plates, and filled them with the delicious assortment of foods arrayed before them. Plates piled high, they sprinkled themselves amidst the adults, who had wisely garnered food ahead of their ravenous offspring and were already engaged in a lively debate.

The teens picked up on the thread and added their opinions. The debate progressed with proposed arguments and required rebuttals, the tone kept light with raucous ribbing whenever someone spouted an unsupported speculation.

Jaden leaned back, watching Kayla soak it in, her intrigue with the easy camaraderie between adults and teens obvious. Then her gaze went to Atu, taking a seat next to her on the side opposite to Jaden. His face expressed his sadness at not having his own family present.

Whispering, Kayla asked, "How are you holding up?"

Atu shrugged. "It beats sitting back in a cave in the desert all by yourself."

"You know that's not what I mean," Kayla said.

"I do." Atu sighed. "But right now, there's nothing I can do about my folks not being here. So I'm doing my best to just enjoy the time I have with everyone here—and hoping that, one day, my parents can join us."

Kayla took his hand. "I hope so too."

"Thanks. It's uplifting to have friends who care about me enough to want to find my parents as much as I do."

Jaden listened to the quiet conversation, grateful Kayla had reached out to Atu. They were just as much a part of his world now as his childhood friends.

Leaning back on his elbows, Jaden surveyed the group as they bantered: Markov, the center of attention as usual; Stovan, quietly keeping the peace; Shianna, bouncing around with her infinite energy; Bree, chuckling at them all; and Tarise, quietly observing.

But as Jaden studied Tarise, he noticed she kept cutting her eyes back to Kayla. And her unusually stormy gaze wasn't friendly. *What's up with that?* If he didn't know better, he'd say she had an axe to grind with Kayla. Although why that would be, he couldn't fathom.

"More food?" his mom asked, interrupting his contemplations.

"Absolutely. Atu, you keeping up?"

Atu groaned. "I'm stuffed. I don't think I could eat another thing."

"Hope you at least saved room for Bree's cake—it's something you don't want to miss."

"Maybe later," Atu murmured, pushing his plate aside and stretching out on the blanket. Closing his eyes, he said, "After a nap."

Jaden chuckled and then ambled back to the food, helping himself to a second generous portion. Strolling back, he dropped next to Kayla. Biting into his chicken, he remembered the last time he'd eaten chicken up in the mountains. It had been with his parents, and the Gaptors were an unknown entity then.

Sneaking a glance skyward, Jaden didn't spot their gliders. But he knew they were up there, somewhere close. This trip had not thrilled them, and they argued before finally succumbing to his pleas with about as much grace as hamstrung ballerinas.

But Jaden was thankful they had. He had needed this time, to bask in this fellowship, to treasure the simple pleasures of fine friends and family. These people around him were the reason he couldn't fail. They would give him the courage he would need in the dark times that were surely coming—the ones he would fight for. He surveyed the group once more. This was where it all began. With family. Where would it end?

Kayla nudged him. "What are you thinking?"

"This," Jaden said, gesturing toward their friends and family gathered around them, "is all the reason we need to succeed."

For the second time that day, she took his hand. "We will." Leaning over to Atu, who had been listening, she grabbed his hand too. "And we'll find your parents along the way."

Atu gripped Kayla's hand. "Yes, we will."

Sensing someone was watching, Jaden's gaze roamed until it found Markov's. Their eyes met. Reading Markov's expression, Jaden knew he was aware there was more happening than Jaden had let on. Markov wouldn't tolerate Jaden misleading him.

Darting a glance around the group, it was a relief to confirm Markov was the only one who had witnessed the exchange between the seekers. Returning his gaze to Markov, Jaden found him still watching them. Markov raised an eyebrow. Jaden sighed and nodded his head. The corner of Markov's mouth tipped up on one side as he half-smiled acknowledgement. Yeah, Jaden knew that look. Markov surely couldn't wait to hear what he had to say.

Only he would *have* to wait. No opportunity presented itself that afternoon for Jaden to speak with Markov alone. And when they reached the end of the path leading down from the mountain to the parking area where the families had berthed their transports, there was only time for goodbyes. They all exchanged hugs. With Tarise, Jaden sensed an awkwardness that had never been there before.

Tarise hugged him quickly, then pulled back and stared up at him with her huge gray eyes. "So, you and Kayla, huh?"

Jaden mentally grimaced. *Duh, I'm dense! How did I not figure this out before?* But there was no way around it. "Yes. I'm sorry, I didn't realize . . ." He waved a helpless hand in the air.

Tarise shrugged. "It's nothing."

Tarise opened her mouth as though she wanted to say more, but then closed it and turned, stomping away. Jaden watched her retreat. The tight set of her shoulders, the grim line of her jaw, and her clenched fists told him it was far from nothing. He scrubbed a hand over his face. *Ugh!* He hadn't foreseen this complication. Regrettably, there was nothing he could do about it now.

Turning, Jaden felt that strange, familiar tingle run down his spine. Snapping his head back, he caught Tarise's face at the window of their terraporter. And he *knew.* This terrible feeling—it had something to do with Tarise.

Jaden stared after her family's departing terraporter, hoping she wasn't planning on doing anything stupid. Then he sighed. What could he possibly do to stop it? When he got these feelings, they were almost always right, despite any attempts he made to negate them. Perhaps treading carefully around her would somehow mitigate whatever she was considering. He debated calling Tarise's mom and asking her to monitor Tarise. But that would just alarm her. And what if Jaden was wrong? But as he walked away, Jaden couldn't shake the sense he wasn't.

The Melmiques and Jamesons waited until the others departed before gathering around Jaden, Kayla, and Atu. The parents had come up together in the Jamesons' terraporter and would travel home the same way. It had been one of Taz's stipulations—that the teens travel with them and not in the transports, to keep both them and their parents safe.

"First to arrive and last to leave," Vicken remarked. "Who would ever have said that of our family?"

Kayla smiled. "Yes, especially the 'last to leave' part. We're not normally in any one place for long."

Vicken gave the ghost of a smile. "Maybe the time has come to do something about that."

"Really?" Kayla said, her eyes lighting up. "You mean it?"

"I'm not promising anything. But I like the people here. And it would be an excellent area to set up a base of operations."

Kayla threw her arms around her father. "Oh, I'd like that very much!" Stepping back, she found her mother smiling. "You knew?"

"Yes. Your father and I have been discussing the possibility for a while now. And with all you three find yourselves involved in, the timing seems right."

Silence followed her statement. Clara Jameson broke it. "Well, I for one am delighted to hear you hope to settle here. It'll make all this . . . uncertainty a lot easier to bear."

Tears welled up unexpectedly in Clara's eyes. Her husband drew her toward him. "There, there. Jaden, Kayla, and Atu have exceptional helpers up there—and from what they say, the kids are quite amazing themselves."

Clara tried to smile. "Yes, that's true. I suppose it's time we left them to practice whatever Tazanna had in mind."

The parents embraced each of the teens, warning them to be careful. Then they clambered into the terraporter, and the teens stepped back as the engines fired up and the transport sped away.

"Think they'll be okay?" Kayla asked, looking a little tearful herself.

Jaden put an arm around her. "Yes, they'll make it through this. They have each other and that's more than they had before."

Atu grinned. "Looks like they aren't the only ones."

Kayla smiled sweetly. "Well, who knows? Zareh said the last seeker is a girl, and maybe she'll be just your type."

Atu laughed. "As long as we find her, I don't really care about much else. It'll just mean I'm one step closer to finding my parents."

"I hear you," Jaden said, clapping him on the back.

Opening the snack bags his mom had left for them, they sat on the rocks edging the parking area and chatted while they ate, waiting out the time it would take the parents to get home. With the time freeze that went into effect with their gliders, they had to delay joining up with their flying friends again until their parents were back home. This way, when they returned, their parents would already be there instead of just starting the trip home. Jaden's PAL beeped. He glanced at the display. "They're home. Now where are our gliders?"

On cue, Han, Taz and Aren swooped into view.

"Ready to fly?" Jaden asked.

"Am I ever! I've missed it, and the trip up here this morning wasn't long enough," Kayla admitted, smiling.

The teens spread out over the vacant parking lot, giving their friends plenty of space to glide by. Aerial connecting, they were airborne in seconds. Glorious, open, empty air. Jaden flung his arms wide, stretching them on either side, indulging in the liberating sensation.

Han grinned. "Enjoying yourself?"

"More than you know."

"Where to?"

"Well, home will always be our ultimate destination," Jaden mused. "For now though, why don't we just settle for the sheer joy of flying?"

Han chortled, his immense frame quaking under Jaden. "Now you're talking."

Taz sniffed. "A suitable short-term solution. But after an hour, we must run through some routines."

"Party pooper," Kayla teased, rubbing Taz's neck.

"I didn't say no," Taz countered. "I could've."

Jaden, hearing her dismay, took pity on her. "She's right, you know. We'd better use the time we have wisely."

Taz smiled at him. "Thank you, Seeker."

Jaden nodded. He could commiserate, understanding how always being the responsible one felt. Just as the task had fallen to him with Kayla and Atu, it had fallen to Taz with their gliders. And what she had said was true. They needed the practice if they were going to stay sharp. They had to be if they were to stand a chance.

But for now, they would fly. They would clear their minds and strengthen their bodies. They would release their burdens for a brief time. Then, when their time of rest was over, they would step into the roles assigned to them, and they would face their destiny.

ALSO BY BRONWYN LEROUX

Jaden and Kayla are finally together! They have the first artifact. Getting the rest of them should be easy, right? Want to know if they survive the quest? Pick up *Doors of Destiny,* the next book in the *Destiny* series.

Feel like a change of pace? Curious about how this all this began? Pick up *Breach,* the *Destiny* companion novella, FOR FREE!

Other books by Bronwyn Leroux:

Breach (A *Destiny* companion novella)

Dawn of Dreams (*Destiny*, Book 1 - this book)

Dogs of Doom (*Destiny*, Book 2)

Doors of Destiny (*Destiny*, Book 3)

Duel of Death (*Destiny*, Book 4)

Forecast of Shadows

IF YOU ENJOYED THIS BOOK . . .

I would love it if you would please share it!

Reviews are the fairy dust that keep my wheels turning, thinking up fresh and exciting books for you - and they help other readers just like you discover new books to enjoy.

You can leave a review at https://bronwynleroux.com/DogsReview

GET THE FIRST BOOK IN THIS SERIES FOR FREE!

I love interacting with my readers and getting to know them as people. I also understand my readers hate spam as much as I do. For this reason, I only send the occasional newsletter with details on new releases, special offers and other bits of news you may find noteworthy. If you are interested in writing your own book, you can opt in for the additional bonus of weekly writing tips.

Enjoy these wonderful benefits, including your above-mentioned welcome gift, by signing up at https://bronwynleroux.com/FreeBreach

For my family who have always been there for me.

ABOUT THE AUTHOR

Born near the famed gold mines of South Africa (where dwarves are sure to prowl), it was the perfect place for Bronwyn to begin her adventures. They took her to another province, her Prince Charming and finally, half a world away to the dark palace of San Francisco. While the majestic Golden Gate Bridge and its Bay views were spectacular, the magical pull of the Colorado Rockies was irresistible. Bronwyn's family set off to explore yet again. Finding a sanctuary at last, this is Bronwyn's perfect place to create alternative universes. Here, her mind can roam and explore and she can conjure up fantastical books for young adults.

facebook.com/AuthorBronwynLeroux
twitter.com/bronwyn_leroux
instagram.com/bronwyn.leroux

www.ingramcontent.com/pod-product-compliance
Lightning Source LLC
Chambersburg PA
CBHW030346200726
48286CB00013B/363